LOST

IN

TIME

John M. Taylor

In association with Thomas Harrison
1887 – 1959

Fen to Pen Publishing
Fen2Pen@outlook.com

Thanks and Acknowledgements:

Robber Barons and Fighting Bishops
By Derek Richings and Roger Rudderham.

Lisette Brodey
Charles Roth
Janine 'Spike' Hornsby.
Pat Bunting

John Taylor was born in Ely and raised in Littleport, UK.
He has been married to Elisabeth for 48 years.
John has three children.
Sadly, his youngest son was lost to a brain tumour.

John has worked in 20 different countries and lived in
England, Switzerland, Saudi Arabia, South Africa,
New Zealand, Papua New Guinea, and Australia.
He now calls Australia home.

Dedicated to my dear wife, Elisabeth,
for her love, constant support and encouragement.

The Fens of East Anglia were drained in the mid 1600s. Since then the land has sunk, with shrinkage now measured in tens of feet. Strange and mysterious objects from the distant past often appear at the surface. Who knows what mysteries they harbour and what strange tales they could tell.

Chapter 1

Thomas Harrison was Head Horseman, tending and working Clydesdales on Mitchell's Farm, near Ely, deep in the Fens of East Anglia; a position he had inherited from his father, as he had from Tom's grandfather. Tom was fond of the horses in his care and thought of them as extended family. He knew their individual likes, dislikes, characters, and temperaments. In return, they sensed his affection and responded well to his management.

Their intelligent understanding of his gentle commands helped him become one of the most accomplished ploughmen in the county. Their teamwork had won Tom the title of East Anglian Ploughman of the Year three times in the past five years. His skill was well known and he attracted the largest audience at the annual ploughing competition.

Like all accomplished horsemen, he had a favourite team for competitions. Their blinkered eye for a straight line was as keen as his own, so he was able to compete with minimal need for control or instruction. Once started, they instinctively knew what to do. Only an occasional quiet word of guidance was ever needed. This impressed the judges and had scored him extra valuable points. Tom was well liked and had won admiration from the local press. When interviewed, he would say his team had done it, not him. Then joking, "I just follow along behind."

He had started working with horses whilst a boy, learning the basics from his father, who, like all good horsemen, was considered extremely valuable to landowners. The fundamentals of horsemanship were common knowledge, but to be really good you needed to know the secrets only more experienced men knew. Most secrets were held until close to the end of a man's working life. Only then were they passed on, and only if it was felt their replacement had a true understanding and feeling for the animals. Tom's father had recognised this quality in his oldest son at an early age and considered him a natural replacement for himself. So over time, Tom was privy to the innermost secrets of horsemanship and groomed to be one of the best.

Now, as an adult, he quietly enjoyed the prestige that came with winning ploughing competitions and seeing his name in the newspaper. Sometimes he played up to the press and onlookers for his casual amusement.

On one occasion, knowing that horses have a keen sense of smell, and knowing how to control them with their likes and dislikes, he used his knowledge for a little fun. After being presented with the winner's shield, he unhitched his mare and went to her ear and whispered, "Thank you". The judges and onlookers could only just hear what was said but thought it an unusual, endearing gesture. Then, deliberately loud enough for everyone to hear, he added, "Now I want you to follow me wherever I go. Have you got that?"

Onlookers laughed as Tom turned and walked away with the horse following close behind wherever he went.

Spectators were astonished, while Tom smiled to himself in the simple knowledge that horses love the scent of aniseed and would follow it anywhere. Nobody noticed that he had rubbed a little of the oil on his collar before going to the mare.

When the war came on 28th July 1914 Tom was considered an essential worker and not required to enlist for military service, much to the farm manager's relief. His contribution to the national effort was to work the land, help feed the nation and the fighting men in France. He accepted, with some satisfaction, that he was contributing to the common good, but still felt guilty at "not doing his bit in uniform". Other men were responding to the patriotic call to fight for their king and country, while he stayed safely at home. His guilt became more acute when in early 1915, his younger brother, Peter, marched off behind a military band and was now fighting in France. Tom was uneasy. His ageing mother knew he was troubled and pleaded with him not to enlist, so risking the loss of both her sons. Consequently, he was even more torn. He knew Ma was already deeply afraid for her youngest son.

Later that year, Peter returned to England on a stretcher with his right leg missing from just above the knee. He was told that he would be hospitalised for up to four months, then after six months, he would be fitted with an artificial leg if enough healing had taken place. He considered himself lucky in having lost only a leg, whilst so many others had lost their lives. Now he was pleased to be back in England, but he was no longer the mischievous teenager who had left home to join the army.

The first time Tom approached his brother's hospital bed, it was with the trepidation of not knowing what to expect. On entering the ward, he saw a dozen beds lined up along each side, each occupied by a wounded soldier. Most were bandaged and some were restrained into precise positions. Some were in bed while others sat on a chair beside it. A few were reading, others looked lost in thought as they lay staring at the ceiling. Those nearest the door looked to see if the visitor was for them. Then, to turn away with looks of disappointment, making Tom feel awkward.

He didn't see Peter at first. Then, on staring at the young man who eagerly beckoned him, he recognised the aged face of his younger brother, and was shocked. Peter was no longer the innocent boy he last saw, a boy who only months earlier had been his playful little brother, full of life and practical jokes. He now seemed misplaced here and appeared like an artist's impression of how he might look when much older. But it was today, and he now look as old as Tom himself. He seemed misplaced here. Gone were his innocent looks; his fresh-tanned cheeks were now sallow and the mischievous sparkle in his eyes was replaced with a dullness that only extreme tiredness, fear, and trauma can bring.

Peter stretched out his arms in anticipation of holding his brother close. After a moment or two, Tom relaxed his embrace to move back a little, but Peter clung to him, gently sobbing.

Tom tried not to show his pain and forced a smile. "Hello, little brother."

Peter sniffed and rubbed the back of his hand under his nose before taking a finger to mop the corners of his eyes. "Hello, Tom. Sorry about that. You have no idea how good it is to see you."

"And you, Pete, and you too, mate." Tom pulled a

chair to the bedside and held Peter's hand…something he had not done since they were boys.

"How are you feeling, Pete? What the hell happened to you?"

"There's not as much pain now. That is until the doctors and nurses start changing the dressings and messing the stub about. Then it gives me gyp for a few hours. Funny thing is, the foot I don't have itches like hell, but I've got nothing there to scratch. Anyway, on the bright side, I should get my shoes at half price from now on. What do you think old Ron Barber would say if I went into his shop and asked for just one left shoe?"

Tom was too pained to laugh at the joke, although he knew it was Peter's way of dealing with the handicap.

"Me and some of the other one-legged blokes have been comparing shoe sizes. George over there lost his left leg, he takes size eight, the same as me, so we exchanged the shoes we don't need, and now we are both winners."

Tom acknowledged the irony with half a smile.

"Everyone at home has been worried about you, and really upset that you got injured. Ma cried a lot, but she was pleased you hadn't been killed. Everyone sends their love. Anyway, we are pleased you're back now, and Ma is coming to see you tomorrow. She desperately wanted to come with me today, but I persuaded her to wait. I told her you would be tired, but the truth is that I didn't know what to expect, and I wondered if I would need to prepare her. She's been worried sick about you. Anyway, looking at you now, I think she'll be fine."

"Good. It'll be great to see her again, but please tell her not to fuss and blab. I couldn't handle it, especially her tears."

"Is there anything you'd like that she can bring?"

"No, they look after us fairly well here. But I'll tell you what; she can bring a couple of sticks of rhubarb from the patch at the back of the house."

"Rhubarb?"

"The truth is, Tom, all this sitting and lying around makes me constipated. Raw rhubarb goes straight through! It's better than a dose of salts, and tastes better than what they give us here."

Tom laughed. "Okay, I'll tell her."

Now that some of the tensions were lifted, Tom joked, "I suppose we'll have to find a parrot for your shoulder and call you Long Pete Silver from now on."

"I was wondering how long it would take for someone to say something like that. Me and some of the lads are running a sweepstake on how soon someone would mention a bloody parrot. I think you did it in less time than anyone expected!"

It felt good to laugh again. Something Peter had not done for a while. It seemed to confirm he was home, safe, with loved ones, and far from the horrors of war. He went quiet when the sudden realisation of his condition struck home. His eyes glazed.

Tom looked serious and squeezed Peter's hand. "What happened to you, Pete? I mean, how did it happen?"

Peter knew the question would be asked sooner rather than later, and hoped he would not have to relive the events of the last few weeks too often. "Listen, Tom, you don't want to know the details, and I don't think I could cope with telling you. It's hell over there - bloody hell, fields of slaughter, just noise, slub, blood, bodies, fleas, and rats."

"What do you mean?" Tom's eyes widened hoping Peter might be exaggerating.

"Men are dying in their hundreds, maybe thousands every day. You stand at the bottom of a trench with slub up to your ankles…they tell you to get ready to go over the top in five minutes, then two. In those two minutes, some blokes prayed; I saw one wet his pants while another threw up. A couple of mates near me hugged each other 'cos they knew it could be their last day. Some swapped notes to be sent to mothers, wives, or girlfriends. God only knows how many will ever get delivered. One poor sod, further along from me, cried and talked out loud to his mother, begging her to take him away. The poor lad was younger than me, he didn't even shave yet. I never saw him again. But for all that, most of us stood in terrified silence. I know I did. It's no place for man nor beast. But we all did as we were told, even though we were frightened to death. I gotta tell you, Tom. Just being there takes real bloody courage, it really does."

Tom was speechless while he stared at his brother.

"The whistle went and we climbed outta the trench. It was like running into a huge firing squad and hoping not to get shot. It's madness. Sheer bloody madness. It's not a war, it's a wholesale slaughter, I tell you, and you got shells bursting close by, too. The boys what went over the top just before us were all cut down in less than a minute…not one survived. Just knowing that was enough to loosen everyone's bowels. It was surreal, totally crazy as if it wasn't real, but we knew it was, and too terrible to believe. So at the last minute, your brain sort of numbs you…it's like you are not there, but you know you are."

There was silence while Peter regained his composure.

"Anyway, when our turn came, we ran towards the Hun trying not to step on the bodies of the first wave. It was hard to run in the mud. Some blokes fell over in it, only to get up and be mowed down straight away. It was a slaughter, a bloody slaughter. I was lucky I suppose, my leg was shot from under me before I got a few paces."

Tom's eyes widened. "What do you mean by 'lucky'?"

"When I got hit, it spun me right round and I fell back, face down towards our trench. I was lucky, I suppose, 'cos the first-aid blokes could reach and drag me back into the trench. If I'd copped it further away, it would have been a while before anyone could help me, and I would probably have bled to death. I didn't feel anything for a minute and wondered what had happened. It was confusing. Then, by Christ, it hurt so much that I couldn't even yell." Peter's eyes filled with tears.

"Bloody hell, mate, I had no idea."

"And do you know what? When the first-aid boys go out to get the wounded, the bloody Germans shoot at 'em! The bastards shoot 'em. You gotta take your hat off to them lads. They don't even carry a gun to shoot back. Brave boys every one of 'em. They all deserve a bloody medal. When we saw one get shot it really pissed us off, and we started to hate the Germans, so we didn't mind trying to shoot a few. But do you know what! It don't help, 'cos we knew they are just lads like us, doing what they are told."

Tom's jaw dropped in amazement. He'd never thought of his little brother shooting and killing someone. Then he realised that it's exactly what soldiers are trained to do. "What did you mean by man nor beast?"

"Knowing how you feel about horses you'll be upset, but you might as well know. They got some beautiful animals over there, thousands of 'em. The poor blighters are terrified by all the noise and that, especially the cavalry horses. You can see it in their eyes. The heavy horses work hard doing impossibly heavy work for hours on end until they're fit to drop, and they're not cared for like they should be. I suppose it's not easy under the circumstances, but what can you do? The poor creatures are worked to death, and if they are injured, they just get shot. I don't think they've got enough experienced men who understand or care about 'em…so they just work, suffer, and die."

Tom was as upset about the horses as he was for the men. Thinking there must be something that could be done, but not knowing what.

Both felt enough had been said about the war, so the conversation moved to discuss farm work and local people's affairs.

"How are the young'uns, Tom?"

"They're fine. Susie turned three a couple of months ago. Ma and Dora put on a bit of a party for her. It was bedlam for a while with all the kids there. Alfie will be five in a couple of months. He's a little sod sometimes, but I suppose he's a typical boy. He often reminds me of you at that age." Both men laughed. "He's full of beans and is into everything. Nothing is sacred when he's around. He starts school soon. No doubt they'll sort him out. His little sister follows him everywhere and tries to copy what he does. I say tries, ah' but you'll soon see what I mean. She's a little sweetheart, and do you know what? Alfie takes good care of her when they are out and about. He sort of protects her and keeps an eye on her. They'll be in to see you soon, so you'll see for yourself."

The loud slamming of a door echoed down the ward. Peter shuddered, squeezed his eyes tightly shut, went rigid, and broke into a sweat. Although there was only one bang, it continued in his head a dozen more times.

Tom felt Peter's hand grip harder.

When Peter eventually opened his eyes, still shaking, he saw Tom's concern and said, "Sorry about that."

Tom could see things were not right, far beyond Peter losing his leg. Then, in what seemed like minutes, an hour had passed and a nurse, in her starched white apron and bonnet, was walking down the ward announcing that visiting time was over.

"Okay, Pete, it looks like I have to go. Take care of yourself, and remember Ma is coming tomorrow. I don't think you should tell her too much about the war, you know how upset she gets. Do you want her to bring anything besides the rhubarb?"

"The local newspaper would be good if she's got one."

"I'll get one for her on my way home."

Peter smiled, they embraced, and Tom left.

The next day, while his mother was at the hospital and without telling anyone, Tom took a bus to the recruiting office in Wisbech, where he signed up with the Cambridgeshire Regiment. There was little formality. An immaculately dressed, larger-than-life Colour Sergeant asked why he wanted to go to war.

"I don't want to go to war, but I hear the horses have a bad time of it over there. I work with Clydesdales all the time, I know about them, and can look after 'em."

"You should be exempt from military service. You sound like an essential worker to me."

"I know, but there are others who can work the horses on my farm. My brother just came back from France saying the horses need attending to, and I can keep them working for you longer."

"That's a good enough reason for me, me lad. We need experienced horsemen. The horses are valuable.

We can get plenty of men, but not horses. They could do with a bit o' looking after all right. Go over to the table and give 'em your details, son."

Tom was amused at being called "son". He didn't tell his mother what he had done right away. That evening she just wanted to talk about Peter, his recovery, and what he could do once he became mobile again.

The next day, Tom told Ma he had enlisted. Knowing she would be upset, he carefully explained that he was not going to the trenches, and they may not even give him a gun. "I'll be attending to the Cart Horses, the ones that carry supplies back and forth. That's all, Ma. There's nothing to worry about." But his words gave little comfort.

After six weeks of basic training, in late 1916, Tom was taught how to care for horses, military-style. He was aware of much of it already, and sometimes he knew more than the instructors. Yet, the nature of their possible injuries and the conditions he would expect to find in France worried him. Not so much for the want of treating them, but the thought of horses getting such injuries. He hoped he would never have to shoot a horse and wondered how he would cope.

Later, he sometimes found the conditions in France far worse than he had expected. For the next two years, he worked mostly with Clydesdales and Shire Horses, pulling the heaviest of loads to and from the front. A few motorised vehicles were available, but they were unreliable and a problem in mud. There were many times when he and a team were called upon to drag heavy field guns or vehicles from the quagmire. He said little to their drivers, who sometimes interpreted his quiet pride as smugness.

He attended to the horse's strains, cuts, and abrasions with care, resting them as often as he could. Of concern was how to calm their fears in the noise and turmoil when they neared the front. He noted, with some disgust, that when shells began to fall nearby, his comrades took cover, leaving their horses to whatever fate may bring. Tom was often ridiculed for staying to steady and comfort his animals, but he didn't care.

He rotated the workloads as conditions allowed, in the hope of reducing their fatigue. Things were bad most of the time, although much better in the summer. Natural feed was more plentiful then, it was warmer and there was less mud to make their tasks more difficult. He was upset whenever he saw a horse die of debility. In his opinion, it was unnecessary, and usually brought on by exposure, overwork, hunger, and resulting illness. Tom quietly cursed the hierarchy for their perceived lack of concern. When he pleaded for more fodder and medication, he was told that he already had all that was available. A working horse was rationed to less than a quarter of its daily needs, so when he had the opportunity he would walk them back a mile or two hoping to find grassy areas to graze. In winter he scrounged blankets to cover them. Sadly there were always some left behind in the trenches. Medicines were scarce, so much of the time, he made do with natural remedies. They worked more slowly and sometimes not at all if the animal's condition was too advanced.

He was fond of the horses in his care and treated them kindly, spending much time grooming and massaging their limbs. When they were stressed, frightened or in pain, he comforted and calmed them by placing his cheek to theirs. Then, gently rubbing their other cheek, he talked quietly to relax them. He was sure the vibrations and sound of his voice were comforting. "There you go, my beauty, just relax, Tom is here to take care of you. Never mind them loud noises…I'm here to protect you and see you don't come to any harm. I know you are hungry, and I'll do what I can to get you more to eat. This won't last forever, you'll see. Then you can spend the rest of your days in peace and quiet, in a lush green meadow, just resting in the sun. Imagine that, my lovely."

It was a great comfort for Tom too, who wanted to believe it was true, and at times, he thought they understood his words. After a while they looked for his comfort, lowering their heads to place a cheek next to his. He never disappointed them, even if he could only spare a moment or two.

His care and affection for the horses did not go unnoticed by his officers, who soon developed a great respect and rewarded him with a corporal's stripe. One of the senior officers offered him a job on his estate when the war was over.

"Thank you, but let's see if we survive this lot first, sir." The officer smiled in agreement.

When the war ended, Tom wanted to take some of the horses back to the Fens. But transportation was difficult and he couldn't afford the cost. So he spent his last day in France at the stables with his horses, grooming and talking to them, to leave them in the best condition he could. They seemed to know he was leaving and craved his caresses even more. Or was it Tom's imagination?

On that last evening, he went to say a final, painful goodbye, hoping they would all find good homes on French or Belgian farms after being auctioned. Unlike many of the cavalry horses which were unceremoniously disposed of.

Chapter 2

Tom was home from France by the end of November 1918. Autumn ploughing had been delayed due to the weather, so he was pleased to help catch up. Early persistent frosts had hardened the ground, making it too strenuous for a horse to plough. Now, in a late milder spell, with the correctly bladed plough and teamwork, Tom could minimise the horse's stress, even though it took a little longer to complete the work.

Often, he was paired with a younger, less experienced man, as the boss had said, "To keep an eye on him and teach him a thing or two." They would plough the same field a little apart from each other, but close enough for Tom to see what he was doing.

There was a day when young Ron's horse was quickly becoming exhausted and was suffering by mid morning. Tom couldn't fail to notice that Ron had been shouting at it, and driving it to do more than was its natural pace. "You know, Ron, if you keep that up, you'll kill your mare before the day is out."

"Narr, she could do with a good workout. I'll impress the boss, show him how much can 'really' get done in a day."

"Be careful you don't show him the wrong things, or

he'll kick your sorry backside off the farm."

Ron's attitude annoyed Tom. He was there to help the lad, but his advice was taken too lightly. Ron always thought he knew best. They were halfway through eating their dockey before the animal stopped panting, her head hung low, and Tom could see she was tired and stressed. Again, Ron was warned to ease up on her.

"Narr, she can manage; I'll see how she goes."

"Well it's up to you, mate, but she looks stressed out to me. I can't see her lasting the day the way you are pushing her. She's smart. When she's had enough, she'll just stop and there won't be a darn thing you can do to move her."

Ron's experience was limited, but he clearly thought he knew more than he did. Tom considered him a "young smart arse" and felt sorry for the horse, so decided to teach Ron a lesson. Having eaten their bread, cheese, and pickles, they drank cold black tea from bottles. Tom went to his horse to give her an apple and have a quiet chat, as he put it. He saw the apple as her little treat for the day. Then, while Ron was relieving himself in a ditch, Tom took the opportunity to cut a short thorny piece of bramble and placed it under the collar of Ron's mare.

"We'd better get back to it then," Tom called, as he returned to his plough. He didn't look back but heard Ron shouting at his mare again. She had taken only one step and would move no further. When her collar pulled back the thorns pricked her neck.

"What's up, mate?"

"She won't bloody well move!"

Knowing what the problem was, Tom walked across. "She knows you're driving her too hard, so I'm telling you, right now, to raise that plough! You are cutting too deep, it's too much for her. I told you, these animals are smart. She's not going to kill herself trying. She can't cut that deep in this hard ground, no horse can. A month or two ago you might have stood a chance, but not now. You'll have to raise the blade a notch, and do what you can, or the boss will get shitty with you for not doing your quota and dock your pay."

Tom knew it would take Ron a minute or two to raise the heavy blade and would not be paying attention to what he was doing. So he went to the mare, and while talking quietly to her, he removed the piece of bramble before gently rubbing where it had been. "I'll leave you to it then," he called, as he returned to his own horse, feeling guilty that he'd caused the mare some discomfirt. Ten minutes later, he saw Ron happily ploughing further across the field and chuckled. "I might just tell him one day…Mmm maybe not."

Over the years, Tom had gathered many little stories about his tricks and adventures with horses, especially those from his army days. So, that evening he decided to begin making notes. His wife, Dora, didn't see the point. "People might not be interested. Anyway, most farms are using traction engines and tractors now."

"Exactly my point, Dora, you never know, someone might be interested in this one day, and even if they're not, I'll still enjoy writing it all down. Who knows, maybe what I've got in my head might get lost if them machines completely take over like you say. Anyway, it's not just about farming, it's about horses, how to look after them, keep them happy, and how to get the best out of 'em. This stuff might end up in a book one day."

"Huh, and pigs might fly!"

Whilst ignoring her remark, the thought gelled in Tom's mind and his enthusiasm welled at the notion. Then, as if he had not heard her, he said, "I could even write it myself! I could throw in a bit or two about poaching and Fen life."

After enthusiastically pumping up the Tilley Lamp, he placed it on the table and prepared to start writing. After a moment or two, he decided to make notes of all the individual events and practices he could remember, and stitch them together later.

Chapter 3

It was not unusual for ploughmen to find odd-looking items that turned up in the freshly tilled soil. Tom had lost count of the number of pieces of white clay tobacco pipes he'd found. There were so many that he now ignored them. Over the years, he had found a Bronze Age spearhead, a few Roman coins, pieces of Roman pottery, and some unusually large bones.

Unfortunately, by far the most common offering from the past was bog oaks. These remains of ancient forests were a problem, the largest pieces being up to twenty feet long and weighing two tons or more. Removing them could hold up ploughing for a day or two. Horses strained when the plough found one, and they seemed to know it couldn't be moved, so instinctively stopped, content to conserve their energy before being asked to drag it to the edge of the field once it was dug out. The heavy, black, moisture-soaked timbers would be left to dry, before being cut up for winter logs.

Ploughmen often joked about becoming rich beyond their wildest dreams when King John's treasure would turn up at their feet. It was a Fenland legend, with the historical events being taught in schools. History books described King John as an unpopular king, who upset people so much that he had to run from the English Barons and the French Nobles. He chose to pass through the Washes of East Anglia via King's Lynn, once Bishop's Lynn, hoping nobody would follow him into such a forbidding area, choosing it as a preferred route to safety at Newark Castle. The king's reputation for collecting jewels and great finery was well known. Even his clothes were described as extravagantly opulent.

As Tom told his children, "Legend has it that, in 1216, he lost his treasures in the boggy salt marshes of The Wash, long before the land was drained, and to this day they have never been found."

Alfie and Susie were fascinated and stared at him in amazement. "Why has nobody dug it up?" They asked.

"Because nobody knows where to find it."

Many a farmworker speculated in jest over a beer about what they would do if they ever found King John's treasure. Everyone was sure that one day it would reappear and make someone very rich. But the speculation was never taken seriously as the loss was far to the north of the Isle of Ely, somewhere northwest of King's Lynn.

Chilled, clear mornings often heralded a beautiful day in the fields. It could take up to half an hour for the sun to burn off the low Fenland fog that carpeted the land. Sometimes it rose only a few feet from the ground, creating the eerie sensation of walking waist-deep through cloud as it slowly crept across the fields for as far as the eye could see. There were few large trees to cast the weakest of shadows, but the view of the huge sky covering these great flatlands was rewarding enough for Tom. The land was so flat that approaching changes in the weather could be seen coming from many miles away. He would often stop and admire the cathedral at Ely, which stood proud and could be seen for almost twenty miles. He loved the open flat Fens, and in admiration, often said he could never live in a place where he had to look up to see the sky.

Something rolled from the freshly tilled soil, catching Tom's attention. It was quite different to anything he had seen or found before. A spherical earthenware object about six inches in diameter. Wiping some of the dirt away, he first thought it was a ball of some sort, maybe a cannonball, but soon found it was much too light. His horse was still moving, so he put the find inside his shirt until he reached the far end of the field. After calling his mare to a halt, he took the object to the bottom of a ditch to wash away the remaining black soil. He would take it home later for a closer inspection.

Tom and Dora lived with their two children in a tied house near the edge of the village, just where a drove led from the surfaced road to deep into the Fens. Their small brick farmhouse was built on soft Fen soil and was beginning to sink and lean forwards. The movement had long since caused the walls to crack, but Tom didn't complain or worry since nothing could be done to save it. The house came with his job, and his boss didn't seem concerned. Tom and Dora were pleased with what they had, especially since they paid no rent. The kitchen was dim, having only one small window and had the faint, but persistent, smell of paraffin from the Tilly Lamp that hung from a hook on a beam across the yellowing ceiling. The lounge, or "best room" as Dora called it, was out of bounds, except on special occasions.

"We'll keep it nice for when visitors come," she had

decreed. However, apart from neighbours, who were not important enough to be shown into the best room, visitors were rare. Although it was used at Christmas time and occasionally when Dora's sister came for a few days, but that was not often.

So like most families, they lived in the kitchen, which was warmed by a blackened iron stove, making it especially cosy in winter. In the evening, Tom liked to turn the lamp down to dim the room even more, then open the front of the stove for a comfortable, warm red glow. Dora complained at his idea of a romantic atmosphere, even though it rarely led further. He'd take great pleasure in making toast on a long fork in front of the vertical grill, then spreading vast amounts of homemade butter and crab apple-jelly, or beef dripping onto it.

Dora complained, "How can I see to sew or darn in this light?"

"Sorry, my Duck, I'll turn the lamp up again," Tom would say with disappointment.

She frowned when he spread an old newspaper over part of the wooden table, before proudly positioning his find there for careful inspection.

"Not more junk you're bringing home? And be careful, I scrubbed that table today."

"Don't be like that, my duck, you never know what things are when you first find 'em. It might be valuable, for all we know."

"Well, it don't look like nothing valuable to me."

Tom thought a moment. "You can't tell. It might not be, but then again, it could be if it's rare. Anyway, I'm curious about it. I've not seen nothing like it before."

He filled a bowl with water from the outside pump before taking a stiff brush to scrub the object clean. Once dried, a brown, unglazed, ceramic vessel was revealed. It seemed to have a lid which time had sealed in place. There was no knob or handle on it. Tom thought it a little strange, adding to his curiosity. There were no markings or impressions to show where it was made or who had made it. A shallow, flat surface had been pressed into it to form a base, enabling it to stand precariously upright with the lid uppermost. He could only guess that it had not been mass-produced, so was likely to be quite old. It offered no clue of what it was used for, of its age, or what it might have contained. It was a little heavier than he would now have expected and cool to touch, typical of thick ceramic items. Leaning back in his chair he stared and pondered intensively over it. "What do you reckon might be inside?"

"How am I supposed to know?" Dora replied, suggesting it was a silly question and clearly of no interest. She was not in the best of moods again.

"Looks like it's got a lid, but it's stuck in place. I'm a bit reluctant to open it and afraid of breaking it trying. You never know what might be inside, but anyway, it would be interesting to know."

Tom got up and put it next to the clock on the mantelpiece.

"Tell you what, Dora. The next time we go to Cambridge, we'll take it to the museum, like I did that Saxon sword handle that our Peter found. I bet they'll know what it is."

"If you must." Dora grudgingly replied. "I suppose it'll be stuck up there a while then. I dunno why you keep bringing that rubbish home."

Tom was frustrated with Dora's persistent negativity, finding it depressing and annoying, but to keep the peace he said nothing. There was a time before the war when he would have challenged her, but now he let things pass rather than argue. He sometimes got mischievous satisfaction from believing Dora wanted to argue and denying her the opportunity. The war had given him different perspectives on what was important and what was not. What was worth chasing and what was best left. He'd noticed that Dora was not the same after Susie was born believing she had depression and decided she would eventually come out of it. Nonetheless, it was taking a long time and their relationship was suffering as a result.

During the next week, Tom's curiosity began to get the better of him. Twice, he'd sat by the evening stove, pondering whilst he fondled the spherical object. Placing it on the table, he noticed that whichever way up he put it, it rolled to stand in the same position, always on the flat area with the lid at the top. He decided it must be weighted in some way or contain something stuck inside at the bottom. "There's something inside it, Dora. You know, I'm sure it's really old. I bet whatever's in it is putrid by now. It's an odd sort of thing."

"It might be a Stone Age bottle'a cold tea," she said with a sarcastic giggle.

Tom shrugged in mild contempt. Frustrated his attempt at congeniality had, once again, been cast down.

In the morning, he took the ball to the big barn, next to the haystacks, and left it on a ledge, thinking he'd get round to examining it more thoroughly another day. Or perhaps let the experts in Cambridge do it.

Dora had not always been so negative. They had known each other since their school days but had taken little notice of each other then. She was pleasant enough and Tom liked her. However, it was not the "done thing" for a boy of his age to be seen being friendly with a girl. Not unless he was prepared to get constant ribbing from his peers. It was two years after leaving school before they acknowledged each other in any meaningful way. Tom remembered the first time. It was at a village fete. They courted for a while and eventually fell in love. Both were in their late teens, were affectionate, and enjoyed each other's company. So it came as no surprise when they announced their engagement.

Both had been reluctant to wait long before marrying but did so to appease their parents, who thought the whole romance was too quick to be serious, and certainly not decent. Eventually, with their family's satisfaction that the relationship would stand the test of time, their wedding took place in the village church.

Three years passed before Dora announced she was pregnant. Tom was ecstatic and overprotective, fussing over her to a level she found irritating. Then, as the changes took place in her body, she became prone to mood swings. Tom was frustrated but sympathetic, so tried not to respond negatively, putting it down to her condition, as was to be expected. At these times, he tried to show Dora more love and understanding, gestures which often went unappreciated, but he tried not to show his disappointment. Unfortunately, four months before the birth was due, Dora tripped over their dog in the kitchen, falling awkwardly. She miscarried and was unwell for some weeks.

When she came home from the hospital, she was a changed woman. At first, she was quiet and reclusive, then later, falling into a depression. Tom was understanding and tried to gently ease her back, but his kindness and consideration worked slowly, he sometimes wondered if at all.

"Is there anything you need before I go to work, my duck?"

"No."

"Would you like me to call in at the shop for anything on my way home?"

"No."

"Tell you what! We'll go to Ely on Saturday and buy you something nice. Perhaps a new dress, or a hat."

"Maybe."

Tom's frustration was turning despondency.

"She'll be right enough when she gets over it, just give her a bit o' time, son," his mother told him.

It took many months for her to respond to Tom with any degree of affection and she seemed happier in the company of her friend Vera, from the village. Tom was grateful to Vera, hoping Dora would eventually be brought out of her depressed state with the help of a good female friend. Yet, it was almost a year before they had anything like a normal relationship again. Tom had watched their marriage become like that of a much older couple who had begun to grow apart, or where love had turned into the habit of just living together. In his disappointment, he remembered the words "for better or for worse", so felt obligated to persevere and not give up on her. It was with patience and frequent displays of affection that he eventually encouraged a return to a more congenial relationship.

All went well for a while, and even life in the bedroom became more satisfying. When Alfie was born, it seemed to draw them closer still, and all was fine until Susie was born. Then it was as though the clock had been turned back to the bad old days. With frustration and sadness, Tom reluctantly accepted this was how Dora would be, calling it "her way." She showed him little affection and seemed resentful of her situation, even negative about life itself. Satisfying Tom's sexual needs became rare again. Yet, she was fiercely jealous of other women being around him. When they did make love, it was not satisfying and Tom was made to feel that her rare consent was from obligation, rather than desire, love, or affection.

Because she had once miscarried, both Alfie and Susie were born in a hospital. Dora became paranoid while having Susie, wondering what Tom was up to, whilst her imagination played tricks. She was jealous of Rose, the farm manager's daughter, who was single, attractive, and in Dora's opinion, "a bit of a floozy".

It began when Tom told her that Rose came in a couple of times a week to clean and do his laundry. He said it was the boss's idea, not his, and that it felt strange having another woman in the house, even just for an hour or two. Dora was protective of her domain and resented another woman being there, especially in her kitchen. She trusted Tom up to a point, but in her troubled state imagined what could develop between him and the younger woman. Deciding in advance that it would be Rose who would make the advances, she nevertheless questioned Tom's resolve to refuse, especially given her own coolness towards him in the bedroom. Dora had previously liked Rose but now resented her.

Tom thought the name "Rose" suited her as she always seemed to carry the fragrance of summer roses. He treated her with respect and constantly thanked her, always mindful that she was his boss's daughter. She teased him now and again with looks and suggestive remarks, which he felt were not always intended to be simply playful. One morning, she picked up a pair of his long johns, stuck her forefinger through the fly and wiggled it at him, calling, "Coo'eee," before giggling and giving him suggestively sensual looks whilst she straightened and stiffened her finger. The situation became more serious one morning when Rose issued a clear invitation. "Why don't you come and help me make your bed?"

"Don't be silly, Rose, I've got other things to do." Tom was embarrassed at the intimation while trying not to show it.

"What's more important than me showing you how things are done in the bedroom? You might like it."

"Stop it, Rose! Behave yourself. I'm a married man." Tom glared at her.

She contorted her face to display what she thought would be a sexy pout of sulking innocence while staring him in the eye, attempting to hold his gaze. Tom quickly but awkwardly turned away, not daring to think what might happen next if he didn't. Secretly, his hormones were galloping, whilst his mind speculated on what it would be like between her thighs; but he would not betray Dora, and so retain his self-respect.

It bothered him all day. On rationalising the event, he could see he had done the right thing. It was near impossible to keep a secret in the village and everyone would soon know, including Dora, and his boss, who would shortly retire from the farm manager's position, which Tom hoped to be promoted to. There would be no question of that if he bedded his daughter. He was thankful she only came for an hour or two but noticed it was always when he was there. Yet, for all his self-control, he couldn't help wondering what she would be like in bed.

Tom was relieved when Dora came home, but there was little conversation. Instead, he read the newspaper or a book and Dora knitted or sewed while they sat in front of their old blackened iron stove. On a few occasions, they were more congenial, usually after Dora had bought an old knitted jumper or two at a jumble sale. She would pull them down and reuse the wool for darning, or for knitting something else. It was times like this that gave Tom hope. But it rarely lasted beyond the time it took for him to hold up the garment allowing the wool to unravel as Dora wound it into a ball.

Evenings were often difficult for Tom and he often thought of going to the village pub for a change of scene and a chat with friends, but he didn't go, believing it would only allow Dora to complain about being left alone.

"Why do you have to hang you wet socks over the oven door?"

"We always dry them there, my duck."

"But they stink."

"I can't help it, they get wet sometimes. Anyway, it saves you washing them and giving me clean ones. I'll move my boots and spats away if they bother you."

"No, you'd better leave them now."

Tom settled again with the newspaper.

"Why do you have to rustle the paper folding it inside out. It's irritating."

"Well look at it. It's so big that it makes my arms ache holding it out. This way it's easier to hold. I'll be done in a second or two."

Dora huffed, wriggled in her seat and returnrd to her knitting. Sometimes she would hold her knitting in her lap, pinch her lips, and stare disapprovingly at Tom as he finished folding the newspaper.

After the children were put to bed he enjoyed his evening pipe, being able to relax and savour the moment in peace and comfort. The smell annoyed Dora, so he restricted himself to only one pipe in the quietness of the evening. Occasionally, in the summer, when he fancied a second one, he would wander around the farmyard, mentally noting what needed to be done while he smoked. On those occasions, he often wondered why Dora had to be so difficult.

He remembered with amusement that Dora had once smoked far more than him. She didn't complain about his pipe then. He had discouraged her many times and smiled when remembering how he'd caused her to stop smoking without her knowing what he'd done. After taking a packet of her cigarettes, and with a fine needle he had carefully threaded a single horse hair through the length of each cigarette. When she smoked one, it made her feel ill. Then, after trying a few more, with the same result, she decided to give up smoking, having concluded they were not good for her if they made her sick. Tom said little more than, "A good idea, my duck, as you like."

Sometimes, as he sat by the stove, he would look across at Dora and realise that he still loved her, even though she was no longer the slim, joyful country girl he had once married. After her miscarriage and the birth of Alfie and Susie, she had steadily put on weight to become a matronly farmer's wife.

In a moment of warm conciliation and nostalgia, he pointed with the stem of his pipe at the clock on the mantelpiece. "Do you remember your mother and father giving us that clock for a wedding present?"

"Of course I do."

"Well, have you ever noticed how it ticks louder at night?"

"Mmm."

"Funny that." Tom added, before giving up on the subject.

"You know what? I was thinking we should get one of them wirelesses they are talking about. Most folks have already got one. It would brighten up our evenings. We could listen to the news, plays, and concerts. What do you think?"

"What for? Anyway, we don't have electricity."

"Ah, but you can run them on an accumulator now."

"I know, but you'll have to take it to Ely every week to get it charged. That's two trips each time, once to take it, then the next day to collect it. You won't want to do that for long…and I'm not going."

"We could get two and alternate them each week."

"More expense!"

"So you don't want one then?"

"It's up to you," she shrugged.

"OK, maybe not."

Frustrated, and trying not to get annoyed, his mind involuntarily wandered to Rose, speculating on what it would be like to live with her instead. She'd be a lot more fun than Dora, but could a man really trust her? She's a bit of a flirt. You'd never know if she means half of what she says, or if she's being faithful. One of these days some bloke is going to take her teasing seriously. I bet one or two already have.

Chapter 4

It was raining the day an ambulance brought Peter to his mother's cottage in the centre of the village. Even so, and as expected, the handful of village children who gathered to watch were pleased to see Peter, and realised how much they had missed him. They had always enjoyed sitting by the river, listening to his 'true' adventure stories which he made up as he went along. One called, "Welcome home, Uncle Peter," as they liked to call him. He waved back giving a half a smile, self-conscious of showing his disability.

Refusing to be taken to the door in an invalid chair, he preferred his crutches to show a level of independence and determination, even though he harboured resentment at his condition. His mother stretched out her arms and greeted him with what seemed an everlasting embrace. He clumsily hugged her back, but without the joyful emotion his mother was showing. Nor did he match her tears. He was just pleased to be home and wanted to get inside.

"Welcome home, my love. Mind the step. Here, take your dad's old seat by the fire. I expect you'd like a nice cup of tea."

"Thanks." He replied softly, lowering himself into the

old wooden carver. The words "mind the step" bothered him. He didn't want to be fussed over, it made him feel like a cripple who needed to be watched. All he wanted was to get back to what was once normal. Yet, deep down, he knew it would never be the same again. He felt cheated and tricked into enlisting into the army. "A great adventure, honour your King and Country, become a real man, be a hero," he was told.

"It's lovely to have you back, dear, you must be glad to be home again."

"Yes."

There was no, "Yes Ma, thank you." Just a bland, "Yes."

She immediately sensed that settling him down was going to be tricky, that it may take a while, and she would need to be careful not to upset him.

"Gosh, it must be nine or ten months since you were last here." There was no reply. "Anyway, dear, it's lovely to have you home again."

He sat quietly waiting for his tea.

"Biscuit, dear?"

"No thanks."

"I made your favourite shortbread ones."

"I said, no thanks!"

Ma pulled her head back at his abruptness but thought better of challenging him, so they drank their tea in silence. Peter poured his into the saucer a little at a time, blew it and slurped from its edge.

"Another cup, dear?"

"No." Then checking himself. "No, thanks, sorry, Ma."

She paused. "What's the matter, dear?" There was no answer. "Look, son, I know you are having a difficult time of it, but we'll work things out and you'll be back to normal soon enough, especially when you get your new leg."

There was a long silence whilst Peter stared at the floor.

"Listen, Ma, I can never be the same again. I'm a bloody cripple, and that's the truth of it. All I know is farm work, a bit about horses what Tom taught me, and soldiering. I can't stay in the army and I'll be useless on the farm! So what can I do? Nothing! Except be a burden to everyone. The government gives us injured Tommies a putty medal and tells us to piss off home, expecting our families to look after us. They sure are grateful for the sacrifice. There's no proper help to get a job or work training after hospital. Just a thank you very much, a pat on the head, now bugger off home."

Typical of Fen people, Ma had never been one for self-pity and was offended at the language, especially from her son. "Now you just listen to me, young man…you are better off than many of them other poor lads what have come home, and a lot better off than them what never will. You got two perfectly good arms and hands, you'll be able to walk soon, and you got a perfectly good head on your shoulders. So let's not have any more of this nonsense. You got no cause for being so negative!"

Peter stared down at his hands.

Ma's expression softened. "Son, we all love you very much and want to see you back on your feet, just as soon as much as you do."

"Don't you mean foot, Ma?"

Before anything more could be said, Tom blustered in. This was once his home and he had never felt the need to knock. "I just had to come and welcome my little brother home. Hello, Ma. How are you, Pete? Welcome home, mate, it's great to see you."

Peter managed a weak smile with a gentle nod, not allowing Tom to catch his eye for more than a second. Tom immediately sensed the strained atmosphere. "What's up, mate? Aren't you glad to be home?"

"Suppose so."

"My word, you are in the dumps. Tell you what. As soon as you are up to it, we'll go down to the pub. Half the blokes in the village are waiting to catch up with you."

Ma reached for Tom's arm, squeezing it just hard enough for him to know he shouldn't continue. "I expect you'd like a cup of tea, Tom? There's still one in the pot." Said to distract from the moment.

Tom smiled. "Yes, thanks, Ma."

She added more hot water to the pot and swirled it around before pouring. Suddenly, the outside door opened with an excited commotion. Ma didn't hesitate. "You young'uns can get them mucky boots off for a start. I don't want you bringing none'a that there slub in 'ere."

The children stopped short, backed into the little wooden porch and hurriedly pulled their boots off without undoing the laces.

"Hello, Uncle Peter," Alfie called, while Susie tried to climb onto his lap.

Peter winced, Tom quickly grabbed her away.

"Sorry, sweetheart, but your, Uncle Peter has a bad leg. Why don't you sit on the arm of the chair and hold his hand?"

Peter was fond of the children. Seeing them now visibly lifted his spirits, and there would be no serious talk in their presence, so allowing him to relax.

Saying nothing, Susie put her arm around his neck

and kissed his cheek, bringing a lump to his throat. He was beginning to enjoy being home. The children loved their uncle Peter and responded well to him. He was always kind and talked with them as equals. He had often said that one of the nicest things you could do for children is to remember what it was like to be their age, whatever that age is.

In the following days, Peter began to slip into depression with periods of frustration and irrationality. It was only when the children came that he had a few minutes of what seemed to be his old self.

He was eventually fitted with an artificial leg, and after a few weeks of being mobile, he would visit the village shop for a newspaper or tobacco. Although he enjoyed his ability to move without a walking stick, he was selfconscious of his limp, and tried to conceal it. Occassionally looking to see if anyone had noticed. At first, everyone was pleased to see him, but it was not long before they learned to tiptoe around him, afraid of saying something to trigger a rebuff or negative remark. Even, "How are you today, dear?" from the village shopkeeper, only promoted a resentful grunt. So she stopped asking.

He refused to go to church, despite the vicar trying to offer comfort and spiritual guidance. His jaw dropped when Peter asked, "Where was your God of love and affection when tens of thousands of men and boys like me were being killed or maimed in France? Where was he then? Was he the loving, caring God you go on about?"

Vicar Parsons was taken aback and at that moment he could only say, "God moves in mysterious ways, my son."

"Yeah, a bit too bloody mysterious for my liking!"

"That's a blasphemous thing to say, young man. I

shall pray for your forgiveness."

"Yeah, yeah, as you like, Vicar."

The vicar stood with his mouth agape.

Ma was embarrassed; she had never seen the vicar get angry, but now he was close. After this encounter, he stopped visiting. Ma noticed and a few weeks later mentioned it to Peter, asking if he would now be accepting of the vicar's guidance, but he responded negatively.

"I thought he was supposed to follow the Bible. You won't see that old bugger here again. He's a bloody hypocrite."

Ma stared at him. "Just what do you mean by that?"

"The Bible says to go forth and find the lost sheep and bring 'em back into the fold. He knows I'm a lost sheep, but he dropped me like a hot potato. Not that I'm bothered, I prefer it when he keeps away."

"Would you have listened, if he'd tried?" she asked, knowing he would not.

Ma said nothing more, but her eyes showed her pain and disappointment. Reluctantly, she now accepted why village folk were thinking him difficult, bad-tempered and a little strange.

More and more, Peter wanted to be alone and often sat in the long grass on the banks of the Great Ouse, just outside the village. He'd watch the ducks, swans, and moorhens for hours on fine days. Ma had suggested he took his father's old fishing rod to catch a few fish or eels like he used to, lamenting, "Your dad loved a bit of jellied eel, you know. The best ones come down from London. Them Cockney folks do it best."

But Peter no longer had the motivation for fishing. Sometimes children sat with him, enjoying his company, as he enjoyed theirs and their wide-eyed innocence.

Some had secretly disobeyed their mothers to be with him. He remembered the times before he had gone to France when days were happy, long and carefree. Now, for an hour or two, he was content and able to forget his worries, but the stories he told the children's didn't come so easily now. He was comforted by the thought that he had fought the war to end all wars, and the children would not have to do what he had done, and risk being killed in another war.

When alone, he sometimes lay back to lose himself in the depths of a blue sky, but it was often cut short when the banging in his head started. Sweating and trembling, he'd desperately try to calm the noise. Those moments were terrifying and lasted too long. In more rational times, he knew it was only in his head, but it didn't kill the reality of the moment or dull his panic and fear when imaginary shells burst around him. It was all too real.

Chapter 5

Dora had decreed that Friday night was bath night. "Where are them kids? It's nearly six o'clock. They know they have to be here long before now for their bath! I lit the copper two hours ago, the water's hot and the bath is in front of the fire ready. Who knows where they are. Do you? The little devils!"

Tom was not bothered but interrupted his newspaper to appease her. "I got no idea, my duck."

"You know what your son is like. He don't go much on having a bath anyway, and his sister takes more notice of what he tells her than what I do. I bet they're up to no good."

"He's your son too, you know! Would you like me to go and see if they are in the yard or one of the barns?"

"No, I suppose they'll come in soon enough," she huffed in annoyance.

Tom shrugged and returned to his newspaper.

"And their dinner'll be all dried up in the oven too. It won't be worth eating soon!"

Tom lowered his newspaper again. "All right, all right, don't go on about them. They'll turn up when they are good and ready. You can tell them off when they get here."

As always, Dora had to have the last word. "In that

case, you better have your bath now. They'll just have to wait till later and have theirs in dirty water."

"Yes, dear. What if the kids come in?"

"I'll give them their dinner and hold the towel for you."

After Dora had emptied a few buckets of hot water into the galvanised iron bath. He sighed as he undressed and stepped into the water, groaning with stiffness as he lowered himself into the water. It felt good, and helped to relax his aching muscles.

Dora placed a scrubbing brush, a block of soap and a facecloth on a chair close by, then, hung a towel over its back. After washing, Tom relaxed, sliding down into the warm water. With his knees raised and with the water to his chin, he closed his eyes to enjoy the best part of having a bath.

Dora quickly brought him back from his daydreams. "I wouldn't get too comfortable in there if I were you. Them kids should be home by now. I wonder where the little beggars have got to? It'll be dark soon. You'd better get dressed unless you want them to see you naked."

"I thought you said…oh, never mind."

Reluctantly, he raised himself from the comforting bathwater as Dora passed the towel. He dried himself in front of the stove, dressed in clean clothes for the week ahead and settled back with his newspaper again, momentarily savouring the feeling of fresh, clean clothes next to his skin. After a short while, he peered over the pages. "You know what, it's dark, Alfie and Susie *really should* be home by now. I'll slip my coat on and see if they are in the big barn, or somewhere in the yard."

Worried, Dora agreed. "If you hadn't offered, I was going to ask you, or go myself."

Fifteen minutes later, Tom returned to the house. "I can't see any sign of 'em, goodness knows where they are. They know they have to be home before dark. Do you think they could be at a friend's house?"

"I doubt it. They'd tell me if they were going to stay out late, or at least come and ask if they could."

Tom suggested they allow another fifteen minutes, then, if they didn't turn up, Dora should go to their friends' houses to see if they were there or see if anyone knew where they were.

Dora agreed to wait, putting her coat and shoes on in readiness. Tom could see she was seriously worried, but did not comment, trying to avoid an agitated, negative response from her sharp tongue.

"It's no good! I can't wait here doing nothing. I'm going now," she said as she went to the door.

"Shall I come with you?"

"No, stay here in case they turn up."

It was a small village, mostly spread along one main street. There were two short roads off each side which led to a few cottages, a field or two and the church. The village shop was small but sold everything from postage stamps to Wellington boots, brooms, soap, tinned food, bread, and most other essentials. It was closed on Saturday afternoons and all day on Sundays. The Sunday newspapers were dropped in a bundle at the door, next to an honesty box. If someone didn't have change, they would pay in the shop on Monday morning. It was where women went to catch up on village gossip. The pub served the same purpose for men, but to them, it was not gossip, but local news. An enterprising ex-army barber cut men's hair in his shed two evenings a week for threepence, and a farmer sold fresh milk and sacks

of potatoes from his barn. Such was village l
where only the seasons changed.

Dora thought of three possibilities where A
Susie might be and went to those first. She tried not to
sound too upset when asking if her children were there.
Being parents themselves, they immediately recognised
her anguish and answered apologetically in caring tones.
At Susie's best friend's house, she was told, "No, dear,
they're not here, I don't know where they could be.
They've not been here at all today, sorry, love. Come in,
while I ask my Lizzie if she's seen them."

"The last time I saw them was this afternoon. They
were with Uncle Peter down by the river," Lizzie said.

After receiving a few words of sympathy and attempts
at reassurance, Dora went to other houses, where the
responses were much the same. One more said that Alfie
and Susie were seen by the river. Dora was beginning
to panic. It was impossible for her to not consider they
might have fallen in and drowned. Her last call was to
her mother-in-law's cottage, desperately hoping to find
them there, but they were not.

"Peter, a couple of people said they saw Alfie and
Susie with you down by the river this afternoon, is that
right?"

"Yes, they came for a while. I was telling them about
the birds, how swans pair for life and other stuff like that.
They were all right when they left. It must have been well
before five o'clock."

"Do you know where they went?" A tears began to
well in Dora's eye.

"No, they went off as happy as Larry, saying they had
to get home 'cos it was bath night. The last I saw of 'em
they were going over the bridge back towards the village."

"Did they say if they were going anywhere else first?"

"No, not a word, but I did think it was a bit early for their bath. I hope they're all right."

"So do I." Dora bit her bottom lip.

After a few minutes of anxiety and speculation with Peter and Ma, she hurried back to Tythe Farm to tell Tom she hadn't found them and that nobody knew where they were. By now both Dora and Tom were beginning to panic. In a positive moment, between painful thoughts, Tom said, "Well, I think we can rule out them falling in the river if Peter saw them leave."

Dora raised her voice. "Yes, but where the hell are they?" Tom was agitated and angry with the kids for causing so much distress. "I don't know, my duck. I'll get my coat, and box their bloody ears when I find 'em."

It was almost midnight before he returned, having found no trace of the children. He called into the Plough and Harrow to see if anyone had seen them. Being Friday night, it was busy. The air was thick with smoke and loud voices. Shouts of "Nice one!" and "Bad luck!" came from the direction of the dartboard.

Nobody had seen the children during the evening, although one man said he had seen them by the river as he cycled home from work that afternoon. "They were with that strange brother of yours. He's a right grumpy little sod is that Peter. I wouldn't trust him near my kids."

Someone else grunted something which Tom couldn't hear clearly. His instinct was to challenge the remark but thought better of it. So he showed his opinion with a dirty look and a shrug of contempt.

When he arrived home, he had nothing positive to tell Dora, causing her tears to flow. Tom was not sure how to handle her in this state. Their relationship had been strained for so long and he couldn't remember the last time he had seen her cry. With his arm around her shoulder, he spoke quietly. "I don't know what else to suggest, my duck. Perhaps I should go to Ely and tell the police, they'll know what to do."

"It's late, there might not be anyone at the police station."

"Oh, I think there will be. It's Friday, remember: payday. The'll be rounding up a few drunks for the night. When they've got someone in the cells, at least one officer has to be there all the time."

Tom took his cycle clips from a nail in the porch, and his bike from the old timber shed at the back of the house, then rode off into the night. His bicycle had no lights, but he didn't care about being legal. He could see well enough in the moonlight, which for a few seconds prompted him to marvel at the wide expanse of the Fenland sky and how brightly it sparkled. "There's a sharp frost tonight," he muttered. "The kids will be frozen if they are out. It'll teach them a lesson."

Anyone entering the police station could be seen from the back office when its door was open. As Tom approached the front counter, a rotund sergeant puffed and grunted his way forwards. Seeing how he waddled, Tom thought he wouldn't do well if he had to chase a crook or get anywhere in a hurry.

The policeman's double chin wobbled when he spoke, hiding the knot in his tie. "Yes, sir. What can I do for you at this late hour?" His sigh and tone suggested that Tom was not a welcome visitor.

"My children have gone missing and I need your help to find them."

"Missing, you say…are you sure?"

"Of course I'm sure, why else would I be here?"

"All right, sir, just relax. You'd better tell me about it."

As the officer made notes, Tom described the children, gave their ages and where and when they had last been seen. He described their habits and haunts as best he could but was unable to say what they were wearing.

The sergeant looked up. "Would you say your Alfred is an adventurous sort of a lad?"

"Yes, well, as much as any other boy of his age, I suppose. But as I said, his sister is missing too."

Sergeant Bowles put his pencil down, leaned back and looked at the ceiling as if about to utter profound words of wisdom with great authority. "You know, sir, when I was about their age, I was up to all sorts of things. Once I made a camp shelter out of sticks, ferns, reeds, and the like. I thought it would be fun to sleep in it overnight, so I did. Didn't tell anybody because I thought I'd get told I couldn't. My mother, poor thing, God bless her, was worried sick. When I went home in the morning, all cold and hungry, my father took his belt off and gave me a good thrashing for worrying everyone to death. I can tell you it warmed me up, but I don't suppose it did me any harm. Now, sir, my experience in these matters is that you can expect them youngsters to show up of their own accord when they are good and ready. Why don't you go home and wait for them? If they're not back by mid-morning, let us know. We'll have a bit of a search and ask a few questions about the place."

Tom's face reddened. "Is that it? Go home and wait? So you are quite happy to leave two small children out all night and do nothing about it, except hope they turn up!"

"As I said, sir…they usually do at some time or other."

"Some time or other…some time or other, sergeant! Is that the best you can do?"

"There's no need to adopt that attitude with us, sir. In the meantime I suggest you calm down, go home and wait."

Tom had little choice, other than to follow the sergeant's suggestion, so left disgruntled. Cycling home was hard. The sharp wind that cut across the open Fen from the north stung his face. Yet, the adrenalin pumping through his veins provided unnatural energy, helping him maintain a steady pace. His hands and fingers were numb, his eyes watered, and his nose ran in the freezing air. As he sniffed, he thought of how Dora would react, and how he could comfort her. Desperately worried about Alfie and Susie, he was close to tears, while knowing he had to hold himself together for Dora. No doubt she would be tearful, panicking, and thinking of the worst possible things that could have happened to the children.

Tom didn't put his bicycle away or remove his boots. Just pushed the door open and walked into the warmth of the kitchen where Dora had kept the fire going for his return.

As she stood, twisting a damp handkerchief in her fingers, she spoke before he had a chance to say anything. "Was there anyone there? What did they say? Are they coming to look for them? Did you tell them what the children look like and how old they are?"

"Slow down, my duck, and I'll tell you what they said. Yes, a sergeant was there. I told him everything I know, but he didn't seem too concerned just yet, but…"

"Not concerned? Not concerned! Two little children have gone missing and the police are not concerned!"

"Now that's not what I'm saying. Hold your horses for a minute or two and I'll tell you exactly what was said. Why don't you put the kettle on, I need something to warm me up. You can put a spot of that brandy we got left over from last Christmas in it too."

Dora turned to the stove with a gruff, "Tell me then!"

Tom was already upset and now agitated at Dora's impatience. "Just let me finish speaking before you start up again, will you! The police explained that they would not be too concerned 'just yet', unless the children were still missing come mid-morning tomorrow and that we should let them know. They didn't seem to think it was unusual that a couple of kids might stay out overnight and said we shouldn't be too concerned. I just hope that fat old sergeant is right."

"I can't wait that long." Dora's frustration bubbled over. "Anyway, it's already tomorrow! I'm going out to look for them. I looked all around the yard and the barns while you were away. I'll check the ditches and anywhere else they might be."

Tom tried to calm her. "Listen, there's not much point in going out now. It's too dark, you won't see anything. Not only that, if they turn up at any time, they'll want their mother, and you'll want to be the first to know. Best stay here for now. I'll go looking again as soon as it gets light."

It was after three a.m. before they had exhausted their worried conversation, but neither went to bed, just dozed in chairs by the stove when tiredness eventually overcame them. Tom sat up at the sound of cockerels crowing in the yard. They always seemed at their loudest before the sun had broken the horizon. Rubbing his eyes, he went to the children's bedroom, hoping they had crept in quietly without being heard. The beds were empty and undisturbed. When he returned to the kitchen, Dora was awake.

"Not there, are they?"

"No, I didn't expect they would be, but I had to look. I just can't think where the little blighters could have got to." Tom spoke through his tiredness. "As soon as there's a bit'a light, I'll be out looking for 'em."

"Where will you go?"

"I dunno yet. Give me a minute to think. I'll look everywhere! I'll look anywhere and everywhere!"

"I'll go too."

"No, like we said last night, stay here in case they turn up."

"But I can't just sit here and wait."

Tom didn't argue. He saw the tears of desperation well in her eyes before she turned away to conceal them. Dora had always been a strong woman and wanted to be seen to be so now, at least on the outside. Seeing her now left him feeling helpless, and he didn't know what to do for her. His instinct was to hold her, embrace and comfort her, but he resisted, knowing she would shrug him away.

"Okay then, my duck, let's do this in some sort of order, so we don't go over the same ground twice. I suggest you look around the village and ask if anyone has seen 'em, especially at the shop. I'll look in all the barns, stables, milking sheds, and chicken huts I can find. If we don't find 'em after that, I'll nip to the main farm and tell the boss what's going on and that I won't be at work today. Saturday is only a half-day anyway. He won't be happy, but it's too bad. Then, if we don't find 'em, I'll go to the police station again."

Dora agreed, and by the time they had drunk their tea, it was almost light. The wind from the north was still bitterly cold, but it didn't deter folks from going about their business. She asked everyone she met if they had seen Alfie and Susie, but none had. Naturally, everyone wanted to know why she was asking and showed their concern. Some said they would help to search later. Others made suggestions as to where they might be. Eventually, Dora became agitated at the need to keep explaining and hearing the same comments in return. Her only comfort was that everyone said they would keep an eye open for the children and send them home if they saw them. The last time anyone could remember seeing Alfie and Susie was by the river, with Peter.

Two boys suggested they might be hiding in the big barn back at Tythe Farm. "We like to play in there. It's good fun."

Dora knew the village children played in the barn, especially when the weather was bad. She and Tom didn't mind as long as they were careful. At least, she would know where Alfie and Susie were. Tom checked every shed and barn he could find, even when he knew he was trespassing. Such things were insignificant now, but he could find no trace of the children. It was as though they had simply vanished.

As arranged, it was ten-thirty when Tom and Dora met back at the house, neither having anything positive to contribute. The only helpful news was that folks had offered to check their immediate areas.

"Will you be all right while I go to Ely to get the police?" Tom asked.

"Yes, yes, go and get them. I'll stay here in case they turn up, or if someone knows something."

"I dunno how long I'll be, but with a bit of luck I should be back by dockey time."

Tom called back as he took his bicycle from the wall. "Oh, last night I couldn't tell them what the kids were wearing. Do you remember?"

As expected of a mother, she knew.

He had been gone for little more than half an hour when there was a knock at the door. Dora's heart leapt but it sank again when she opened it. "Oh, hello, Vicar, do come in."

"Thank you, Mrs Harrison; I won't stay long. I just wanted you to know that as soon as I heard your children were missing, I checked every corner of the church, graveyard, church hall, and chapel. I regret to say that I could find no trace of your little ones."

"Thank you, Vicar."

"Do you have any idea where they might have got to?"

She thought it was a silly question. Did he think we hadn't already checked everywhere we could think of? What's more, if we had any idea where they might be, we would have probably found them by now.

"No, Vicar, me and Tom have searched everywhere we could think of. Tom has gone to Ely to get the police. Something's happened to them, I just know it. I can feel it in my bones!"

"My dear Mrs Harrison, I don't want you to fret so. I know it must be stressful for you…but they will turn up; just you wait and see. I know the Good Lord will take care of them. I'm going to organise as many people as I can to search around for your little ones."

"As you like, Vicar." Dora's contemptuous expression portrayed her feelings. She was not a religious woman, had never respected the vicar and now wished he would go away. In the past, she had never missed an opportunity to make jokes about him and his name. "Whoever heard of a vicar named, Parsons? It's as daft as a parson named, Vicars," she'd say, then wait for her listener to laugh. Some believed it was bad luck, or even blasphemous to ridicule a vicar. One woman had told her she shouldn't take the mickey, as she may never know when she might need him, and her negative remarks would come home to roost. But Dora had taken no notice.

It was in this moment of awkwardness that vicar Parsons quietly stepped back and left. In the yard, Vera Brown hurried past him.

"Vicar," was her only acknowledgement when he raised his hat and briefly smiled with a polite mechanical reflex.

"Hello, Dora my love, have you found them yet? A terrible business. I've come to keep you company; you must be worried to death, I can't imagine how you must be feeling. Where's Tom? What did the Vicar want?"

Dora and Vera had been friends for as long as Dora could remember, or at least since they had started school together. Both had lived in the village all their lives and shared the trials and tribulations of Fen life. They had never been happier than when they were working side by side in the fields, be they potato picking, onion wringing or beet singling. The worrying times, when their husbands were at the war, had brought them even closer, having shared their innermost thoughts and fears. Both women had put on considerable weight over the years and could now only lament the passing of their youthful figures. They had often joked about their past girlish exploits but were now content at being farmer's wives, and mothers to their children. Accepting this was their life's purpose.

"What did old Parsons want?" Vera asked again.

"I think he felt he ought to show his face and a bit of concern. At least I didn't get a sermon. I think he knew better. Said he was going to organise a search party. I suppose I shouldn't be too hard on him. At least he's doing something that might be helpful."

"Well, that makes a change from him just hovering about, giving silly advice. The old fool creeps around the village as timid as a church mouse. I remember when he first introduced himself, he almost apologised for being here. When I shook hands with him, it was like flapping a bit 'o wet fish."

Dora was more concerned about her children. "I ought to go and look too, but Tom said I should stay here in case they turn up. He's gone to Ely police station. He went last night as well, but they told him to go back today. The police thought the kids might turn up this morning."

"So what are they going to do if they don't turn up?"

"I don't know yet, but we'll see when Tom gets back."

The ladies fretted and speculated for almost an hour before Tom returned just after midday. The policeman with him had come to take statements from anyone who might have useful information. His first task was to ask Dora to reconfirm what the children were wearing, their favourite haunts, who their best friends were and where to find them.

"Mothers always know," he had told Tom.

When the policeman had finished, Tom said, "Dora my duck, I made a statement at the police station… they're gonna start searching the whole area right away.

I'm not hanging about either. I'm going to check the local drains…especially the weed filters in front of the pumping houses."

The look of shock on Dora's face said he should have been more tactful.

Alarmed, Vera reached for Dora's hand as she spoke. "What! You mean we are looking for their bodies?"

Vera gently, but firmly now held Dora's arm with both hands.

"We are not making assumptions, Mrs Harrison, only trying not to leave any stone unturned. I'm sure you would want us to be thorough, wouldn't you?"

Dora nodded gently as she pulled a handkerchief from her apron pocket. Tom excused himself and promptly left, annoyed at his lack of tact.

"Your husband is just helping us check everywhere, Mrs Harrison, as we asked him to. Being a local man, he knows the area like the back of his hand. Now, I need to ask you a few more questions, if I may? Do you mind if I call you Dora?"

She gave an approving nod as the policeman took a notebook from his pocket.

"I'm, Constable Brian Cornwell, you can call me Brian if you like. I'd prefer that anyway," he said with a weak smile, trying to relax her and show a little compassion. "May I sit next to you at the table, Dora?" Not waiting for a reply he positioned a chair close to her.

Dora gestured toward her friend. "Sorry, officer, I should have said, this is my friend Vera, she lives in the village." She hesitated. "Aren't you going to start searching? Taking notes won't find my children."

He spoke softly. "Well, Dora, you'll be pleased to know that we are doing both, and with a lot of help, I might say. As we speak, my sergeant is checking with the bus company and the railway station to see if your children have been seen there, just in case they had decided to run away."

"My Alfie and Susie would never run off! Why would they?"

"You know, Mrs Harrison, some children do. I bet your two have threatened to run away before now. Most children do at some time or other, especially after being told off, or had a bit of a walloping. Has young Alfie or Susie been in trouble lately?"

"No. Well, no more than usual, just little things, kid's stuff, but nothing serious."

"Have you noticed anything missing?"

"What sort of things do you mean?"

"Do they have piggy banks they could take money from? Is there any food missing from the pantry? Have any of their clothes gone? Or anything else they would find useful if they'd planned to run away? What about a favourite toy, especially Susie, does she have a special doll, teddy-bear, or a golliwog?"

Dora blushed, suddenly feeling inadequate, realising she should have already checked. Now she was more receptive to the constable and decided that he really was being thorough.

"Sorry, no, I haven't checked yet."

"Not to worry, Dora, you've got a lot on your mind. We can't think of everything at the same time, can we? We'll check before I leave if it's all right with you."

Before he could ask more questions, Vera asked if he would like a cup of tea. "I can soon put one in the pot."

The constable smiled. "Would you like a cup of tea is my favourite tune, Vera? Thank you. I think the world must revolve around a cup of tea, don't you?"

The kettle was filled and placed on the stove.

"Dora, I have just a few more questions if you don't mind. Where and when did you last see the children?"

"Susie was with me most of the day. Then, when Alfie came home from school they went off together."

"What time was that?"

"Just after three o'clock."

"Were they with any other children?"

"Not that I know of."

"Did they seem upset at all?"

"No. They just went off to play as usual."

"Did they have a bag with them, or were they carrying anything?"

"I don't think so, not that I noticed."

"What time did you expect them home?"

"As it was bath night, they knew to be home by five at the latest."

"Do you know where they went?"

"No, not everywhere, but I know they went to the river at some time."

"Have they stayed out overnight before without letting you know?"

"No, never."

"Before they left, did they say anything unusual that you think might help us?"

"Not really."

Dora responded to his questions worrying that her answers were not helping. She hadn't thought of them running away, only drowning, staying with friends, or getting lost in the fields, although the latter was the most unlikely.

"Dora, I don't want you to jump to any conclusions,

but have any strangers or gypsies been seen in the village lately?"

The women stiffened.

"No, I don't think so."

"That's good, thank you." He touched the point of his pencil on his tongue again. "It might sound a bit unpleasant ladies, but I need to ask. Have you checked the lavatory pit?"

"What!" Dora almost shouted.

"It's worth checking. Some of the holes are rather deep and it's not unknown for a little one to fall in headfirst. I hate to tell you, but we had a case only last year."

Shocked, Dora stood. "That can't be! 'Cos they are both missing. Alfie is old enough to know better and too big to fall in. If Susie had fallen in he would have run and told us!"

"It's all right, Dora, it's all right. It's just that I had to ask."

As he was speaking, Dora took a torch from the mantelpiece and was heading for the door. Vera and the constable followed. At the back of the house, the timber lavatory door was ajar. A few small square sheets of newspaper had fallen from the string loop to land across the floor. Vera hung back at the last moment thinking it was not proper to go looking into other people's toilets. Dora hesitated, too afraid of what she might find, so gave the torch to the policeman. Cornwell held his breath as he pointed the torch down the hole and squinted into the darkness. Those few seconds of silence seemed like an eternity to Dora.

"No, there's nothing down there that shouldn't be." Dora's shoulders dropped with relief as he continued.

"Dora, as for young Alfie telling you, he could have been too afraid to, and ran off to hide, especially if he was supposed to be looking after his little sister."

Dora didn't answer, partly from relief, but mostly because she was too distressed.

"Okay, Dora, let's go back inside and check if anything has gone."

It took only a few minutes to see if the children's clothes and toys were still where they would normally be, and that nothing was missing from the pantry.

"You see, they haven't run off. I just know they have been abducted or had an accident! So when are you going to start looking for them?"

"As I said, others have already started searching. Later I'll go back to the station and see what the sergeant has discovered. I expect he'll organise a bigger search here if we need to. He might even bring one or two others in from Littleport or Soham to help, and maybe from as far away as March if need be. We'll let you know what's going on as soon as he decides."

It was comforting that something official was now being done, but Dora's anxiety was mounting. Although she wanted the police to help, now they were involved and taking it seriously, it took on an even more worrying tone. She slumped onto a kitchen chair, and as she began to cry Vera put an arm around her shoulder. "I just want my Alfie and Susie back."

Constable Cornwell politely excused himself to go and search the buildings in the yard.

"You won't find nothing there. My Tom and me have already looked," Dora said through her tears.

"Just the same, I'll take a look."

After fifteen minutes, he returned to confirm that

Dora was right, and to excuse himself again, saying he would go into the village and ask a few questions. Tom returned to share his mixed feelings. Relieved that he had not found the children's bodies in the drains, but now with greater anxiety for where they might be.

"I met a few people who helped me look. It seems the last time anyone can remember seeing either of them was with our Peter down by the river. Old Mrs Featherstone thought she might have seen them coming home sometime just before five o'clock. But she couldn't be sure. You know how it is. You see kids about the village all the time and think nothing of it. You hardly notice them, unless they are up to mischief."

Chapter 6

The arrival of a police car at two in the afternoon did not go unnoticed. The village grape-vine sprang into action and almost everyone knew about it within an hour. The car pulled into the muddy yard at Tythe Farm. Dora watched from the kitchen window as an overweight police sergeant struggled from the car, straightened his ill-fitting uniform, and made for the house. She opened the door, but before she had a chance to speak he stated, "Mrs Harrison I presume," then looking past her, "hello, Mr Harrison, we meet again."

"Yes," Dora replied, gesturing for him to enter.

The policeman took a moment to regain his breath before pushing his great round chest forward. "I am Sergeant Bowles come to organise things here." Tom thought he showed a pompous streak. "Well, Mr and Mrs Harrison, you'll be pleased to know we have every available officer looking for your children. I have even asked for extra help from Downham Market, and Wisbech. But they won't be here until tomorrow. Now I don't want you to worry…"

"Don't worry! That's easier said than done, they are not your children, are they!" Dora's face turned red.

"Let the officer finish, my duck, he's doing the best

he can, and trying to be helpful." Tom thought a little patronising might encourage him.

"Thank you, sir. What I'm trying to say is that I expect this will all work out nicely and things will get back to normal for you very soon. Rest assured we'll be doing everything we can to find your little ones. I've asked for extra help because of the large area we need to cover. I'm sure you want us to be thorough, Mrs Harrison."

Tom thanked him in a friendly manner, trying to detract from the tensions in Dora's remark.

"Can we go outside, Mr Harrison? I want to know where you have already looked. You can show me your barns and the rest of the yard."

Dora was indignant at being left out but didn't follow. As they entered the largest barn Sergeant Bowles turned to face Tom.

"Look, Mr Harrison, I'll let a constable search around here, if he hasn't done so already. I just wanted to let you know that we will be dragging the river and all the drains. I didn't want to say so in front of your wife, she's upset enough already. I hope we don't find anything, it's just that we have to consider every possibility, you understand. Leave no stones unturned, so to speak."

"Of course. What can I do to help?"

Bowles produced a neatly folded survey map from inside his tunic. "You can start by showing us where the open drains are on this map. The blokes from Wisbech won't know, and they'll be doing the dragging." Then as an afterthought, "And I want you to stay away from them when they do."

"Can't I help?"

"No, the truth is, Mr Harrison, if we do find something, you won't like what you see."

"It couldn't be any worse than what I saw in the war."

"I know, sir, but when it's your own, and especially children, it's a bit different. Like I said, what you can do is show us on this map where the main drains and the pumping stations are. Then arrange to get the pumps turned on. It's best if we have the drains as low as possible. After that, I suggest you stay and comfort your wife, she'll be getting more upset by the hour."

Tom reluctantly agreed but wanted to be involved in the search. It didn't feel right, just sitting around doing nothing when he could be out searching.

An hour later he was home again. The local pumps were turned on and water from the drainage channels was already gushing into the river. Again and again, he wracked his brains and debated with Dora and Vera where the children could be, wondering if they had missed anything. Yet, after mentally revisiting all the places they could think of, there were no new suggestions. For now, their most hopeful conclusions were that they had been abducted, got lost, or had run away. The thought of them having died or been abducted was too terrible to consider, or even discuss, but the unspoken fears remained.

The sergeant returned at dusk and spread his map on the kitchen table. Tom lit and pumped up the Tilley Lamp, placing it next to the map. Then pointing with his pencil Bowles began, "I've had officers out all afternoon looking in this, this and this area. There's no sign of the children, not even a clue. The constables who searched the village and asked around reported nothing positive either. That is, except to say the last place there were definite sightings was with your brother, Peter, down by the river yesterday afternoon. An officer spoke with him and said he seemed agitated, and a bit stressed. Not quite normal, if you get my meaning. He wouldn't look the constable in the eye either. That in itself raises questions. Anyway, an officer went to search the river bank where they were last seen, but he found nothing worth mentioning."

"You'll have to excuse my brother, sergeant. He's not been well since he came back from the war. Shell-shock affected him badly, you see, and he didn't just lose a leg, it messed him up in the head too. Some of the villagers don't understand and take the mickey behind his back. They annoy me, but it's just his way. That's how he is now. He can't help it."

"Ah, that might explain it then."

Tom felt concern that suspicion might be falling on his younger brother. He wanted to say that Peter would never do anything to harm Alfie or Susie, that he loved them and enjoyed their company, but he said nothing, not wanting to draw more attention to Peter and cause the sergeant to speculate on why he might feel the need to defend him.

But Dora responded to the intimation. "Peter wouldn't hurt a fly, he loves the children."

"As well may be the case, Mrs Harrison, but I still need to go and have a word with him myself before I return to the station." Then, after folding his map he added. "We'll be on the job again bright and early tomorrow morning, and every day until we find them children of yours, you can be sure of that. The blokes from Wisbech and Downham Market will be here too." Attempting to show his diligence, he gave Tom a look of sincerity before excusing himself.

Mrs Harrison's cottage was easy to find. Bowles introduced himself and was asked inside, where he found Peter sitting in front of the fire with a poker in his hand. On leaning forwards, he pushed it through the front grille, causing ash to drop into the tray below, so brightening the fire above.

"Ah, you must be Peter Harrison, is that right?"

"Yes," his mother answered.

Peter didn't look up.

"He's already told your constable all he knows, why can't you leave the poor lad alone? He don't know nothing anyway."

"I'm sorry, Mrs Harrison, but I need to hear for myself. He might have remembered something more since the constable was here."

Uninvited, the sergeant took a chair from the table and sat opposite Peter. Then he took a pencil and notebook from a top pocket.

"So you were the last person to see young Alfie and Susie, were you?"

"I don't know, was I?"

"Well, the information we have suggests that you were."

Peter shrugged without looking up.

"Right, lad. Let me ask if you saw your nephew and niece down by the river yesterday afternoon?"

"Yes."

"What time was that?"

"After half-past three, probably about four o'clock, I don't know exactly."

"Thank you, son. How long were they with you?"

Mrs Harrison interrupted. "They might not have been down there with Peter all the time. They might have gone off mucking about somewhere else."

The Sergeant gave her an enquiring look.

"It was probably about half an hour," Peter replied.

"What were you doing?"

"Nothing much, we just sat and talked."

"What about?"

"I dunno. About the swans and that, about wildfowling, and how some birds are now protected, stuff like that." Peter was getting agitated and turned to face Bowles for the first time, unwittingly waving the poker towards him. "Look, I dunno nothing! So leave me alone!"

"Now don't you get testy with me young man, and I think you'd better put that poker down before I charge you with threatening a police officer."

Peter hesitated before putting the poker down.

"Now then, that's better. Some people think you know more than you are letting on, so you'd better tell me here and now what you know. We need to find them kids quickly, so start talking."

"I told you, I dunno nothing!" Peter began to twitch and gently shake. Mrs Harrison had seen how difficult and reclusive Peter became when he was upset. It pained her to see him this way, and she didn't want to go through another day of difficulty. So trying to be tactful she said, "Why don't you stop pestering him, Sergeant! You can see he don't know nothing, and how upset he is. Leave him with me for an hour or two and we'll have a good talk. If he knows anything useful he'll tell me, and I'll let you know. We want them children found as much as anyone else."

Sergeant Bowles was taken aback at Peter's involuntary movements and agreed to leave it to his mother. "Very well, Mrs Harrison, but I expect you to be honest with me, and tell me everything, especially if you care about your grandchildren as you say." With that, he left.

The next day dragging the drains and the river began, but nothing was found, apart from rubbish, a bicycle or two, and a few old sacks containing a couple of bricks and decomposing kittens, found next to the bridge. An officer from Downham Market calculated how far a body might drift, so it was agreed that dragging would continue in an area further downstream. But nothing was found. The day ended with no trace or clues as to where the children might be, or what may have happened to them.

Sergeant Bowles visited Mrs Harrison's cottage twice more but received no additional information from Peter or his mother. It frustrated him since he had decided the young man knew more than he was saying. It was now three days since the children's disappearance and Bowles still had no idea what had happened to them. Yet, in a short time, he had managed to convince himself that Peter Harrison was, in some way, involved. He was embarrassed because villagers had expected him to have found the children by now. When they stopped him in the street to ask, it only created awkward moments. Most of all, Bowles had nothing to report to his superiors. Which he felt made him look inadequate. Nonetheless, he went to see Tom and Dora at the end of each day to report what had been done, while trying not to sound pessimistic.

The *Ely Gazette* was quick to make the story front page news, with the headline: *Missing Children Mystery.*

A reporter had conducted an awkward interview with the reluctant Sergeant Bowles, who had little to say other than to describe his efforts to find Alfred and Susan Harrison. Although prompted, Bowles would not speculate on what had happened to them, except to say that for now, they seemed to have simply vanished. In the mind of the reporter, the words "simply vanished" conjured up great mystery and intrigue, while at the same time it told him the police had no idea of what may have happened to the children. Sensationalising his article, the reporter speculated: *Could the children have drowned and been swept away in the river? Could they have been abducted?* Adding that gypsies were known to steal children. Or had they simply run away?

He had tried to interview Tom and Dora, but Constable Cornwell turned him away under instructions to allow only close friends and relatives onto Tythe Farm. As a result, the newspaper attempted to appear public-spirited by requesting that anyone who spotted the children or knew anything helpful should contact the newspaper in confidence. The paper would then inform the police without mentioning their source. Bowles was furious, see it as a sneaky way of getting information before the police and he was afraid of seeing things in print before he knew about them. Also, he didn't want to be in a position where he owed the newspaper any favours.

By the next day, the story had reached the national newspaper offices in London. As a result, the village and the Ely police station were pestered by reporters and photographers. Most unsettling for Bowles was the arrival of his Chief Constable, who demanded an immediate, up-to-date report on events. After listening to Bowles he was satisfied that all that could be done with the available resources had been done.

Looking the sergeant in the eye he said, "All right, Bowles, you have done your bit. Keep a few constables poking around for a day or two, the locals will expect it, while I get a detective here to take over. Let's see what he can dig up."

Feeling this was a result of his failure, Bowles was embarrassed. When he had met plain-clothed officers in the past he had gained the impression they considered themselves superior to uniformed officers. Consequently, a dislike for them had grown. What is more, he was resentful of his authority being diminished in his domain.

"How are the parents taking it all?"

"Just as you might expect, sir, they are worried sick."

"Yes, no doubt they are quite frantic. Get their doctor to see them. They might need something to calm them down, or who knows what they might do."

"Right away, sir." Bowles cursed himself for needing to be told.

"I think it might show our greater concern if I went to see the Harrisons myself, especially now there is a national interest. An officer of higher authority, you see. We'll take my car then I'll head back to Cambridge."

Bowles felt put down by the words "of higher authority."

Before leaving, he barked a few instructions to the young officer at the front desk. "Constable, get Harrison's doctor to make a house call to see how they are. Make sure you keep them newspaper blokes away from here too, and don't you go saying anything. Do you hear, not a single word to them!"

Within half an hour the chief constable was sitting with Dora and Tom, explaining just how seriously the police were taking the matter, and that no effort would be spared to find their children. Being a father, he could not prevent his official demeanour from wavering. "I understand that you must be getting frantic, so I am authorising a very experienced senior detective to work on this for you, in addition to other things we are doing.

Our searches have already been very thorough as you know."

He didn't mention the scaling back of officers on the ground but went on to say that the detective would want to talk to them and Peter Harrison, "Just in case any of you remember something more. I can assure you we will not stop until we find your children."

Tom and Dora hadn't much to say but seemed to take a little solace from the chief constable's assurances. Distress was obvious in their constant frowns and worried expressions, while the dark areas under their eyes revealed a lack of sleep.

True to the senior officer's word, a detective arrived the next morning to interview Tom and Dora, then Ma and Peter, before talking to the village folk. There was no mistaking his rank when he stopped to speak to Constable Cornwell at the farm entrance. An exceptionally tall man, he made Cornwell look short when he stood in front to him. His brown belted raincoat fell open to reveal a dark, double-breasted suit. In his grey trilby, he looked as though he was wearing a typical detective's uniform.

Detective Sergeant Mills stayed for an hour, asking many of the same questions Tom and Dora had answered previously. However, he was more inquisitive than Bowles, asking why, where, and when, more often. Tom did his best to be as helpful as possible, while Dora was mostly content to let him answer. She cried and sniffed into her handkerchief at some of the questions.

"Do you have a recent photograph of them?"

"We've only got two or three," Dora sniffed, "one when they were babies and the most recent is of them at a wedding last year."

"That should do."

Dora stood, saying she would fetch it from the dresser in the best room.

Mills' final question was. "Where can I find your brother, Peter?"

Tom was quick to reply, "He's stressed enough as it is. Please don't push him too hard. Some of the village folk have already accused him of being involved."

"Why would they do that, Mr Harrison?"

Tom kicked himself. "Because, as you already know, Alfie and Susie were last seen with him. He's disabled, had a bad time of it during the war and it's still in his head, he's not over it yet. Let's say he's a bit different, sort of disturbed by his experiences."

"Disturbed, you say… in what way?"

Tom now thought he had said too much so tried to explain, hoping he hadn't created problems for Peter. "It's like this, officer. When he came home from France he'd lost a leg and had shell shock, still has, although he's getting better now. Ma says she hears him crying out in the night. He struggles to accept that he's handicapped and calls himself a cripple. He thinks he's useless and a burden so gets withdrawn and reclusive at times. He's patient and good with kids though, but he's got little time for authority. I think he blames it for how he finds himself now. He used to be a fun lad before he joined up, but now he can be a little difficult at times. I have to admit that he can be rude too, but he don't mean it. It's just his way. So go easy on him and you might find he'll tell you more."

"Mmm…strange, is he?" the detective said quietly.

"No, he's not! He's just trying to recover from what the war did to him, nothing more. I tell you he loved our kids and they loved him. He was never happier than when he was with them. He used to say he didn't feel threatened by them, and they accepted him for how he was. Come to that, he was great with all the village kids. They liked him telling them stories, he enjoyed it too. It sort of took him out of himself, if you know what I mean. He wouldn't have hurt one hair on any of their heads. He just gets upset sometimes 'cos some of their parents don't like him and told their kids to stay away from him. They painted him as some sort of a monster. It frightened some of the real little ones what didn't understand."

"You talk in the past tense, Mr Harrison?"

Tom looked down and shook his head. In that moment Mills accepted the sincerity of what Tom was saying.

Dora held out a photograph. "Will this do? You can keep it. We've got two of them."

"Perfect, Mrs Harrison, thank you." He then turned to Tom. "All right, Mr Harrison, I understand. Where can I find him?"

"I'll go with you and show you where he lives."

"Thank you, but when we get there it's better if I see him by myself."

"Okay, but at least let me introduce you in a way that won't upset him. If he's scared he won't tell you anything, so you might as well let me."

Even with Tom's delicate introduction, Peter quickly became agitated. His mother's attempts to calm him had little effect.

Mills tried to be tactful and spoke quietly. "Peter, I want those children found as much as you do. So, if you would just help with my questions as best you can, I'd be really pleased. There is no need for you to be upset. You are not being accused or blamed for anything and my questions are about the children, not you."

After half an hour with Peter and his mother, Mills left no wiser, yet feeling he would get nothing more from Peter. He spent two more days in the village, interviewing those he thought might know something, whilst picking his way through much gossip and speculation. He believed he'd only managed to discover three things of any consequence. Firstly, was that several people confirmed they had seen the children with Peter Harrison by the river on the afternoon they went missing. Next, Peter was a little strange and appeared uncooperative, so raising suspicions. Then last, one old lady thought she may have seen the children walking back to the village, but she wasn't sure.

Mills spent the next morning in Ely with Sergeant Bowles going over their notes, comparing them with what the local officers had gathered. At lunchtime, he voiced his opinion. "We're not getting to the bottom of this, are we? And I still don't think, Peter Harrison is as innocent as his family would have us believe. Someone knows something, there's always someone who does, and I think it is Peter Harrison."

"I'm inclined to agree," Bowles replied, not knowing what else to say.

"I think we should bring him in for questioning, get him out of his comfort zone, such as it is, away from his mother, and put him under a bit of pressure to see what he comes out with."

"When?" asked Bowles.

"No time like the present, Bowles."

They drove to the village and pulled up outside Mrs Harrison's cottage. As always, village folk noticed and a fresh round of speculation ensued. Inquisitive children stopped to look at the car, not knowing what they might see. Some peered inside. A boy wrote down the registration number, adding it to his collection.

Mills was deliberately blunt. There was no courteous introduction or explanation this time. Bowles was taken by surprise, but said nothing, leaving things to the detective.

"All right, young man, you are coming with us."

"What for?" Peter asked.

Mrs Harrison stepped between them. "I told you he's done nothing, leave him alone!"

"Sorry, Madam, but we have to take him to the station for further questioning." Mills paused, then increasing the pressure he added, "I can't say when he'll be back, or if at all. It depends on what he tells us."

"I told you, he's done nothing!" Ma shouted.

"We'll see about that, but he knows more than he's letting on. Now we can walk out of here quietly or do it the hard way. Which is it to be, Mr Harrison?"

"I'm coming too."

"No, Madam, that won't be possible."

She watched as Bowles guided her son to the car by his arm.

Expressionless, Peter looked back to see his mother standing by the cottage door in tears while she fidgeted with her apron. She watched from the doorway as the car drove off, before backing inside to get her coat and going to tell Tom what had happened.

A few village women and children watched the events unfold from across the road, their faces full of speculation, believing this was a significant event. Ma ignored them, expecting the whole village would know within an hour that her Peter had been taken away.

Tom was both puzzled and furious, especially at seeing his mother so upset. "I'm going to Ely to see what the hell is going on."

Ma stayed with Dora for mutual comfort. It was more than an hour before Tom returned, looking flustered and still angry.

"I didn't see him! They wouldn't let me past the front desk. Just said they were holding him for further questioning. When I said I'd wait until they were finished, they told me not to bother because they might be keeping him there. They said that if they do let him go today, they'll bring him home."

"Then I'd better go to be there for him when he arrives," Ma said, wringing her hands.

Peter was scared, and didn't know how to handle the interview, but had the presence of mind to remember that he was completely innocent. Even so, he was afraid of being accused of things he hadn't done or even knew about. He couldn't prove his innocence but was comforted in the knowledge that the police couldn't prove anything against him either. In his mind, they had nothing bad on him, and could only speculate. So he just needed to stay composed.

He was told to sit at a bare wooden table while Detective Mills stood opposite. Leaning forward with his knuckles resting hard on the table, Mills deliberately stared down at his suspect to intimidate him. "It's time you stopped playing games with me, young man. Just come to your senses and tell us what you know. Now let's get it straight, you were the last person to be seen with Alfred and Susan Harrison on the afternoon of the day they went missing. In fact, only minutes before they disappeared! What time was that?"

"I don't know for sure. I didn't check, and I don't know if anyone saw them after me."

"There have been no definite sightings of them since, so that makes you the last known person to be seen with them. Now you have to admit that it puts you in an awkward position. So just tell us what happened and put an end to this nonsense!"

"I've already told you, I don't know any more."

Mills leaned further forward to glare into Peter's eyes. Peter turned away.

The detective's voice carried undertones of sarcasm and threat. "Well, you will excuse me if I say I don't believe you. Now stop pissing me about or it will go bad for you!"

The fear in Peter's eyes was obvious. Mills hoped he was beginning to push his suspect into saying something incriminating.

"They were all right when they left me. That's all I know."

"That's not good enough, young fella! I'm convinced you know more about this than you are saying! Now what the hell happened on that riverbank?"

Peter's eyes began to widen and glaze as he raised his voice, "I don't know nothing! Nothing happened!"

Mills slammed his hand down hard on the table, making Bowles jump. Peter shuddered and clasped his head with both hands to cover his ears. Then turned sideways to the table and curled into a foetal position. He didn't know where he was, but shells were bursting all around him. Bowles expected Mills to stop the interrogation, but to his surprise, he continued. Shouting, "Come on! What did you do to those children?"

But Peter couldn't hear him for the noise of battle. Mills repeated his question with the same ferocity.

Bowles stepped in. "Excuse me, sir, but he can't tell you anything while he's like this. Let's take a break, and I'll get a constable to make us a brew."

Mills gathered his breath and agreed with a silent gesture. After fifteen minutes the questions began again. Peter was pale, weak, and stressed. His shirt was wet with perspiration, sticking to his back and chest as the questions kept coming. Mills was careful not to bang the table again, although he kept pressing Peter for answers he didn't have. Questions turned into accusations. It was too much for Peter to handle.

"Half the village think you've got something to do with the kids' disappearance, why would they think that? I'll tell you why. Because they know you are weird, and they don't trust you, that's why. They can't all be wrong, can they? So, bloody well tell me the truth!"

Peter was so stressed that he was on the verge of making up a story of guilt to satisfy Mills and get this over with when the questions stopped. He was shaking, feeling nauseous, and so weak that he didn't know if he could stand.

The policemen went to another room leaving Peter alone. "That little devil is not going to talk, is he? I'm bloody sure he knows something. He must. We've got nothing on him at all, just suspicion. So until we find some evidence, or he confesses, we'll have to let the little one-legged sod go."

"What if he's telling the truth and really doesn't know anything?" Bowles suggested.

"He bloody well does!"

Bowles didn't pursue his point, but after a few

moments of silence, he asked. "Shall I take him home?"

"What are your cells like, Sergeant?"

"OK. Like any other police cell, I suppose. Basic but clean."

"We could hold him here overnight to put a bit more pressure on him."

Bowles was quick to reply. "I don't think that's a good idea, sir, if you don't mind me saying. He's already in a bad way, and I don't think we want to be responsible for him. You never know what he might do to himself in his current state."

"Okay, you could be right. Take him home. But you can tell him I'm not finished with him."

When Bowles returned to the interview room Peter was still sitting, now leaning forward with his elbows on the table, holding his face in both hands. For the first time, Bowles felt sorry for him and wondered if his lack of information really was because he had none to give. "All right lad, that will be all for today. Let's get you home."

Peter was slow to stand, trembling as he did. Staring at the floor, he made his way to the door without speaking. He didn't look at Mills when they passed. Showing a little compassion, Bowles decided to drive him home himself, believing that Peter wouldn't appreciate a constable trying to make conversation along the way. He was still in a fragile state when Bowles dropped him off at his mother's cottage. Although a short journey, it gave Peter time to relax and recover a little.

Watching, as he slowly limped to the door, Ma didn't need to ask how he was. "Hello, sweetheart. I expect you'd like a nice cup of tea?"

Peter gave a half-smile, "No, thanks, Ma." Then after

a moment, he said, "Yes, I think I would like one if you don't mind."

Ma removed the round iron cover from the hottest part of the stove then, taking a cloth to the handle of her blackened kettle she slid it over the hole. She wanted to know how it went at the police station but knew better than to ask right now. Peter's drained look deterred her, believing he would tell her in his own time. She didn't have to wait long.

In a pained, weak voice he said, "They think I did away with Alfie and Susie, Ma. How could they possibly think that? I love them kids." Tears ran down his cheeks as he blew his nose.

"We all know that, dear, you wouldn't hurt a fly."

"They said half the village think I'm weird and that I did something to them."

"Let them think what they like, son, we know the truth. If they think that then it's them what's got the problem, not you. You can expect they'll whisper behind their hands. They got nothing better to do, but you know what they say, don't you? 'whispers tell lies and fools listen', and you know you never hear anything good from a whisper."

Mother and son sat in silence by the stove for almost half an hour. As the daylight dimmed, Peter decided to go to bed. It was early, but Ma understood, she could see he was exhausted. Kissing his forehead she told him not to fret, and bid him goodnight. Then she sat, worrying about the events of the past week, fearful of what was to come, and the fate of her grandchildren. The door squeaked as Tom entered.

"Is Pete back yet, Ma?"

"Yes. Just over an hour ago, but he's gone to bed, the

poor boy is drained. They must have given him a hard time. I do worry about him. I don't know what they did at that police station, but he looked terrible when he came in." She repeated what Peter had told her.

"That's ridiculous, Ma. Pete wouldn't hurt a fly."

"My words exactly, son. It's times like this I wish your father was here."

"The poor lad is not well to start with, what did they think they would achieve by frightening and upsetting him like that?" I'll come back in the morning, Ma. I don't like to leave Dora alone for long. I think she's beginning to go off the rails with the worry of it all."

Chapter 7

It was another four days before a police car arrived at Ma's cottage, bringing Sergeant Bowles and a constable who waited by the car. Bowles was sympathetic to Peter's condition and had hoped to encourage him, in a non-threatening manner, into remembering something more. Or at least tell him if and how he had been involved in the children's disappearance. But Peter could add nothing more, and the sergeant left after half an hour.

Ma warmed to the sergeant's kindly manner and walked with him to the car. "So what's happening to find the children?"

"Well, Mrs Harrison, we have looked everywhere possible, and as you know, we found nothing, not a single clue as to what might have happened to them. Nobody we have spoken to can tell us anything that might be helpful either. As Detective Mills said, there is always someone out there who knows something. We just have to wait until we find them, or if they come out with it." Hastily adding, "In the meantime, please be assured that we'll still be keeping an eye open for the children."

"So what's being done about it right now? They can't just disappear into thin air."

Bowles was defensive. "Of course not, like I said,

somewhere, someone knows something. So we'll keep asking questions. At the moment all we have to go on is little more than gossip and what some folks 'think' they know or saw. Detective Mills has alerted the police further afield, telling them to keep a lookout for them. That's why he asked for the photograph. He's had it copied and passed around all the police stations in the county, and even further afield."

"And has anyone seen them?"

"No, Mrs Harrison, you would already know if they had, and just between you and me, it's a long shot, so don't go getting your hopes up too high. I'd hoped your Peter might have been able to tell us a bit more. After all, the last positive sighting of them was with him. Personally, I think he knows something more."

"Then you must think he's involved!"

"No, I didn't say that. What I mean is…he might have been able to give us a clue or two without even realising it."

Ma didn't quite believe him but asked no more questions.

No sightings or news of Alfie and Susie over the following weeks were found, and no clues to give anyone hope. The enormous stress, anxiety, and fading optimism caused Dora to be more impatient and disagreeable with Tom. He, in turn, became increasingly frustrated with her cutting remarks, as though she was blaming him for their children's disappearance, or at least, for them not being found. Most times he would let her words pass without comment. Consequently, they fell into many hours of thought whilst not speaking to each other, causing the stress between them to mount.

Just as the doctor had advised, Tom eventually returned to work to keep occupied and not dwell too long on things. Yet, he couldn't forget the children for more than a few minutes at a time. His thoughts drifted for long periods, and on several occasions, when he refocused his mind back to his work, he was surprised to see how much he had done while not concentrating.

He and Dora were becoming introverted and reclusive. Even the village folk behaved differently now, not knowing what to say or to talk to them about. It was an awkward sympathy. Periodic questions to the police provided no answers that would encourage a little optimism. It seemed inevitable that they would have to accept their children had simply vanished, in what was now a surreal, unacceptable world.

Life in the village around them began to carry on as before, upsetting Dora. "Don't they know my children are still missing? How can they carry on like normal?" she snapped more than once.

Tom didn't know what to say. There was no closure, no ability to move on, even if they had wanted to. Not unless they were to give up hope, which they would never do. It would be a total betrayal of their love for Alfie and Susie. Conversations were sparse and their presentation to the outside world was nothing more than a thin veneer covering their innermost feelings. Villagers eventually stopped asking Dora if there was any news, as she would get upset and start to cry. Mostly, she didn't answer at all, just shook her head and hurried away to hide her fresh tears.

Tom took a little comfort from being reunited with his team and liked nothing more than to be alone with them in the fields. Sometimes he confided his innermost thoughts to them. Sharing his fears and anxieties as they worked, asking them questions about Alfie and Susie. "What do you think has happened to them? What else can I do to find them?" It was safe to talk aloud there and the horses would never betray his confidence. He always felt better after a chat. It was like an exorcism when the Devil nagged at his heart.

Now more reclusive than ever, Peter's reluctance to leave the cottage had grown, although he occasionally went to Tythe Farm to ease his boredom. There he'd potter, collect eggs for Dora, play with the dogs, cut up bog oakes for firewood, and do other small tasks to occupy himself. Mending sacks and cob baskets in the big barn occupied him for a few hours on rainy days. It helped him feel useful again, even though he was lonely. He particularly liked swirling new potatoes with a stick in a bucket, peeling them for Dora or his mother. It had been his job when he was a boy. Silly, he thought, but it was satisfying, taking his mind back to happier times.

"How are them spuds coming on? They gotta be done before your father gets home for his dinner, you know," his mother would joke. Peter smiled at the memory, wishing his father was still here.

Dora always offered him something to eat, which he mostly declined, just settling for a mug of tea and perhaps a homemade biscuit. Neither he nor Dora was disposed to much conversation, but there was always a sense of wanting to chat, albeit with difficulty starting.

Afraid he might become more introverted, his mother encouraged him to go out, get some fresh air, see something different, and feel the sun on his face again. "Go down to the river," she'd say, hoping it would help bring him out of his depression.

He liked the river, but it held uncomfortable connotations now, making him reluctant, saying. "Don't push me, Ma." Then to appease her, "I'll go when I'm ready…you'll see." Deep down, part of him wanted to go and sit quietly on the bank, there was always something different to see by the river. But he was afraid of the villagers' scorn, especially as he'd seldom been seen of late. His mind churned, speculating over what might happen. Would he get strange looks? Would he be chastised or abused? Would people avoid him and turn away? Would the village children run away or stand and stare at him? The more he thought about it, the greater his fears became. The detective's words echoed in his head time and again. "They know you are weird and don't trust you."

However, rising very early one morning, and in a moment of confident defiance of his fears, he decided to go to the river. Taking comfort from knowing it was Sunday, he would see few people as he cycled through the village. Then, if anyone saw him, they might not recognise him with his army greatcoat collar turned up, hiding much of his face. As it was, he only saw one person, a man cycling fifty yards ahead. Peter held back. Now and again the man disappeared into thick patches of fog that drifted slowly over the road like a blanket.

By the time he reached the river his good leg ached with the exertion of propelling himself on a single pedal. He had fitted a clip to hold his foot in place and removed the other pedal allowing his artificial leg to hang unencumbered. He slipped as he climbed the dew-covered grassy bank.

The early sun was beginning to evaporate the fog, offering a little warmth as he spread his coat on the grass.

Sitting quietly, he began to realise how much he missed these happy times. There were moments of euphoria when he watched moorhens forage amongst the lily pads, and when a water rat, oblivious to his presence, emerged from the reeds to nibble on a piece of flotsam only a yard from his foot. For a while he was happy, forgetting his stump which so often pained him, especially when the weather changed. This was how it used to be and how he thought it should always be. He watched as the last of the mist crept gently across the water, evaporating as it neared the far bank. He remembered the early mornings when he was a boy, coming here to check his eel traps, and taking the catch home in a bucket to proudly present to his mother. He knew the eels were not always welcome, but she had praised him and always turned them into a meal. He smiled, comforted by the memory.

As the rays of the morning sun warmed his face, he felt a warm inner glow. His mind wandered back to the long hot summer days when, after school, he and his friends would come here to swim. Yelling and shouting as they jumped and dived into the water. There was the annual swimming gala with races across the river and diving from the bridge. The whole village turned out for it. They were such happy times.

A noisy traction engine travelling behind the bank brought him back to the present, causing his mind to move into darker places. Feeling sad, he doubted if he would ever sit here again with the village children, telling them stories about the river, its wildlife and how to catch eels in a sack of straw. He wondered how long the villagers would take to give up their suspicion of him, or if they ever would. It made him desperately unhappy and he hated his forced seclusion.

Then, while squinting at the reflected sunlight on the water he thought, *I wonder what it's like to drown, to breathe water instead of air? Would it make me cough and choke? I wonder if it's painful? Would I see a bright light at the end of a tunnel just before I die, like they say you do? If I walked into the river to end it all, would I panic at the last minute? There's nothing for me here, so I've nothing to lose. Some say drowning is peaceful if you don't fight it. I wonder how they know? Has anyone drowned and come back to tell? Would I still get into heaven if I did away with myself? If there is a God, would he still accept me?* Then after a little contemplation, *No, I can't do that. If I do people will really believe I did something to Susie and Alfie and had to do away with myself because I couldn't cope with the guilt. Or that I was afraid of being found out and hanged. Anyway, Ma would be devastated, especially after losing her grandchildren. Perhaps I should have just died in the war.*

Undisturbed, he spent another hour or two on the riverbank. If he was lucky, he would be home before the villagers came out of church and be able to sit quietly with the Sunday newspaper for the rest of the day.

Ma studied him. "It looks as though your little outing did you some good. You'll get some colour back in your cheeks before you know it!"

The next morning, just as old Mrs Harrison was taking her quart milk churn to be filled, a police car stopped outside her cottage. Sergeant Bowles clumsily scrambled out. "Ah! Mrs Harrison. Is your son, Peter, at home?"

"Yes. Why? What do you want with him?"

"We'll talk inside if you don't mind."

Feelings of trepidation flirted with optimism as they went into the cottage. "So what's this all about? Have you found the children?"

"No, Mrs Harrison. Two more children have gone missing from the village, so I need to talk to your son."

"Oh, dear God, no! Who are they?"

"It's a boy and girl again, the Fletcher twins, Mary and Alan. Do you know them?"

"Yes, but what has it got to do with our Peter? Why don't you go and upset someone else?"

"Listen to me, Mrs Harrison…with his suspected involvement in your own grandchildren's disappearance I have no choice but to question him. Like it or not."

The sergeant walked past her and into the cottage where he confronted Peter. "Now, young man, where were you on Saturday afternoon?"

"At home."

"Can you prove it?"

"Ma will tell you."

"Yes, he was here all day, I can vouch for that."

"Unfortunately, the word of a mother, or any other relative, is unacceptable as an alibi." Bowles wanted to believe her but she was his mother and would be expected to protect him.

Then how on earth do we 'prove' he was here?"

Bowles didn't answer. For now, he had no option other than to consider she may be telling the truth, unless he could prove otherwise, so continued with his questions.

Peter soon became distressed and wouldn't look Bowles in the eye, giving short, seemingly unhelpful answers.

"Why can't you leave him alone? He's done nothing," Ma pleaded.

"Look, Mrs Harrison, the children were last seen in the vicinity of Tythe Farm and we know that your Peter goes there. I'm just doing my job and it would go a lot easier for everyone if you would both cooperate. Even if he's not involved he might have seen something that would help. Then, at least we could eliminate him from our enquiries."

"How could he see anything when he was here all day?" We've got nothing to cooperate with. Can't you see that? And look how upset he is, just as he was beginning to come out of his shell."

"Upset he might be, but not as much as the parents of the missing children, I can assure you."

Ma thought it strange that she didn't already know about the twins being missing, then realised the village grapevine was excluding the Harrisons.

"Now, about Tythe Farm…"

"All the village kids go there to play in my Tom's big barn at some time or other. Our Alfie used to take them, especially on mucky days. It's nice and dry in there and they have a bit of harmless fun."

"Thank you, Mrs Harrison; it's one of the places we are going to look. We'll be doing much the same as we did when your grandchildren went missing."

"Huh! I'd have thought you'd do better than that! You didn't find them, did you?"

Apart from a dirty look, the sergeant ignored her remark and left, only to return later in the day with more questions for Peter.

"Now then, young fella-me-lad, what do you know about this?" The sergeant held out a grubby pink ribbon.

"What is it?" Peter asked. Ma moved closer to see.

"It's a ribbon. We found it in the big barn at Tythe Farm."

"So?"

"You go there, don't you? Do you know anything

about it, or who it belongs to?"

"No, why should I?" Peter stared at the sergeant for the first time, challenging him for a logical answer.

"I'll tell you why. I've just come from the Fletcher's house where Mrs Fletcher identified it as belonging to her Mary! Or at least she confirmed that Mary had ribbons just like it."

"I still don't know nothing about it!"

"Well, I think you do!"

"Hang you on there a minute, Sergeant Bowles!" Ma demanded in her strong Fen accent.

Bowles was surprised, not accustomed to being spoken to in this way, especially by a woman; his face reddened.

"That there ribbon could've been there a long time and could've belonged to any one of them village girls what play in that barn. Most all of 'em got ribbons of some colour or other for their pigtails. So don't you go accusing my Peter of things he don't know nothing about, do you hear!"

"I was not accusing him, Mrs Harrison," he said by way of an unconvincing apology.

"Well, that's just in case you were then!" Ma had to have the last word.

The village was rife with debate and speculation for weeks, but the Fletcher twins remained missing. An underlying fear was always present, and again, strangers were treated with suspicion. Even gypsies, hearing of the events, stayed away knowing they would automatically be suspected. Commercial travellers who were already known to the villagers, and who visited the shop and the pub regularly, were also treated with suspicion. Not a day passed when a policeman was not seen asking questions or searching. Mothers were now more fearful for their children than ever before and for a week or two youngsters were rarely seen without an adult close by. None were allowed to walk to and from the village school alone as they had once done. In the afternoons, some women escorted the children of working mothers to their homes. Speculation was fuelled by fear, and once again, in the absence of any clues, Peter Harrison came under suspicion.

National newspapers kept track of events and didn't help as they sensationalised and speculated on what terrible things might have happened to the children. Headlines such as "Another Two Children Vanish", "Is There a Monster Lurking?" and "Who's Children Will Be Next?" only heightened the tension. One newspaper commented that a local man, Peter Harrison, was being questioned and closely watched by the police, causing alarm and near panic in the village, adding that a demon may be living amongst them. Peter became even more afraid and reclusive.

After Peter was named, Sergeant Bowles made a press announcement on the steps of Ely Police Station. "This dangerous, sensationalised scaremongering has to stop immediately! If it does not, there will be no more press briefings, you will be kept out of the village and left in the dark." Then alluding to Peter Harrison, "And nobody will be tried or convicted by the press! Do you understand?"

As if he had not heard, a reporter shouted, "What involvement is Peter Harrison suspected of?"

Bowles clenched his fists and glared at the reporter without answering, before going back into the police station. The gathering dispersed amongst low mutterings.

No trace of the Fletcher twins emerged. A month later a six-year-old girl named Polly Brown went missing. Once more a child had disappeared without a trace. Never before did the village get so much attention from the newspapers, radio, and police. Again, Peter Harrison was the first to be questioned, which created more suspicion and fear of him in the minds of the villagers. As far as some folks were concerned, he was guilty of the most horrible crimes against all the missing children.

"Why else would the police keep questioning him? They must suspect him but can't prove anything," was the common thought.

The Harrison family were shunned, leaving only the village shopkeeper who would speak to them. Old Mrs Harrison was marginally tolerated, although she soon realised that most people only wanted to get information from her to fuel their gossip. But she had nothing to offer, which was interpreted as having something to hide. Consequently, her little chats became rare.

Eventually, extra officers needed to be assigned to keep the press from the village. They were a nuisance and were indirectly undermining police investigations. The final straw for Bowles was seeing potentially useful information published before it had been reported to him. On investigation, much of it was found to be incorrect and potentially dangerous. He decided that all future announcements to the press would be made at the police station in Ely, where no questions would be answered unless approved by a visiting senior officer.

Five children had now mysteriously disappeared without a trace, leaving the police embarrassed at having no leads whatsoever. Nor could they explain, only speculate, so keeping the press at a distance to avoid awkward questions was not easy. When announcements were to be made, they were carefully scripted and read verbatim. All information provided was of what the police had done, were doing, or intended to do. However, it didn't prevent the reporters from calling out questions.

With the noticeable lack of evidence, leads, suspects, or bodies, two specialist police officers from Cambridge were sent to Ely. Their task was to review all the statements and other information for clues and possible connections between each event. By the end of their stay, they had only found two common points of interest in all three cases. First, was that the five children had disappeared leaving no tangible trace or clue. Except for the ribbon found in the barn, which was considered very weak evidence of anything suspicious. It could have belonged to any girl and may have been there for a while. The second point was the vague connection with Peter Harrison, but they found no proof of anything untoward and were only left with suspicion and speculation.

Over the following months, it became clear that life in the village would never be the same again. Some families refused to allow their children out alone. Two families moved to another village. Eventually, a few parents began to relax. In time, the police presence in the village decreased and the press moved on. Now and then an investigative reporter would arrive in the hope of discovering what the police had not, so making a name for himself.

From the parents' desperation, pressure was put on the Parish Council to "do something positive", although no one had any suggestions of what it might be. Until now, the council had been silent, so a meeting was called in the village hall. Although unspoken, most felt the

Parish Council would have few ideas of what else could be done or have the authority to do much more. But it was felt they were, at least, doing something and not allowing the matter to rest.

The meeting was to be chaired by Councillor Richard Cole, an unusually short skinny man with a red face and an ego that had blossomed when he was elected Chairman of the Parish Council. He'd become unpopular since then, especially after insisting on being called Councillor Cole, or at the very least, Mr Cole, when he had always been known to everyone as Dick. Some folks described him as a beggar on horseback, while others simply said he was a big fish in a small pond. As he was unlikely to be re-elected, some joked about how he would handle his ego when he was no longer a councillor. Others wondered if he would continue to present himself as an authority on all matters concerning the village.

His attempts to promote his perceived superior intellect, and appear more erudite, were often unsuccessful, as he was guilty of misusing words, much to the amusement of his audience. It was with some surprise that he had been reluctant to chair the meeting since villagers expected it would pamper his ego. Some decided it was because he wouldn't know what to do or say. However, his demeanour made him the perfect target for folks to vent their frustration on.

As the little village hall filled, Chairman Cole banged on the head table with his knuckles and raised his voice, calling the meeting to order. At that moment, Sergeant Bowles entered at the back of the room. He was hardly recognisable in his brown suit. Without his sergeant's cap, he showed the sharp contrast of a weathered face against his white balding head. People nearer the front were unaware of his presence.

Cole hesitated before taking a deep breath. "Ladies and gentlemen, we are here pacifically to discuss the disappearance of five village children and what can be done about finding them. Mrs Reed will take notes for the Council minutes. Before we open the meeting to comments, suggestions, and questions, let me say, on behalf of the Council, how dreadfully sorry we are for those poor children and our symphonies go out to each of their parents. I know how you must feel…"

"No, you don't, how can you know? You've never had any children. Cut the waffle and let's get to what you intend to do about it!" a male voice called out.

A murmur of approval went through the gathering, setting the tone for the meeting, making Cole nervous.

Taken off guard he stammered, "Well, the police have, er, done everything they can to find the children. They have looked far and wide, and er, it's difficult to see what more can be done."

"Sounds like you are defeated before you start then, you old fool" the same man shouted.

Cole became even more flustered and a little annoyed as he hesitated to regain his composure. "Now look here, let's not make this personal. I thought this meeting was going to be constructive and hopefully provide some ideas on what is to be done. So let's settle down and put our flusterations and unhelpful comments aside, shall we?"

To Cole's obvious relief, there were signs of agreement, albeit with an air of contempt, and a few sniggers for the man and his use of words. The gathering settled while they listened to Cole's summary of what the police had already done.

After recapping the events surrounding each disappearance, and hearing a few impromptu accusations and theories, someone asked, "Why isn't Peter Harrison here? He's involved in some way, he must know more than most. The police always go to him first, so they obviously suspect him of something. He should be here. I don't trust the little beggar!" Others sounded their agreement.

Tom's blood pressure rose as he raised his voice to speak for the first time. "Just listen to me, you lot! This all started because my brother was the last person to see my Alfie and Susie. That doesn't mean he's involved or guilty of anything, whatever your twisted, nasty little minds might think! If he was guilty of anything, the police would have locked him up long ago. Instead, he sits at home terrified to go out because of you. The police go to him first because he enjoyed the kids' company and they liked him. He understands them better than most. They'd tell him things they wouldn't dare tell their parents, 'cos they trusted him and he'd give them good advice. He never judged them or ever told them off, just guided them to do the right things. The police go to him because he might know best about where they go and what they do."

Tom's chest pounded as he became increasingly angry. When he stopped to take a breath, Vicar Parsons stood and raised a hand to intervene and hopefully avoid an ugly scene. It took more than half a minute for everyone to settle while he patiently waited. Eventually, Cole had to call for silence to allow the vicar to speak.

"Excuse me for saying so, but I feel it is grossly unfair to start apportioning blame on some poor soul who is so clearly unwell and not here to defend himself. I am as satisfied as the police are that Peter Harrison is not involved. It's high time you opened your hearts to him. You have no concept of the pain and suffering you cause him with these nasty, unfounded accusations. You should be ashamed of yourselves."

There was a surprised silence when the vicar, looking a little embarrassed, sat down. It was unusual for him to be so outspoken.

The meeting returned to order, but the mood remained. After much debate, it was accepted that, as far as anyone could see, the police had done all the obvious things, and a few more besides. It was noted with some comfort that no more children had gone missing since Polly Brown's disappearance. However, it provided no satisfaction for the parents of those children who were still missing and did not relieve the fears of others.

The consensus of opinion was that, although the police had done their best, they had now given up. True or not, it was found to be unacceptable. Mr Brown described them as, "a useless bunch."

At that, Sergeant Bowles called out, "That's unfair!"

People turned to see Bowles at the back of the room.

"The police have spent many months searching everywhere we could think of. We even brought in extra officers from around the county, dragged rivers and drains, interviewed dozens of people, including every gypsy we could find. We've distributed photographs to all the police stations in the country, and investigated every possible sighting. Believe me, we are as frustrated and as anxious as you are to find the children, and we have certainly *not* given up!" He paused for breath. "Look, I came here this evening in my own time as a concerned private citizen, hoping to contribute something positive, if I could, and to listen to your views and comments in the hope I might hear something that'll be useful for when I've got my cap on tomorrow morning. So let's cut out the talk of the police giving up. I can assure you that we have not!"

After a short silence Cole said, "Thank you, Sergeant, I'm sure we are all very statisfied with the great effort you and your officers have put into helping us find our children."

Bowles was appreciative of the sentiment, but a little indignant at the intimation of the police being second in the search effort.

Much was debated as the meeting continued and it soon became obvious there was little confidence that more children might not disappear. This led to the idea of a policeman being resident in the village as a precautionary measure. It was agreed that a letter would be sent by the Parish Council to the Chief Constable with the request. Sergeant Bowles agreed to support the move.

In an opportune moment of quiet, before the meeting closed, Mavis Strawson stood. "Can I please say a few words?"

Cole acknowledged her and called for silence.

"Thank you, Dick. Now you all know me. I'm probably the oldest person in the village and have done more living'n most on'ya. After my Albert died, I took to religion for a bit'o comfort. The vicar here was very kind and helpful. I soon discovered there were more to it than just going to church or chapel on a Sunday. An' I don't mean putting out a few flowers, doing a bit'a cleaning, or playing the organ either. There's a bit'a spiritualism involved. What I mean is, there are people what are proper gifted and knows how to reach people on the other side. In't that right, Vicar?"

The vicar looked uncomfortable, shuffled his feet and hesitated before giving a gentle nod knowing that his personal opinion was not fully aligned with the church.

"Yes, an' now I talks with my Albert quite often, 'e tells me things in a funny sort'o way, private like. Sometimes he don't talk at all, he just does things, and makes things happen. So why don't we get one'a them mediums or spiritualists in 'ere to try and see what's happened to them poor children? We might even find out where they are."

The vicar stared at the floor. A few people scoffed at the idea, while others thought anything was worth trying. A show of hands was called for and the decision was made to find a credible medium. A task which fell to the vicar.

Chapter 8

Eager to console the villagers and recognising the need to rebuild credibility, the Chief Constable granted their request, and within a few days, a policeman was billeted in the village. Folks began to relax and were satisfied they had been listened to.

Vicar Parsons went to see the Bishop of Ely to explain the unusual circumstances and ask for his approval to enlist the services of a spiritualist.

The bishop paced his study. "I am aware the church has an exorcist, although we don't broadcast the fact. As for a spiritualist, you should know better than to ask considering the scepticism that surrounds them and our official view of these… people."

"But surely, Your Grace, if we in the church do not believe in spiritualism, are we not hypocrites?"

The bishop's face reddened. There was no answer, but the question did not endear Parsons to the Bishop, who, through his silence, avoided further debate on the interpretations of spiritualism.

Much against church doctrine, the vicar set out to find a spiritualist minister. Loyalty to his flock and his doubtful interpretation of the church's position on spiritualism, he decided to risk the bishop's wrath.

Two weeks later Mr Bentley arrived at the vicarage, where he was to lodge and execute his mission. The following morning, Parsons told Tom and Dora that he had found a spiritualist of some considerable repute and that he had already arrived from Nottingham. It was a quick visit with little discussion as the vicar was keen to inform the other parents. They were all invited to meet Mr Bentley in the vicarage at seven o'clock the next evening. Then, if everyone agreed, Mr Bentley would see if he could 'make contact'.

During the day, the vicar told Bentley what he knew of the families, the missing children, and the limited knowledge of their disappearance. They also visited the big barn at Tythe Farm to see if Bentley could detect a presence. He explained that everyone wanted to know what had happened to the children, where they were and if they were still alive and safe.

Bentley was concerned at the expectation placed on him. "Please understand that I am a psychic medium with the gifts of clairaudience and clairsentience. I gather and harness the energies of those who have passed over and receive their messages. As such, I may need to interpret any message I receive. On a few occasions, I have found it prudent not to relay a message for fear of causing distress. On other occasions, and only a few, I was privileged with evidential powers. This, I believe, was due to the strength of the spirit's own will and determination, not to my gift."

The vicar expressed his understanding.

"I will have to remind everyone that I am unable to contact or receive messages from any spirit that does not wish to be contacted or is not yet ready to be contacted, and certainly not someone who is yet to pass over. Therefore, if I am unable to contact a spirit it may be because the spirit in question does not wish to be contacted, or the person is still with us since their spirit is still within them. I will not be able to tell the difference in these circumstances because I will have nothing to go on. There will simply be a void, a silence. I do hope your good people will understand."

The first parents arrived at the large Victorian house next to the church shortly before 7 o'clock. Not all were full of optimism, even though they didn't know what to expect. Mr Brown and Mr Fletcher were cynical and complained that they came only because their wives had forced them to. Nonetheless, they were curious. Both had protested their need to wear a suit and tie. Neither of them looked natural nor felt comfortable in formal wear. The ladies were more open-minded, eager for any positive result.

Mrs Parsons invited everyone into the large entrance hall, where most felt uncomfortable in the perceived opulence. Playing the perfect host, she took everyone to the drawing-room, inviting them to sit. Her soft, exaggerated tone of compassion was noticeable. The fading evening light, which crept between the heavy velvet curtains, did nothing to brighten the room or improve the austere atmosphere. "I'll bring some tea in a moment or two," she said, before excusing herself and scurrying away.

Dining room chairs were placed in an arc facing a small round table, a few feet away. Vicar Parsons and Mr Bentley stood across the room by an open fire. As the parents entered, they crossed to greet them, each with an extended hand, while the vicar introduced everyone.

Through small talk, Parsons sensed tension and an occasional wave of speculative doubt, so made a conscious effort to relax everyone with playful attempts at jest, all of which failed to overcome the stiffness in the air.

Mrs Parsons brought tea and biscuits as she had promised. Mrs Fletcher saw fit to insist that her husband not to pour the tea into his saucer or dip a biscuit into the tea. "Don't you dare embarrass me. It's not the done thing in polite company!"

"I expect you'll want me to cock my little finger next!" He grumbled.

After ten minutes, Mr Bentley decided it was time to be more formal. "Let's get started, shall we? Please take a seat."

Mrs Parsons interrupted, "I'll just take the cups away and get out of your hair."

"Oh, please leave the biscuits on the table if you don't mind," Bentley asked. The vicar placed two chairs behind the table for himself and the canon.

"First, I would like to say how sorry I am to each of you for your apparent loss. I say 'apparent' because I understand there is much still to be learned, which hopefully I will be able to assist with. I am what is known as a psychic medium, which means the Good Lord has endowed me with the gift of being able to communicate with the spirits of those who reside on the other side. I listen to their messages and pass them on to those loved ones who are still with us. However, I add caution to this evening's events in that we may still not resolve our mystery. To explain, my gifts are to hear and feel the presence of spirits, and to communicate with them. The Good Lord has given me two ears and one mouth, so I will be listening more than speaking. Whatever I may tell you will come from them, not me. On only two occasions have I been able to be very specific with detail, by that I mean, able to relay dates, times, and places. It is usually left for the recipient to interpret. I am not able to communicate with the living in this way as I am not a mind reader, nor can I hear the words of any spirit which does not wish to be contacted. Do you understand?"

There were a few quiet utterances of "Yes", while everyone nodded.

"Do any of you have questions at this time?"

The parents shook their heads.

"Good. Now I'm going to place these six candles in a bundle on the table and ask our vicar to light them. We'll keep the biscuits there too. Some believe that light, warmth, and food attract spirits. To be honest, I have my doubts, but let us do everything possible."

The vicar took a taper from the fire and lit the candles.

Sitting, Bentley waited before continuing, "There will be no trickery, odd chanting, or fainting, and I certainly don't expect things to fly around the room. We will be attempting simple spiritual contact. So, you can relax, it's not going to be like a melodramatic Victorian séance. I shall remain seated, as you must, and I ask you to be quiet and still while I concentrate. Only speak to me if I ask you something. It may take a while, so please be patient."

After a short prayer for divine blessing and guidance, the canon closed his eyes and placed his hands flat on the table with his palms uppermost. "We, the loved ones of Alfred and Susie Harrison, Mary and Alan Fletcher, and Polly Brown, wish to make contact with your spirits. If any of you are with us this evening, please reveal yourselves now."

Nothing happened. Canon Bentley paused before repeating his words a few more times, but there was no communication. After a short break, he continued for a further ten minutes, only to achieve the same negative result. Yet, at one point, the onlookers noticed a slight change in the Canon's expression, leading them to believe he may have something to tell them.

"Well, my dear friends, I must say, with some regret, that I have not been able to make contact with any of your children's spirits. Although I did experience a most unusual feeling…or call it intuition, that your children may well have passed away, but then again, they may not have."

The parents' look of confusion was obvious.

"I know it sounds contradictory, but I have not experienced this before and I apologise for it not being helpful. If I may explain, when we pass over, our spirits move to another dimension, one where I may be able to contact them. Yet, what I experienced this evening was somewhat different. Clearly, your children cannot be contacted, or should I say, possibly don't want to be. Everything seemed so distant. Yes, distant is probably the best word. It was a very odd sensation."

The parent's fidgeted as they moved to readjust their seating, while Mrs Fletcher took her handkerchief to the corners of her eyes.

"Please do remember that my failure to communicate may be because they do not wish to be contacted at this time, should they have passed over. Hopefully, it will be because they have not yet done so. It's all most strange, as children usually want to communicate with their parents if only to tell them not to be upset."

The ladies' optimism faded to disappointment, the

sceptics were satisfied and one could not resist a quiet, "I told you so."

The vicar spoke, ignoring the remark. "Thank you, Mr Bentley. I confess that we are all a little disappointed, but please do understand these things are so often beyond anyone's earthly influence or control." Then, to appease the parents more, "I do hope you understand that when we 'pass over', as we all surely will one day, it is not the end. Our spirits simply live on the other side, and one day we shall all be together again. So when a loved one leaves this psychical world we must think of them as simply, 'going on ahead', and waiting for us on the other side."

Mr Fletcher was impatient. "So you think they are all dead do you, Vicar?"

Bentley saw the vicar's hesitation and replied on his behalf. "I'm sure our dear vicar did not mean it quite that way. The truth is that we really don't know. Very sadly, I do not doubt that over the past months those same thoughts must have crossed your own minds."

From amongst the grief of loss, came a reluctant murmur of agreement. Openly acknowledging that their children may have died was painful beyond words. The men were silent, whilst the ladies sniffed into their handkerchiefs. Tom returned home to update his notes.

Chapter 9

Six months passed before village life began to take on a veneer of normality, one where the missing children were not always the main topic of conversation. However, the pain of the children's disappearance always lingered beneath the surface. That was until eight-year-old Michael Green disappeared one Friday afternoon and panic returned once more. All the old fears hit like a great tsunami of emotions rushing through the village. The constable stationed there was embarrassed and felt helplessly inadequate, especially after being read the riot act by his sergeant, who blamed him for allowing it to happen.

The police were quick to respond, flooding the area with officers. Some searched while others interviewed as many people as possible in the shortest time. Detectives from Scotland Yard were summoned, arriving in Ely by train the next morning. Their afternoon and evening were spent reviewing the information in the files of the other missing children and being updated on the most recent events. Sergeant Bowles treated them with reverence, hovering to answer questions as best he could. On Sunday morning, one of the detectives was escorted by Bowles to their first interview, which was to be with

Michael Green's parents.

After the obvious questions and request for a photograph, the detective asked if there was anything else they could think of which might help. Mrs Green was too distraught to answer. "What about you, Mr Green?"

"Not really, like I said, I was at work all day Friday and when I come 'ome Marge was upset 'cos Michael and Terry were late. She were already think'n the worst. Then when young Terry come in we asked where Mick were, he said he didn't know. Said they'd been playing hide-and-seek. Then when he couldn't find Mick, he come 'ome."

The detective took the closest chair and moved to sit face to face with Terry. "Okay, son, why don't you tell me, in as much detail as possible and in your own way, what happened with you and your brother?"

"We were playing hide-and-seek and it was his turn to go and hide, so I counted. When I got to a hundred, I shouted 'I'm coming' and went to look for 'im. But I couldn't find 'im. After looking everywhere I could think of, I called out saying, 'I give up', but he didn't come out, so I called a few more times." He gave his mother a worried look. "Then, Mrs Harrison came to see what the shouting was all about.'

"Mrs Harrison? Were you down at Tythe Farm? How many times have I told you, boys, to stay away from there!"

The detective raised his palm to silence Mrs Green and quietly asked Terry to continue.

"I know, Mum, but we have a lot of fun down there in their big barn and Mrs Harrison don't mind. She knows we like to play there, especially jumping and rolling in the hay. I didn't tell you before 'cos I didn't want to get into trouble."

The policemen glanced at each other at the mention of Tythe Farm and the big barn.

"It's all right son, you've done the right thing by telling us now. I'm glad you did; so carry on. What happened next?"

"When Mick didn't come out, I thought he was messing about and gone home. He does things like that. He's always mucking about. He'd think it was funny leaving me there to look for him."

"And then what?"

"I came 'ome, but he wasn't here either."

"That's fine, son, you did well, thank you. Is there anything else you can remember that might be helpful? Did you see any strangers about?"

"Not what I can remember."

"Thank you, Mr and Mrs Green, we'll be off now. The sergeant or I will be in touch with you as soon as we know something more. Thank you again, especially you, young Terry."

The boy grinned. Mrs Green grabbed the detective's arm, and with tears in her eyes she pleaded, "Find my boy, please find him. I want him back."

"You can be sure we'll do our very best, Mrs Green. You can count on that."

The door closed quietly behind them.

"Okay, Sergeant, let's go and take a look at Tythe Farm and this 'big barn' we keep hearing about, the scene of the crime, so to speak."

"Excuse me, sir, but do you think we should take young

Terry Green with us? He could show us where the

kids usually hide. It'll make his day to have a ride in a police car."

"Yes, a good idea."

Bowles was pleased with himself and went back to get Terry.

Dora had expected the police would eventually get round to visiting, so the arrival of a police car in the yard came as no surprise. She took her apron off and pulled back a few loose strands of hair, whilst waiting for a knock at the door, which didn't come. Moving the net curtains, she peered through to see Sergeant Bowles, another man, and a boy standing with their backs to the house whilst surveying the yard in the direction of the biggest barn. Sergeant Bowles was pointing and talking, but Dora couldn't hear what was being said. After a moment of deliberation, she went out to meet them. "Hello, Sergeant. What can I do for you this time?"

"Ah, Mrs Harrison, this is a detective, who's come from Scotland Yard to investigate Michael Green's disappearance. We want to have a look around, especially in your big barn..."

Before he had finished speaking the detective turned to face her. "I am Detective Banner. I'll need to ask you a few questions, so please don't go away."

"All right, I'll be in the house, but I don't know what I can tell you."

After Terry Green had shown them all the typical hiding places, he was sent home. The policemen went to the big barn, entering through the large open front. From the inside, it seemed much bigger. Most of the contents were unfamiliar to the London policeman, but he admitted it looked like an adventurous place for children to play. He wandered around, mostly looking at the floor to see if there were any clues. After ten minutes, they went to the house.

The detective spoke first. "Mrs Harrison, I understand that you saw Michael and Terry Green here on Friday afternoon?"

"Yes. Well, no, not exactly."

"What do you mean?"

"Well, I knew kids were playing in the barn and around the yard. Me and Tom don't mind, we know the kids like it in there. There's not a lot of places for them to go in the village. My Tom likes to keep them on side 'cos they come in handy when the men take the haystacks down. They clobber the rats and mice with sticks, you see. A proper sight it is. Not many get away, but I have to make sure I keep my door shut, just in case."

"Yes, yes, Mrs Harrison, as you say. Now tell me what happened here last Friday."

"Anyway, I did see young Terry Green. I heard him first but not his brother. Terry was calling and looking for him, so I went and asked what was up. He said they were playing hide-and-seek, but he couldn't find his brother, so when he didn't come out, young Terry gave up. I said, 'Michael must have gone home without telling you.' So I think Terry went home too. That's all I know."

"Did you see anyone else around, maybe a stranger?"

"No, nobody. Village folk here keep their eyes open for strangers and gypsies these days. We'd soon see anyone we don't know."

Banner thanked her, then addressed both the sergeant and Mrs Harrison. "With your permission, we'll get a couple of men down here to go through that barn of yours with a fine-tooth comb. Who knows, we might find something of interest." Then, looking at Bowles he said,

"Get them to drag some of that hay out, in case he's under there."

They thanked her again and left to see if the officers searching elsewhere had anything useful to report. As before, there were no clues, except to say that the barn and Peter Harrison once more came under scrutiny by the villagers. Someone had even suggested the barn should be burned down.

"I'll take a walk down to Granny Harrison's cottage, Sergeant, and have a word with this Peter Harrison fellow. You can get Tythe Farm thoroughly searched in the meantime…and I mean thoroughly."

Bowles obeyed, but after an hour of searching nothing of any consequence was found.

The detective's timing was fortunate for Ma and Peter as a noisy crowd of a dozen or so men and women had gathered outside Mrs Harrison's cottage. Banner could see there was going to be trouble. Shouting and jeering, they demanded that Peter come out. They quietened when the detective approached.

"What's all this about?"

"We want Peter Harrison out here, now!" someone shouted.

"What for?"

"You'll find out soon enough," the man replied while others jeered their approval.

"Okay, you lot! "I'm Detective Banner from Scotland Yard, so you'd better listen to me. You are not going to achieve anything with this behaviour, so I suggest you all go home and let us do our job."

Constable Cornwell arrived with his truncheon drawn and stood next to the detective. The gathering shuffled backwards a few feet.

"We want Harrison out here!" someone shouted again.

"Now look here, if you don't disperse, I'll book the lot of you for causing a public disturbance, and for threatening behaviour. The magistrate can deal with you tomorrow morning."

Cornwell stepped forward. "Come on now, you all know me, let's be sensible and go home. We'll sort this out soon enough."

Again a voice came from the gathering, "Get Peter Harrison out here!"

"Right!" Banner said as he took a notebook and pencil from his pocket. "Let's have your names!"

There was disgruntled muttering from the crowd as they hesitated and slowly turned away. The policemen waited a few minutes to watch the gathering disperse.

Mrs Harrison, still clutching her copper stick, opened the door to invite the policemen in. "Thank you, officers, you was just in time. I was frightened of what they might do next. Proper frit I were. I dunno what the world is coming to."

The detective apologised for what had gone on outside. Peter was sitting across the room, badly shaken, with his face in his hands.

"If you'll excuse me, sir, I'll stay outside by the gate in case anyone comes back." Cornwell offered.

Banner agreed. Then after a few minutes of sympathetic small talk to help Peter relax, he began his questions, but Peter was not able to contribute anything helpful. Eventually, Banner was satisfied that he knew nothing about this most recent disappearance. He thanked him and his mother for their time and left.

"I'd like you to stay by the gate for an hour, Constable,

and then be seen near the cottage from time to time. I don't expect that mob to return but it will make them inside feel more comfortable. They've had enough for one day."

Hearing about the commotion, Sergeant Bowles arrived.

Sergeant, is there a pub in the village?

"Yes, sir, The Plough and Harrow," Bowles replied, thinking it a strange question knowing every village has at least one pub.

"You had better make sure it's kept closed this evening. We don't want any of that mob getting tanked up and coming back to get Peter Harrison or setting fire to that barn. They wouldn't be so manageable full of booze."

"Right, I'll see it doesn't open tonight."

"You know what, Bowles, that young man in there needs help. The poor lad is in a bad way and those idiots in the village are making him worse. What sort of a life is he supposed to have, I ask you?"

"I know what you mean, sir. Fen people have long memories and once they get something into their heads you can't move it. If they think he's involved they'll haunt the poor lad for the rest of his life."

Early on Monday evening Michael Green walked into his mother's kitchen just as she was washing the dinner dishes. She turned and almost dropped one on seeing him. "Where the hell have you been?" Tears rolled down her cheeks as she rushed to hold him, her embrace lasting a full minute.

Michael was confused. "Sorry, Mum, am I late for dinner?"

"Late for dinner! Never mind, you're home now.

Where have you been?”

“Me and Terry were playing in the barn at Tythe Farm. Sorry, Mum, I don't know what happened, but I think I must have fallen asleep or something. Where's Dad?”

“He's out looking for you.”

“Suppose I'll be in trouble when he gets back. I don't want the strap.”

“No, dear, he'll be pleased you are home safe and sound. We thought you had gone missing like them other children. Where were you all this time?”

“In the big barn at Tythe Farm.”

“But the police almost emptied that barn looking for you.”

“I don't understand. I must have fallen asleep there, because that's where I woke up. I had the strangest dream. It was so real that I thought it really was, but it couldn't be. I'm hungry. Is there anything to eat?”

She turned to Terry, who had been watching in amazement.

“Go and find a policeman, anyone will do, and tell him our Michael is home. Go on, as quickly as you can.”

She reheated the dinner leftovers, which Michael ate with gusto.

Within ten minutes, Bowles arrived at the house. “Well, young man, it's good to know you are home safe and sound. Would you mind telling me where you have been since Friday afternoon?”

“What do you mean? It's only Friday now.” Michael frowned and looked around the room.

“Excuse me, young man, but it's Monday evening!”

“It can't be.” He looked at his mother. “Is it Monday, Mum?”

"Yes. You've been missing for three days. We went to church yesterday to pray for you. Even your dad went, and you missed school today. Why do you think the police are here looking for you? There are even two detectives come from London to help find you." She was now wondering about her son's mental state.

Michael still had difficulty comprehending his apparent loss of time.

"Come on, Mick, we need to know where you have been, and what happened to you."

"I don't know, Mum, I honestly don't. I must have fallen asleep in the barn like I said. I had this weird dream…it was so real."

Bowles wondered if the boy had been drugged, taken away, and later returned to the barn. But he said nothing, hoping Michael would remember something from his drugged state. "Where was this place you dreamed about son?"

"I don't know. It was all very queer. Sort of old-fashioned. Like some of the pictures in the history books at school. It was hard to understand what people were saying, they all talked funny. It was like being in another country with a lot of foreigners."

"Where was it? Do you remember seeing anyone you know or recognise?"

"No, I don't think so."

Bowles was now convinced that Michael was drugged and had been hallucinating. "Do you remember what happened when you were playing with your brother up to when you fell asleep?"

"Only that we were playing hide and seek around the yard and when Terry went to find me, I crept back to the big barn, like you are supposed to. I called 'home,' but I don't think, Terry heard me 'cos he was off somewhere looking for me. After that, I don't properly remember anything much until I woke up there just now. I don't even remember where I fell asleep, but it must have been in the hay 'cos that's where I woke up. That's all I know. I don't understand what all the fuss is about."

"All right, son, that'll do for now, but if you remember anything else I'd like to know right away." Then turning to Mrs Green he said, "I'll be off now. I have to let everyone know the boy is home safe and well, call off the dogs so to speak."

He was buoyant when he approached Detective Banner. "Ah, you will be pleased to hear that Michael Green has turned up in one piece."

"Yes, I heard, I'm pleased to hear that, but are you telling me that I was brought all the way from London on a fool's errand? Don't you know that most missing kids turn up after a day or two! Wasting my time is a serious thing, Sergeant."

The redness in Bowles' face deepened. "Well, sir, what with the other children and all…"

"Don't bother, Sergeant, where is the boy now?"

"At home, sir."

"You'd better organise a doctor to look him over."

"I'll get a constable onto it."

"Okay, we'd better go and see the kid. I need to talk to him. When we get there, I want you to take young Terry away and keep him occupied while I talk with his brother."

After greeting Mr and Mrs Green, Banner said how pleased he was that Michael had returned home safe and sound. Also that he needed to talk to the boys before he could close the case.

Then, he chatted casually with Mick for twenty minutes, hoping that a relaxed approach might help him remember more and encourage him to talk. He repeated the same questions, phrased differently, to test the boy's recollections and accuracy. Eventually, asking for his brother to be brought in, then with the same approach, he asked Terry similar questions, listening carefully to the answers to see if they matched his brother's. He watched carefully for any interaction and body language between the boys. He noticed the darkness under Michael's eyes and how wide his pupils were, and moved nearer to his face for a closer look. "Did anyone give you something to drink, or some tablets to take while you were at Harrison's farm?"

"No, there was only me and Terry there."

"What about before you went?"

"No, sir, we had nothing."

The detective gave Bowles a knowing look.

"My thoughts exactly, sir," Bowles said, hoping to endear himself.

"What about something to drink?"

"No," they said in unison. They shuffled to stand side by side, each clasping their hands in front of them.

Sensing their concern, Banner leaned back, hesitated and smiled. "What about smoking? I know when I was a boy I experimented with smoking. The first time was with tea leaves in one of my father's old pipes. It made me sick, so I didn't do it again."

They all chuckled.

"So, did anyone give you something to smoke or ask you to take a puff, just for fun?"

"No."

"And did you see or speak to any strangers in the

village on Friday afternoon?"

"No, there weren't any."

"Now, Michael, why don't you tell me where you went to for all that time?"

The boy gave the same confused answer he had given Bowles.

Banner believed the boys and was content that he had achieved as much as he could for now. He thanked Mr and Mrs Green before returning to the Ely police station with Bowles. On the way, the sergeant said he thought it strange that if they had been drugged, why both boys had not disappeared. Banner agreed.

The doctor concluded that the boy had not been drugged. So the detectives completed their report, leaving open the question of where Michael Green had been, how he got there and had returned. As far as they were concerned their task was to find the boy, so their work was finished. Sergeant Bowles kept a low profile, impatient for the detectives to leave. Yet he was surprised at their decision to go without further investigation, believing that Michael Green's circumstances may help lead to finding the other children.

The press had long since descended on the village, each reporter trying to find an angle on which to speculate about what had happened to Michael Green. Under instructions from the police, the Greens were told not to talk to the press, or at least, not for a while, adding frustration and desperation to the reporters' efforts. All police officers had been instructed not to talk to newspaper reporters, or give a hint of any developments. Detective Banner refused to be drawn on any of the questions he was bombarded with before leaving the village. Only saying the police will make an announcement the next morning at Ely Police Station.

It was mainly to appease the press, giving them something positive and accurate to write about. While at the same time, to draw them away from the village where they were becoming a nuisance. Some villagers had already answered questions and offered their opinions on what might have happened to Michael Green. Reporters then added their spin to embroider their stories. Some protected themselves by saying, "It is suggested that," or "Local people believe." Consequently, the police felt obligated to set the record straight, which they were pleased to do on this occasion as there had been a happy outcome.

As the most senior local officer based in Ely, Sergeant Bowles was delegated the task of reading a prepared statement. At the appointed time he stepped onto the patio above the steps at the front of the police station. He was surprised at the number of people gathered there and nervous at having two Scotland Yard detectives looking over his shoulder. Flash bulbs illuminated his face. He waited for everyone to settle before speaking.

"Good morning, ladies and gentlemen. As you know, a boy named Michael Green from a nearby village went missing on Friday afternoon. The police conducted an extensive search and questioned many village folks, seeking information to help us find the boy. Two senior officers from Scotland Yard came to manage the investigation. We are pleased to say that yesterday evening, Michael Green was found unharmed, and is now at home with his family, following a check-up by his doctor. The Green family have experienced great stress and anxiety these past few days, so we ask that you respect their privacy by leaving them in peace. Thank you."

The sergeant stood for a moment as though he didn't know what to do next. Reporters were scribbling their shorthand notes when a voice shouted. "Tony Brown, *Daily Telegraph*. Did you find the boy or did he turn up of his own accord?"

Red-faced, Bowles turned to leave.

"We heard the boy turned up without your help! What about the other missing children, Sergeant, where are they?"

Followed by the two London detectives, Bowles continued into the police station, ignoring the questions called after them.

The detectives glanced at each other. "Glad he didn't try to answer them. He'd probably dig a hole for himself. You know what these country coppers are like," one said.

"Yeah, but I suppose they are good at seeing school kids across the road and catching poachers." Banner smiled.

"Those city newspaper blokes can be a bloody nuisance. They are more concerned about making us look inadequate than reporting the news. One once told me that 'good news is no news, and bad news is good news'. Apparently, good news doesn't sell newspapers."

Bowles muttered his opinion of Londoners. Thinking he'd done things properly, he'd expected at least a, 'Well done, Sergeant.'

Tom had gone along to see what the police had to say and to update his notes. He noticed that since starting to keep them, he recognised more about people's characters and their way of doing things. Sometimes, he could even predict what they would do or say next, an intuition he was beginning to enjoy.

By the time autumn had shortened the days, he'd written more than forty pages of notes and had a pile of newspaper cuttings. Through the long winter evenings, he sat at the kitchen table trying to make sense of them as he looked for clues, desperate to find something that would lead him to Alfie and Susie.

He had included as many facts as he could find about the missing children, especially his own. Tom described his and Dora's feelings and how events had affected their lives and relationship. There were times when he wanted to talk to the other parents, but was afraid they would become upset or angry, especially since his brother was suspected of being involved. They seemed to have ignored the fact that, when asked later, Michael Green stated that he had not seen Peter Harrison that day, nor had he had anything to do with him for some time.

Many hours were spent pawing through the newspaper cuttings to determine what was true and what was not. To his surprise, as many as half the articles were no more than speculation, opinion, or were simply untrue. He had previously believed that what he read in the newspapers was completely true, now he would never be sure again.

Chapter 10

It was a miserable, empty winter for Tom and Dora without their children. They missed so many of the little things, some pleasing, some amusing, even those which had seemed frustrating at the time now didn't matter. It was with sadness that Tom considered the many things he had not noticed before. Things only mothers might see, which Dora now commented on. They hated each day that passed without Susie and Alfie and dreaded the thought of Christmas without them.

Tom lamented, "Kids are funny, you struggle to get them out of bed in the morning, then fight to get them back in the evening."

Dora sighed. "When it snowed, they'd spend hours making a snowman and throwing snowballs with the other kids. They loved the snow."

"Yeah, and Alfie loved to skate on the drains too. Do you remember how we used to worry about him, wondering if the ice was thick enough?"

Tom noticed that Dora spoke as though the children might never return, which he also painfully believed, yet was hesitant to admit. He took sad comfort from seeing her beginning to accept the inevitable and to talk a little more. He hoped her distress would continue to diminish with time. Or that she would learn to manage it better.

On starlit winter evenings, Tom watched Dora as she sat by the window, staring at the heavens. He knew exactly what she was thinking while feeling her pain and anguish on top of his own. He wanted to hold and comfort her but knew she would be better left to grieve quietly in her own way. Some evenings, when the grass glistened white with frost and the moon was bright enough to cast a shadow, Dora would go for a walk, returning after half an hour. Tom would ask where she went, but her reply was always the same.

"Oh, just through the village to get some fresh air."

He knew that in her heart she was looking for Alfie and Susie.

"It must have been cold out. Would you like a nice mug of hot cocoa?"

"No, I'll just go up to bed," she'd say.

Tom accepted that Dora sometimes wanted to be alone with her thoughts, but he was still disappointed when she shut him out. As a result, they had few meaningful conversations. Mostly they spoke to each other in passing comments or with simple questions and answers, but it was a start. With only slight improvements, the uneasy atmosphere continued into spring and summer. Sometimes, Tom was thankful for the long summer days in the fields as it meant less time at home where he was likely to upset himself pondering over the children's fate. But he was always left with a twinge of guilt at leaving Dora for so long.

Little of any great consequence happened in the village beyond church fetes, jumble sales, and the annual Maypole dance. People were thankful that no more children had gone missing, but the fear of past events being repeated always hovered in the background.

Like other parents, the image that Tom and Dora projected in the village was little more than a thin veneer of normality, hiding their feelings of irreplaceable loss.

Little things triggered sad memories and sometimes anger laced with frustration. In the spring, when Dora first saw the daffodils pushing through the long grass in their modest orchard, it reminded her of when Susie had picked them to give her. "They'll last longer left where they are, don't pick them again!" Dora sighed at the memory, wishing she had not been so harsh when Susie was only trying to please her. "Silly I suppose", she would say. "But I can't help feeling guilty when those daffodils come out."

Harvesting was done, and as the signs of autumn were approaching, Tom decided to tidy the big barn before ploughing began. The inside was a mess. To the right, hay was scattered over twice the area it needed. Cob baskets were stacked along the back wall. Those near the top sported intricate dust-laden cobwebs while piles of hessian sacks hid many of the others. Some were scattered where children had left them after returning them from sack races at the village fete, but most were neatly stacked. To the left, harrows and heavy rollers waited for the spring.

"Mmm, the rollers need a bit of grease before they go out again," Tom muttered. Most farmers didn't bother and left rollers outside to rust, but he knew it made them harder for a horse to pull. Half a dozen scythes hung on a wall next to sickles and beet hooks, all placed out of the children's reach. Along a ledge lay half a dozen long, worn sharpening stones. In a corner, spades, pitchforks, and hoes leaned against the wall. Looking around, he had no difficulty seeing where children played. He smiled as he visualised them climbing onto one of the beams and jumping down into the hay.

With a little surprise, he noticed the round earthenware container he had discovered more than a year ago still on a ledge not far from the open side of the barn. He'd forgotten about it with everything else that had happened. Picking it up, it now seemed a little lighter than he remembered. It had dried and the lid looked as though it would now come off easily. At first, he thought to take it back to the house and open it, then changed his mind, expecting Dora would complain and mock again him for what he brought home. No, he would open it right here in the barn and there was no time like the present.

He found an old cob basket with a missing handle and turned it upside down for a seat. Then, he draped a sack across his lap in anticipation of what might spill out. Like all countrymen, he carried a sharp shut knife in his pocket. Gripping the bone handle, he carefully scratched around the lid, trying not to damage the rim. He need not have been so careful since it came off easily, almost as though it had been opened before.

With inquisitive anticipation, he looked inside to see a dark, congealed liquid at the bottom. Not able to tell its colour in the dim light of the barn, he turned to catch the light from the open side. All he could see was that it was dark and looked sticky. Putting his nose to the open container, he cautiously sniffed. It was a sweet, inviting smell with the light scent of cinnamon. Seconds later, he felt a sharp pain surge through his temples as if someone had pushed a rod through his head. Then as quickly as the pain had come, it diminished to a low ache. He stood and moved to get fresh air. After standing for only a few seconds, his legs became weak and he was lightheaded. Realising something was wrong he quickly placed the lid on the container and put it back on the ledge. That was the last thing he could remember.

Chapter 11

When Tom regained consciousness, and before he opened his eyes, he detected the familiar smell of hay and horses but had no idea where he was, or what had happened to him. For a second or two, he thought his senses were playing tricks and believed he was in the military stables in France. On regaining his composure he wondered if he was dreaming. But if this was a dream it's a bit too darn real.

He lay on his back for a full two minutes, gathering his strength. Adding to his confusion, he didn't recognise the timber roof beams he was staring at. "My God, what the hell is in that flask?" he said aloud.

Struggling to his feet, he looked around expecting to see the inside of his barn but he didn't recognise this place. Confused, pushing his cap back to scratch his head, he could see that he was in a stable. There were two rows of six stalls on each side facing each other down a central walkway. He could feel and smell the presence of horses, although not see them behind their gates.

Making his way to the outer door, he stopped to look over some of the gates to find a horse behind each one. Pushing the door open, he looked for something familiar but there was nothing, and his confusion almost caused him to panic. Before he had walked three paces, he was grabbed and held by two odd-looking characters each wearing what appeared to be grubby, medieval fancy dress. Tom twisted and pulled, trying to free himself.

"Get off me, you idiots!"

But they only tightened their grip.

"What were you doing in there with them horses?" One of the men demanded.

Tom thought this must a medieval fete or pageant. Then more calmly said, "Stop messing about lads, let me go."

"What, you think we'll let you go? The knights will want to know about this. You could be a spy!"

Tom considered it must be a fundraising stunt, typical of the Cambridge students on Rag Day. "Okay, okay. If I play along and let you auction me, can I go afterwards?"

"Go? You are not going anywhere, except to the stocks, my good fellow! The knights will decide what's to become of you. We are ostlers, sent to look after the knight's mounts."

"Come on lads, who are you really? What's all this in aid of?" Tom smiled.

The men looked at each other, and the question went unanswered. Their dialect was odd, so Tom had to listen carefully to understand what they were saying, assuming it must all be part of an act. It soon became clear they were not going to step out of character. Tom felt this was taking on a more serious tone and he was beginning to get annoyed. As he was escorted through cobbled streets lined with old buildings, he noticed there were no Edwardian, Victorian, or more modern buildings. They were all of a medieval style. The smaller ones were timber-framed and thatched, larger stone and flint buildings had split stone or slate roofs. He struggled to find a logical explanation. "Where is this? Are you making a film here?"

"What! You don't even know where you are? This is Bishop's Lynn, you fool."

"Where is that?"

"North of the Washes," one of the men said, rolling his eyes at Tom's ignorance.

Tom thought they must have meant King's Lynn since he had not heard of Bishop's Lynn. Still confused, he could only conclude this was all a dream and hoped he'd wake in his bed at home sooner or later. Yet when he pinched himself, the pain was real. The notion of a dream quickly disappeared.

His captors questioned if he was quite right in the head. Dressed in a way they had not seen before, he spoke differently and appeared confused. Ignoring his presence, one asked, "Where do you think he's from?"

"I know not. Maybe he's from one of the foreign trading ships."

"He certainly is an odd sort, and talks strange too."

Tom had no choice other than to go with them. As they made their way, two striking figures approached. Each wearing chain mail, covered by dirty white sleeveless smocks that reached their ankles back and front. Slits at each side, from the bottom to the waist, caused the wind to treat them as flags. A large, blood-red Christian cross was blazed across their chests. Both carried swords slung from sashes, and daggers in their belts.

"Who are they?" Tom asked.

"Templars, Knights of the Temple to you. Approved by the Pope, they are. They're commissioned by King John to guard him. So you'd better show them respect."

"What have we here?" One of the knights asked as they looked Tom up and down.

"He was in the stables with your horses and those of the king, so we grabbed him, Sir Knight. We are taking him to the Royal Guards."

At the mention of the king's horses, Tom thought of Humpty Dumpty and made the mistake of grinning.

"What is the idiot smirking at?" One of the knights demanded while the other stared at Tom.

"What is your name?"

Tom was confused, so joked to lighten the atmosphere. "Tom, but everyone calls me, Tom."

"A jester! Smart with your tongue, hey! What were you doing in the stables?"

"You wouldn't believe me if I told you," Tom said, grinning, still not taking things seriously.

The knight raised his hand to cuff him for his insolence, but was distracted by his accent, and lowered his arm.

Tom flinched.

"All right, you ostlers get back to the stables. We'll take this rogue, and be sure the stables are clean for the king's arrival. The replacement horses will need fresh hay and feed."

They stooped a little, stepped back, and tugged their forelocks before returning to the stables.

Thinking on his feet, Tom decided to play along. "I'm sorry if I caused any offence or was somewhere I shouldn't have been. I was tired and looked for somewhere to sleep. Stables are out of the wind and usually have fresh hay, so they seemed like a good place to rest. I didn't know whose horses they were. When I woke up and went to leave, the ostlers grabbed me. Honestly, there is nothing more to tell you than that."

"Where are you from?"

"South of here," Tom said, deliberately not naming the place or saying how far.

"There's a lot south of here and precious little to the north, so don't play games with us."

"The Isle of Ely,"

"You mean The Isles of Eels don't you?"

"Yes."

"So what are you doing here?"

Still playing along, Tom thought quickly. "I heard the king was coming to Bishop's Lynn, and I've never seen a king before, so I thought this might be my only chance. It was a long journey and by the time I got here, I was dead on my feet. I don't have any money, so I chose to sleep in the stables. As I said, I didn't know they were yours or the king's horses."

"They are ours, but the king will take all the stables when he arrives. We tell the ostlers they are mostly the king's horses, so they tend them more carefully."

"But we do not tell them which is which," the other knight added with a laugh.

Tom was pleased with himself for sounding convincing.

"I say you have two things wrong today, scoundrel. First, you are too early. King John is not expected to arrive for a few days hence and second, you picked the wrong place to sleep."

"I'm sorry, but I had no way of knowing and had to rely on gossip. If the king doesn't arrive until later, what are his knights doing here today?"

They looked at each other in surprise, not accustomed to being questioned by a serf. "Cheeky, hey! If you must know, we travel in advance to make arrangements for the king's arrival. You don't think he could simply arrive and have a place to rest and eat, ready and waiting for him, do you?"

"No, I don't suppose so," Tom said, still not able to comprehend what this was all about.

"We'll take you somewhere we can watch over you. You might be telling the truth or you could be a baron's spy, up to no good. The king has many enemies hereabouts, so we take no chances."

They lessened their grip on Tom's arms as they walked, but he knew better than to try to run. He didn't know where he was and had no idea where he would go. He hoped the knights had believed his story and accepted his innocence. As they continued to walk they met more knights and other oddly dressed characters.

A Templar Knight approached leading his horse. "What have you here?"

"Ostlers found him lurking where our horses are stabled. We do not yet know if he is up to mischief, a baron's informer, French spy, or just a stupid serf."

While the knights were exchanging words, Tom noticed the horse was breathing heavily, as though it had just been run but he could see no sweat from hard exercise. Reaching out slowly, so as not to be threatening, he placed the palm of his hand on the horse's neck. It was hot, but as Tom expected, completely dry.

The horse flinched. "Steady there, my beauty," Tom whispered, attracting the knight's attention.

"Get your hands off my charger!"

"Sorry, but the animal is sick."

"What do you mean, sick?"

"It's got The Puffs. Didn't you notice its breathing, or

should I say panting? Just look at it. If you don't treat the poor thing soon, it will probably die of organ failure."

"You seem to know much about horses for a mere serf?"

"It's what I do. I've worked with horses all my life, and during the Great War…well what I mean is, I'm trained in horse medicine, I know how to care for them."

Tom checked himself just in time, not wanting to add to the knight's intrigue of him with a misplaced comment. "If you can't find a vet, you need to make a brew of dandelion roots, nettle, red clover, borage and add some kelp if you can find some. Brew it slowly for an hour and mix it into the horse's feed. You should give it twice a day for a few days. Oh yes, and if you can find some fenugreek seeds, make a tea with them and get the horse to drink it."

The knights looked at each other in surprise.

"Vet?"

Tom rolled his eyes and said "Animal doctor."

They shrugged, giving him complacent looks.

"And don't run the animal until its breathing is better, or you could kill it."

"You dare with such audacity to tell a knight how to tend his mount! Since you claim to know much about the beasts, how would you treat these leg wounds?" another knight asked, pointing to the animal's front hocks.

Tom went down on one knee to inspect the wounds and saw they were made by chafing from a heavy decorative harness that hung across its front legs. "To start with, you could leave this harness off until the wounds are healed, then pad it to stop it from happening again. You need to bandage the legs. But first, dissolve a small amount of salt in boiled water. It has to be boiled to kill any germs in it. Otherwise, it won't be clean and could cause infection. Let it cool, then, gently wash the wounds with it at least once every day. It will clean the area and help it heal. After that, crush some fresh garlic to a pulp, mix in a tiny amount of salt, make a poultice and strap it over the wounds."

The knights raised their eyebrows as they began to develop cautious respect for Tom, and said "Well then since you know so much, you can care for all our mounts."

Tom's agreement was assumed and although he didn't object, he had been pressed into some sort of service. The mystery of what he was doing in the stables seemed forgotten. But he was still at a loss to fully comprehend where he was. This whole experience was wildly surreal and confusing. He expected that at any moment someone would appear and explain. Or that he would spot a policeman keeping onlookers away. Yet, his instincts told him to go along with events, at least for the time being.

As they walked, Tom said, "I have to hand it to you blokes, you certainly play your parts well. Very convincing, I must say."

There was no reply. The knights gave each other questioning looks. One rotated a forefinger at his temple.

Chapter 12

Within ten minutes Tom was sitting at a long table in the public room of an inn. The air was grey with the smoke that wafted from an open fire each time the outer door was opened. Several knights were talking and drinking ale, while they monopolised the seats closest to the burning logs. Although Tom wanted to warm himself, he thought better of disturbing them. The more they drank the louder and more brazen they became. Their raucous voices and laughter eventually dominated the inn. The innkeeper watched them carefully…worried they might leave without paying. He had challenged a knight to pay for his ale once before and although he received payment, it came with a painful cuff from the back of a strong right hand "for being an insolent bastard," he was told.

The local men who congregated here most evenings were resentful of the knights. A foreign sailor or two from one of the trading ships was an accepted novelty, but a group of rowdy Templar Knights was different. Tom saw the locals' resentment for the way they commandeered anything that took their fancy. The knights knew this, but their arrogance prevented any concern. They boasted an air of great authority at being Templar Knights and demanded reverence for being on the king's business. Word had spread quickly that King John was expected to arrive soon.

"Have you eaten today, scoundrel?" one of the knights called to Tom.

"No, not yet."

Instructions were issued to the serving wench and within minutes Tom was brought a steaming bowl of broth containing vegetables and a little meat, accompanied by bread and a flagon of ale. The broth looked unappetising, but he was hungry. To his surprise, it tasted good and was rich in vegetables and herbs of some kind.

Tom's confusion was changing to speculation of this being the real thing. Was he really back in the days of King John? But it was not possible.

"Let that be advance payment for curing my horse's ills, which you had better achieve or I'll hang your innards from the inn sign." The other knights laughed.

Tom knew that relief for the horse would take a few days, but he would explain that later.

Having eaten his fill, he was warmed and satisfied. As he sipped his ale, a tall lean, grey-bearded man with a deep frown came into the room. His dark robes dusted the stone floor as he made his way to the open fire. When he pushed past the knights, they looked at him with contempt but didn't complain.

"What is the king's physician doing here amongst us common folk?" one knight asked in sarcastic jest, causing the other knights to laugh.

"I'll not talk until I am warmed and have eaten. Yet my business is none of yours."

The knights hooted and laughed at the rebuff.

"Where is the serving wench?" The physician called to the landlord. "Bring me ale and warm food. This cold, damp air reaches into my bones." He stood with his back to the open fire, raising his clothes to warm his buttocks.

The knights' laughter amplified. "Come, physician, shall we join you bare-arsed to the heat? Don't break wind, lest you scorch your buttocks."

"Leave him while he warms the *hole* of his body," another added.

The laughter continued at the physician's expense, as did the banter until the landlord beckoned him to a table, where a steaming bowl of broth and bread was placed. Only then did the man respond to the knights. "Mock as you will, scoundrels…the day will come when you may need me and I will ask myself if I should bother to attend you. Think on that, my friends."

"Tis but a jape, physician, where is your humour?"

"I'm saving it for when you ask me to repair your bodies."

The knights fell silent, allowing the physician the last word, so letting him eat in peace. Tom, sitting close by, watching as the man eagerly devoured his food.

"You look as though you needed that," Tom said trying to make polite conversation.

The physician didn't answer.

"My name's Thomas. People call me Tom. I gather you're a doctor, sorry, I mean physician. I'm pleased to meet you, sir."

"Thank you. My name is Rauin. Do not call me 'sir', I am not a knight, and never wish to be confused with one. I serve the king's health only, not his battles. These are troubled times enough without him being in poor health.

141

"What ails the king?"

"He has carried sickness for some days and worsens. He worries about the barons and the French, as he rightly should. I may yet manage to cure his body, but I am unable to settle his mind.

"Why is he worried?" Tom asked, already knowing the answer from his school history lessons.

The physician turned to face Tom. "You speak strangely, where are you from, my good man?"

"Oh, my home is deep in the washes south of here, on a small isolated island. We have our own dialect, quite different to most other parts of the country." He was pleased with himself for thinking so quickly. "You were about to tell me why the king is worried by the barons."

"He needs to finance his wars with the French and to compensate for his losses in France and Ireland. He has increased taxes several times and now the barons and his subjects claim to be overtaxed. They revolt as we speak. The king fears they plot to bring him down. That is why we journey here…to avoid their threat. The king is sick with worry and ill of health. Now, such is the burden of my responsibility to heal him."

Memories of Tom's school lessons came flooding back. "But surely the Magna Carta treaty should have put an end to their quarrels?" Again, Tom already knew the answer but listened intently to humour the physician. He was unwittingly behaving as though he had accepted that he had been transported back to the early thirteenth century.

"The road to hell is paved with good intentions, my friend. Neither the king nor the barons have paid heed to those nobly crafted words, certainly not to the first Charter. Yet, even the second struggles to survive, even though it was more readily accepted at Runneymede. I fear it may appear an almost worthless document in these troubled times."

"Why is that?"

"You ask many questions. What is your interest?"

"Oh, I'm the knights' horse physician."

"I didn't know there was such a person. I have not seen or heard of you before."

"I keep a low profile and attend to my duties. It's not often I meet such an eminent person as yourself, so I'm inquisitive. I like to hear of our king and the state of affairs, especially, as you say, in these troubled times."

"Mmm…then you must have known that the king has lost his lands in France and Ireland, thus much income. No doubt he will be called John Lackland once more, should his throne survive. It is painful for him to know that Louis III has taken Winchester and even Lundan. The king's saving grace may yet be the great wealth he has amassed in jewels, gold, and other finery. He believes wealth is power, but it has not prevented Dauphin Louis from taking Norwich, even now as we sit and dine. This fair land is greatly troubled. Even to the north Alexander of Scotland takes advantage of the turmoil to create more threat and discord."

"But if the king has such wealth, why doesn't he use it to raise a larger army and defeat the French, instead of turning the barons against him? Surely they would support him rather than lose their land to a Frenchman?"

"Ah, that is a question for King John himself. I dare not answer lest I be accused of treason. As such, it is not my affair. Yet, I agree that hoarded wealth in itself has little power if it is not put to good use."

Tom played along with the scene and was regaining

his speculation of where he might be. As his concern came to the fore he asked, "I know the history. Is this all some sort of a pageant or re-enactment, I must say it's very realistic?"

The physician looked at him in confused amazement. "This is no pageant, I assure you! The king is plagued by his enemies and seriously at risk. You speak strangely and your dress is…well, let me say, 'somewhat different'. Where did you say you are from?"

Tom put on his best apologetic face and spoke quietly. "I'm sorry, as I said I live in the southern washes, in the Isles of Eels. I'm a physician of sorts myself, I attend sick horses, manage their recovery and see they are worked properly. I apologise if I offended you."

Rauin relaxed. "Then we have something in common. I have just returned from those very Isles myself, but I saw none such as you. Ah, but I only attended the monastery so met none of the common folk. The monks at Ely have a great knowledge of herbal remedies and I sought their help to cure the king's ills."

"That's an arduous journey," Tom said sympathetically, encouraging the physician to continue.

"Only after making a considerable payment with an assurance that, if their cure was successful, the king would reward them handsomely would the monks agree to help. They never miss an opportunity to enrich themselves. Even the king is not exempt from their exploitation. They sent a novice monk south to Denny Abbey for rare herbs the nuns cultivate there. On his return, they made up a flask containing a potion for which they gave strict instructions, nay a warning no less. Their reluctance to part with it was clear and they fervently refused to enlighten me of its formula."

"But why?"

Some monks would prefer to see the king die, but dare not speak of it so openly. I believe their reluctance was from a dislike of the king as much as it was of keeping the secrets of the potion. Even my demands to know what I would be administering were of no avail. For as much as I know, they may have concocted a poison to kill King John. I must be diligent as he is so unpopular. Those plotting monks would draw favour from the barons for their deed, yet I would be blamed. You must understand that in such a circumstance my head would be worthless.

"So what happened?"

"I was given an unusual looking vessel, completely round like a ball." Rauin cupped his hands to describe its size and shape. "I was to meet the king here in Bishop's Lynn to administer the cure."

Tom's eye's widened. He straightened and leaned forwards to face Rauin, wanting to hear more without appearing too eager, but his body language betrayed him.

"You are curious beyond your need, Thomas. However, the king was pleased that he may eventually be free of his illness. I had assured him that the monks at Ely would find a cure if anyone could. But now it will likely be my head for failing him, metaphorically speaking that is, if he is of ill mood."

"Why would you fail him?"

"As you must know, the journey through these great marshes is strained with many obstacles, even though much of it is by watercraft. On my return journey, I had momentarily placed the urn on the prow of a vessel, but it rolled into the river and could not be recovered. So the cure was lost. Now I have to attempt my own cures once more and face the king's displeasure should they fail. He is a man of extreme moods."

"Where did you lose the flask?" Tom stared urgently into Rauin's eyes.

"It was about two hours' journey to the north of Ely where the river winds, not far from the island of the Little Port."

Tom immediately thought of the old river bank, as it was known locally, and how it sweeps in a long bend not far from Littleport and Prickwillow. He had played on it as a child and later poached rabbits there. Goose pimples rose on Tom's arms and neck as he remembered the ceramic container he had found in the very area Rauin had described. Without blinking, he stared at Rauin. "What were the warnings the monks gave you?"

"They said the potion must be administered twice each day, both at sunrise and sunset, for four days and that after one week it would no longer work as intended. I was told it would thicken, and develop the sweet smell of cinnamon. When I asked what would happen if it was then taken by mouth, they were uneasy and would not speak more of it. When I insisted they walked away."

"But why? Surely, they would expect the king's physician to be careful and want to know what he's dealing with as if his own life depended on it. You have a right to know!"

"True, my friend, but none would speak of it. However, as

I was about to leave, an old friar took me into cloisters and quietly explained. Only then was I comfortable at administering it to the king. I can tell you no more without breaking my word, other than to say he told me the effects of the potion after ageing for seven days. Of which, I agreed not to tell."

"But as you no longer have the potion, anything you were told might be considered hearsay, to be believed or not. Can you tell me in strict confidence, as one physician to another, and share the knowledge as physicians do?"

Rauin hesitated for a full minute while sipping his ale. "I will tell you, but only on your oath to never repeat it. You must understand that what I tell you now is only because we must share knowledge if we are to progress our profession. Although, I doubt this will contribute greatly, as nobody will believe you since it will appear to border on witchcraft."

Rauin paused again, "I am still uneasy about this, Thomas."

"You have my solemn word," Tom said with sincerity.

"Well then, on your oath. The friar said that after seven days of fermentation the potion takes on mystical properties. A monk once sniffed the sticky residue and thereafter could not be found for two days. When he reappeared, he claimed to have been transported back to the time of King Alfred, when he was attempting to banish the Danes from Wessex. The poor soul had been terrified for his life and was pleased to return. Not that the security of our lives may be any better here.

"But I digress. Of course, no one believed where he had been, yet he insisted and his story did not waver. So, from frustration and a desire to prove his truth, he sniffed the potion again in front of witnesses. Then as before, he disappeared and was missing for two days, having been transported back in time. However, before the potion wore off, he gathered a few small items to bring back to the present. On his return, when the other monks saw the artefacts he had brought, they had no choice but to believe where he had been. The old friar went on to say that another monk tasted the ageing potion and he too disappeared but has never returned. I was advised that after seven days the potion should be destroyed, suggesting it was the work of the devil….You look pale, Thomas."

At that moment Tom's mind leapt in wild speculation as a thought hit him. *My God! So that's it. What if the children found the flask and are here?* They haven't returned, so if they did find it, they must have tasted it. He had to find them, but how on earth would he get them home again?'

"How far north of Ely did you say you were when you lost the urn?"

"I would estimate about one league. Why do you ask?"

"Oh, just curiosity". Tom quickly calculated it to be a little over three miles. Right about where he had found it. Surely it couldn't be the same flask? But it must be! The monks said the fellow who sniffed it first was transported back in time and returned after two days. If that was true, he really must be back in mediaeval times. So this was real, and he should go back to his own time before long. *My God, the children!* he thought, and felt his pulse pounding in his temples.

Tom's mind was galloping with another astounding thought. If this is the time King John lost his gold and jewels in The Wash, perhaps I could discover where it happened and find the exact spot. Then, when I get back to my time, go and recover it.' His heart rate almost doubled. 'No. He must find the children first.' But his curiosity got the better of him. "Forgive my ignorance, Rauin, please remind me what year this is?"

"1216. Why do you ask?"

Tom didn't reply. He was consumed with excitement as he tried to remember the history.

"And what date is it?"

"The fifth day of October. Why?" Rauin looked at him strangely.

"When exactly does the king arrive in Bishop's Lynn?"

"Again, your curiosity exceeds your need, Thomas. To be sure, it is difficult to know. In truth, rumours abound. It could be tomorrow, the day after tomorrow, or after that. All are speculated upon, so the barons may not be correctly informed. In truth, I am uncertain myself, and would not dare to tell if I knew. If the king is not fit to travel he may choose to wait or travel slowly. I have not had word since I returned from the Isles."

From memory, Tom calculated that if this was October 5th, the king would lose his treasure four days from now, on the 9th, following two nights here. He was to have stayed longer but decided to continue to Newark Castle for greater safety.

Seeing that Tom was lost in thought, Rauin excused himself. He was weary after the journey from Ely and retired to a room in the inn.

Tom pondered how he might search for the children if they were here. Who would be most likely to know if strange children had appeared in the past? Where would they be now and how would he get them home if he found them?

The knights had exhausted much of their bravado and now sat quietly by the smouldering logs. One, who had overindulged on ale, was sleeping as he slumped against the wall. Tom smiled at the scene. It was only a short time before they began to leave. The rattles and squeaks of armour and the clatter of helmets woke the sleeping knight who staggered behind. Stopping at the door, one turned to look back. "Thomas, go to the stables and tell the ostlers to find you warm hay for the night. If they are not there, go to the hay loft…and you'd better be there in the morning!"

Tom saw the latter as a threat. He had no intention of absconding and decided it would be prudent to stay close to the knights, and Rauin, with whom he had struck a congenial relationship. His mind raced in many directions, leaving him unable to make rational decisions. Confused, he retired to the stables. Having slept with horses many times before, it didn't bother him, but there was too much on his mind to allow sleep. In the darkness of the night, when thoughts and ideas are not always practical, he pondered the children and the royal treasure. He loved Alfie and Susie dearly and wanted to take them home, so it weighed on his conscience when he considered the extreme wealth the royal treasure would bring if he took the time to locate it first.

Chapter 13

Tom drifted into an uneasy sleep just before dawn and was woken by the sound of voices from outside the stable door. The ostlers were bringing feed for the horses and preparing to groom them for the day. As the stable door opened Tom shielded his eyes from the sudden light.

"What in the name of hell are you doing in here again?" one man shouted.

"Relax, will you?" Tom said as he stood brushing himself off, before continuing in a tone of authority. "There's no mischief. I'm employed by some of the knights to attend their mounts. I'm a horse physician. The inn was full so I slept with the animals as I often do. And who might you be?"

The men's demeanour changed, as he had hoped, expecting they would not care to be chastised by the knights for interfering.

"Oh, that's all right then. But how were we to know you were with the knights? You didn't say."

"Well you know now, so let's have no more nonsense."

Tom gave them a smug glance as he left the stables, amused at their newfound respect. He was learning that hierarchy was important here. In the same way that he was obliged to show respect to the knights, even though none of it sat comfortably with his principles. Yet, he accepted that hierarchy and respect for position was often needed to impose and maintain order. When in the Army, he didn't think of officers as better people. To him, they were just others who had different responsibilities. Even though he didn't like some of them, he still respected their position and authority.

At the inn, Tom was given bread, cheese, a coarse porridge, and ale. He thought it a strange breakfast and declined the ale in favour of water, which he drank very little of since it tasted worse than the ale he had drunk the night before. Not permitted to sit at the same table as the knights, he watched and listened from another as they discussed their plans for the arrival of the king's entourage. After eating, he stood beside the knights, waiting to be noticed.

"Well, what is it?"

"I'll go now and find the ingredients for your horse's cure, mix a poultice, and prepare a mixture for the Puffs."

"Yes, go. The mounts will not be needed before noon. Until then they can remain stabled."

"I'll need the use of a kitchen to prepare the mixtures. Would you ask the innkeeper to allow me to use theirs?"

"Ask? Allow? I'll tell him you will be using it!"

"I hope you are aware there are no instant cures for your horse's problem. It may take some days for the results to show. It's the same with horses as it is with humans. Your mount will not be cured by noon."

The knight grunted his reluctant acceptance. "Take your leave now, we have much to discuss here."

The salt was easily obtained as was the nettle, dandelion root, and red clover. Tom couldn't find kelp but discovered seaweed growing in small quantities at the base of structures by the quay. Most people had not heard of borage seed, as it came from foreign parts. Tom's only hope was that he might locate some on one of the foreign trading ships at the quay. Luckily, he found a small amount on a vessel newly returned from the East.

"Pay for it, you must," the quartermaster demanded in broken English.

"It's for the Templar Knights and I have no coin."

"Huh, that is typical of ze English. Go."

It was well known that if the knights wanted something, they would take it irrespective of protest or the need for payment. For such a small item they would not ask, just take. Tom was relieved as the only money he had was a two shillings piece, a half-crown, and a few coppers. Coins nobody would recognise, and showing them would raise awkward questions.

On returning to the inn, he asked for the kitchen. An untidy-looking woman, wearing a plain blue dress, and a once-white apron, which like her dress reached her ankles, was measuring flour for bread. She had been told that Tom needed space but resented others using her kitchen, no matter who they were.

"Don't think you're taking over my kitchen, mister. I'll need this 'ere big table to put me dough on, so you'd better do whatever it is you gotta do over on that there bench."

"That will do just fine, madam, thank you."

"Madam! madam, is it? I expect you'll be wanting to borrow something next."

She was right.

"Don't think I've been called Madam afore, sounds real proper like," she muttered with a smile. Then after recomposing herself to her usual demeanour, she asked, in a disgruntled tone, "So what is it you want then?"

"I need a bowl of boiled water, a small jug, a pestle and mortar, and a clean cloth if you please."

Before the woman had time to respond, Rauin spoke from the doorway.

"Good morning, Thomas. You may borrow my pestle and mortar. I'll be interested to see what a horse physician does with it. But I need it back soon to prepare the king's tonic."

"I don't know, the last time I looked this was *my* kitchen," the woman complained.

Rauin stared at her. "You will mind your manners, woman, if you know what is good for you. We are on the king's business here."

Replying with an indignant "Huh", she looked down and aggressively pounded her dough, causing clouds of flour to rise and linger in the air.

Rauin moved closer to where Tom was working. "I did not expect to see you here this morning." He watched before jovially adding, "I can see you have done this before, Master Thomas. Will it work?"

"Yes, given time. But it will depend on the ostlers giving the doses as and when I tell them. It might be best if I do it."

Then, leaning closer Rauin spoke so only Tom could hear: "I must confess my uncertainty of the ability of my potion to cure the king's ills. It failed previously, but now I have fresher ingredients, so there may yet be hope."

"What exactly is wrong with the king?"

"He struggles to keep food inside. It either comes back up, but mostly it passes through him quickly as a tanned liquid. I fear he overindulges and eats inappropriate foods, believing it will compensate for his increasing weakness.

Yet, he rejects my advice and demands medicinal cures. I have tried with all my knowledge but to little effect, which is why I went to the monks at Ely. I can only make my potion stronger and pray that it works."

"Have you tried giving him fenugreek seeds to chew? It can work wonders. My mother used to give it to my brother and me when we had diarrhoea. We were given it three times a day, and within two days we were both fine again. You might try to keep him away from fresh fruit, especially apples, and give him cider vinegar to drink. Hard-boiled eggs will help bind him too."

"You speak strangely, Thomas. What is fenugreek? Where can I find it? And what is diarrhoea? I know not these names."

Tom realised that in his enthusiasm he had probably said too much from a different time. In the future, he would need to be careful how he explained himself.

"Fenugreek comes from foreign parts, where King Richard fought his Crusades, and also much further to the east. It's used to treat many ills. I think you would only get it from a trading ship returning from those parts unless a merchant already has some. Diarrhoea is another name for when food passes through someone suddenly and quickly, like the brown liquid you described."

"But the king complains of gut ache much of the time and my medication has little effect," Rauin sighed. "I have given him belladonna to ease the pain and induce sleep and help him rest, but alas, it is to no avail. Even its properties of causing firmness in what he passes have failed him."

"Have you tried giving him blackberry tea? You should be able to find a few berries hereabouts,"

"No. How is it prepared?"

"It's easy. Just boil a handful of berries in water for five minutes, strain the crap out, let it cool, and take a good mouthful two to four times a day. It's not a cure, but it helps make the stomach more comfortable and it'll replace his lost fluids. Hopefully, the king should find it soothing."

"Thank you, Thomas. Again, you use another strange word. What is crap? Do you mean the remains of the berries?"

"Yes," Tom said, cursing himself again for not being careful.

Rauin squinted as he peered into Tom's eyes. "Just where are you from, Thomas? I have never before met anyone quite like you. You dress and talk so differently. You have knowledge that I have not heard before. I suspect there is more to the truth of you than you divulge."

Tom's thoughts returned to his home, of Dora, and his children. The hope of finding them here swelled his emotions.

He considered carefully before speaking, trying not to be overheard. "Well, my friend, in a manner of speaking, I have already told you the truth. However, I admit there is much more. Some things are hard to explain, even to myself. There are lots of things I have difficulty understanding. But, as you have shared your confidences with me, I'll share mine with you."

"You have my word that whatever secrets you hold will be safe with me. I shall not betray your trust."

"Thank you. First, I have to take this to the stables, attend to the knights' horses, and instruct the ostlers. Then, I'll come back here to inform the knights about their conditions. That should give you time to finish the king's medicines. After that, we can talk privately." He winked at Rauin and nodded towards the woman who was struggling to overhear.

Tom pulled on the small chain that led to his waistcoat pocket and lifted out his fob-watch. After staring at the face for a few seconds, he said, "Let's say about eleven o'clock, shall we? Here at the inn." Before dropping the watch back into his waistcoat pocket.

Wide-eyed, Rauin stared at Tom's pocket.

"I can see you are puzzled by my fob-watch, I'll explain it later."

The physician arrived early but didn't have to wait long for Tom, who asked if they could walk in the streets to avoid being overheard.

"You will probably find it hard to believe or understand much of what I tell you, Rauin. But when you remember what you have already told me, you might believe. You see, I am from the south of here, as I said, and not too far either. Just near Ely, so still in the area you know as The Washes, or The Isles of Eels, which I know as The Fens and The Isle of Ely. That was all true, but I come from a different time, I've come from 1925 to be exact, and I was born in1890."

Rauin stopped to stare at him.

"I believe I found your flask, the one you lost while coming here, but centuries later. I can see that it's hard for you to accept and I can hardly believe what's happening either."

"But that is seven hundred years hence!" Rauin gasped. "It cannot be so."

"I know it's a long way into your future. Please believe me when I say I know something about your time. I'll explain shortly. But first, may I ask if you believe what you were told in Ely about the king's cure?"

"Do you mean that it would cure the king?"

"No, I mean what happens to the cure after seven days and the story about the monk who went back to King Arthur's time."

"Well…I have no reason to disbelieve."

"Good, then I'll explain how I found your flask. As I said, I am from far into the future and I know a lot about what will happen from now until 1900." Do you understand?"

"Yes, of course. But…"

"In about four hundred years from now, the Duke of Bedford will get permission from King Charles the first to drain this whole area and for a long way south, well past Ely, almost to Cambridge. The course of some rivers will be changed and new ones made. Once drained, it will be rich, fertile farmland and provide most of England's food as well as enough for export. As the water is removed, the ground will sink. The way an apple shrinks when the juice has gone. When the land sinks, lost items from the past eventually appear at the surface. The whole landscape will become known as The Fens, with each area having its own Fen name."

Rauin blinked hard in amazement before fixing his stare back into Tom's eyes.

"I have worked with horses all my life, and when a great war started in France in 1914, my job was to care for the big working horses there. I already knew a lot about them, but the army taught me more. That's how I know about treating horses and can see when they have a problem or are sick. After the war, I returned to my farm. I tilled the soil ready for winter and spring seeding. One day, I was ploughing in the area of the old river course, right where you say you lost your flask. In my time, it's known by local people as The Old Bank. Anyway, one day, a round ceramic object, like a ball, rolled off the plough's blade."

As Rauin had done, Tom cupped his hands to show the approximate size. The physician's eyes widened with the realisation that Tom had found his flask. "The fields I worked were about three miles north of Ely. I can see what you are thinking, Rauin. I also believe it was the flask you lost a few days ago, or should I say, hundreds of years ago."

"Then you must have smelled the potion and transported yourself here." Rauin's eyes sparkled. "So the old friar was right! Go on, go on!"

"Yes, absolutely."

"This is taking some moments to comprehend. "Where is the flask now?"

"I hope it's where I left it, on a ledge in my barn, back in 1925."

Rauin paused, still struggling with the facts. "But how can I know you are telling the truth and that you have not made this up after I told you of the friar's words?"

"Please trust me, Rauin, I have no reason to lie to you. I could tell you about coming events and you would eventually know I'm telling the truth." Taking the coins from his pocket he offered Rauin a penny. "Look, these are coins from my time. Like yours, they carry an image of our king or queen while they reign, but look at the date, what you see."

"It says 1874. Yet, it is not gold or silver. It is brown and worn, not unlike copper. How do you know its worth?"

"It says on it, look, one penny."

"Ah, we have a penny too, but it is unlike this."

"I know, but gold and silver have not been used for a long time. They are too precious, too soft, and wear quickly. As you know, people can take a nick from the edge, and over time, collect the precious metal. But in my time, the value is not in the metal. Its value is in what it represents and what you can buy with it. It's a different sort of value. This one is worn because, even in my time, it's considered quite old and has had a lot of use. It will have passed through thousands of pockets and purses. Do you see the queen on the other side? That's Queen Victoria. She died in1901."

"It's difficult to understand how I could exchange this for goods, or food and lodgings. If I offered this to an innkeeper in payment, he would have me thrown out."

"That's because it's not valid here. He would think it foreign and worthless, which of course it would be to him. We are from different times, my friend. Things have changed over the centuries. Here, look at this other one, it's the same value but minted later. It's not so worn but is the same value as the other one. See, it has the head of King Edward the Seventh, and the date is 1910. Look, it still says one penny."

"I don't know, Thomas, yet I feel you are truthful." Rauin's mind raced. "What of that device you chained to your pocket? The 'fob' I believe you called it."

"Oh, that's my watch, some people call it a fob-watch. I have no idea why. It's a small machine for telling the time. Here, listen to its movement."

Tom held it to Rauin's ear.

"It has a heart of its own! I can hear the beat! Why is it kept in your pocket? Why is it chained there? Where do you find such a thing?"

"Slow down, Rauin. It doesn't have a heart, just a spring. It's a miniature machine to tell the time, made by men with special knowledge and skills. Tell me, how do you know the time of day now?"

"Well, if the day is bright, I consult the nearest sundial. Many churches have them and they are to be found in noble gardens and castles. Always on a part of the building which receives the most sun. If there is no dial, I look at the angle of the sun and the shadows to estimate the hour."

"And if there is no sun, or it's dark, what then?"

"Ah, that is not so easy. I estimate according to the moonlight and the length of the day so far, also by the position of the stars, if there is no cloud. Also, my stomach tells me," Rauin joked.

Tom laughed. "So you would mostly guess."

"Yes, I suppose so. No, Thomas, I estimate."

"Exactly. To be more accurate, men invented this little machine and much larger ones too. See here, the short pointer moves at almost the same speed as the sun and moon so tells the hour. The longer pointer sweeps around the dial exactly once every hour to give the minutes. So you can know the time to within one minute, day or night, rain or shine. Almost every man has one in my time, and we all set them to the same time. If you had one, we could arrange to meet at fifteen minutes past nine in the morning. We would both know exactly to the minute when that is. The chain is simply to save it, should it fall out of my pocket. It was invented long before I was born."

"Amazing! Next, you will tell me that man has learned to fly like a bird."

Tom grinned. "Let's not talk about that."

Without either man realising it, they were beginning to bond. Each had something of benefit to offer the other. Although they were from completely different times, they felt a kinship that encouraged trust.

"Do you have one of your pennies, Rauin?"

Rauin produced a leather pouch from inside his tunic and took out a coin.

"This is a silver penny. See, the king's image is on one side and a Christian cross on the other."

Tom inspected it with interest. The coin was indeed silver, and approximately round. He thought the workmanship was crude. The image of King John was unflattering, lacking any recognisable features, and showing bulging, staring eyes. Even so, Tom was complimentary, saying it was interesting, before suggesting they exchange coins. Ruain eagerly agreed as they accepted the other's penny. "Thank you, Rauin, I'll treasure it," he said, putting the Silver Cross penny in his coat pocket. "You mentioned that a monk went back to King Arthur's time and returned after a short while. Do you know how long he was away?"

"I can't be sure, but I understand, from what the friar said, it depends on how much and how deeply he had breathed the odour. Why? Are you concerned about returning to your time?"

"Not exactly, well yes and no. It would be nice to know approximately when it will be and if I could come back again later." Eventually finding the children here uppermost in his mind, but he didn't mention them, just searched faces as they walked. Nor did he mention his speculation of discovering where King John was about to lose his treasure. He didn't think Rauin would find it possible that the king would allow it to happen. No more than believing the king will die in just over two weeks, irrespective of his efforts to save him. No, he thought it best to say nothing. His emotions were running high at the hopeful possibility of finding the children. For now, he had enough on his mind.

Rauin frowned. "The king could arrive here this day and I must be ready to administer his potion. He could arrive soon, at any hour, but it is not known. Although, the common word is that he will not be here on the morrow. He is to stay at the bishop's manor, but for how long I know not. He can be secretive, which is as well given the many enemies he harbours. If I receive word that he is delaying, then I must go to him, and not dally here. I do not know how long he will stay in Bishop's Lynn. Even those he sends ahead to plan his arrival do not know with certainty when he will appear. My king has been known to send word ahead to a destination and never journey there for fear his enemies may have discovered his movements.

"Surely a king should be a popular figure, a powerful man, to be revered and obeyed?"

"I tell you privately, Thomas. I serve my king honestly and well, but he can be an odd fellow. When he is unwell and his innards pain him, he blames me and demands an immediate cure. I am not a magician. I advise rest, medicines, and to eat modestly of plain food. I do what I can, but he becomes impatient and angers quickly. He can be kind, witty, and generous one day, and full of pettiness, cruelty, and spitefulness the next. He is a man of many moods. As for being revered and respected, that might have been so once. But now he hangs onto his throne and such lands as he has left in desperation and with little support.

"Why? Surely he has great wealth and the support of his subjects." Tom knew it to be untrue but wanted to hear more from Rauin.

"He certainly has wealth in gold and jewels. Like a magpie, he has hoarded for many years. He continues to want more, yet he is reluctant to use his own wealth to finance his battles. He inherited lands in Ireland, Anjou, and Normandy, but has now lost them and the revenue they provided. He treated the nobles badly, so they revolted taking back their lands by force. I'm afraid King John is no great politician or warrior. Consequently, he pressures the English nobles into providing more taxes. They, in turn, have no choice but to increase taxes on the monasteries and common folk. Most cannot afford the additional burden, become destitute, and turn against both the nobles and the king.

Much of King John's wealth and lands were inherited from his brother, Richard, who most thought was a good king and highly respected. Unfortunately, he ignored matters of state at home, being away on crusades too often. These crusades created great debts which John inherited. Always resentful of his brother's talents and popularity, John could hardly wait to take the crown and prove himself a worthy king. However, while Richard was away, John meddled in matters beyond his authority, creating discord and unrest. His wealth is now such that he has engaged two thousand or more of the Knights Templar to guard it and himself. Ah, but what I say is strictly between ourselves lest I would be accused of treason."

"You do not need to worry, Rauin. My lips are sealed, but you may be pleased to know that history will record your words as the truth."

Rauin gave a weak smile of appreciation.

"But what brings him to Bishop's Lynn? It's a small tidal port, miles from anywhere and of no great significance."

"No, my friend, you misjudge the town. It is most wealthy, with traders and merchants. Many own fishing fleets that bring whale oil, cod, and herring from the northern seas. Reed, live eels, grain, and wool are exported to foreign lands from here. Many traders sponsor expeditions to the east, returning with spices, silks, and other finery. Many rich merchants live here. They are wealthy and pay taxes directly to the king. Hence, he favours them and this town. Yet to answer your question with accuracy is difficult. The king is losing lands to the south and west as we speak, and the country is at war with itself. I cannot be sure how to answer your question with complete truth. He may be running from defeat, he may be intending to regroup in a place where others might be reluctant to follow, or he may sail away to a friendly country. If there is such a place left for him. Time will reveal the truth. But for now, he is not strong, often bad-tempered, and I fear his judgement may be impaired."

"If the English barons have revolted around him, and his enemy is to the west and south, it seems he is trying to avoid an inevitable fate?"

"Sadly, I feel that too. Do not venture these opinions elsewhere, or you may lose your head. There is a fellow, who once resided not too many miles from here, who was outspoken in matters of state and so was declared an outlaw. Had he been a truly common man he would have been held and executed, as he yet may be if King John has his way."

"Would that be the Earl of Huntingdon?"

Rauin frowned. "I have not heard of such a nobleman."

"I ask because centuries later, in my time, he is considered a romantic folk hero, commonly known as Robin Hood, and not so commonly as The Earl of Huntingdon. It's said that he was a great supporter of King Richard, which made him unpopular with King John. Legend has it that he robbed the rich and gave to the poor."

"Ah, you refer to Robin Hode of Loxley, a little to the north of Huntingdon. He is no folk hero, Thomas. So that is how history remembers him." Rauin laughed aloud.

"Then who is he?"

"His father is a landowner of some modest title. Robin became a Yeoman of the Crown at the court of King Richard, to whom he was fiercely loyal, especially in his absence. Hode was not a truly common man and had been educated by monks at his father's expense. He became bold and outspoken of John's 'mischief and meddling' as he called it. He also empathised greatly with the plight of the common folk, and it seems he may have deliberately fostered discontent amongst them. So, when John became king, he decided to silence Hode once and for all, but Hode was warned by a courtier and fled. The king ordered that he be found and brought back. It is believed that Hode first dwelt in these very marshes, it being a forbidding place where few men might venture. So the king declared him outlawed. As such, any person suspected of helping or harbouring him could be executed without trial. The purpose was to draw him into the open for capture. It was much less costly than offering a reward for information for his capture. Rumour has it that Hode disliked these cold, damp marshes and left after only a few months."

"Where did he go?" Tom asked, looking for confirmation of the legend.

"He is talked of in the Nottingham area, described as the common folk's champion. They gave him sustenance and secrecy because he once argued with the barons against their poverty. He achieved little but had at least tried. Hode lives feral and hunts the king's game for food, giving his surplus to the village folk. Of course, they are grateful, being near to starvation, and not daring to hunt game themselves. I hear a few ruffians and common folk have joined him, but he is no great hero of our day. It seems he is destined to spend his last days in fear of betrayal, and the loss of his head."

"What has happened to him?"

"It is not known with any certainty. Rumours have him seen in many places. Some say he is dead, but the king will not believe it until his head appears on a pike."

"What of Maid Marion? Where does she fit into his life, or is there no such person?"

"Ah, now, Thomas, you touch a royal nerve. Some believe she is the true reason King John so fiercely hates Hode."

Tom leaned towards Rauin. "Why?"

Rauin hesitated to gather his thoughts. "Well, my friend, it is a tragedy in itself. Robert FitzWalter, the Lord of Dunmow, had a very beautiful daughter named Matilda. My king fell in love with her and desired her for his mistress, but Matilda refused his advances. She became distraught by the king's continued attention and feared what he might do. You see, Thomas, as king, he is accustomed to getting his way in all matters. Matilda fled to Sherwood, where she met and fell in love with Hode. She stayed with him and his 'band of rogues' for three years, where she became known as 'The Fair Maid Marion.' When news reached her that her father had fled to France, she decided to return to Dunmow and manage her family's estate. When the king heard, he once more courted her with letters of love and affection, which she ignored, still being in love with Hode.

The king was enraged and intensely jealous. In his despair, he decided that if he could not have her then no other man would. He engaged Robert de Medewe to take her a bracelet, so beautiful that she could not refuse it. However, de Medewe was unaware of the bracelet being coated with a deadly poison. He was dazzled by her beauty and charm, so he too fell in love with her. He dared not speak of his affection when he returned to court, lest the king should hear of it.

After some days, he could not clear Matilda from his mind and went back to Dunmow, only to find that she was dead. Her body lay on a bier covered in flowers. The beautiful bracelet was still on her wrist, but the skin on her arm was blackened by the poison. Poor Robert was devastated that he had been an instrument in her demise. He refused to return to the service of King John and is now a reclusive Brother of the Order of St. Augustine, housed in a priory serving God alone."

"That's amazing, I had no idea."

"Speaking of the king, I must prepare to greet him. I shall brew your blackberry tea and pray it helps."

Each went their own way. During the remainder of the day, Tom searched the streets for the children. By late afternoon, Rauin was attending the king.

The town was overrun with Knights Templar, who occupied almost every house, supposedly on the king's authority. There were two thousand of them, with other folks in attendance. Many had to camp in pastures and on common land where heavy carts cut deep into the soft ground. A wondrous spectacle for Tom, who thought the town would run out of ale and food long before they left. His anxious task of finding the familiar faces of his children in this melee was difficult.

Tom and Rauin spent only a short time together at the inn that evening where they mostly discussed medicine. Their conversation was occasionally interrupted when Rauin responded to sarcastic banter from the knights. But he didn't stay long, being required to attend to the king at the manor house.

After eating and savouring the warmth of the inn, Tom retired to the stables where he found fresh hay and was greeted by the waft of fresh horse dung. Much had happened today and once more his mind was racing with thoughts of his children. He decided that tomorrow he would ask people if they had been seen.

Chapter 14

Tom was in a puzzled daze before he recognised the inside of his barn at Tythe Farm. Gathering his senses, he clambered to his feet, dusted himself off and began to wonder what had happened and where he had been. Was it a dream or was it real? He couldn't be sure.

Hollow iced puddles in cart tracks crackled under his feet as he walked back to the house. The air was cold and crisp. Instinctively, he put his hands into his pockets. His fingers touched something hard. He fondled it, then remembering what it was, he quickly brought the object to his eyes. He was holding a rough silver coin. One side carried the poor image of King John, and the other a Christian cross. Tom stopped, staring at it in astonishment, now contemplating that his experience might not have been a dream.

He reached the farmhouse door with a feeling of trepidation, knowing he was about to have a lot of explaining to do. He took a breath, turned the doorknob and entered. Dora was standing at the sink with her back to the door. She turned sharply when it opened. Staring at her, Tom didn't know what to say.

"Where on earth have you been? Everyone has been looking for you!"

"I'm sorry, my duck, but I don't really know myself, so I can't tell you exactly."

"Can't tell me exactly. Can't tell me! I'm your wife. I have a right to know." She glared at him, waiting for an answer.

"Well, what I mean is, I don't know where to start, and you probably wouldn't believe me anyway. I have to sort things out in my head for a minute or two."

"Sort things out! Don't you know where you were these past two days?"

"Yes, sort of, no, but you wouldn't understand. I'm not even sure myself."

"Try me! I've been worried sick."

"Give me a few minutes…and don't attack me, woman. You said you were worried, but you don't seem at all pleased to see me!"

Dora put her hands on her hips. Short of an immediate answer she rocked her head.

Tom quietly broke the silence. "I could do with a cup of tea, my duck, I'm parched."

"I expect you'll be wanting some breakfast too," Dora said as she filled the kettle.

"Yes, please, I could eat a horse."

After hanging his coat on the back of the door, Tom cut two thick slices of bread, took the long fork from its hook by the hearth, and sat at the stove to make toast. Dora cracked two eggs into a bowl, and with a small amount of milk, whisked them with far more aggression than was needed.

"I don't know why I bother. You disappear for two days without as much as a by-your-leave, then turn up as though you have just come in from work like it was any other day. If I could smell beer on you, I'd think you'd drunk too much at the pub and had been sleeping it off somewhere."

Tom didn't respond, but wondered how he could explain without sounding ridiculous.

As Dora put a mug of tea on the table she interrupted his thoughts. "You haven't been off with that Rose, have you?"

"No, no, of course not."

"There's no 'of course not' about it. I've always known you fancy her and she'll go with anything in trousers. Who knows what went on when I was in the hospital!"

"Now don't be like that, Dora. She might flirt a bit, but that's all. You're just being nasty and nothing went on. So let's not get silly about her!"

Tom took a deep breath and exhaled between his teeth. He thought he could hardly be blamed if he was with Rose, especially given his and Dora's relationship over the past couple of years. It fleetingly crossed his mind to falsely say that he really was with Rose. It would be more believable than the truth, but it would cause distress and embarrassment for everyone. He might even lose his job and he'd be scorned by the village women. Tom allowed himself a mischievous thought, *He'd be envied by most of the men.*

Dora was right. He did like Rose, in a funny sort of way, and he would have courted her had he been single and nearer her age, although knowing he would need to tame her a little. Tom returned from his fantasy, saying nothing. He could have tried to explain, but it would only escalate the argument and dig an even bigger hole for himself. Dora's suspicions would have to rest where they are for now.

"Come on, Tom. What am I supposed to believe? I'm waiting!"

"Dora, I have *not* been with Rose! Why don't you go and ask her?"

"Why should I? She'd only lie!"

Tom exhaled heavily and shook his head. He wanted to tell her that he may have found where the children had disappeared to, but until he knew for sure, decided it was best to say nothing. There would be too many questions, too much speculation, and no doubt ridicule when he tried to explain. None of which he could cope with right now. Then, remembering King John's treasure, he said, "Look, my duck, the best I can tell you is that I've been away looking at an unexpected opportunity that could make us both a fortune. If it works out, you can have a nice house, wherever you want and live like a lady."

"Well, you'd better tell me about it then," she snapped.

"I can't right now, but I will soon, I promise. Don't get upset. You wouldn't believe me anyway, nor would you understand if I told you. All I can say is that it's nothing immoral or criminal and it won't get anyone into trouble. What's more, there is no other woman involved, so get that out of your head once and for all. You have to trust me on this, and please stop being so aggressive. How about showing me a little kindness once in a while, or even a little caring, if it's not too much trouble?"

"Of course, I care or I wouldn't get upset, would I?" She went quiet as she looked down at her hands.

"Good, then I wish you'd show it now and again. Just trust me, and I'll tell you right here and now that I have to go away again, for at least another day or two."

"When?" she asked.

"Later today or maybe tomorrow morning, I've not decided yet."

"Why? Where to?"

"I can't tell you, Dora, and you can't tell anyone what I have told you either. Like I said, just trust me, please!"

Dora huffed. "What'll I tell people about you being away? I've already told Lilly in the shop I don't know where you are…and your boss has been looking for you too. I even told the police you were missing."

Tom thought a moment, wishing she had not gone to the police. "Tell them you have just found a note I left, saying I had to go to London suddenly to help my cousin with a private matter. Say it got pushed behind the clock or something so you didn't notice it sooner."

By now Tom had toasted his two slices on both sides and placed them on a plate for Dora to cover with butter and scrambled eggs.

When he had finished eating, he went to a bookshelf in the best room to get a volume of the history of East Anglia and the Fens, which went back to pre-medieval times. Then, taking it back to the warmth of the kitchen, he sat by the stove again. His fingers glided through the index to stop at 1100 AD to 1300 AD, where he found the events of 1216. It confirmed what he thought, that King John left Bishop's Lynn on 9th October for Newark.

"Remind me what the date is today, Dora?"

"It's the seventh of October. Fancy that, you have even forgotten what day it is."

Tom ignored her sarcasm. "Then I have to go back today."

"Back where?"

Tom didn't reply, knowing she would think him mad if he told her. His main thought now was of what to take with him.

"Can we please stop playing silly-beggars! Where the hell are you going, and why? I'm your wife. I have a right to know."

Tom turned towards her, gripped her firmly by the upper arms, and giving her a gentle shake, he stared into her eyes. "Look, Dora, you'll know everything in good time, but for now you have to trust me. How many more times must I tell you?"

She was neither consoled nor satisfied.

Tom returned to the best room where he placed the Encyclopaedia of History in his old army rucksack, along with a book of herbal medicines, a handful of postcards, and a few photographs of Dora and his children. He then searched in a cupboard for his old army compass, which he put in his pocket.

He decided to update his notes while events were still fresh in his mind, unsure where to begin and what to say, but it came as he wrote. When finished, he thought of leaving a sealed envelope with information about where he had gone should he not be able to return. Although he doubted that anyone would believe him unless they eventually discovered the urn and tested its contents. He smiled at the thought of Constable Cornwell turning up in his uniform, helmet on and truncheon in hand, at the court of King John. No, he would not leave word. Dora would not resist opening the envelope as soon as he was gone.

Returning to the kitchen he placed much of the meagre contents of their medicine cabinet into the rucksack.

"I have to go now, Dora. Don't worry. I'll be back."
"When?"

"I don't know exactly. It could be tomorrow or a day or two, I just don't know right now. Please do as I told you, and stop people looking for me. Oh, and don't forget to let the police know. They won't be pleased with you for not finding the note sooner, so just play innocent and apologise. They'll get over it."

"What if they want to see the note?"

"Show them. Here, give me some paper and I'll write it for you now."

He signed it "Love, Tom." It felt strange. He had not told Dora he loved her for a long time. It didn't go unnoticed by Dora, who had a melancholic moment. It occurred to him that maybe it was for him to begin the thawing process. He had always blamed Dora, so it was a profound moment. A thought he'd consider later. With that, Tom made his way to the big barn.

Dora didn't look to see where he went, just stood wringing her hands into her apron when he left the kitchen. Tom had promised he would return and she could only hope he would.

Sniffing the opened flask deeper than the first time, he wanted to stay away longer. Then, after quickly replacing the lid, he put the flask on a higher ledge than before and tensed, waiting for the pain through his temples.

Chapter 15

Once again, Tom woke to the familiar smell of the stables, but this time he knew where he was. The autumn chill had permeated the air and the horses would soon welcome their blankets. The sound of voices from outside prompted him to quickly orientate himself. The outer door at the end of the stalls opened to reveal the ostlers who had previously apprehended him. As they entered, Tom assumed an air of authority to take the upper hand. Deliberately failing to greet them, he immediately gave orders. "These stalls need mucking out, it should have been done by now. See to it! Make sure the fresh hay is dampened. We don't want these poor animals coughing and sneezing all morning, or the knights will see you in the stocks! I'll be back to check later."

It worked. There was no challenge. They simply doffed their hats in obedience. To discourage any discussion, he didn't look at them as he left. They moved aside when he passed between them on his way to the door. Not being accustomed to giving orders in such an autocratic manner, it didn't feel natural, but he enjoyed the moment and waited until he was outside before allowing himself a grin of satisfaction.

The streets were busy. Men were driving horse, and

ox-drawn carts to and from the docks. At times, the clatter of steel rims and hooves on the cobbles was almost deafening. Tom watched as children collected horse dung, which he presumed was to fertilise their family plots. He thought it a good thing or the streets would soon become a stinking slurry when it rained. There was an air of great purpose as traders hurried with small carts of vegetables, fruit, meat, and fish, none having time to stop and chat with the other. He stopped when a boy herded a gaggle of geese across his path, only to disappear in an alleyway. A dog or two, of doubtful breed, scavenged for scraps. Angry growls caught his attention when two challenged each other for possession of a morsel. A woman poured wastewater into the street while gulls screeched overhead as they squabbled over scraps. All the time Tom searched faces for his children.

As he neared the inn, there was a scene of increased activity with Knights Templar talking in small groups. Some had already retrieved their mounts from the meadows, while others were on foot. One of the knights stepped out at seeing Tom. "Where have you been, scoundrel?"

"Inspecting your mounts and looking for herbs to make their cures. They are scarce at this time of the year, so it took a while." Tom's answer was accepted with a slight grumble. "May I ask if you have seen the king's physician this morning, Sir Knight?"

"He's in the kitchen, here at the inn, making mud and horseshit pies." The other knights laughed.

Tom turned to the inn but was held back by his shoulder. One of the knights placed his face close to his. Tom winced, pulling his head back at the smell of bad breath and rotting teeth.

"Listen. There are many knights here, all willing to buy your services. If you are asked, you must say you are already commissioned to Sir Gillaume de Chartres, do you hear? Sir Gillaume de Chartres! No one will argue with you then."

The closer knights looked at each other and smiled in a way that made Tom doubt the truth of what he was being told. So he smiled, nodded, and made to leave. He was told to wait while the knight fumbled in a leather pouch producing a coin, which he gave Tom.

"See, you have been paid in advance before witnesses. You are indentured to me and my brother knights now. By accepting payment our contract is sealed."

When Tom entered the kitchen. Rauin was already at work.

The landlord's wife looked to see who had entered. "So you're back 'ere again, are you!"

Rauin quickly turned to her. "Watch your mouth, woman, he is my companion. Any more insolence from you and I'll see you in stocks for the rest of the day."

She pinched her lips, grunted and looked away.

"Where have you been, Thomas?"

"I've been looking for fresh herbs. Some are hard to find at this time of the year, so I needed to find a merchant who had dried ones." Then, with his back to the woman, he winked and flicked his eyes in her direction. Rauin immediately understood.

"What do you want, woman, be gone. We are about the king's private business here."

She waddled off to another room, mumbling her complaints as she went.

Tom moved closer. "I've been back to my time. There doesn't seem to be any way of controlling exactly when the potion will act, so I couldn't let you know in advance. If I disappear again, you'll know why."

"Speak slowly, Thomas, your manner with words needs great concentration."

Tom slowed and relaxed, swinging the rucksack from his shoulder. "Sorry. It's a good thing that others believe I'm from foreign parts. Look, I brought a few things for you which may help with the king's illness, or at least make him more comfortable."

He was tempted to tell Rauin that no matter what he did, the king would not be cured and was destined to die of his illness soon after reaching Newark Castle. Tom thought it a pity as modern medicine and professional care could save him, but then it would change the course of history. Hesitating, he decided to leave it for the physician to discover for himself from the history book he'd brought, or from the event itself, whichever was first. Rauin wouldn't want to hear that he was about to fail in his efforts to cure the king. So a stressed discussion was avoided.

"Can we talk, Rauin?"

"I must finish here first. Then if there is time before my Liege demands my attention, it may be possible. Thereafter, much of my time will be spent at the manor house."

"Can we talk while you work?"

"Yes, of course. You may help with the mixing too."

"When I went back to my time, I checked the history books to discover more about King John and his illness. Did you know he was not only known as John Lackland, but also John Softsword, and later as Bad King John?"

"Lackland and Softsword I have heard, but Bad King John does not surprise me. Is that how history records him?"

"Yes, I'm afraid it does. But I'm digressing. Anyway, I discovered that he is fond of fruit. Especially peaches. Is that correct?"

"Do your books record such small detail?"

"Yes, sometimes."

"The king would eat his way through a full cob of them at one sitting if he could."

"Rauin, that's a big part of the reason he passes solid foods like a liquid and why he is in pain."

"How did your books know about his bowels? He does not like talk of it, but I suppose it's hard to keep secret."

"You have to try and stop the king eating peaches. Some fruits are not good for him in his current condition. Try to keep him from greasy meats or food cooked in fat. He should also avoid acidic foods as much as possible. I tell you honestly, it will not cure him, but he will be more comfortable."

Rauin sucked air through his teeth, doubting that he could control the king's eating habits. He could advise, but would the king comply? "Then what must he eat and drink?"

"Things that will help to bind his bowels and settle his stomach, such as plain toasted bread, eggs boiled hard, and chicken breast with no skin. He should drink clean boiled water and plenty of it to replace his lost fluids. You can put a little lemon juice in it too. I know I said to avoid acids, but lemons have other properties too and they will be diluted. There are lots of things that will help. Ginger is very good, fennel, mint tea, a sauce made from apples, cinnamon and apple cider vinegar will all help reduce his diarrhoea. You might already know some of these things."

Rauin was impressed. "I know of some but not all."

Tom took a small dark blue, hexagonal, glass bottle from his rucksack and held it up.

Rauin stared at it. "I have not seen such a vessel before."

"It contains something we use in the twentieth century. It settles the stomach and eases pain."

"What is it?"

"Oil of caraway. It's not a cure, but it may help relieve the king's stomach cramps. It's best taken after meals, and only when he has pain. Just one spoonful will do. Some other time when we have the seeds, I'll show you how to extract the oil."

"He can be a difficult patient according to his mood. I hope he will accept it."

Tom unscrewed the lid. Rauin was as fascinated with the bottle as he was with the contents.

"Smell it. Doesn't taste bad either, most people like it. If it makes him feel comfortable, he might be in a better mood for a while."

He smiled as Tom handed it over. His curiosity was obvious as he inspected the bottle.

Tom watched for a moment or two. "Just twist the top and it'll come off…that's it."

Grinning, he removed and replaced the cap several times.

"Sorry Rauin, I'm delaying you from your work, but later I have more to show you."

"No matter, no matter. Thank you for bringing your medicine. If I can get away, we can meet this evening here at the inn." As Tom made to leave, Rauin added, "I don't suppose you have a cure for head pains, do you?"

"Yours or the king's?"

"Both."

They laughed. Tom moved closer. "Well, as it happens, I do have something that might help."

Tom rummaged in his rucksack to produce another small glass bottle which he held for Rauin to see.

"Surely, you jest with me, Thomas?"

Tom was enjoying the moment. "No, really," he said as he pulled the cork, lifted out the cotton wool wadding, and tipped a few white tablets into his palm. "These are called, aspirin. They work well, just swallow two every four hours until the pain goes. Oh, and don't crunch them up, they taste terrible. They should be swallowed whole with water. I suggest you don't give these to the king, they could aggravate his condition. They are good for pain in the head but bad for an ailing stomach."

"Do you mean there is no need to inhale salts and the like?"

"I'd say, if it works, do it, it's up to you. There are other things you can try too," Tom said with a mischievous grin. "In my village, the old ladies say that crushing a small amount of charcoal into a glass of water, then drinking it, works. Sorry, I mean 'goblet'. But I have never tried it. Then, there's drinking herbal tea while soaking your feet in hot water for twenty minutes. But that has to be an old wifes' tale. If I get a headache that's not too bad, I massage my temples for a few minutes."

"An old wifes' tale?"

"It's just an expression meaning that it's something old ladies would make up and say."

"You should be a physician, Thomas."

"A doctor, not really. Most people know these things in my time. I'm happier with horses. I'll go now and see you here this evening. Oh, may I ask if you have heard of Sir Guillaume de Chartres?"

"Yes, of course. The entire king's household and the Knights Templar all have. He is the grandmaster of the Knights and spends much time with my Liege. He may be with him as we speak. How do you know him?"

"I don't. I'll explain later."

Tom returned to the stable where the ostlers were busy cleaning and about to start grooming. They worked harder and their chatter stopped on seeing him enter, much to Tom's amusement. He spent an hour checking the horses and applying remedies where necessary, even though he didn't know who each horse belonged to. It didn't matter. He believed that if an animal needed attention, it should get it. Some were in good condition while others, in his opinion, had been neglected. "When you have done cleaning, I want to see these mounts gleaming." Tom then left to look for Alfie, Susie and the other children.

He searched every street and alleyway he could find but was disappointed with the result. He asked people about them, some said they knew nothing and had not seen the children he described. Some simply walked away without answering and he was beginning to believe the children were not here.

It was late afternoon. He was hungry and thirsty. A mug of Dora's tea would be perfect right now. Even a bottle of cold tea with a bit of dockey would hit the right spot, but that was another world and a different time. After searching most of the day, he took his time going to the inn to meet Rauin.

There was a growing buzz in the air with much activity about the town, even more than this morning. The news of King John's arrival had travelled quickly and people from outlying areas came into the town with their wares and produce in the hope of selling to the royal entourage. Some accosted the knights and other visitors, while those with edible produce focussed their efforts on the inns, and any likely place where visitors would rest and eat. The market square was now a crowded centre of activity. Some costermongers made their way to the common grounds where many of the visitors were camped.

The inn was bustling with Knights Templar when Tom entered, many of whom he had not seen before. Scanning the faces for those who employed him was not easy. It was noisy and the smell of smoke from the open fire mixed with pungent body odours from the many unwashed bodies. Tom winced and rubbed a finger under his nose. He seemed to be the only one who noticed. Apart from their stature, the knights all looked very similar in their chainmail, uniforms, and full facial hair. It was difficult to see faces clearly in the dim light, especially of those turned towards the fire. They were a rowdy bunch with no apparent respect for others.

A teenage girl ran the gauntlet of lecherous hands whilst she attempted to deliver tankards of ale through the melee of boisterous knights, many of whom had already drunk enough to lower their few remaining inhibitions. They laughed at her rebuffs as she passed through. Tom was annoyed with them but restrained his instinct to defend her. The landlord ignored sarcastic jibes about his ale, and Tom saw how awkward he was while politely, even humbly, asking for payment. His flustered wife appeared with bowls of broth and lumps of bread, only to disappear with empty vessels as she huffed and puffed her way back to the kitchen.

It had been a dull day and it was getting dark early. Tom watched as a boy lit oil lamps around the walls and placed a few candles on the tables where people were eating.

He thought that a soldier's demeanour had not changed much over the years. To him, the scene reminiscent of off-duty soldiers in a French town during the Great War. The boisterous camaraderie was just the same, except in France, there would be alcohol-induced singing as the evening wore on, usually in some doubtful tune and language.

The landlord's wife ushered people away from the table once they had finished eating. Her abrupt demands might have started an altercation but no one cared to argue with her. Tom took the opportunity to sit as soon as a place became available. Feeling more relaxed and at ease, he was learning how things were done. Within minutes he was asked what he wanted. Feeling mischievously playful, he said, "I'll have roast pork with a little crackling, apple saurce, roast potatoes, sprouts, and carrots. Oh yes, and with a little gravy please." Then, after an expression of intense thought, he added, "Followed by…"

Not amused, the woman cut him short: "You'll have pottage with bread like everyone else, and lump it!"

"Lump it must be dessert. Well then, after careful consideration I think I'll have the pottage with bread. Then if you don't mind, I would like to have a little custard on my lump it, my good woman."

"Don't you come here from them foreign parts with your fancy talk, and don't you go 'my good womaning' me neither or I'll clip your ear'ole."

Tom chuckled. She left for the kitchen feeling

satisfied that she had put him in his place. He felt good. It had been a long time since he had last pulled someone's leg. His stew arrived in good time, and it was hot and tasty. There were small pieces of meat amongst the vegetables along with small, brittle bones. The bread was fresh, although he thought he might break his teeth on the crust. But after noticing that others dipped theirs into the stew, he did the same. In a moment of curiosity, when the landlady passed, he asked what the meat was.

"Well now, it could be a bit'a blackbird or even a bit'a thrush. You'll soon know according to what tune you start a whistling - you might even quack!" She waddled off as before, pleased that she had teased the foreigner again and gained a few laughs from other customers.

Tom didn't mind…he had seen men eat more unusual things in the trenches. Feeling well fed he studied the scene. By the time Rauin arrived, he had finished and left the table.

"Ah, there you are, my friend. My apologies, I was delayed with the king."

"No need to apologise, Rauin. We didn't set a time to meet."

"I can stay but one minute. I came only to keep my word, as I must be on hand at the manor house for the king's pleasure. I have been granted a small chamber there, so I shall not be staying at the inn while the king is here."

"So when can we talk privately?"

Rauin thought a moment. "If we tell the guards that you are my trusted assistant, you could come with me to the manor house. Please remember that I am obliged to give the king priority in all I do, so if he calls, I must leave you. Who knows, in an unlikely event, you may even get to meet the king."

Tom was beside himself with anticipation and excitement at the thought, although a little nervous. This was beyond anything he could have imagined. His mind raced. *Here I am, I've travelled back in time from the twentieth century, might find my children and could actually meet King John in the flesh only days before he loses his jewels, and a week or so before he dies! Nobody will believe me. They'll think I'm completely mad. I can hardly believe it myself.*

He eagerly accepted Rauin's offer, who instructed him to follow his lead in all matters, to say as little as possible and leave the talking to him.

"Have you eaten, Thomas?"

"Yes, I finished just before you arrived."

"Good." Rauin placed a coin on the table and made to leave.

"Thank you, but I could have paid."

"My friend, they think you are foreign and would have cheated you. Anyway, I am indebted to you for your advice and medicines."

As they walked, he asked Rauin if he had seen the king today. At times, it was difficult to hear each other above the busy street clatter, so they often waited for the noise to subside.

"Yes, but I regret that his illness remains as before. He is pale, and from his words, I fear he may soon replace me as his physician."

"Did you give him the oil of caraway?"

"Yes. It calmed his innards for a while, thank you. He asked what manner of medicine it was. I had to tell him that it came from caraway seed, brought here from foreign parts by one of the trading ships. Unfortunately, it was only a short time before he again took to a private chamber for relief."

"Did you discuss his diet with him?"

"I tried, but he would not listen."

As they approached the manor house it was obvious that someone of importance was there, given the number of Templar Knights on guard. Tom was nervous. He studied the grand stone mansion with its large cobbled courtyard, quite different to many of the other houses, which were mostly timber and lath, roofed with reed. Only the merchants' houses and the bishop's mansion were built of stone and flint. Knights guarded the gates and inner doors, while others stood in small groups with swords and shields to hand. Tom assumed these must be the king's bodyguards. Six brightly coloured wagons and a more highly decorated coach stood at the end of the courtyard. The guards stared at Tom.

The physician spoke with authority before they could be questioned. "This man is my assistant, here for the king's benefit." They were allowed to pass without further question, but the same routine was not as successful at the main door, where a knight demanded to know more of Tom's business.

"He has cures and knowledge to aid the king," Rauin replied, expecting the guard would not dare to interfere with the king's welfare.

"He's an odd-looking character."

"He's from deep in the Washes. You must know people are different there. He brings potions for our king from the monks in the Isles of Eels,"

The knight stepped back allowing them to pass but watched as they made their way down the hall to a stairway on one side.

"You may relax, Thomas, they fear the baron's spies or of an assassin entering. They trust few, but as long as you are with me you are safe. They know me and the privileges of my status."

Rauin's room was small, it had a fireplace, a high narrow window, a wooden framed bed, stool, a small chair, and a modest table. The wide floorboards creaked with every step. By the fire was an animal skin rug, which Tom guessed was once a fully grown bear.

"This is my chamber. Not much as you may see, but quieter and more private than the inn. You can stay here too if you wish. The mansion was built for the bishop and his many visitors. All the rooms are occupied now the king is here, and I doubt you will acquire a room at the inn for a day or two."

Tom thanked him.

"I must advise you of a little court etiquette, Thomas, should you happen to meet the king. Wherever and whenever, you must always hold a deep bow until he has passed. Should you enter any room he occupies, you must immediately stop, bow and wait for his approval to enter and approach. Once in front of him, you must bow deeply and go down on one knee. Do not look at him until you are told to rise. Do not ask questions, wait until you are spoken to, and only answer his questions. When you leave, you must walk backwards towards the door…do not turn your back to him. Bow when you are far from him, then wait until he waves you away. Only then are you free to turn and leave."

"I'll try to remember all that."

"Before we settle, I must advise the court that I am back should the king need me. I shall not be long. Please do not leave the room."

When Tom was alone, a feeling of vulnerability came over him. What if a knight or someone else came in and asked questions? He hoped Rauin would return soon. Minutes later there was a knock at the door. Tom's heart skipped a beat. If he answered and it was a knight, he would surely be questioned. If he didn't answer and a knight came in, there would be even more questions, all laced with suspicion. He felt trapped between the two, so apprehensively opened the door.

To his relief, a teenage girl holding a large basket of wood and tinder stood waiting.

"Excuse me, sir. I've come to make up the fire," she said, whilst giving a slight, but respectful curtsy.

"Come in, come in," Tom said, quickly shutting the door behind her. While crossing to the fireplace, she couldn't resist examining Tom through sideways glances. Then, placing tinder in the fireplace, she lit it by striking flint onto a piece of metal. The tinder smoked and flared. A few thin sticks, followed by larger pieces of wood which were placed on top. She stood, wiped her hands on her apron, gave a little curtsy, and said she would return later with more logs. Tom stepped forward to open the door for her.

"Ooo, thank you, sir," she said with a guarded smile.

The door was only closed for a few seconds when he heard voices in the hallway. It sounded as though someone in authority was questioning the maid. As the voices came closer, Tom tensed. He couldn't hear the conversation clearly but recognised the louder, final words, "Be off with you, wench."

There was no knock, the door swung open by the hand of a Templar Knight with his other hand readied on the hilt of his sword.

"And who might you be?"

"My name is Thomas Harrison. I'm here to help the king's physician."

"Then why are you not with him?"

"He has gone to let the court know he is here."

"As may be, but you do not look or sound much like a physician's ward. Come with me."

The knight grabbed Tom by the arm and led him to the door.

"Can we please wait until Rauin returns? He'll confirm who I am and why I'm here."

"What! Waste my time and chance you to escape! You are coming with me."

Tom had no choice but to comply. Fighting off the knight was not an option. "You don't need to hold onto me. I'm not going to run away, I have no need to."

The knight didn't release his hold. They continued along the hallway to the stairs, and down to a small room at the side of the main entrance. On entering, three knights turned to stare at Tom. He was thrust forward by the arm, almost causing him to stumble into the room. The door slammed shut behind him.

"Well, well, what manner of rogue do we have here?" One asked.

"I found him lurking in one of the rooms above."

"And just what were you doing there, rogue?"

"I was waiting for Rauin to return to his room."

"And what business do you have with him?"

"I'm helping with medicines for the king."

"Then why were you not with him?"

"He is letting the court know he is here, should he be needed."

"You have a strange manner of speech and about

your dress. Where are you from?"

Tom had to think on his feet again. "I come from deep in the marshes, towards the Isles of Eels. Some parts are isolated and cut off, so our ways are different to others."

"Inbred you mean!" a knight added, making the others laugh.

"But you sound foreign to me. You could be a spy from over the channel." Tom didn't respond.

"How did you enter here?"

"I came with Rauin and without a problem. Ask the guards at the gate."

"Maybe we should find the physician and see if he recognises you."

"Yes, please do," Tom eagerly agreed.

He was pushed to a corner, told to sit on a stool and not to move if he valued his life. One of the knights left the room to find Rauin. Tom was tense while repeatedly receiving stern, inquisitive looks, but he was not spoken to. They taunted him by discussing what they would do to him if he was lying. One suggested he might be a French spy come here on one of the trading ships. Another added that spies don't live very long. They debated which they would remove first, his eyes or his tongue. Tom felt his bowels weaken and his mouth go dry. He began to perspire and wished the potion would weaken and send him home. Almost fifteen agonising minutes passed before the knight returned.

"The physician is not to be found."

One of the knights drew a dagger and held it to Tom's throat. "You had better start telling the truth if you don't want your throat cut and your gizzards spread across the floor."

Tom was sweating and beginning to tremble. "Look,

just because you couldn't find the physician, doesn't mean I'm not telling you the truth."

"Bah! You were caught in the king's refuge. You say you are with a man who cannot be found, so what is to be done with you?"

The dagger was pressed harder against Tom's throat, and he could feel the cold sharpness of its point. In desperation, he had nothing to lose. "Like I said, because you couldn't find him at this very moment doesn't mean I'm not his ward. He could be anywhere, even with the king. Did you check in the king's chambers?"

The knight who had searched looked at the others, slowly closed his eyes and gently shook his head. "We do not disturb the king for every matter."

"But surely, that's where you would expect to find a doctor, I mean a physician, with his patient. I have cures and treatments for the king that Rauin will give him. You can be sure that His Highness will not be pleased if you harm or delay me."

"As you say, but we have not seen you before and we do not know you. You dress and speak strangely, and you were found loitering in a chamber in the very manor where our king now rests."

"I was not loitering. Rauin asked me to wait in his room until he returned. Where else would you expect a physician's helper to be?"

"With his master," Another knight interrupted whilst drawing his sword. Then, with a menacing grin, he pointed the weapon at Tom as he approached. "This rogue's tongue is too smooth. I say we cut it off and run him through."

The dagger was removed. Tom watched the sword point as it came closer to his face, hoping this was only a gesture to frighten him, or a bad dream, even a surreal nightmare. The knight drew his elbow back and lowered the blade to Tom's heart.

He heard himself say, "Oh, Dear God!"

At that moment, the door burst open.

"What are you doing? Unhand him, you ignorant fools. The king shall hear of this!"

The knights shuffled back. Tom watched as the sword was replaced in its scabbard. Blinking a few times to clear his eyes, he saw Rauin standing in the doorway. Tom's shoulders dropped with relief as he closed his eyes. His head fell forwards to rest his chin on his chest. He almost cried with relief.

"We found him loitering in one of the rooms above," a knight explained. They were cautious about arguing with Rauin on serious matters, knowing he had the king's ear.

"You fools are strong in the arm and weak in the head. You carry your brains between your thighs! This man was not loitering. He was in my chamber waiting for my return. He is a trusted physician from other parts, here to assist me with care and medication for King John. If you have harmed him in any way, the king shall hear of it and certainly have you flogged. He will at least hear of your molestation."

The knights shuffled awkwardly but didn't speak. Their expressions were enough. Rauin had made his point and put fear into their souls.

"Come, Thomas, we'll leave these poor fools to contemplate their futures." He spoke loud enough for the knights to hear and leave them worried.

As they walked away Tom asked if he would tell the king.

"No, the king has more than enough matters to bother him without these vagabonds." Then he gave a mischievous grin. "Did they harm you?"

"Not really, but they gave me one hell of a fright."

"I warrant they would have been unwise to harm you, but they will be courteous in future, my friend."

"How did you know where I was?"

"When I returned to my chamber, you were gone. The maid brought logs so I asked if she had seen you. She told me what had happened and where you were taken…It looks as though I arrived just in time. Rauin added with a chuckle.

"I didn't think it was that funny! My whole life flashed before my eyes."

"I know not your meaning, Thomas?"

"It's said that just before you die your whole life flashes before your eyes, like a fast film."

"A fast film?"

"Oh, it's something from my time. Don't worry about it now, I'll explain later."

By the time they reached the room, the fire was burning briskly. There was bread, meat, fruit, two goblets, and a cask of wine on the table. The stool and chair had been placed close to the table.

Rauin noticed Tom's surprise and smiled. "Courtesy of His Majesty. See, you even have a blanket warming by the fire should you wish to sleep there tonight."

Taking the stool, Tom allowed Rauin the chair when they sat. Having eaten earlier, Tom took very little and embarked on small talk and drinking the wine, helping him to recover from his ordeal.

"In the future Bishop's Lynn will be called Kings Lynn, which is what it's known as in my time. Why is it called Bishop's Lynn now?"

"Ah, my friend, long before it was Bishop's Lynn it was just Lyn, meaning by a lake or water. It became Bishop's Lynn when Bishop De Losinga from Norwich built this mansion and made it his home. He all but owned the town. It was he who built the Abbey, the Benedictine Priory, and The Church of St. Margaret.

"When does the town become Kings Lynn?"

"Not for another two hundred and fifty years," Tom replied, before changing the subject.

"Where do all these Knights Templar come from? I'm surprised there are so many?"

"They are a mixed bunch and come from many countries. At best, they are a private army, well trained, well equipped, and brutally efficient in battle, even bloodthirsty. Sometimes killing when there is no need. They were sanctioned by Rome to support King Richard on his crusades, which is why they carry the Christian cross on their tunics. In former days there were but a few score, assigned with the task of protecting missionaries to the Holy Land who were often robbed of the taxes they carried.

"How do they become Templar Knights?"

"In my opinion, it is a satanic process which you will shudder to hear of. The order began at Gisors Castle in France. Mostly, they came from families of some note, able to donate their entry fee with gold, land, or influence. They are a law unto themselves, and their actions are highly questionable. They are often cruel, showing no mercy. A bunch of bloodthirsty rogues, I fear."

"That doesn't sound very Christian-like to me, or how I had understood them to be. Why doesn't the Pope stop them?"

"Thomas, if I tell you what I know both our lives would be in mortal danger." He hesitated and stroked his beard, daring himself to take Tom further into his confidence as the wine tempered his caution. "Should I tell you, you must swear on all that is holy, never to utter a word of it to a living soul."

Tom was surprised at the seriousness in his tone and waited a second before answering, "I swear, but what can be so terrible? Most history books describe them as honourable Christian Knights, to be revered and respected."

"Then your books are wrong. I tell you, Thomas, they are more pagan, nay satanic than Christian." After a silence lasting almost half a minute, he continued, "I once attended a knight on his death bed. He asked for a priest, but one was not to be found. He said he wanted to confess his great sins, that he had done terrible, blasphemous things. Now, as he neared his earthly end, he feared the wrath of God, wanted to make his peace and ask his forgiveness. I offered to listen to his confession, saying I would find a priest to absolve him of his sins and save his soul."

Although they were alone in the room, he lowered his voice before explaining further.

Tom leaned towards him.

"The wretched man described their initiation ceremony in much detail, declaring that he had blasphemed greatly. Along with three others, he was blindfolded and taken to a dull cave-like place, where there were no windows and natural light. When his blindfold was removed, he observed a crude altar with the skull of a goat in the centre. A lighted candle stood on each side. A few older knights stood back in the shadows to observe the proceedings. As expected, he and his companions were made to swear allegiance to the order. A crucifix was produced, inverted, and he was told to damn Christ, kiss the inverted cross. Then, to his horror, spit or urinate on it. He was made to vow that, from then on, he would worship only the skull and The Black Madonna. When the ceremony was completed, he was taken to see proof of the magic the skull possessed and its mysterious mystical powers."

"That's terrible! How could they get away with such things?"

"Secrecy enforced under the threat of death, Thomas, which is why you must never utter a word of this."

Tom gasped.

"But that is not all. They are cruel in the extreme. To prove the magic of the skull, he was told it could make a man's severed head speak and a demonstration was provided. He was taken to another dimly lit place, where a common man had been paid to be buried so only his head could be seen. The recruits were invited to talk to the head, which responded to their questions. After leaving in amazement, the group debated amongst themselves how this could be. The way curiosity leads us to discover how a jester might do his magic tricks. Then, to their astonishment, the man's severed head was brought to them on a platter as proof of the skull's magic."

Bile rose to the back of Tom's throat. Rauin saw the paleness in his face and said nothing more.

It took several minutes for Tom to regain his composure. "Why in God's name does the Pope allow this to continue?"

"It is an odd situation. Pope Innocent the Third

has long since withdrawn his support for King John, yet he permits his protection by the Knights Templar. I fear there are sinister motives at play. It would be a most convenient way for the Vatican to spy on our king. I suspect the Pope is in league with the king's enemies, both here and in foreign parts. It is not wise to upset the Pope, my friend, no matter who you are. He rules and interferes in many lands in a clandestine manner."

Wanting to change the subject, Tom reached for his rucksack. "I've brought a few things from the twentieth century that I'm sure will interest you."

Tom produced a small brown hexagonal bottle and removed the cork, placing a finger over the top he turning it upside down. He held out his yellow-brown fingertip. "This is iodine. It's for killing germs in and around open wounds. You don't need much, just dab it on. You can wash your instruments in it too…it helps prevent infections. When this is finished, use boiled, salted water. It does much the same thing."

He gave Rauin a few packed bandages and went on to explain the need for cleanliness in all things relating to wounds. "It saves a lot of amputations and deaths later."

"Where can I get more of this iodine?"

"I don't think you can get it as I've given it to you, but it's mostly found in seaweed. Please remember what I said about cleanliness. Always place instruments in boiling water for ten minutes before you use them. If you have to put them down, make sure it's on a clean cloth that's been boiled, and don't touch the blades with your fingers. Make sure your hands are clean too. Again, it will all help prevent infection. If you don't have boiled water and it's an emergency, then urinate on them."

Rauin raised his voice. "What! Piss on them?"

"Yes. If you pee on a plant it dies, right? It will kill infections the same way. I know it's a last resort, but it works. If you have salt, as I said, mix some with clean boiled water. It will also kill germs. You could make a pad laden with crushed garlic to place on a wound after cleaning. That helps too. It's what I sometimes did with horses in the Great War."

Tom steadied himself, realising his comments may require him to provide lengthy explanations. He was already bursting with things with which to amaze, without the need to explain about the World War.

He reached into the rucksack again. "I've brought you a book of herbal medicines. It tells you where to find the herbs, how to make the cures, and how and when to apply them. Please don't be offended, I expect you already know many, if not far more than what's written here. I thought you might like to have it."

Tom was enjoying the moment when it crossed his mind how wonderful it would be if he could take Rauin to the twentieth century. He would show him so much, knowing he would be fascinated.

Rauin was immediately taken with the book's appearance and said nothing for a full minute as he enthusiastically flipped through the pages before repeatedly thanking Tom.

"The print is strange and the pages are so fine, there are so many of them for a volume of this size. I can easily carry it in my sack. It takes so little space compared to my bulky parchments."

"All books are like this in the twentieth century. Some are even smaller. Do you think you will be able to read it?"

"Yes, I think so, given time. Once I am familiar with the print and the strangeness of the words."

"If you don't recognise the names of some of the plants or berries, just look at the sketch. You might recognise them. Don't worry about the exact quantities, just keep the ingredients in the same proportions as it says."

Rauin smiled his appreciation and wonder, whilst offering his thanks again.

Tom steadied himself as his enthusiasm grew again. He had impressed his friend, and now he was about to introduce him to photography. "I am married. My wife's name is Dora. This is a picture of us on our wedding day."

Rauin took the black-and-white photograph and stared at it. First at arm's length, then closer to his eyes, and again at arm's length. "What manner of parchment is this? It shines, is smooth like glass and there is no colour, yet the image is perfect as though I am seeing these people in life. It is better than an artist's painting."

"It's not a painting but a chemical process on special paper called photo card."

"Surely, it is witchcraft to capture and hold such an image."

Tom smiled, wondering how to keep his explanation simple but it took a few minutes to explain the process.

"Well, if it's not witchcraft then it is surely magic."

"Look here's another picture. We call it a photograph. It's of my children Susan and Alfred." Tom smiled. "It's very clever, you are looking at children who will not be born for hundreds of years to come." He went quiet as a lump came to his throat. Then blinking and swallowing hard to regain his composure before saying that he must find them. After a moment or two, he took out a few postcards. "These are photographs too. Look, this is what my village and the river looks like in the early twentieth century."

Rauin stared intently.

"Look, here's one of Ely Cathedral."

"But the building is not yet complete. It is no more than half-finished. I saw with my own eyes only days ago."

Tom laughed. "This picture was made seven hundred years into your future. In my time it's a very old building. Glorious as it is, it can be seen from miles away in almost every direction. It's often called The Ship of the Fens."

"Why?"

"Because it stands out above the flat landscape like a huge ship at sea."

"No, no, this is some kind of trickery." Rauin continued to stare at the picture.

Tom laughed, but Rauin was looking serious. At that moment, Tom decided not to give him the history book just yet. His eyes were heavy, he yawned and they had finished the wine, so he said he would lie down. After placing more logs on the fire, Tom slept on the rug in front of it, while Rauin studied the book of herbal medicines by candlelight.

When Tom woke, it was dark, and he was pleased to find that he was still in Bishop's Lynn. The fire was little more than dying embers. Rauin was sleeping on his bed with the book open, face down on his chest. The candle he had placed on the ledge above his head was now no more than a molten spoil of wax clogging the holder. It was cold. Tom opened his pocket knife and shaved one of the logs for tinder to restart the fire. Getting down on his knees, he blew gently on the embers, first bringing smoke, then a small flame, just enough to kindle another blaze. By the time Rauin woke, the room was warming.

"Good morrow, Thomas, I trust you slept well this past night?"

"Yes, fine, I've slept in more comfortable beds and some a lot worse but yes, I slept well, thank you."

Rauin stood, leaned backwards, stretched his back and arms, then moved to warm himself by the fire.

"Your book is difficult to read, but with some practice I have come to recognise many words, certainly enough to comprehend their meaning. Yet, there are still many words I do not know. Perhaps you will advise me when we have time?"

"Yes, of course."

"Nonetheless, Thomas, what it contains is of great interest. It is most like a bible of cures. Ah! I must see how the king is this morning and I shall return soon. I hope he is cleansed by this time. Fortunately, he is obsessed with bathing. Truly, what he eats passes through him like galloping horses to emerge an uncontrollable stream. Please do not leave the room until I return."

Tom didn't need to be told. Alone again he wondered what the day would bring. There was a gentle knock on the door, gentle enough for him to confidently say. "Come in," knowing it would most likely be the servant girl. She carried a heavy basket of logs but still managed a small curtsy. Tom reached to carry her basket, but she turned away to prevent him.

"No, sir. It is for me to carry."

Tom's thoughtfulness was overshadowed by his awkward compliance. He didn't consider himself any better than her, and it had come naturally for him to offer. She scurried to the fireplace, leaving the basket and retrieving the empty one.

"Oh, I see the fire has already been stoked! I'll just leave the logs, sir."

She turned to face him and again and gave her customary curtsy. "I'll be back soon to tidy the fireplace and the room. Someone else will bring you food, sir."

Two breakfasts of vegetable pottage, bread, eggs, and thinly sliced, salted pork arrived soon after. Tom didn't wait and ate before the pottage became cold. Knowing he must soon leave to attend the knights' horses, he was anxious, and hoped Rauin would return soon.

Minutes later, he hurried into the room. "My bag, I need my bag," he said urgently.

Tom said he had to leave for the stables.

"Then I shall see you from this place and give orders for your re-admittance. Come now, quickly."

They hurried to the main door and the gated entrance, where the guards were given stern instructions. "This man is on King John's personal business. Do not delay him with your idle trivia at any time."

With that, they went their separate ways. When Tom arrived at the stables, the ostlers were loading dirty hay and horse dung into a barrow. He found a stable boy grooming one of the horses. As he inspected each stable, he noted that all but one had fresh straw and asked the boy why not.

"The ostlers said not to bother because there was no dung in there to clear, sir."

"Listen to me, young man. Every horse is to have fresh hay and straw each day, horse shit or not. Do you understand? I'll have a word with the ostlers."

The boy looked frightened. Seeing his face, Tom felt sorry for him, gave a half-smile and put his hand on the boy's shoulder.

"I was only doing what I was told to, sir."

"Yes, I know, son, and you are doing well. How many days has there been no dung?"

"This is the second, Sir."

"Fetch the ostlers here please, and don't take no for an answer. I want to see them right now."

The boy hurried off to return a minute later. From the men's demeanour, it was obvious the boy had told him Tom was not happy. They stood facing Tom, heads slightly bowed, twisting their caps in their hands. "Yes, Sir?"

"First, each horse is to have fresh straw and hay every day, no exceptions! Got that?"

"Yes sir."

"How long has this animal been constipated?"

"Sorry, sir?"

"How long has it been since it had a shit?"

"Just over two days, sir."

"Call yourself an ostler! Can't you see how agitated the poor animal is? Now get to it and help the poor creature to shit."

The boy spoke up: "How do we do that, sir?"

Tom shook his head then spoke to the ostlers. "Okay, wash your hands and right arm in clean water, smear it with olive oil or fat, then stick it up the horse's backside and pull the dung out. As much as you can get hold of. Oh, and you'd better hobble its back legs if you don't want to get kicked through the wall. And you, young man, you can stroke the horse's chin and talk gently to it. Got that?"

They grimaced as they looked at each other.

"Then, you can give it two apples to eat, and do so for a few days. It will help keep it free. I'll be back in a while to see if you have done it…and give it fresh hay!"

Tom checked on the other horses, then went to the inn looking into the faces of children along the way. It was almost midday and he was longing for a mug of tea, but the only drink he'd get was red wine, ale, milk or water. Approaching the knights, he told them of their horses' progress. They were satisfied, and to Tom's surprise, each one gave him a silver coin which he now recognised as a silver penny. They were being pleasant, making him suspicious. He believed the coins were not only payment but given to endear themselves to him. One even offered to buy his ale. Another, who seemed ready to talk. "Thomas, you say your name is Thomas?"

"Yes."

"How would you like to be a permanent horse physician to us Templar Knights?"

Tom hesitated, searching for words to tactfully decline, but before he could speak, the knight continued.

"We would pay you fairly, and see you are well catered for. Just imagine, you would travel the world, experience great adventures and gain prestige. What do you say?"

Tom remembered what he had been told him about the knights and didn't trust them. "I am flattered at such an offer, but I already have the commitments of a farm, a wife, and family."

"Then you must do such as others and bring your family with you."

"Thank you, sir, but I would not want to move them against their will."

"Will! Does your family have a will? Do they not do as the master of the house commands?"

Tom smiled, hoping to lessen the frustration that was slowly developing.

"Please allow me time to consider your kind offer, sir."

"Very well, Thomas, but we expect to leave here very soon and wish you to travel with us, so do not procrastinate long."

The landlord provided Tom with a perfectly timed distraction, saying there was now space at the long table if he wanted to eat. Tom excused himself, saying he was hungry. His mind raced, and he could feel his heart beating much faster than normal. 'The children, I have to find them. But they may not be here, and the opportunity to see where King John's treasure will be lost is a godsend. He couldn't have asked for a better opportunity.

"Oh, so you're here again, are you!"

"No, my good woman, this is a wooden replica of myself." Tom rolled his eyes. "When the king and his entourage have left, you will have fewer customers and be pleased to serve me without being so rude."

She walked away with her usual disgruntled mumbles.

Tom relaxed and took his notebook from the rucksack. He recorded his interactions with Rauin, going on to describe the inn, the landlady, events at the stables, and the knights. He was relieved that no one had asked about his school exercise book and the pencil he was using, or the style of his writing. After placing the notes back in his rucksack, he leaned back to survey the scene once more, drink his ale, and listen to the chatter, taking special notice of what the knights were saying.

One group was debating what the king would do next. The main question seemed to be how long they would stay in Bishop's Lynn. Some had been told to be ready to move on immediately should the king be fit to travel. If that were the case, they would travel northeast, as any other direction would place them under threat from the invading French. This was followed by talk of how to best guard the king. But at times voices were lowered and Tom was unable to hear what conclusions were reached. At first, he thought it was for security, but as he watched their body language, he gained the impression there was something more afoot.

It was October 8th and Tom knew the royal party would leave tomorrow. Yet the king's intentions remained unknown to his guards. Although he knew when the king would leave, he only had a vague idea of his exact route, or the one his jewels would take…just that they would go different ways. He had only a short time to discover what time the separate columns would leave. Trying to find out would be difficult. He had to be careful not to arouse suspicion, especially after some of the knights had once suspected him of being a spy. Weighing up the facts, he realised he was very lucky so far in being involved with both the king's physician and the Knights Templar, even if it didn't happen by design.

One of the knights came to the table. "Well, Thomas, have you decided?"

"Not quite, sir. May I ask if you will travel with the king's column or the Crown Jewels?"

The knight was visibly shocked that Tom should know about the two being separated. Not to mention knowing the king's wealth was travelling with them.

Tom's face flushed as he realised the implications of what he had asked.

The knight leaned close to his face to stare into his eyes. "What makes you think the king will be separated from his wealth? Or that he even carries his wealth with him? Why do you suggest such things?"

"I don't know. I mean, I didn't know until I overheard some of the knights at the manor house talking about which column they would accompany."

"At the manor house. What were you doing there? You appear a very accomplished spy!"

"No, no, I was invited there to assist the king's physician. Remember you saw me with him here. He invited me to the manor to discuss medications for King John. I spent the night there. Ask him."

On remembering he had seen them together, the knight eased back. "It may be as you say. Some at the manor should watch their loose tongues. Well, will you join us?"

"I'm not sure. I will if the king's physician can spare me. I'm required to give Rauin and the king priority."

Tom hoped he had bought a little time, hoping no knight would openly argue against the king's welfare. The exchange told him that some may already know of the king's plan, but that it was to be kept secret. He was afraid of unwittingly being drawn into doing something he didn't want to do, but afraid of the consequences if he refused.

"I harbour doubts of you, horse physician. You will travel with my column where I, Sir David of Lyon, can personally keep watch over you, like it or not. I trust I will not need to run you through as a spy. There will be no consequence for me. Maybe even praise for protecting the king. I shall tell you in good time when to be ready."

Tom was taken by surprise at his tone. Worried for his safety, he responded with a simple nod.

Sir David turned back to scowl at him. "And keep what you hear to yourself if you value your tongue!"

After a few minutes of contemplation, Tom left the

inn and made his way back to the stables. The street scene had not changed, but the smell of burning wood and peat was more noticeable as more fires announced the arrival of cold autumn winds from the North Sea. The ostlers were nowhere to be seen, but Tom could see the horses were groomed and the stables were clean. After checking the dressings on the horse with chafed legs, he decided to head for the manor house and talk with Rauin.

Still fascinated by the scene, he took his time, absorbing all that was unfamiliar. Now and again he stopped to look at the rough timber-framed buildings and the people who busied themselves in the street while all the time looking for the children. Again, he was tempted to ask if they had been seen. A few people appeared wealthy, while others looked desperately poor. Some looked at him for a second or two out of curiosity, but none spoke. The presence of a man dressed differently was not unusual in this port town and seldom generated a second look. As he watched a group of grubby-looking monks pass along the cobbled street, a little girl's voice called out, "Daddy? Daddy!"

Tom recognised the voice and froze.

Chapter 16

For a second Tom thought his mind was playing tricks, but on spinning around, he saw Susie and Alfie hand in hand. He steadied himself and tightly closed his eyes. This had to be a dream, but when he opened them, the children were still there. They hesitated a moment to be sure it was him. With his arms outstretched, Tom dropped to his knees as the children rushed towards him. They cried with joy while hugging their father. Tom repeatedly kissed them, unable to speak.

Susie eventually spoke through her tears. "We knew you would come, Daddy…we knew you would come for us. I always said you would!"

"It's alright, sweetheart, I'm here now," Tom croaked.

"We want to go home, Daddy. Please take us home."

"I'll try to take you, Susie. I'll certainly try."

After a long embrace, he eased Susie and Alfie away and stood to feast his eyes on them as if to confirm this was real. His first impressions told him they were healthy and well-fed, if a little grubby. "Look at you. If your mother could see you now, she'd want to give you both a spit wash right here in the street, then take you home to dump you in the bath together! There would be no waiting till Friday night." With tears still in their eyes, they all laughed.

Neither Alfie nor Susie wore proper shoes. Pieces of soft leather-covered their feet, each tied above the ankles with leather laces. The remnants of their old clothes were now much too small. Both wore short, hooded cloaks covering their heads and shoulders with tie cords just below their chins.

Tom pulled Susie and Alfie towards him again, holding them tight, while the lump in his throat stifled his words. He guided them to the marketplace where they could sit and talk. Susie chatted excitedly along the way, while Alfie struggled to be heard. They found an octagonal shelter with wooden benches circled beneath it. An old lady sat to one side with a goose wrapped tightly in a cloth, allowing only its head to protrude. Next to her was an elderly man clutching a basket of vegetables and four small fish threaded through their gills onto a loop of twine. They watched with curiosity when Tom and the children sat opposite, but soon lost interest and left.

"Where have you been, Dad?" Alfie asked. "We don't like it here and want to go home."

"I know you do, and I want to take you, but I have to find out how to get you there first. It could be difficult."

"Why, Daddy? Can't we get a bus or a train and just go?" Susie asked.

"No, sweetheart. It's hard to explain. Tell me how you got here...although I think I already know."

Alfie began to explain. "We were playing in the big barn and saw this thing that looked like a ball sitting on a ledge, so we got it down. I managed to get the lid off with my pocketknife. There was some stuff in the bottom. It looked a bit like when Mum makes toffee, so we stuck our fingers in to taste it. Then we felt strange and put the ball back on the ledge. Me and Susie got a bad pain in our heads, and the next thing we knew, we woke up in a stable not far from here."

Tom felt guilty for leaving the flask where the children could find it.

"Please, Daddy, can we go home now?"

Tom saw the tears well in Susie's eyes. He became emotional and once more his own eyes glazed. Putting his arm around her, he swallowed hard before replying, "We'll see what we can do, sweetheart. Have you seen the Fletcher twins, Mary and Alan, or Polly Brown? Are they here too?"

"Yes, but they came later. We think Michael Green was here too. We are sure we saw him for a few minutes, but he didn't see us. It was market day, so there were a lot of people and we couldn't find him again. We don't know where he is."

"Where have you been living all this time?"

"We stay with the nuns at the convent. The first two nights we slept in a barn. It was cold and we got hungry, so we ate raw mangel-wurzels, blackberries, and wild mushrooms. When we came into the town, other kids made fun of us because of how we looked and the way we speak. We were really scared. They all talk funny here, Daddy. We didn't properly understand where we were and was frightened all the time. One day some of the local kids were throwing stuff at us in the street, laughing and calling us names. Two nuns came and stopped them, then talked to us. They could see we were lost and hungry, so took us back to their convent."

"Where is the convent, sweetheart?"

"It's not far from the new church. It's funny, cos it

looks new but it's sort of old fashioned. The convent is like that too."

"Are you all right now?"

"Yes, but we want to go home," Alfie pleaded.

"Are you hungry?"

"A bit."

"Then let's get something warm inside you, and I'll explain things as best I can. We'll go to an inn I know."

They chatted continuously along the way. "Everyone at home is missing you and the other children. Nobody has any idea where you all got to. You just disappeared. The police didn't know either and sent detectives from London to find you."

Alfie looked serious. "Are we in trouble, Dad?"

"No, certainly not. Where are the Fletcher twins and Polly Brown now?"

"Probably at the convent. They look after us there, but we have to work. The nuns make us peel vegetables, wash clothes, and clean the floors most days. It's the others' turn to do the floors today. They say it's to repay them for looking after us."

"And where do you sleep?"

"We all have to sleep in the same room. I don't like sleeping with the boys 'cos they tease the girls at night. It's cold, but we all have a mattress, a sort of bag filled with hay. They give us blankets too, but they're really scratchy. Alfie and me sometimes cuddle up together to keep warm. The nuns have got fires in their bedrooms, but we don't. We know 'cos we sometimes have to clean the ashes out and take the firewood in."

Alfie cut in. "Twice a day we have to go to some sort of church service. Half the time we don't know what they are on about, so we just pretend to. Then we go to the kitchen and help do the vegetables. Do you know they have never heard of potatoes?"

Tom smiled. "I'm not surprised."

As they entered the inn, the landlady looked up from her cleaning and rolled her eyes in their direction.

Tom stared and pointed to her face. "Not one word from you, woman! Not…one…word!"

She rocked her head. "We don't allow no waifs and strays in here mister!"

"Good, because I don't see any. Now bring two bowls of your best pottage. Make sure it's hot and bring some fresh bread too."

"I dunno who you think you are comin' in 'ere, a-tellin' me what to do. This inn is my husbands' and mine, I'll have you know."

"Madam! As you have been told, I am here on the king's business, along with his physician. Now you can serve these children or answer to the Royal Court. The choice is yours!"

Alfie and Susie stood wide-eyed at the exchange. As usual, the woman grumbled and left. She returned five minutes later with two wooden bowls of steaming pottage, half a loaf of bread, and two spoons in her apron pocket. The bowls were clumsily placed on the table, spilling gravy from one of them. She then used the corner of her apron to wipe it away. Tom glared at her.

"So, who's paying for this?"

Tom said nothing, just gave her a look of contempt as he placed a silver penny on the table. It was obvious the children were hungry. They didn't stop to speak as they devoured large mouthfuls. Tom watched with pain in his heart, wondering how he was going to explain the difficulty of getting them home again, or even if it could be done. Telling them where they are would be hard enough, since they would struggle to understand. The children finished their meal with a warm look of satisfaction.

"How did you get here, Daddy? Were you looking for us?" Susie asked.

"The same way you did." He didn't want to go into detail. "Lots of people have been looking for you for a long time. We have all been very worried and nobody had any idea where you were."

Alfie interrupted. "But now you've found us, can we please go home? We want to go home, Dad."

"Tom's anguish was obvious. "It might take a while, son."

"Why?" Susie asked. "I want my mummy and I want to see Uncle Peter and Nanny too."

"I know, sweetheart. I know you do, and they miss you too. I'll do everything I can, I promise. You see it was, well a sort of magic that brought you here. It was the same magic that brought me here too, and now we have to find a way to undo it. We have all gone back in time for hundreds of years, so it's not as easy as getting on a bus or train to go home, because they have not been invented yet. If this was just another country in our own time, it would be much easier. We could get on a ship and go back to England, but we can't because this *is* England, only it's hundreds of years ago."

The children were puzzled, but their innocence helped them understand the concept of magic. Tom explained about the earthenware flask and the potion, how it came to be in the barn, and what it had done to them. He stopped short of telling them about the monks in Ely who had concocted the brew, only saying it was from the olden days and that he had found it in a field while ploughing, which they understood. He was tempted to say they should have left it alone but didn't. Now was certainly not a time to chastise them, if at all. He believed it was his fault they were here for leaving the flask where they could find it. "Now listen carefully, I may have to leave you here a little longer while I try to find a way to get you home. Do you understand?"

Susie started to cry while Alfie looked down in silence. Tom moved to give them both comforting hugs. "Please don't be upset. It's just that I have to find out how to do it. First, I'll talk to the people who made that stuff in the flask." Tom saw the children's disappointment. "Please don't be upset. Look, something very special happened today…we found each other, didn't we! Don't you think that's a big step in the right direction, something to be happy about?" They nodded their agreement. Tom tried to brighten the moment. "Why don't you show me where you have been living? I can meet the nuns and thank them. I bet Mary, Polly, and Alan will be excited to know you have all been found. Let's go and tell them."

Susie smiled as she wiped her tears away on the back of her hand, while Alfie took her other hand. Tom was flushed with pride on seeing Alfie was still looking out for his sister. Little was said until they arrived at a large heavy wooden door embedded in a high wall of stone and flint.

"It's here," Alfie said as he banged the heavy iron ring.

After a minute, a small, barred inspection hatch opened, allowing Tom to see the top of a nun's veil. After Alfie had called out their names, the hatch closed. They heard bolts being pulled on the other side of the door before it opened just enough for a nun to peer through.

On seeing the children, she beckoned them inside. Puzzled by Tom's appearance she asked, "Who are you, sir? What do you want with these children?"

Before Tom could answer, Susie shouted, "This is our daddy."

Not knowing what to say, the nun stared at him.

"What Susie says is true. I'd like to talk to Mother Superior if I may."

The nun opened the door a little further and stepped back. The door was closed and bolted behind them.

"You had better wait here while I fetch Mother Superior."

She hurried away, returning a few minutes later with an older woman who wore a long grey gown with a full-length, sleeveless, white smock over the top. It draped from her shoulders, down her back to her heels and her toes at the front, like a wide scarf with a hole for her head. Clutching a wooden cross attached to a necklace of wooden beads, she asked, "Who do you say you are, my good man?"

"My name is Thomas Harrison. I am Susie and Alfie Harrison's father. I'd like to thank you for looking after them and their friends."

"Hmm, father, you say, but how do you know these other strange children?"

Tom detected no warmth in her voice or manner. "Mother Superior, we are all from the same small village far south of here, where everyone knows everyone else. Ask the children." He smiled whilst trying to show respect and warm her to him, but she didn't respond. "They are the Fletcher twins, Mary and Alan, and Polly Brown. As I said, we are all from a village far to the south, deep in the Washes."

She was more satisfied at the mention of the other children's names. "We thought they were orphans from another country. Maybe they had run away from one of the trading ships where they had stowed away or had been kidnapped. They have such strange stories to tell, their dress is unusual, and like you, they speak strangely. Sadly, they have little knowledge of the scriptures, but we are teaching them. Do you know how they came to be here?"

"It is a long story that would take a lot of explaining."

"Then we shall pray before we talk, it's that time. You may join us if you wish, Mr Harrison."

Tom felt obligated to say, "Yes."

Mother Superior turned to Alfie. "Bring the other children to the chapel." He scurried away without hesitation.

Tom, Susie, and Mother Superior walked down wide arched corridors, some framed with heavy timbers, while others were of grey stone. Having expected a small intimate setting, Tom was amazed at the chapel being big enough to accommodate at least a hundred people. However, there were no pews. In contrast to the rest of the building, it was not sombre, but bright and colourful with beautiful stained glass windows. The walls were covered with tapestries and paintings of biblical scenes, stretching up to twenty feet from the floor.

He was fascinated but was not allowed time to study them. High above the paintings, on each side, was a row of evenly spaced statues of Saints, each one looking down on the congregation. In front of him stood a magnificent altar that would be the envy of any church. Tom stopped in front of it and dipped his head in reverence.

Mother Superior noticed, was pleased and did the same.

Before anything could be said, he heard the children arrive at the entrance behind him. Turning quickly, he didn't recognise Mary, Alan, or Polly straight away. There were more than a dozen children, making him search their faces. However, it was not difficult as Mary, Alan and, Polly had the biggest smiles. Alfie had already told them how they had found his father.

Their faces lit up even more when Tom gave a discreet wave and smiled. At that moment the air was electrified with the children's excitement. They wanted to run to him but were restrained by the nun's discipline. The chapel was a serious place of worship and they didn't want to be punished for what the nuns called, "disrespecting the Lord's sanctuary." They had fidgeted and whispered once before during chants and had come to regret it.

The service was over in half an hour. Being conducted in Latin, which only the nuns understood, made it appear lengthy and especially boring for the children. The singing and chanting echoed through the rafters of the high-arched ceiling to create a moving, spiritual atmosphere. The beautiful sounds caused Tom's emotions to rise. It seemed fitting that he should experience such an inspiring event on the very day he had found the children. No one heard him say, "Thank you, Lord. Thank you from the bottom of my heart."

They all put their hands together and closed their eyes, copying the nuns' movements for the final prayer. Then there was silence as each nun passed the altar to curtsy and cross herself before quietly filing out of the chapel. Tom and the children followed.

Mother Superior told one of the nuns to take the children and feed them while she talked to Mr Harrison.

They were disappointed at not being able to get close to Tom, especially as they had waited impatiently through the service. Yet they knew better than to disobey or question Mother Superior. Even the nuns obeyed her without hesitation. Alfie and Suzie desperately wanted to stay with their father but were waved away with the others. Tom saw their disappointment, gave a gentle nod and a wink, suggesting it's best to obey.

Tom was led to a cool, grey stone-walled room, offering only a small slit window for light. Mother Superior sat on a wooden chair with her back to the light while Tom was gestured to sit on the bench opposite. "Be aware, Mr Harrison, you are greatly privileged to enter our sanctury. Male children are accepted but adult males are usually not. Now, please tell me about yourself and what you know of these children."

"First, Mother Superior, I would like to thank you and your nuns for taking the children in and caring for them. It was kind of you and I am very grateful."

"Yes, yes. It's what we do here with orphaned children. But from what I now understand, some may not be true orphans. Five of the children seem to know you, as you appear to know them. How is this, and why are they so different to the other children?"

"Well, you see, like me, they are not from these parts. You have noticed that we speak and dress differently. We have a different culture altogether."

"And where might you be from that is so different, some strange foreign part, no doubt?"

"No. As I mentioned before, we live in an isolated community far to the south." Tom was trying not to be specific.

"How far south?"

"We are from The Isles of Eels, deep in the Washes."

"Yes, I know where it is, Mr Harrison. I have been to the Abbey at Ely and further south to Denny Abbey. I met none who talk and dress such as you."

"We are from one of the more remote, smaller islands which is seldom visited. So our culture has developed in isolation."

Tom was pleased with his half-truth and spur-of-the-moment explanation. Yet he was still not comfortable. He wanted to be as honest as he could but knew he would have even bigger problems if he dared to talk about coming from seven hundred years in the future. The look on Mother Superior's face suggested she was not entirely convinced, but fortunately, she chose not to pursue the matter.

"And what, may I ask, is your purpose here in Bishop's Lynn?"

"I'm attending to the knights' horses and assisting Rauin, the king's physician. I treat the animals for their complaints and injuries. You might say I am a horse physician. I know about certain cures for people too." In emphasising the *king's physician,* he hoped it would add credibility, importance, and maybe slow her enquiry.

"And why are the children here for so long without you?"

"The children went missing some time ago and were never found. It was as though they had wandered into the marshes and drowned, got lost, or had been abducted. I was lucky to find them here, safe and sound, thanks to you. Many people have been looking for them. They have certainly come a long way, and again I thank you for caring for them. They seem happy and are well-fed," Tom said, trying to please her.

"Well then, no doubt you will wish to take them back?"

"Yes, just as soon as I have finished with the knights' horses and my assistance to Rauin. I have been asked to travel with the Knights Templar for some days, so it may be a while before I come for the children. May I ask if you will please care for them for a little longer until I get back?"

"Yes, of course. But if you must go with those heathen, be very careful. They are not to be trusted."

"Thank you…and I will. May I now have a little time alone with the children?"

"Yes, certainly, wait here," she said as she stood, gesturing for him to sit where she had been.

Alone, Tom looked around the small, grey, dimly lit room. Apart from simple wooden furniture and the filtered light from the window, the only adornment was a wooden cross on one wall.

He was forced to think ahead and hoped to buy a little time. There was a dilemma looming for which he had no immediate answer. Should he forget about tracing the king's lost treasure, or try to get the children home as soon as possible? If he found the treasure then and got them home afterwards, he could give them a much better life. They had already been here for a long time, so he speculated that a few extra days would make no difference. However, the notion did not overpower his conscience. The children were so anxious to go home and he didn't want to disappoint them. He needed to confide in Rauin, tell him how they went missing, that they were now found and ask if he knew of an antidote to the monk's potion.

Minutes later the children rushed in. Susie was the

first, running to her father, throwing her arms around his neck to hang on tightly. Alfie's hug was made clumsy by Susie's clinging, but it didn't matter. He loved his father and just wanted to be close.

Aware of the other children standing by, Tom smiled and beckoned them. Their inhibitions disappeared as they came forward. Susie, Alfie, Mary, Polly and Alan stood as close as they could to Tom, who tried to embrace them all. No one spoke while some shed joyful tears.

"Okay, why don't we sit for a minute and I'll tell you what we'll do or at least hope we can do to get you home."

Mary, Polly, and Alan moved to the wooden bench where they sat, whilst Tom thought for a moment. Susie climbed on his lap, keeping an arm around his neck. Alfie stood on the opposite side, leaning on him with an arm across his father's shoulders. Tom didn't want to raise their hopes about getting home. He couldn't be sure of anything but wanted to be honest without upsetting them.

"First, let me say that all your mums and dads are very worried about you and want you back home. Everyone in the village has been looking for you for a long time. Some people thought you had fallen in the river, others thought you might have run away, and some even believed you had been taken by gypsies."

The children looked serious.

"Are we in a lot of trouble?" Alan asked.

"Good Heavens. No! Just imagine how pleased and excited everyone will be to see you again." They smiled and relaxed again.

"I know how you got here, but I must be honest and say that, at this moment, I don't know how to get you home again. I have to talk to some other people and find out what can be done."

The children's smiles disappeared as they looked at each other.

"Can't we just go home?" Polly asked.

"It's not that easy," Tom said sympathetically. "You see, that sweet sticky treacle you tasted in the barn was, well, it was sort of a magic potion. It not only took you to a different place but also a different time. In fact, seven hundred years back to when there were no cars, buses, or trains and only a few proper roads.

"So is there magic to get us back home again, to my mummy and daddy?" Polly asked.

"I don't know yet, but I hope so. You see, I have to speak to the people who made the first potion to find out. It's not as easy as just getting on a bus and taking you home, as much as I would like to. I could take you back to our village, or at least to where it was before you left. But it might not even exist. Your houses wouldn't have been built and your mothers and fathers won't have been born yet."

The children looked confused. In a moment of strange speculation, Tom considered if these children could become their own parents' ancestors. No, that was too outrageous. Or could they? Was it possible?

Polly looked worried. "When will you go?"

"Just as soon as I can. I might be away for a few days or even a week or two, but I'll do my very best, you can be sure of that. You'll have to wait here a little longer while I check things out."

"How long? We want to go home now," Alan lamented.

There was a chorus of agreement.

Again, Tom felt the pressure of his predicament. "I know you do, and I'd like to take you right away, but I don't know how long it will take. You see…the people I need to talk to are miles away in Ely. As I said, I'll do everything I can, as quickly as I can. I promise."

Tom stood when Mother Superior entered.

"It's time for the children's lessons, Mr Harrison."

"Yes, of course. Thank you, Mother Superior." Tom looked lovingly at the children. "Don't worry. I'll do everything I can, and I promise to come back and see you again very soon." He dropped to his knees to hug each child. Alfie and Susie didn't want to let go, and it was a painful parting.

"Stay here with these kind ladies for now and don't worry. I'll come back, I promise."

Mother Superior relaxed her stern persona. As the children said goodbye, and Susie cried, she could see genuine love, erasing any doubt of Tom's story. She led him to the main door. "Thank you, Mr Harrison. No doubt we shall see you again."

Chapter 17

Tom went back to the manor house where he hoped to find Rauin. Passing the knights at the entrance was daunting, but he entered without being questioned, although he did receive suspicious looks. Rauin was in his room, intensely deciphering pages of the book Tom had given him.

He looked up to see who had entered. "Ah Thomas, I most certainly need your knowledge to deal with this language.

"Not just now, if you don't mind, there are things I must talk to you about."

"Can they not wait?" Rauin's attention was still on the book.

"No, I'm sorry, my friend."

The book was closed.

"You remember what I told you about the flask and how I came to be here. Well, there is much more to tell you, and I need your help. You see, I hid the flask, well not exactly hid it, but put it in one of my barns. My son, daughter, and three of the village children found it and tasted the potion. They are here in Bishop's Lynn, right now! I found them today. Well, to be honest, they found me. They are being cared for by the nuns at the convent."

"Dear God above! Are they fit of body and mind?"

"Yes, the nuns have looked after them well. But I have to say they are not as energenic as I remember them, they are unhappy, sometimes afraid, and suppressed by the nun's strict discipline. They desperately want to go home…Is there an antidote to the potion that will return them to their own time?"

"Not that I know of, but I did not ask the monks or the friar about that. All they said was that if you taste it after it has aged for seven days, you will depart, never to return. Reversing the effect was never discussed."

"So there may be a remedy?"

"Maybe, but I have grave doubts as the latter effects were unforeseen."

"I have to get them back home, I have to. I was careless with the flask, so it's my fault they are here in the first place. I wish I'd never found the cursed thing."

"Do not chastise yourself, Thomas. Some things in life are meant to be, ordained by a higher authority. I might just as easily say it was my fault for carelessly losing the flask. That said, if circumstances were different at this time, I would journey to Ely for you and see what can be done."

"Thank you. I understand that you can't leave the king, but I could go!"

"Sadly the king is no better and he informs me of his wish to leave this place soon. I have doubted his fitness to travel since his condition worsens. Yet his mind is set, and he refuses to be persuaded. He is anxious to reach Newark Castle, where he will feel less vulnerable. He commands me to ensure his fitness to travel."

"There are two thousand or more Knights Templar to protect him. Surely he is safe enough here?"

"The king prefers the feel of thick castle walls about him. He not only fears the French and the English Barons, but in private he proffers that he does not trust the knights either. He believes they will first serve those who pay the greatest reward, so change their allegiance. At times I fear he may be somewhat paranoid, but regarding the knights, I am not sure myself. I believe they are traitorous."

"Why? I thought they were loyal protectors."

"Thomas, some guard the king, and others his treasures, which includes the Crown Jewels. The wealth they guard is many times greater than the king pays them, even though he rewards them handsomely. If they had a mind to plunder King John's treasures, there is no one to stop them. Certainly, the barons would not interfere. They are more likely to be conspirators in such a plot."

"But I have always believed that the Knights Templar were honourable and loyal."

"Ah yes, but as we have discussed this before Thomas, only to their own causes, whatever they may be at any time. They are supposed to be a religious order, they were required to swear religious vows of obedience, chastity, poverty, and piety to the Vatican and honour any noble cause approved by the pope. All fine words, but with the years their wealth and power has grown, as has greed and corruption within their ranks. They have become exceedingly wealthy in their own right. Frankly, I do not trust them.

"Nor do I." Tom thought a moment. "I'll go to Ely myself. What is the best way in these times?"

"The safest is by river, as I did. You will be less likely to be accosted and robbed along the way. I will provide you with a letter of introduction to the abbot. Showing it may afford you free passage and perhaps a little comfort. The Royal Physician's seal should also encourage the monks to treat you with courtesy. Even though they are not fond of the king, they respect our profession. Yet many of the monks are arrogant, undisciplined scoundrels. Their sincerity to duty is nothing more than a veneer. However, they can be clever in many ways.

Tom listened intently.

"A grand cathedral is being built on the high ground at Ely and some of the timber arrives in Bishop's Lynn by ship. From where I know not, but it is loaded onto river barges to be transported to Ely. The journey takes about two days depending on the weather and tide. Hulks leave here each day, so it should not be difficult to obtain passage.

More concerns flooded Tom's mind; What if I leave here and return to my own time during the journey. I don't have control over when it'll happen. Of course, I could come back, but I'll find myself back in the stables and have to start again. Two days' travel, one day there, then two days to return. That's five days at best! Will the potion last that long? Once more Tom wressled with his conscience. I won't see where the crown jewels are lost and the knights will have left by the time I get back.

A courtier knocked at the door, and without waiting entered, taking them by surprise.

"You know better than to enter here without my beckoning, knave!"

"My apologies, Master Physician, but the king asks for you with urgency."

Rauin placed the book on his bed. "I know not how long I shall be gone, Thomas." He gathered his bag as he made for the door.

"Not to worry. I have to attend to the horses anyway."

"I will seal a letter for you on my return. You may use it as you see fit."

Rauin hurried to the king's chambers. Tom went about his business at the stables. Later, he returned to the children to explain why he was going to Ely. This time he was greeted more favourably by Mother Superior. The children were pleased to see him but were saddened when he told them it might take some days, or a week or more. Although unhappy, they trusted him, realising they had little choice other than to wait.

Tom was invited to share a meal with the nuns but was reluctant, preferring to eat with the children. He was not introduced, just offered a seat at a long table. Food was brought and prayers were said. It was only Mother Superior who looked directly at him, but he was aware of inquisitive glances from some of the nuns. He had once begun to speak but Mother Superior quickly raised a vertical forefinger to her lips. Later he was allowed to spend time with the children. Before leaving, he told Mother Superior that he might not be able to return for the children for a week or two. After a moment of hesitation, she confirmed her agreement to continue caring for them until he came.

On returning to the inn, Tom reported the condition of the horses. Pleased with his services, the knights took him aside. Each one gave him a silver coin. Again, they were noticeably friendly causing him to be suspicious. His intuition was correct. One of the knights, who Tom knew as Sir Michael of Worcester, came nearer, placing his face close. "Thomas, I tell you in great confidence that we will leave here tomorrow to travel north to Newark. As you know, we wish you to continue attending our mounts, on the journey and thereafter. The column is to be split. The king will take the longer safer route to the southwest and then north, while the remainder will accompany his wealth across the Washes. Will you come with us? We shall reward you well."

Tom felt trapped, and he was expecting this, already knowing the procession would be split and which train he wanted to travel with. He decided to play along until he could go to Ely. "I must tell you that Sir David of Lyon has already demanded I travel with him."

"Do not trouble yourself with Sir David. He is but a French buffoon. As for me, I will be protecting King John."

"It would be best for me to travel with the other column. Your horses are well enough for the journey to Newark without me, but some of your friends who travel across the Washes may need me. I might also be useful along the path, as I'm familiar with this country. It can be dangerous with bogs, quicksand, and rushing tides nearer the coast."

"But I expect you to be with me."

"I would join you again in Newark, and may even be there before you. I think I can serve the king's mission better this way."

Sir Michael shrugged. "As you wish, Thomas,"

"Thank you." Tom relaxed.

"Then I must introduce you to Sir Richard De Vere. He sits by the fire with his ale. I believe he is responsible for the route, but he may not welcome you."

Tom was worried that he was becoming more deeply involved.

"Sir Richard," Sir Michael called as they approached. "I wish you to meet Thomas Harrison. He is what you might call a horse physician. He also assists the king's physician. Although I doubt the king has horse ailments." A wry grin creased his face.

"Am I supposed to know this knave?" Sir Richard said without looking up.

"Now, now, Sir Richard, relax. Thomas is a local man with much skill at treating whatever may ail our mounts. He has attended my own, Bruce's, John's, and Sir Casper's horse well. We have come to respect his skill and knowledge. He would be useful to you on your journey."

Sir Richard looked disparagingly at Tom. "So what is it you wish of me, horse physician?"

"Sir Richard. I am to meet Sir Michael in Newark in a few days, but I would better serve you and the king by travelling across the Washes with your train. I ask for nothing other than approval to travel with you and attend the horses."

"How do you know these details of our journey?"

Before Tom could reply, Sir Michael interrupted, "I told him of our plans. He may be trusted. He is a known friend and companion of the king's physician."

"As you say, but can he silence his tongue or does it flap out of control?"

"He is trusted well enough to deliver advice and cures for our king, so I'm certain it is safe to bring him into our confidence. What is more, he may be useful as a guide across the Washes."

Tom wished he was not involved in this and stood quietly by.

"I tell you, Sir Michael, we want only knights and our trusted wagon drivers as we journey! No one else… and we need no guide. If this 'Thomas' is so valuable, I suggest you attach him to your own column on the morrow. Now leave me to my ale and the warming of my extremities."

Tom already knew from his history books that they would not take a guide, but he was surprised that Sir Richard was so adamant. Once again, he suspected the knights may have an ulterior motive. Was it because he feared being led into an ambush when he had only half the complement of knights or did he have other reasons? Tom had no way of knowing for sure, but it seemed rather strange as the Washes are a place where only those who know their moods would dare to venture, especially with wagons. He said nothing other than to excuse himself. "Sir Michael, I must return to the manor house and discuss the king's condition with his physician."

"We will see you at the stables just after sunrise then," Sir Michael called after him.

Tom waved but didn't reply. In ten minutes, he was back in the little room at the manor house. It had become chilly outside and the sight of an open fire was welcome. He was still warming himself when Rauin entered.

"Ah, you are back, Thomas."

"I arrived a few minutes ago. What was so urgent earlier?

How is the king?"

"His condition is unchanged, but he found comfort from the liquid you gave and wanted more. When he is distressed, everything is urgent and his patience wanes. I fear he has taken all there is of the precious gold liquid and now demands I provide more."

"I'm sorry, my friend, I don't have any more, but give me a moment to remember other ways to ease his discomfort. In the meantime, get him to chew caraway seeds."

"I fear we don't have much time if the king is to leave at dawn."

Tom thought quickly. "Well, there are a couple of things you could try…I don't know if they will work or are old wives' tales, but my grandmother used to swear by them."

"You talk strangely again, Thomas, but what are these cures?"

"If you have, or you can get rice, boil it in water until most has evaporated. Strain out the rice and keep the remaining liquid. Then stir in a good helping of honey."

"Will it work?"

"I don't know, but my grandmother always said it worked on my grandfather when he had the trots."

"The trots?" Rauin frowned.

"The same bowel problem the king has. Sometimes she would give him oats, applesauce and toast, with lots of ginger. Ginger in almost any form will soothe the stomach. I thought I had mentioned that before."

"Thank you. Anything is worth trying at this time. Excuse me while I send someone to find these things. I will also see if the kitchen has ginger."

Tom stood with his back to the fire whilst waiting for Rauin to return, which was not long.

"My apologies, I'm sure you understand my priorities."

Tom nodded, anxious to discuss his concerns. "I understand the king is to go north tomorrow by a safe inland route, while his treasures are to be left in the hands of the knights who will cross the Washes."

Surprised, Rauin cut in. "How do you know these things?"

"Sir Michael of Worcester took me into his confidence."

"He should be careful. If Sir Guillaume de Charters were to discover his indiscretion, he may consider it treasonable."

"I feel backed into a corner. One way or another I am expected to travel with the knights. However, I prefer to go to Ely as we discussed. Part of me is fascinated with the opportunity of crossing the Washes with the knights…but I'm afraid of what they might do if I don't show up."

"If you must go to Newark, surely it would be safer and more comfortable to take the inland route? Yet what of your intent to journey to the Isles?"

"Yes, I am going but unfortunately it may have to be later." Tom hesitated, considering if he should tell the whole story. Then, given their relationship, as short as it has been and that it was based on mutual trust, he said, "Rauin, I know what is going to happen over the next few days."

"How can you possibly know?"

Tom took the history book from his rucksack and holding it flat in the palm of his hand, he patted it with the other. "To me its history, all recorded here in this book, hundreds of years from now, taken from chronicles written in your own time." He opened the book to the first pages. "Do you see? It says published in London, 1919."

Rauin was wide eyed with expectation.

Tom opened the book. "See, it describes the events up to this day and beyond. See, it describes King Richard's crusades, how he became known as, the Lionheart, and how he died. It tells about King John, how unpopular he was, or should I say *is*. It even mentions his illness, which is called dysentery in my time. It tells about the treaty he was forced to sign with the barons at Runneymede, about his failed marriage in France with Isabella of Angouleme, and the lands he lost there and in Ireland. It even explains why he was called John Lackland before he became king. Look, here are sketches of King John signing the Magna Carta. This book explains what happened in England up to my own time."

Amazed, Rauin asked what it said about the next few days.

Tom hesitated to compose himself. "It's not good, I'm afraid. It records that the king took the inland route to Lincoln and on to Newark, while the knights tried to cross the Washes with the king's treasure. But there is something strange about it. You see, the knights refused to take anyone to guide them across the marshes and they took no notice of the tides, which was clear folly. Consequently, their horses and wagons became bogged in a swampy area. Then when the tide came in, many were washed away and drowned with their horses. The wagons were lost to the bogs and tides along with their valuable cargos. They were never recovered. Even in my time nobody knows exactly where they are, although lots of people have tried to find them.

Rauin was shocked, afraid of the forthcoming events and realised the dangerous potential of such a document. "Thomas, you must hide this manuscript and never tell anyone of what it contains. It would be considered treasonous, heresy against the king, or at the very least a product of evil witchcraft. It would frighten people and you and your volume would be burned at the stake."

"You are the only person here who knows it exists. Here, you can have it."

As much as Rauin was fascinated and wanted to read

it, he hesitated. "If it is discovered in my possession, I would be burned also, probably as an evil Druid." Yet, like a moth to the flame, he took the book, his curiosity getting the better of him.

"I shall read what I can and then perhaps destroy it, or return it to you if you prefer. Thomas, if these events are to happen, why would you want to go across the Washes and endanger your life?"

"I think my life will be in danger if I don't go. But if I am forced to, I can see exactly where the jewels are lost. So, in seven hundred years from now, I may be able to find them, if they really were lost as history records. It means I would go to Ely in a few days rather than now."

"Why do you doubt your history book when it is written?"

"My friend, what I tell you is only my personal speculation. I have no evidence to confirm my opinion, but if the knights were to hear of it and it's true, we would both find ourselves having an accident on a Templar's sword, king's physician or not."

"Then is it wise for me to hear?"

"I'm sure you would want to know. There are many accounts of the event in history books. Some give more detail than others, but together they arouse my suspicion."

"I know not what you mean, but my curiosity is compelling."

"I believe the knights know better than to try and cross the tidal washes with a train that includes heavily laden carts and carriages. It's difficult at the best of times and almost impossible without a guide. Yet they want no local man to guide them. They will leave in the morning, irrespective of the conditions and the tides. It's as though they want a disaster to happen. I can only speculate as to why."

"What is it you suggest?"

"Well, just suppose the king's jewels are not on the train at all but have already been taken and hidden by the knights."

"They would not dare! The king would have their heads!"

"And who is there to take their heads? Has anyone seen the jewels in the last few days?"

Rauin slowed as he realised what Tom was suggesting. "No, I doubt the knights would let anyone near them."

"Precisely. History records that the king's treasure was lost in the Washes due to sinking bogs and tidal surges. There was even a loss of life, which I suspect was exaggerated. King John would have to accept the loss, especially after ordering an immediate search when absolutely nothing was found, not even the remains of a single cart or carriage. Which is strange in itself. For hundreds of years men have searched for these treasures, but no trace has ever been found. What is more, nobody knows exactly where they were supposed to have been lost. So what I'm suggesting could be a logical explanation. Wouldn't you expect the place would be known and that every man and his dog would have been out there immediately, looking for the treasure?"

"You make a strong, if controversial, supposition Thomas."

"Not only that, but history also records that shortly after this date, the Templar Knights in England became extremely wealthy, and there are no records explaining how they achieved it so suddenly."

"But if your book is correct and the location is known

tomorrow, surely local people searching will quickly take their plunder away, so there would be little or nothing to find later. What's more, no one would admit to their find."

"You could be right, who knows? But wouldn't you expect that some of the gold or jewels would eventually show up somewhere, even in foreign lands? What if I'm right and nothing was lost in the first place? It answers a lot of questions."

The two men stared at each other. Tom broke the silence. "Now you know why I would cross the Washes."

"But if you believe as you suspect, why do you wish to go?"

"Simply to be sure and to know the location. You see, I don't doubt the tragedy, which could have been staged, I only question the loss of the treasure."

Although he was frustrated and excited at the same time, Tom's dilemma seemed to be resolved. He had been torn between finding an antidote to the potion immediately, or finding where the treasure was supposedly lost. The latter now seemed unavoidable and Tom's conscience weighed heavily.

After almost ten minutes of silence, while Rauin examined the book, he finally looked up. "Does your book tell of what eventually happened to the Knights Templar?"

"Yes, they became very rich indeed, wealthier than some kings and their kingdoms. They had great influence on the authorities, even with the pope. However, they will only exist for a century from now. You might say they create their own downfall."

"How so?"

"The book describes how, over time, they loaned a

huge amount of money to King Philip of France. The debt became so large that he couldn't repay it. So, when the knights pressured him, he had them banned for heresy and blasphemy. Their leader was arrested, tortured and executed, as were many of the other knights. Almost five hundred were imprisoned and executed, but many more fled taking much of their wealth with them."

"It does not surprise me, Thomas. I have long disapproved of their evil ways and had considered it may eventually bring their downfall. It is a pity it will take so long."

Tom didn't respond. His mind was on the children whilst he paced the room. Flushed in a moment of intense guilt, laced with anger, he spoke out. "Why should I allow these evil bastards to prevent me from trying to save my children? Thank you, Rauin, I'll accept your offer of a letter introducing me to the abbot in Ely. I'll go as soon as I can. To hell with those bloody knights, they can keep their stupid treasure."

"I shall draft it for you this evening, Thomas, and pray for your success."

"Thank you. If you will excuse me now, I'll go to the river and find a boat heading to Ely."

Chapter 18

Trying to show casual confidence, Tom walked past the knights when he left the courtyard. He hoped he was not being paranoid but was concerned at the thought of them knowing what he suspected of their plans. If they knew, he would not see tomorrow. He stepped into the street with a sigh of relief.

As he made his way towards the estuary, it seemed less busy now, while the smells of cooking wafted through the air. As he neared the river the odours changed to those of tar, damp fishnets, and stale fish. The port was busy as usual. Walking along the quay, he was fascinated, and wished he had a camera.

Towards the north end of the quay, he noticed two cogs with their cargoes of huge timbers being unloaded. Smaller vessels were tied side by side at the quay while others were moored randomly in the river waiting for their cargoes. Tom watched as an ingenious method of hoisting the huge timbers was used. It consisted of the main beam which swung from the quay over the side of the ship. Ropes and pulleys were controlled from a crude, but effective, windlass. Three men were involved in managing the apparatus while two more in the rivercraft shouted instructions as they guided the cargo down into a secure position. He watched the riverboat sink a full two inches when each timber was loaded. Three of these huge pieces were as much as the twenty-five-foot craft could carry without sinking dangerously close to its gunnels. The port workers were unshaven and dressed poorly in what seemed to be little more than rags. As he watched, a man dressed much better approached.

"Looking for work?"

"No. A passage to Ely."

The man looked him up and down. "Ah, now I see you are not of the labouring class. You're an odd-looking fellow, I must say."

"I'm with King John's party and I need to get to Ely."

"You speak strangely too. Where are you from?"

"Not these parts."

"I thought not. Ely, you say. You might just be lucky. These boats are taking timbers there for the new cathedral. They say it'll be huge. But we'll not see it finished in our lifetime."

Tom was taken by surprise and kicked himself for not remembering. "Of course, it was not finished until almost 1350."

"What's that you say?"

"Oh nothing, I had forgotten about the cathedral. Do you know any of the captains?"

"Captains! Captains, you call'em. A bunch of rogues if you ask me. Yes, I know most of 'em. See that first one, he'll pull away soon's he's finished loading, then he'll tie up further along the wharf to wait the morning tide. No point in fight'n the ebb flow what rips through right now when he can make better time on the morning flood. George Martin owns it. He might take you up the river… for a price o'course. Tell him Michael Cross the docking master sent you, it might help."

Tom thanked him and waited for the boat to be fully loaded. Two men on board clambered onto the cog, across its deck, and onto the quay where a line tied to the bow of the river boat was thrown to them. Hauling on the rope, they brought it slowly forwards, while a man with a pole pushed it clear of the cog. Once the boat and cargo were secured, the men came ashore. Tom stepped forward to the man who appeared to be in charge. "Excuse me, are you George Martin?"

"Some calls me that," he said, eyeing Tom cautiously.

"Good. My name is Thomas Harrison. I need to get to Ely. Will you take me?"

"What do you want in Ely?"

Although thinking it was none of his business, Tom humoured him.

"I'm on the king's business and have to see the monks there."

"I don't know why I should help that king of yours. How do I know you tell the truth?"

"I have a letter from the king's physician for the abbot, and I should tell you that Michael Cross recommended you to me."

"Well, if Cross sent you, I'd better not cross him, if you'll pardon the pun. Now that'll cost ye five silver pennies!"

"Three!" Tom replied. Although he didn't know their worth, he felt the need to bargain.

"Four!" Martin responded.

"Agreed. I'll see you in the morning. What time will you leave?"

"On the turn of the tide, just 'afore daybreak."

"As you say, Mr Martin, thank you."

On his way back to the manor house Tom visited the stables to see if the ostlers had followed his instructions, then decided that something to eat and drink was in order. The inn was quiet with only a few local men sitting by the fire, no doubt pleased to have their regular seats back.

"Where are the knights?" Tom asked.

"Dunno," one of the men replied, adding, "Good to see the back o'them, I say."

"They look like they're getting ready to leave," Another said.

The landlady came to take Tom's order. Feeling mischievous, he gave her a big smile.

"Well, what do you want?" she asked.

"I'll have a large flagon of your very best ale, my good woman."

She grunted and turned away muttering, "I'm nobody's, good woman."

Tom couldn't resist. "That is so true, Madam."

She turned to face him as though looks could kill. Tom thought he may have gone too far, but was saved from her tongue by the landlord's call.

The old men laughed. "She ain't never been known to smile, my friend. An' I gotta say, you're a brave man to take her on. I dunno how her husband puts up with 'er. Fancy waking up every morn with her aside ye?"

They all laughed. Minutes later, his ale was unceremoniously dumped on the nearest table. He wondered if he should order food. As he neared the end of his ale, he got a strange feeling and disappeared. Only one of the old men saw what had happened and quickly stood in shock. "'E's gone, 'e's gone! 'E were there one minute and gone the next. I seed 'im goo."

"Course he's gone, he ain't here, is he?" another said.

"No, no. I mean he disappeared. Gone like a puff a smoke. He just vanished."

The other men ridiculed him, saying he was imagining things and that he had obviously not noticed Tom walk out.

"I knows what I sees, I tell ye! 'E just vanished!"

The landlady came to see what the fuss was about, then placed her fists on her hips. "Well, I'll be damned! That there cheeky foreign fella has run off without paying. Just wait till I see him next time if he ever dares to show his face!"

Chapter 19

When he came round, Tom was on his back in his big barn. He pulled out his watch. It was half-past six in the evening, cold and dark. Crossing to the house, he stopped for a moment or two with reservations about confronting Dora. He took a deep breath while hesitating at the door. So much had happened that he wouldn't know where to begin, or if he should tell her anything at all. Turning the knob, he walked in and was greeted by the familiar faint smell of the paraffin lamp, which no longer lit the room and there was no welcoming glow from the stove. After pumping and lighting the lamp, he could see the room looked as it always had, but now with its lack of warmth was not so welcoming.

Hanging his coat on the back of the door, he wondered where Dora was. His first thoughts were that she may be in the outside toilet at the back of the house or perhaps upstairs. Lifting the latch on the small wooden door to the stairway, he looked up and called her name. There was no reply. Silly, he thought. If she was here the fire and the lamp would be lit.

By the time he had relit the stove and put water in the kettle, she had not returned. Although it was unusual for her not to be at home at this time, he was not too concerned, just a little puzzled. Then, after stoking the fire and adding coal, he decided to take this opportunity to update his notes while he waited for Dora.

On finishing, he looked at the clock on the mantelpiece. To his surprise, it was already past eight-thirty. His concerns grew, knowing Dora would never be out by herself this late. Not in the dark and especially not when it's cold unless she was mooning over their children. After a few minutes, he put his old army greatcoat back on and made his way through the village to his mother's cottage. The evening frost was already turning the grass brittle and white.

"Hello, Tom. Where've you been a-disappearing off to?" was his mother's greeting. Ignoring her question, he noticed Peter sitting by the fire.

"Hullo, Ma. How are things, Pete?"

Peter nodded. "Good, what about you?"

His mother's choice of the word "disappearing" made Tom hesitate.

"Yeah fine, fine, thanks," he said, rubbing his hands in the warmth of the fire. Obviously, Dora was not here.

"Well, I think you should tell us what's going on, Tom."

"Nothing's going on, Ma."

"Where do you keep a-disappearing off to then?"

"I really can't say. Not yet anyway, but I can assure you it's nothing that will get me or anyone else into trouble."

"I know you're up to something, and don't you go a-thinkin' you're too old to go across my knee, young man! Dora told people you'd gone to London to help your cousin. What twaddle! We all know you don't have a cousin in London. So what's this all about?"

Tom ignoring her question. "Have you seen Dora? Do you know where she is? She's not at home."

"We've not seen her all day," Peter replied.

Suddenly a horrible thought flashed through Tom's mind. Then, almost speaking out loud he thought, *Dear God, I hope she's not been sniffing around in the barn...* "Do you have any idea where she might be?"

"No idea at all," Ma replied. "But then how would we? Between the pair of you, you'd put Harry Houdini to shame with all them disappearing tricks."

Peter chuckled, then looking at Tom's anxious face he cleared his throat. "Sorry, mate, but we've not seen much of either of you these past two days."

Ma broke the silence. "I suppose you'd like a cuppa?"

Tom and Peter accepted.

"I'm puzzled, Ma. Dora should be at home by now. Has she said anything about going anywhere? Maybe to her sister's place or off with that friend of hers…Vera Brown?"

"Like Peter says, we've not seen her much, so couldn't say. If she were a-going to her sister's she'd a told us. I don't wanna say nothing out'a turn, but she's not been herself for a while and don't say much. She's been moody too."

They drank their tea in silence. The chinking of cups on saucers and the occasional slurp of tea sounded louder than usual.

"Biscuit?" Ma asked.

They shook their heads, then Tom asked, "Ma, are there any ladies things on in the village tonight?"

"Not as I know. The Woman's Institute meet'n were last night. I dunno if she were there. She don't usually miss her W.I. nights."

Tom agreed. "Well, I can't sit here all night'. I'll go and see if she's home now."

"Are you going away again, or staying put for a while?" Ma asked with a twinge of sarcasm.

"I'll be away for a day or two, Ma."

"Expect you'll eventually tell us what you're up to," Peter said, conveying frustration at his brother's secrecy.

"It's difficult, Pete, but I'll tell you everything in good time, I promise."

"Why not now?" asked Peter.

Tom felt awkward and a little guilty. "Put your coat on, Pete and help me look for Dora, just in case she's not at home yet."

Disgruntled, Ma would have to wait, intuitively knowing that Tom will tell Peter. Then, he in turn would tell her.

"I'll see he gets home safe and sound, Ma, long before he turns into a pumpkin."

She smiled at Tom's joke.

As they walked smartly back to the farm their breaths created clouds of white vapour in the cold moonlit night. Tom noticed how well Peter was walking with only the slightest limp now.

"You go in, Pete, light the lamp and stoke up the fire. I want to check something in the barn."

Tom found the vessel exactly where he had left it, looking as though it had not been disturbed. Peter was still stoking the dying embers when Tom returned.

"Good lad, Pete. We could do with a bit of a warm-up. Won't be a minute, I'm just going upstairs."

Dora's coat and handbag were gone, but nothing else. All her clothes, which Tom could remember, were still there. Everything seemed to be normal. Even their old brown leather suitcase was still on top of the wardrobe. He decided she could not have gone far. As he passed through the kitchen, he said he was going out the back for a pee.

The little wooden structure had a flat wooden seat with a deep hole beneath it. Six-inch squares of newspaper were threaded onto a string that hung from a nail in a side wall. Dora was not there. As Tom slowly closed the frosted door, the frozen latch stuck lightly to his fingers.

Peter was already sitting in one of the chairs by the stove.

"Okay, Tom, you must have asked me here for a reason. What's this all about?"

Tom sat opposite and looked into his brother's eyes. "Peter, you have to solemnly promise me you will not tell a soul, not even Ma. Do you understand?"

"Yes, alright." Peter looked surprised.

"I mean it, Pete. This is serious, not one bloody word, or I'll kick your arse all the way to London and back."

Peter sat upright and looked attentively at his older brother.

"Well, to make a long story short…I have found the missing children and I'm about to try to them back."

"Bloody hell! That's fantastic! What, all of them? Where are they?"

"Yes, all of them. I can't tell you any more now and if I did you wouldn't believe me."

"Try me!"

"No. Not yet."

"Why?"

"Like I said, you would never believe me. It's bizarre and I can hardly believe it myself. I just want to bring them back home, but it's really hard, and I don't know if I can do it. I have to go back again and see how, or even if, I can."

"Back where?"

"I can't say. Look, Pete, I'm telling you as much as it's safe for you to know right now, so please don't push me! Just think of what would happen in the village if they knew. Imagine the state the kids' parents would get into. There's no telling what they would do. There would be so much excitement and uproar. The newspapers would be all over the place, worse than before. The police would want to take over and they couldn't. They would jeopardise the whole thing and lock me up as a lunatic. Nobody else can do it, because I'm the only one who knows where they are and how to get there."

"Are they far away?"

"No. But at the same time, one hell of a long way away."

Peter looked confused. "Can I come with you to help?"

"Absolutely not! And please don't ask again!"

"Are they all right?"

"Yes, they seem to be. But of course, they all want to come home."

"Are they being held by someone?"

"You've got too many questions. I'll tell you more when I can. Now, remember not a word to anyone. Even Dora doesn't know what I've just told you. She thinks I'm off somewhere with Rosie. That's what's worrying me about her not being here. I just hope she's not being silly. You know Ma will question you when you get back. Only tell her that Dora was not here so we were out trying to find her. Okay?"

Peter agreed.

Tom tried to distract Peter's attention from the children. "What have you been doing with yourself while I was away? What's been going on?"

"Ah well, your boss has been looking for you, getting a bit shitty about you not being here too. But you know how it is, a bloke with your experience and reputation with horses is hard to find, so he didn't want to rock the boat too much. He asked if you were moonlighting."

"Huh! Where could I get other work in secret around here?"

"Anyway, he was here and at Ma's place looking for you. He said he was short of someone to look after the horses. Not so much to work the fields, but to get them ready for work, see 'em back in the evening, feed, groom 'em, and see they are all right. So I volunteered and started yesterday."

"That's good news. I'm pleased for you, mate. It's time you got off your arse and on with life."

They both chuckled.

"Yeah, I know. I know you are right. I might be asking you for a few tips now and again. Ma is quite pleased."

"You already know more than most blokes, Pete. Why don't you take it up proper? It's been good to me. I'll give you a couple of books on horse medicines and treatments for you to study."

"Thanks."

Tom now had a decision to make. Should he stay and see if Dora was alright? Or help the children? Whichever he chose would leave him worried. After some consideration, he knew he was already committed to helping the youngsters and convinced himself there would be a logical explanation for Dora's absence. After all, she was an adult and could take care of herself. She was bound to turn up soon.

"Look, Pete, I have to go off again in a few hours, but

I'm worried about Dora. Would you do what you can to see she's all right? You can tell her I was back but had to go off again. For God's sake, don't tell her what I told you about finding the children. There's no telling what she'd do and who she'd tell."

"Don't worry, my lips are sealed."

"Thanks."

Peter stood. "I'll go back to Ma before it gets too late."

Tom hugged his brother before he left. It almost seemed as though Tom thought they may not see each other again.

Noticing his hunger, Tom cut two slices of bread which he toasted and smeared with beef dripping before adding a sprinkle of salt and pepper. It was one of his favourites. As he ate, the warm glow from the grate felt good on his face and shins. Relaxing, he considered what he should take back to the thirteenth century. He needed very little but decided to take food for his journey to Ely, so wrapped a lump of cheese in greaseproof paper and placed it beside the remains of the bread.

"I hope Dora turns up before I leave," he mumbled, sitting by the fire again, but desperately needing his bed. He didn't go for fear of oversleeping and missing the morning boat to Ely. No, he'd wait here until four o'clock. Dora should turn up before then. He sat taking catnaps in the warmth of the stove. Each time he woke, it was with a start and he chastised himself for drifting off. But try as he might, he couldn't stop himself from doing it again. When he woke one more time, the clock showed fifteen minutes to four. The fire was low and the room was beginning to cool. He gathered his thoughts. It's time to be off. Now, had he forgotten anything? Coat, food, rucksack. He seemed to have everything he needed.'

He spotted last week's copy of the Ely Standard newspaper, believing Rauin would be fascinated by it, so he folded it into his rucksack. Again, his thoughts went to Dora. *Where the hell are you Dora?* I don't want to bump into you in Bishop's Lynn.

The yard sparkled, lit with a clear light from a bright moon causing the frosted ground to shine and glisten. Crossing to the barn, he considered what he had to do when he arrived in Bishop's Lynn. Saying, "I'll almost certainly need to be away for a week or more, so I'd better take a few good sniffs from the flask. I'll go straight to the docks and find George Martin. Hell no! I can't do that. I need to collect the letter of introduction from Rauin first!"

Moonbeams filtered into the barn providing just enough light for him to locate the container. As he removed it from its ledge, the idea of taking it back to show Rauin came to him, sure that he would be impressed. It would also dispel any lingering doubt of his story. What's more, it would remove the opportunity for anyone else to tamper with it. Holding the flask in one hand and grasping the lid with the other he gave it a slight twist, sniffed deeply several times, replaced the lid and quickly placed it in his rucksack.

Chapter 20

When Tom left the stables, he couldn't help noticing the brightness of the moon. He smiled, knowing it was the same moon he had seen a few minutes ago, just in a different time and place. It made him feel insignificant in the grand order of things. His mind quickly returned to more pressing matters as he hurried through the empty unlit streets to the manor house. The smell of smouldering fires filled the early morning air. Two knights Tom had not seen before guarded the gates. He approached with trepidation, once more trying to create the impression of confidence and great purpose.

"Who are you, and where do you think you are going?" One demanded.

"My name is Thomas Harrison. I assist Rauin, the king's physician. I'm here to collect a letter to take to the abbot in Ely. The monks are to prepare a cure for me to bring back for the king."

"What? At this hour? An unlikely story, clear off or I'll remove your ears where you stand."

The other knight laughed.

"I'm going to Ely on one of the riverboats. They leave when the tide turns in little more than an hour. You must allow me to collect the letter. Don't worry, I'll leave again as soon as I have it, I promise."

"Oh, you promise, do you? What is the promise of a scoundrel like you worth?"

The knights were not taking him seriously, and having fun at his expense.

"If Sir Guillaume de Chartres were to hear that you prevented me from fetching the king's medicine, you would both be in trouble. Then you might be the ones without ears, or even your heads."

Realising what he had said, Tom was afraid he had pushed his luck too far. However, their faces changed so he knew his bluff was working.

"Do you know Sir Guillaume?" They looked at each other in surprise.

"Yes."

"How?"

"I cared for his mount when it needed attention. He's grateful to me." Tom had nothing to lose.

The knights exchanged expressions suggesting they should not delay him.

"All right, one of us will escort you, but no tricks do you hear? Remember there will be a sword at your back."

"Thank you. I only need to go to the physician's room."

Tom led the way through the courtyard, past two knights at the inner door, and up the stairs to Rauin's accommodation. He had expected to find him sleeping, but he was not there. On the table was a folded letter, closed with the seal of the royal physician, addressed to Abbot Blackthorne at Ely. Besides the letter, was a small leather pouch. Picking them up, he turned to his escort. "Right, let's go."

Tom wasted no time with small talk as they retraced

their steps to the main gate. After holding up the letter for both knights to see, he hurried to the docks. George Martin was nowhere to be seen, but it took only minutes to locate his craft in the flickering light of burning torches. He was relieved to see that Martin had not already left. A few minutes later, a voice from the shadows greeted him.

"So you are here already, are you?"

Tom turned to see George Martin emerge from a warehouse.

"Yes, I didn't want to keep you waiting. It's nice to see you again, Mr Martin. Thanks for waiting for me."

Martin smiled at Tom's respect. "Don't flatter yourself, my friend. I would not have waited long for you."

Before Tom could answer, someone called from the far side of the boat. "I'm over here, George. Just checking the cargo is secure."

"Good man," Martin called before he turned back to Tom. "I'll let you know when you can board, Mr Harrison."

Tom had no measure of George Martin so decided to humour him with respect for his authority, without appearing to patronise. Waiting in the grey light of dawn, in those moments when the water is dead between tides, Tom watched as a loaded vessel was slowly poled past. There was the shadowy figure of a man standing on the bow and another at the stern, a dim lantern hung above head height against the mast. The stillness of the night was passing and a light northerly breeze gently opened the sail to push it further into the estuary.

"Come on, Bruce, let's get this old tub under way," Martin shouted. "Climb aboard, Mr Harrison."

Tom did as he was told. Martin untied the mooring ropes as Bruce put all his weight on a long pole to push away from the quay. Martin climbed aboard and in a few seconds had untied and secured the sail before heading for the stern to take the tiller arm.

"All right, Mr Harrison, you can make yourself comfortable. I'll let you know when we need an extra pair of hands."

"Please call me Tom."

"No, Mr Harrison, it wouldn't be proper, with you being a gentleman on the king's business an'all."

"What'll I call you? George? Mr Martin? Captain?"

"Just 'Master' will do, or Mr Martin if you prefer. This here is Bruce. I call him a few other things as well, but best you stick to Bruce. Mind you, he don't take no orders from nobody but me." Tom wondered if Martin was entirely comfortable at having royal authority aboard, no matter how far removed it might be.

"How long will it take to get to Ely, Mr Martin?"

"Well now…it depends on the wind and the tides. Get it right, and we have done it in a day and a half. Get it wrong, and it could be three days or more."

"How long do you expect this trip to take?"

"Let's see now. We got near on a full moon giving us strong full tides, and if the northerly blow picks up and stays with us, I suppose we might do it comfortably in two days."

Tom hoped it would be less, believing he could walk it in less time on decent roads. But there were none. He had little choice, so smiled, remembering the train does it in thirty-five minutes. Tom was accustomed to early mornings on the farm and by now he would have had breakfast and two mugs of tea. It didn't feel right to start the day without a nice hot brew.

Accompanied by the sound of rippling water from

the bow, the hulk moved out into the river, helped by a light breeze and the start of an incoming tide.

"We should make good time in the next six hours or so. That is until the tide turns, then we'll be under sail, pole or oar. You ever rowed 'afore, Mr Harrison?"

"Yes."

"Good, then you can take an oar when we need you. Are you in a hurry?"

"Not exactly, but it would be helpful to get there as soon as we can."

"Then you won't mind lending a bit of elbow grease?" Martin grinned.

Tom didn't know if it was a statement, a question or just sarcasm.

Bruce sidled up. "Don't mind him, Mr Harrison. He don't recognise breed'n or authority, especially if they got anything to do with the king."

"It's alright, Bruce, I'm not offended."

"He don't like all them taxes what he has to pay. Although he pays to the church and the barons, he knows most of them end up with King John. He says they take half his profits, so he puts a bit by, if you get my meaning." Bruce tapped the side of his nose with a forefinger.

"I'll pretend I don't know that," Tom said and winked. His instinct was to explain that he was just an ordinary man like Bruce but thought better of it.

"It's criminal. Most folks in these parts got nothing much to start with anyway. They got no coin to speak of and make a living as they go out'a what nature provides. Do you know there's a village not far from Ely, Little Port they calls it. They had to make an agreement with the abbot to pay their taxes with eels 'cos they got no coin.

Last year they delivered over seventeen thousand of the slippery little devils." Bruce hesitated. "In a way, it helps us, 'cos when we go back to Bishop's Lynn we take boxes full of 'em for export. O'course, George is happy to get paid for going both ways. He says it's the only way he can turn a decent coin. Anyway, you'll have to excuse him now and again, sometimes his tongue's got a rough edge, but he don't mean nothin' by it."

Eventually, the sun cleared the horizon, and the low mist which had drifted over the water was gone. Both wind and tide had picked up, causing the boat to deliver a healthy wash to the banks. Ducks, coots and moorhens bobbed in the wake close to the reeds, whilst an occasional swan watched nervously as they sailed past. Tom smiled, thinking not much had changed on the river. He could see great distances and thought little of it until he realised there were none of the raised banks he was familiar with. The river ran through vast wetlands that were yet to be drained and dykes built. In many places, the distant views were marred by tall bulrushes, reeds and willow trees. In a few other places, reed was being cut and loaded onto punts. Watching the scene unfold along the way was fascinating.

Martin manned the tiller while Bruce sat at the bow. They didn't pass other craft, nor were they overtaken, but many empty vessels passed as they returned to Bishop's Lynn. By late morning their speed had reduced with the slackening of the tide.

"We'll be on sail and oar soon when the tide is lost," Martin called to no one in particular.

"If the wind don't drop we should still make decent time," Bruce replied.

Tom climbed to sit on top of the heavy cargo of

timbers for a better view. He'd not been there long before Martin called out, "Take that bucket and bail the water from below the cargo, Mr Harrison." It was clearly a command, not a request. Martin looked awkward, and realising his abruptness added, "If you please, sir."

As George Martin had predicted, within half an hour the tide had turned, and they were now relying on sail with their speed reduced to less than a half of what it had been. It became an increasing battle between opposing wind and tide. Fortunately, the tide was less fierce this far up the river, so allowing the wind to dictate their direction, albeit very slowly.

"We'll be lucky to make it to Denver afore dark at this rate," Martin called again.

"What's at Denver, Mr Martin?"

"Not a lot, sir, not a lot. Just a few shacks and a shabby inn by the river. The village proper is a little way off. We try to tie up there overnight if we can. An ale or two is always welcome and sometimes a proper bed if you arrive in good time. But if you don't keep an eye on your cargo, you can lose it overnight to them bloody thieves hereabouts. Some masters have a few ales, then sleep aboard. The inn has only a few beds so it's first come, first served. We'll try and get you one. They may have to turn some poor bastard out, what with you being on a king's mission an all." He laughed. "I can't see anyone running off with one of these bloody great timbers though. He'd need an army and a dozen horses."

Tom and Bruce smiled at the thought. The north wind that blew across the great expanse of marshes was decreasing, although bringing a winter chill to the river. Their progress had slowed with the ebbing tide. Eventually, they were almost at a standstill.

"No point in rowing against this. We'll tie up and wait a while," Martin shouted as he manoeuvred the craft parallel to the side of the river.

Bruce took a pole to the bow. Then, once the vessel had stopped, he raised it vertically as high as he could before thrusting it through the water deep into the mud. Putting all his weight on it, he pressed it further in. Almost simultaneously, Martin did the same at the stern. The craft was held between the poles and the reeds. Hemp ropes were quickly tied around the poles as the boat gently slipped back a few inches.

"Right, Mr Harrison, did you bring some vittles?" Martin called from the stern.

"Yes, bread and cheese," Tom called, holding up his rucksack.

Bruce was already tearing a flat round loaf of bread in half with grubby hands. Martin took a piece in exchange for what looked like a generous piece of chicken or roasted wildfowl of some kind. In the two hours they waited, more than a dozen boats passed on the tide heading north. Most were high in the water and looked empty. Martin seemed to know most of the masters. Waving to each other they exchanged a few words of news and playful insults.

Tom wasn't relaxed. He worried about getting the children home and wondered how he would be received in Ely. Would the monks help him? If they could, would they? He'd undoubtedly have to pay them. Soon his mind drifted to Dora and where she might be.

By the time the outgoing tide had fully slackened, the autumn sun was weakening as it continued its journey to the horizon. Tom remembered the pouch Rauin had left him. Looking inside, he found his friend had been far more generous than he thought necessary. He must have believed the monks would want considerable payment.

Martin stood and arched backwards with his arms held high in a blissful stretch. Then after checking the wind he said, "We'd better be off if we are to make Denver afore dark."

"Then we'll need to row," Bruce called back.

"All right, grab an oar. And if you don't mind, Mr Harrison, your arm to an oar would be appreciated."

Tom moved to the far side of the boat where a long, heavy wooden oar hung beneath the gunnels. Positioning it between the pegs of a crude rowlock, he held the blade clear of the water and waited for instructions. The moorings were removed and the poles stowed as the hulk gently drifted into the river. Martin took the tiller. Bruce hurried to sit opposite Tom on the other side of the cargo. Almost immediately, Bruce called time on the oar until they were perfectly synchronised.

"All right there, Mr Harrison?"

"Fine, thanks."

Bruce spoke in a low voice. "Old Martin's enjoying this. If it weren't for you, he'd 'ave to be down here himself."

Dusk had fallen by the time they reached Denver. It was just as Martin had described. The inn was the largest of the few buildings, all of which were thatched. Two had smoke rising from their chimneys. Four other boats had arrived before them, each laden with huge timber beams. Only a short distance away, Tom noticed a punt stacked high with freshly cut reeds, and another piled high with eel traps. On entering the inn, a cloud of smoke billowed back from the open fire. The candlelit room had an eerie atmosphere and held the added smell of smouldering peat. A dozen faces turned to see who had entered. Martin and Bruce greeted people they knew as they made their way to the fire. "Three ales, please," Martin called.

Tom stood silently until the bravado and posturing between the river men had died. On noticing Tom looking lost, Martin raised his voice and said, gesturing to him across the room, "This 'ere is, Mr Thomas Harrison…on his way to Ely to see the monks."

The onlookers offered a casual greeting. Later Martin quietly told Tom that he had purposely not mentioned he was on the king's business. "We don't want you getting your throat cut, do we? Lots of folks in these parts don't have nothin' to thank King John for. They'd rather see him gone. O'course, they might think you are carrying a few bits of gold or silver. You'd be wise to remember that before you go telling folks what you are about."

It made Tom nervous since he had not previously considered himself to be in any great danger.

Martin saw the look on Tom's face and smiled. "Don't worry, we'll see you get to Ely in one piece."

Tom asked to be allowed to pay for their food and drink. Martin laughed, saying he didn't need to ask. A poorly dressed, short, thin lady with a pale complexion came to ask what they would like to eat.

"You get the best eel pie there is here," Martin stated. The lady attempted a smile but seemed distracted. Not having to pay, Bruce grinned widely, quickly finished his ale, and ordered another. Three eel pies arrived, and Tom agreed that it was excellent. Also, the vegetables were some of the tastiest he'd ever eaten. Bruce had previously said little but the ale loosened his tongue.

"Poor old thing. She's the landlord's wife, gets dumped

on to do most of the work hereabouts. Most nights, after midevening, the old sod is so drunk he can hardly stand, let alone serve anyone. No wonder she gets flustered. He used to give her a beating now and again, till one day she were so bad she couldn't give no service. That's when some of the locals sorted him out, 'in kind' like. He were in bed for three days. 'E leaves her alone now. She needs a bit o' help, but the miserable old devil won't pay anyone to give her a hand, the tight bastard."

The woman returned for the empty plates. "I expect you'll be looking for a room. I already got'em two up. There's only the barn and the stable what might be better than sleeping on that old boat of yours."

Before Martin could reply, Tom reached for his arm. "The stable is fine with me if there's clean hay."

"All right, Maud, as long as them old nags o' yours are out the way," Martin added.

Tom smiled and said, "You know, Mr Martin, sleeping above horses in a hay loft can be nice. I've spent many a warm night in a stable."

Martin raised his eyebrows. "What, a man of your standing?"

"Yes, even me. I'm not as important as you might think."

Bruce joined in. "Not with them old nags out there a-shittin' an' a-fart'n all night long. We'd be better off with the chickens."

Maud laughed, replying, "I won't charge you for the stable."

After two hours the three men retired to bed down on clean hay put aside for winter feed. Bruce and Martin produced a thick coarse blanket apiece. Tom covered himself with his old army greatcoat and, to deter curiosity, used his rucksack as a pillow.

Martin's last words were, "Don't have to be up so early tomorrow, Mr Harrison. The tide's a little later here. It hangs a'hind Lynn as we get further up the river." The night passed uneventfully except for Martin's persistent, ale-induced snoring.

They were woken before dawn by the incessant crowing of cockerels. "Why the hell do they have to do that? Bruce asked. Bloody things are only good for servicing hens and for the spit!"

The sounds reminded Tom of home. After George and Bruce had shaken straw from their blankets and Tom from his coat, they went to the inn.

"What's for breakfast, Maud?" Martin called.

"Gruel with or without lumps, take your pick."

"She's in good form this morn'n, George," one of the other masters chirped.

Maud brought three bowls of gruel to the long wooden table in the centre of the room. Tom looked at what he had been given: a bowl containing a thin grey mixture. It had little flavour but was filling and warming. Joking, he said, "I would love a slice of toast and marmalade right now, or a plate of bacon and eggs with a big mug of hot tea."

"What are you on about?" Martin asked.

"It's what we eat where I come from."

"Where is that?"

"Oh, a long way away."

Martin sensed that Tom didn't want to elaborate further, so didn't pursue his question.

Tom was halfway through his gruel when he swayed, and with a big happy grin said, "I feel light-headed."

Bruce smiled. "That'll be the hemp seed what Maud

puts in the gruel. She'll put a bit'o honey in it too, if you like."

"No, this is fine," Tom replied, still grinning. He couldn't help noticing the hemp had much less effect on Martin and Bruce, so assumed they were more accustomed to it. When they were finished, Maud appeared with eggs, a slice or two of salted pork, and bread, much to Tom's delight.

Martin spoke quietly: "We should make it to Ely by nightfall if all goes well, and if the wind gets up like it did yesterday. We'll go as soon as we are finished here to get ahead of the others so we don't have to wait too long for a berth."

While Tom paid, they gathered their belongings and made their way back to the boat.

Martin turned to Tom saying, "That's right generous of you, Mr Harrison, thank you."

There was no wind to remove the thin low mist that always crept across the river at this early hour. The air felt damp. Two moorhens scurried into the mist with alarm when the men approached.

Martin rubbed his stubbled chin and said, "Might as well pole her, Bruce, until we get a bit of a blow and the tide starts to move. It's shallow enough if we don't go to the middle."

After releasing their moorings, Bruce took one of the long poles and slowly manoeuvred the hulk along the edge of the river, reminding Tom of the punts he had seen in Cambridge. Enthralled with this whole experience, he wanted to tell them about the future and how things would eventually be but was afraid to do so. They would have difficulty believing that one day there would be craft, much larger than these, which would travel without sail, pole, or oars effortlessly into the wind and current in any weather. All they would need is to be steered and the speed controlled. Bishops Lynn to Ely would be achieved in less than one day. No, they would think he was making it up.

Within half an hour a sharper morning light had replaced the greyness of dawn. A gentle northerly breeze was growing, and the river began to flow southward once more. Martin ordered the pole to be put away and for the sail to be set. The dark red canvas billowed and banged when the wind filled it. Tom sat back, opened his rucksack, and added recent events to his notes.

He couldn't help noticing how much the river meandered. There seemed to be no straight stretches lasting more than a few hundred yards. This was not the Great Ouse River he recognised. His fascination heightened when they passed villages he only knew centuries later. In this time some consisted of no more than a small collection of thatched cottages, clustered together on slightly higher ground where they struggled to be seen above the reeds and bulrushes. To Tom's surprise, he saw no churches, only an occasional large timber cross standing tall on the highest part of shallow village islands. He estimated the locations of what he knew as Downham Market and Hilgay. Then, to confirm his calculations, he asked Martin the names of villages as they passed.

"I don't know that this one has a proper name, but some calls it South Island."

Tom decided it must be Southery. The river was noticeably narrowing and meandered more as they journeyed towards Ely. He had expected to pass close to Littleport, but found the river veered far to the east, and even further away once past the village. Two miles from Littleport they passed the confluence of the River Lark.

George Martin pointed. "That takes us to Saint Edmunds, right into the abbey grounds. Been up there a couple of times, but it gets too narrow and mighty shallow in places. The monks are none too friendly either. Got a high opinion of 'emselves if you ask me. I don't go there no more. Anyway, these trips down to Ely will keep me going until I turn my toes up. That cathedral will still be being built long after I'm gone. No, I don't need no more than this."

Bruce took a wooden bucket and began to bail the seepage from below the cargo. Slipping, he bashed the heavy bucket hard against a plank near the keel. Water seeped through the split, which he tried in vain to plug with rags, pushing them in with a knife. But within minutes they were soaked and forced out with the pressure of water.

"Bloody idiot! It's bad enough getting damage from outside without you causing it from inside," Martin cursed.

Bruce's face reddened. He looked down, then turned to

Martin. "What! Have you never slipped on them wet boards

'afore?" Knowing Martin had slipped many times. "Some of the planks on this old tub are past it anyway. If they were sound, they wouldn't a split!"

Martin ignored the remark, knowing Bruce was right. "We can't get her out for a repair now, not with this load aboard. You'll just have to bail now and again until we get to Ely. We'll patch her up there with a bit o' canvas and tar, then do a proper job when we get back to Lynn.

We might find a decent plank or two there."

Both men were now in a bad mood. Tom tried to lighten the atmosphere. "Where does all this timber come from, Mr Martin?"

"I don't know where it comes from 'afore Bishop's Lynn, but they are getting far more overland from up Nottingham way, and a lot further."

"And what about the stone?"

"Ah, now that don't come quite so far. Up Lincoln way, they say. Huge lumps of it, some taller 'an a man. I won't carry it. The weight causes the boat to sit lower in the water and makes it unstable. Not only that, if they drop one while loading or unloading, it would likely go straight through the hull. Many a good tub has been lost carrying stone. No, you won't get me carrying it."

There was only a light breeze now, and Martin wanted to get to Ely as soon as possible. Bruce was told to rig an oil lamp to the mast. Tom had an uncomfortable night, managing only a few hours of sleep on board, but he didn't mind if it would get him to Ely sooner.

At dawn, Tom calculated they were approaching Ely but found it strange not to see the cathedral towering above the landscape. He could make out a large structure of some kind and assumed it was the partly built cathedral.

Pointing, Tom asked, "Is that the cathedral?"

"Yes, sir," Bruce answered. "But it don't seem to change much. It don't hardly look no bigger 'an it did a year ago."

Tom's fascination grew as they neared the island. The river eventually passed within a quarter of a mile of the cathedral site. Several timber jetties protruded into the river, like the prongs of a rake. A little further he saw more jetties, timber-lined and infilled, making a solid base where heavier cargoes could be unloaded.

There was a hive of activity as craft manoeuvred in and out of the quays. It was noisy, with skippers calling instructions, their voices frequently lost in the melee from the quays. The solid jetties were fitted with a sophisticated apparatus, similar to those in Bishop's Lynn. Here much of the weight was being taken on long ropes, tethered to teams of cart horses struggling to hold their ground. Although fascinated, Tom was sad to see the excessive loads placed on the animals. "Is it always this busy?" he asked.

"Not always, it depends when you arrive. We all share the same fortunes of nature on the river, so it's natural for a lot of boats to arrive near the same time," Martin replied. "When you get ashore, I suggest you move on. This is no place for a king's gentleman," he added with a touch of playful sarcasm. The conversation was interrupted by a call from the shore directing Martin to a quay.

"I'll pay you now, Mr Martin, and be off."

Martin was surprised to see the amount of silver Tom was carrying. "I'd keep that pouch out of sight if I were you, Mr Harrison, lest you fancy a blade through your ribs. Not everyone hereabouts is respectfully employed."

"I'll heed your warning Mr Martin, thank you, and thank you for bringing me here."

Chapter 21

Tom tucked the pouch inside his shirt before making his way along one of the sloping muddy tracks to the huge construction site. He often stepped aside to avoid empty carts hurrying back to the river. Others, heavily laden, slowly made their way to the top. Some had teams of up to six horses or oxen. He could see why. Hauling huge lumps of stone weighing up to two tons or more up this hill required great effort. The poor creatures were clearly straining and doing their best, and the shouted insults and occasional whipping upset Tom. A man carrying a heavy wooden pole walked beside each cart, ready to slide it behind the wheels should the animals stop and the cart begin to roll or slide backwards. A few luckier horses pulled lighter carts, containing food, tools, and other supplies. He couldn't resist giving some of the horses an occasional quiet word of encouragement and a friendly pat, earning him strange looks from their masters.

Tom was reminded of his reluctant commitment to the knight's service. *They will be annoyed at my disappearance and wonder where I am. Luckily, they won't be in Bishop's Lynn by the time I get back.*

As he reached higher ground, Tom could clearly

see the cathedral taking shape. Thick stone walls of varying heights were under construction. Most had rickety-looking timber scaffolding against them, all tied together and held in place with rope lashings. Crude ladders were randomly placed to give access to the next level of scaffolding. Heavy beams protruded beyond the scaffolding, each strategically placed at the top of a wall. All were rigged with blocks and tackle for hoisting building materials. It all looked none too safe but the builders seemed unperturbed, even on the highest walls.

Everywhere was a hive of activity. With round wooden mallets and steel chisels, masons chipped away at limestone blocks, shaping them to match the wooden patterns they had been given to ensure consistency and a perfect shape. Carpenters sawed huge timbers, while others chiselled joints and decorative features. Each tradesman worked on a small piece of a giant, three-dimensional jigsaw, which needed to fit together perfectly. Some worked under open-sided thatched shelters, others in the open. A man wandered amongst the craftsmen carrying a basket of newly sharpened chisels, exchanging them for dulled ones. At first, it looked chaotic, but as Tom watched he saw that it was well organised. Fascinated, he again wished he had a camera.

A few better-dressed men walked through the huge site, pointing, questioning, and giving instructions as they consulted scrolls of building plans. Men carried heavy baskets of mortar up ladders on their shoulders, sometimes waiting, holding it there to allow portions to be taken by tradesmen cementing blocks in place. The position of each stone was checked, levelled and tapped into place, only to be checked again with a plumb line. A woman with a bucket of drinking water and a ladle walked amongst the masons, offering to quench their thirsts. One or two others brought food, presumably for their friends or family members. Almost all were shabbily dressed and most were wearing short hooded cloaks covering their heads and shoulders. Children gathered the stone spoil in baskets, taking it to the building to infill the walls. Nothing was going to waste. Even wood shavings were used to maintain warming fires and by blacksmiths to rekindle their forges.

Few people stopped to look at Tom as visiting strangers were frequent. Being dressed differently attracted no more than a casual glance. Curious about the stranger, two little urchins followed him for a few yards through the clatter of mallets and chisels until he turned and smiled at them. They hesitated, exchanged glances and ran away. Their pale, grubby appearances made Tom feel sorry for them, wondering what their lives held in store. Not much, he thought.

As he made his way to what would eventually become the main entrance of the cathedral, he was fascinated to see the construction of the north transept, perfectly matching that of the southern structure. He could now envisage what the main entrance of the cathedral would have looked like before the north transept came down, never to be rebuilt. Forgetting the year, Tom had expected to see St Mary's Church a short distance away, then remembered it had been built much later.

He spotted a monk looking at an open scroll. Standing next to him was a man Tom thought to be a building supervisor of some kind. Staying back a little, he could see the drawing and was surprised to note that the main tower and four transept towers were to have spires, but he knew they would never be erected.

"Excuse me, could you tell me where I will find Abbot Blackthorne?"

"Who wants to know?" the monk curtly responded.

Speaking slowly, Tom looked him in the eye and said, "My name is Thomas Harrison, and I am here on the official business of Rauin, King John's physician. I have a letter under royal seal for the abbot. Will you please tell me where I can find him?"

Tom was never comfortable at not telling the exact truth but had decided to do and say whatever it would take to get the children home. He had no time for argument or debate with a nosy, officious monk.

"He's to be found at the priory annexe over to the south."

The monk pointed in the direction of a place Tom knew as Cherry Hill, where he saw the remains of a timber castle with other smaller buildings nearby.

Tom gave a curt, "Thank you" and walked towards the annexe. On reaching the large timber building, a young monk politely asked his business. Tom explained as before.

"Then I shall take you to him. You are dressed strangely, sir. May I ask where you are from?"

Without thinking, Tom almost said, "Here," then quickly answered, "Foreign parts."

"I thought as much. You will find Abbot Blackthorne a kindly man. He means well but struggles to influence the unsavoury ways of some of my older peers. They cause him much distress and frustration. I hope he has time to see you."

As they reached a heavy wooden door, Tom was asked to wait while the monk went to see if the abbot was available.

"Please tell him I don't have a lot of time, and that I have a letter for him from King John's physician."

The monk acknowledged with a slow lowering of his head, revealing a perfect tonsure. It was only minutes before he returned with hurried steps and a smile. "You are lucky, Mr Harrison. Abbot Blackthorne is free for a few minutes, but he states that he must return to holy administrative matters very soon. Please follow me."

The interior of the building was poorly lit and apart from an occasional cross hanging on bare timber-panelled walls, it was dull and uninspiring. Tom was led to a modest room where the abbot sat at a table littered with documents and scrolls. As Tom entered, he rose from his seat in greeting. The monk discretely stepped backwards, quietly closing the door as he left.

"Welcome, Mr Harrison. I understand you have a letter for me from the king's physician?" He gestured for Tom to sit before returning to his desk. "The letter, if you please."

Tom nervously handed it over, while thanking the abbot for his time.

Facing each other across a thick wooden desk, Tom was silent while Abbot Blackthorne inspected the seal, opened Rauin's letter and read it. Tom was surprised, having expected small talk by way of introduction before getting to business. However, he was relieved that no questions were asked.

"The letter is indeed from the king's physician. He vouches for your association and good character while urging me to offer you the utmost assistance. However, I must tell you that the king is not popular with the church at this time, so if your request involves others here, you may meet with some reluctance. We live in troubled times, Mr Harrison. I tell you truly, there is much concern for the future. Only recently, Sir Falkes de Bréauté sacked and destroyed our modest castle just yonder. Much confusion and stress remains amongst our people as the barons continue to battle, but I digress. Since this letter is addressed to me, I am obligated by my position and faith to assist you. What is it you need my help with, Mr Harrison?"

"You may remember that Rauin visited you some days ago and was given a potion by the monks to help cure King John's illness?"

"Yes, I remember him well. Did the potion help the king?"

"I'm sorry to say, no. There was no doubt about the potion's effectiveness, but it was accidentally lost in the river while returning to Bishop's Lynn."

"I am sorry to hear that, it is most unfortunate. So you would like to ask for more, am I correct?"

Tom considered it prudent to say yes but hesitated before explaining further. "Abbot Blackthorne, the monks here are very knowledgeable in medication and potions. They gave Rauin instructions on how to administer the liquid, along with a private warning."

Blackthorne was surprised and interrupted to test Tom's knowledge of the secret. "And what was the warning?"

"He was told that after seven days the potion would change its properties and no longer be a cure and that it would have a strange mysterious effect."

"What effect might that be?"

"As difficult as it might be to believe, it was said that, if smelled, it will transport a person back in time. However, that person will eventually return to the present at a time dependent on how much was sniffed. But if it is tasted, the person will never return." Tom had expected Blackthorne to scoff or make a disparaging comment, but after a moment of thought, he replied.

"You are correct, Mr Harrison. I am also aware of this. There was a friar here who smelled the aged remains of a similar potion and disappeared for two days. On his return, he claimed to have found himself in the time of King Arthur as he fought with Danish invaders. Naturally, everyone thought him mad or intoxicated. In frustration that nobody would believe him, he sniffed again, intending to return with artefacts as proof of his transportation. Which he eventually did. However, since that time not all has gone well for the poor man or the concoctor of the potion. You see, when Friar De Loy sniffed a second time, he asked for witnesses. Those watching saw him disappear as if by magic. Consequently, Monk Ambrose, who prepared the potion, was, and still is, being held for wizardry. As is Friar De Loy now he has returned. So, Mr Harrison, the monks, friars and myself are sworn to secrecy over the potion, at least until it has been properly investigated. I may suggest the only reason Master Rauin was told is because of his intimate association with King John. Can you imagine the problems if the king were to disappear in such a manner?"

With some amusement, Tom believed there must be times when King John would like to disappear. Maybe now would be one of them.

"And how are you involved in this mystery, Mr Harrison? Are you also sworn to secrecy?"

"No, I have not been sworn to secrecy, but I understand the need for discretion and consider that it's no one else's business so would not tell. Nor would I betray Rauin's confidence." Tom tried not to reveal too much, but he could see the Abbot was still inquisitive.

"Mr Harrison, your dress is unusual, as is your manner of speech. Where are you from?"

Tom pondered the question.

"Well, Mr Harrison?"

He decided to tell the truth, believing it would go no further. "I am here because in the year 1920 I found the container of potion that Rauin lost, and I sniffed its contents. I am from the future, where things are very different."

The Abbot's mouth dropped open and his eyes widened. Staring intently at Tom, he leaned forwards while mulling over this stunning revelation.

"I live in a village not far from here. I found the potion, which had been buried for centuries. I hid it in a barn, but village children found it, tasted the potion, and were transported back to this time. Right now they are in a convent in Bishop's Lynn. The children, two of them are my own, disappeared without a trace, and naturally, we desperately want them back home. None of the parents know where the children are or even if they are alive. When I sniffed the potion, I had no idea that I would also be transported back to this time where, as luck would have it, I unexpectedly found the children. Well…to be honest, they found me."

There was silence for half a minute while the abbot, deep in thought, stared at the ceiling. "It seems your mission here is twofold, Mr Harrison. You would like to return to Bishop's Lynn with a fresh potion for the king and no doubt an antidote to save your children?"

"Yes, exactly."

"Leave this with me, Mr Harrison, while I see what can be done. You may return after noon today, once I have spoken with Monk Ambrose."

Tom stood, thanked the abbot, and left. The next four hours seemed like an eternity as he wandered the medieval streets of Ely. Respectable solid buildings and houses stood within walking distance of the cathedral site, while hundreds of others, which to Tom looked like thatched timber shacks, were spread at the outskirts. Few looked solid enough to stand for long. Yet it occurred to him that families of the masons, carpenters and labourers must live there for all of their lives. No doubt for many generations too, since the cathedral took more than three hundred years to complete. Unavoidably, he found himself trying to visualise the features of Ely as it would be in 1920, comparing locations, streets, and the market square. Not an easy task, but he saw the beginning of the layout. As late morning approached, he became hungry and found an inn where he could eat and drink while waiting for noon.

The abbot was in his chamber. "You intrigue me, Mr Harrison. We have much to discuss about your time. May I ask where will you stay this evening?"

"I've made no plans yet, probably at an inn."

"You will have difficulty finding refuge in the town. I invite you to stay here as my guest. We could spend the evening conversing."

"Thank you, that's very kind, but what did you discover about an antidote…and of course, the king's cure?"

"I see your priorities, Mr Harrison, but first let me address the cure. I regret it is unlikely that a repeat of the potion could be made ready for many days, possibly even weeks. You see, it contains certain ingredients which take many days to ferment before the final preparation can be achieved. They come from rare herbs, which the nuns at Denny Abbey cultivate. The plant has special properties and must be treated with great care. Denny Abbey lies some miles to the south of here. Even if the potion could be reproduced, as you know, there are only a few days when it is effective for its true purpose."

"Can anything be done to get the herbs here quickly?"

"It will take much of a day to walk to the abbey. The nuns may not have the ingredients available, and if they have, they will drive a hard bargain before parting with them. Not to mention the Templar Knights, who visit there often, so our monks are reluctant to go for fear of mistreatment. Even the nuns live in fear of losing their chastity."

"But I can go! If I can borrow a horse, I would be there and back in a day."

"Have you encountered the Temple Knights before, Mr Harrison?"

"Yes, I know they can be arrogant and aggressive, but I have found that mentioning Sir Guillaume de Charters, their Grand Master, works wonders in settling them down."

The abbot smiled in surprise. "Do you know Sir Guillaume? A devil's disciple if ever I saw one."

"I have not met him, but I'm aware of his position from Rauin and some of the knights.

"You attended the knights?"

"Not exactly, I have treated some of their horses' ailments."

"We certainly have much to discuss, Mr Harrison."

Tom fidgeted in his seat. "What about the antidote?"

"I'm afraid there is little or no chance of ever producing one. A need for it has never been perceived, and the friar advises me that it would take many months or even years to develop, if it can be produced at all. We must remember that it is a side effect you wish to address, a complete accident. Also, let us not forget that those involved with it are currently restrained."

"But there must be some way of getting the children back?"

"Not without a miracle. I fear your only hope is for the effect of the potion to weaken over time, but of course, it is in the hands of God. Therefore, we shall pray for your children's continued safety."

Tom was disappointed and inwardly scoffed at the offer of prayers, leaving him with little optimism. "May I talk to the monk myself to discuss what could be done?"

"You may, but I assure you it will give you no comfort as he is most emphatic of there being no chance of an antidote. Please understand that the original potion took more than a year and a half of experimental endeavour to achieve. It was only luck that a portion was available when your physician friend visited us." The abbot held Tom's gaze and gently shook his head. "I fear its power is so strong that it cannot be undone."

Tom stared at the floor in despair.

Showing considerastion, Blackthorne waited before asking when he would return to Bishop's Lynn.

Tom slowly lifted his head and replied, "It's too late to go today, so I may as well leave tomorrow morning."

"Then I shall arrange a sleeping chamber for you here. If you return at dusk, we shall eat and talk longer. I am most intrigued and would discuss your times with you." Then smiling he added, "Now don't go disappearing before this evening."

Tom spent the afternoon by the river arranging his passage back to Bishop's Lynn. When asking after Mr Martin, he discovered that George had already left with a cargo of eels. He eventually came across a skipper who was willing and needed a crewman, as his previous man had decided to stay in Ely.

He was a stocky man with a short neck who seemed to have difficulty facing forwards, so looked at Tom in diagonal glances. His dress was poor by the standards of other skippers, and it was clear he used the fullness of his shoulder cloak to conceal a modest hump on his back. Tom thought of The Hunchback of Notre Dame and was not entirely happy, hoping this man was trustworthy. When asked his name, he replied that he was known as Hutch. After some discussion, it was agreed they would leave at dawn. There would be no fare as Tom would work his passage. Hutch warned him not to be late.

Passing the cathedral at dusk Tom saw the stonemasons and carpenters still hard at work. He introduced himself at the priory door saying the abbot was expecting him. A monk took him to a spacious hall hung with tapestries and where a large welcoming fire blazed. Two long wooden tables stood parallel in the middle of the room, each with benched seating along their outer sides. He had not been there long before two monks hurried in, one with a tray of metal jugs and the other with a tray of goblets. As soon as they were correctly placed on a table, they hurried away. Moments later, they returned to repeat the process at the far table, again leaving in the same hurried fashion. Next, a much younger monk appeared. Taking his time, he set the tables with metal plates, spoons, and knives. Tom was enjoying the warmth of the fire when the abbot entered.

"Ah, Mr Harrison, I am pleased you are here. Come, we shall dine in my chamber and leave this rabble to intoxicate themselves once more." He led the way to a comfortable but not opulent room. A fire burned brightly and a table was already set for two. After inviting Tom to sit, he asked how the afternoon had been for him.

"I went to the river and arranged my passage back to Bishop's Lynn. I need to be at the quay by daybreak tomorrow."

"Good. I am regretful that we could not assist you further in your quest. What will you do now?" the abbot said as he offered a goblet of wine.

"I don't know. I'll consider it on my way back down the river."

"Is there anything the king's physician can do for you?"

"No, we have already discussed it. It was him who recommended I speak to you."

Tom didn't say that by the time he returned, the king and Rauin would have left for Newark.

"Mmm, I would suggest that you be cautious with those river folk as not all have savoury reputations. Pray tell me more about the year you have come from."

Tom wondered where to begin. "Well, the first thing of interest to you will be that in the twentieth century your new cathedral will stand magnificently in the Isles of Eels and be seen for many miles. It will be called 'The Ship of The Fens' standing tall over the flat lands, like a large ship at sea.

The abbot smiled with pleasure.

"These great wetlands will be drained in the1600s to provide the richest farmland in the country. There will only be rivers and drainage channels left to remind us of the great wetlands. The north transept of the cathedral will collapse and never be rebuilt. A few centuries later the building will be defaced by a man named Oliver Cromwell and his army."

Shocked, the abbot stared at him in amazement.

"Also, I believe the cathedral is designed to have several spires, but when it's finished it will have no spires on the main tower or transepts. The central column will eventually collapse and be replaced with a magnificent octagonal tower."

"Fascinating, but if I may play the devil's advocate. How may I know that what you say true? I would certainly not have the means to verify them. You wear strange clothes and speak words in a way I have not heard before. How do I know you are not from foreign parts, and perhaps on some other mission?"

"Abbot Blackthorne, I understand your concern, but if you believe the power of the potion when it is old, then you must surely believe that I, at least, could be telling the truth. I have no reason to mislead you."

"Forgive me for being a doubting Thomas…and please pardon my pun. I do not intend to offend, but it would give me comfort to know the proof of that which you speak."

Tom rummaged in his pocket to find a few coins and described them as he had done to Rauin. Blackthorne inspected them with interest before handing them back, but his doubts lingered in his expression.

Tom remembered the newspaper and took it from his rucksack. "In my time, news of all types is printed on many pages by the thousand. Huge machines do it in only a few hours, to produce what we call newspapers.

They are sold to men and women. Almost everyone knows how to read in my time. They learn about local, national, and international events, sport, the current price of livestock and even tell the weather in coming days."

The abbot was amazed. "But apart from the regular seasons that seem impossible beyond a few hours, or a day, although if we are observant, wildlife will often warn us of coming inclement weather."

"In the twentieth century, it's possible, I assure you. Look, this newspaper is dated just one week ago in my time. Do you see?"

Tom paused as the abbot took the newspaper, first inspecting the fineness and size of the paper, feeling it between finger and thumb before acknowledging the date.

"How often are these documents produced?"

"Some, in the cities, are printed every day, while here in the country, once each week is normal."

"Good Lord above!" The abbot crossed himself.

"What is it?" Tom asked.

"See here, a sketch which claims to be of Ely Cathedral but it is most unlike any I have seen on the plans."

The newspaper was placed open on the table. "Abbot, this is how the cathedral looks in the early twentieth century. It appears different to you because the spires are not there. As I said before, they were never completed. The north transept near the main entrance collapsed and was never rebuilt. That's why it looks a little out of balance. Then, other extensions were added over the next few centuries. The main part of the cathedral will not be finished for another one hundred and fifty years from now." Tom paused to take a breath. "Look, it says plans are being made for a carol service in Ely cathedral before Christmas. See here, it says the date of this paper, October 1924."

"I must say, Mr Harrison, as hard as this is to comprehend, I am inclined to believe you really are from another time. However, these printed words are not familiar to me."

"It's because our language has developed and changed over the centuries. People from my time will have difficulty understanding your written words too."

Blackthorne was fascinated as he continued to scour the newspaper. Tom was pleased when food was brought. Later, a replacement jug of red wine arrived. It was obvious that Tom was expected to assist in draining it, as his pleas not to refill his goblet were jovially ignored. He had not drunk this much wine since he was on leave in France during the Great War. The rest of the evening was spent explaining events leading to the twentieth century, and to answering an endless stream of questions.

There were long pauses when the abbot struggled to comprehend. Gently sucking air through his teeth, he then asked. "What of our king? Do you know how and when this situation with the barons and the French will be settled?"

Tom tried to sidestep the issue. "There will be many wars and much animosity between England, France, and the Vatican for centuries to come."

"You do not surprise me, but what of our king and this current situation where he has turned the Vatican, the French, the barons, landowners and even the common people against him?"

Tom's head was light from the wine, encouraging him to be less cautious, saying, "Abbot, if I tell you, may I have your solemn promise made with your hand on the Holy Bible that you will not tell another living soul."

Shocked, but without questioning, Blackthorne agreed.

"As it happens, you will only need to keep it secret for a few days as I'm sure the news will quickly reach you. The king will travel from Bishop's Lynn by an inland route to Newark where he will die on the 19th of this month from his illness, which I know as dysentery."

With eyes wide open and with his mouth ajar, the Abbot leaned forwards. "What is to become of his court and entourage?"

"Templar Knights will take the wagons on a shorter route across the Washes, but they will never arrive in Newark. The tide will flood their way. Some will be drowned and the crown jewels will be lost forever...or so history books will record."

"I detect your doubt. What do you mean?"

"Well, you must know the reputation of the Templars. Even up to my own time those jewels have never been found. So who knows, maybe there was a plot to hide the truth, and the jewels were never in those wagons?"

"My dear God, we live in troubled times. First, the unscrupulous William Longchamp is placed here in Ely by a doubtful king, who to this day fights with Rome. Now the Templar Knights may seek to rob him. When will this madness end? You must surely know our king is secretly known as Bad King John. But this is too much!" The abbot hesitated, realising he had criticized the king. "You must not quote me, Mr Harrison. You understand this conversation is between us alone. The wine has a habit of loosening our tongues."

"Don't worry, abbot, my lips are sealed, and if I tell

someone in my own time, it won't matter, will it?" Both men smiled.

"I find it hard to believe what will happen to the king's wealth. Surely some must have been recovered?"

Tom noticed that he didn't seem concerned about the king's death. "No. They say it was all lost in the tidal surge, but who knows for sure? It could have been buried for recovery later or hidden in a monastery or church. I think Ely cathedral would be an ideal place. Maybe within wall cavities while it is being built, or at the abbey in Bury St Edmunds. All I can say is that shortly after the king's death, the Knights Templar in England will become extremely rich."

Although Blackthorne was intrigued and wanted to know more, he could see that Tom had difficulty keeping his eyes open, so offered to escort him to his sleeping chamber. Tom was unsteady on his feet and not totally aware of where he was being taken. They entered a small, cold room with no window. A wall candle, providing a dim flickering light, burned on its ledge. The only furniture was a stool and a simple bed on which lay a straw-filled mattress and a woollen blanket. A wooden cross hung on a wall.

"I hope you will be comfortable, Mr Harrison. If you need anything, please call to the novice monk who sleeps next door. His name is Timothy. I will tell him to attend you as may be required." Then, hesitating, he looked back from the doorway. "Must you leave in the morning? I mentioned you to, Bishop Eustace, and he would so like to meet with you."

Knowing that waiting for a reversal of the potion was pointless, Tom quietly answered. "Yes, I'm afraid I have to go. Perhaps another time."

Tom flopped onto the bed, stretched, then rolled onto his back to watch the ceiling slowly rotate. He tried to focus on the candle but eventually gave up because it wouldn't remain still, seeming to wander around the wall. Hardly noticing the discomfort of the mattress, he was pleased just to lie down. His last thoughts were, *What the devil did they put in that wine? I hope I'll wake on time.*

It was dark when Tom opened his eyes. There was no spark of light as the candle had burned to its stub. Disorientated, he was a little afraid and it took a few moments to remember where he was. There was a bad taste in his mouth from the wine, but he was surprised to find he had no hangover, and pleased to know he was still in the early thirteenth century. It took a minute or two for him to find the door. As he opened it, the dim light from oil lamps in the hall filtered into the room. While his memory of how he got there was vague, he looked up and down the passage trying to determine the way out. After a few minutes of exploration, he found himself standing beside the main door. The sun had not yet risen and there was a deep blue-greyness in the twilight clouds. Feeling pleased with himself, he muttered, "I might have been a bit tipsy last night, but the old body clock still works."

Chapter 22

Even at this early hour, workmen were arriving at the cathedral site. A few small fires burned where workers stood rubbing their hands and stamping their feet, while others drank a steaming hot brew of some kind. Tom made his way down one of the slippery, muddy slopes to the river. Unloading had already begun and more boats waited their turn. Now in the grey dim light of dawn, it took only minutes to locate Hutch, who had been waiting to leave.

"A few minutes more and I'd a gone without you!"

"What, without a crew?" Tom grinned.

Seeing the annoyance in Hutch's face, Tom laughed to suggest he was joking. He suspected the man may not have an amiable disposition. Hutch watched as Tom dropped his rucksack into the bow of the boat.

"Okay, when are we off?"

"What is this 'okay'? You speak strangely, sir."

Tom ignored the comment. "Shall I release the moorings or lower the boom first?"

Once the slack was taken in from the boom and the line secured, they were under way with the skipper at the helm. Little was said as they watched the distant sun rise through gaps in the cloud. There would be little for

Tom to do while they sailed, so he settled by the mast. As much had happened in Ely, he sat quietly updating his notes.

Hutch watched with interest. After passing Little Port and then South Island he called, "Here, you take the tiller a while, Mr Harrison. Keep her to the outside of bends. The insides can be shallow, depending on the time of the tide, and take care when passing others."

Having completed his notes, Tom was pleased to have something constructive to do.

Hutch sat where Tom had been. Soon the rucksack caught his eye and his curiosity got the better of him. Tom watched as Hutch picked it up.

"That's private!"

"Oh yeah, and what's so private about it?"

"If I told you it wouldn't be private. There's nothing to interest you in there."

"We'll just see about that!" Sniggering, Hutch made his way aft as he opened the rucksack. Tom let go of the tiller arm and quickly moved towards him. Hutch pulled out a dagger and pointed it at Tom, hesitating just out of reach.

"Don't come any closer, Mr Harrison, or I'll slit your throat."

"You wouldn't dare. Look, what's in there is private and some is the king's business. If you harm me or steal anything, the Templar Knights will hunt you down and kill you."

Hutch laughed. "Nobody knows you are here, so I could slaughter you right now and you'd not be missed.

"The abbot at Ely knows I'm with you," Tom lied.

"To hell with the abbot! When I arrive at the river ports and Bishop's Lynn alone, I will say my crewman stayed in Ely and I'd be believed. They will only need to ask around to find him, and he will confirm my story. Should your abbot have something to add, I would say you didn't show at the appointed time, so not wanting to miss the tide, I sailed without you. I could run you through here and now, take your pouch and your sack, put ballast stones in your shirt and roll you over the side. You would sink to the bottom never to be found, and the fish would enjoy a good meal." Hutch laughed as he faked a lunge towards Tom who stepped sharply back.

"I could dive over the side now, report your activity to the king's knights, who would find you for sure. Remember you are well known on the river, so they would have little difficulty. After posting a small reward, you would be theirs within a day."

Tom had bluffed, but he couldn't leave his rucksack with Hutch. By this time the vessel had drifted sideways and the bow had wedged into thick reeds along the bank.

Hutch pulled out Tom's school notebooks and clumsily flipped the pages. "What manner of document is this?"

"Just notes I make to record daily events, like a diary."

Hutch threw them aside then produced the ball-like container. "And pray what is this charming object?"

"That's no business of yours!"

"Everything is my business today, mister!"

"If you must know, it holds sweet-tasting nectar to freshen your mouth and please the taste buds. The monks at Ely made it for me to take after meals."

Hutch removed the lid.

"I don't think there is much left but you can try a little, and see for yourself."

Hutch sneered. "I shall, I shall." Seconds later he

was inspecting the thick treacle on the end of his finger before sucking it clean. "Mmm" was the only sound he made. Then looking pained, he put the flask down and sat heavily on the gunnels. Raising his hands to his temples and pressing to ease the pain, he grimaced and disappeared.

Tom was unable to prevent a wide grin. He felt a little sorry for the man, but consoled himself knowing Hutch was not dead, just "somewhere else," and chuckled as he imagined Hutch's confusion when he arrived at wherever he was going.

Amusement and relief quickly turned to concern as Tom considered how he would get to Bishop's Lynn. He had learned how the vessel was handled while under sail to and from Ely. If the wind didn't fail or change direction, he could manage the craft back to Denver. After repacking his rucksack, he pushed out from the reeds with a pole, ducking as the sail caught the breeze to bring the boom across the vessel. Taking the tiller, Tom steered a meandering course north. Remembering his journey south, he had a good idea of where he was. A few boats passed him heading south. Occasionally a skipper called to him. Tom didn't reply, just offered a friendly wave and a smile, hoping they would think he was new on the river.

It was not too long before the tide began to slow and turn, to run back towards Ely. As late afternoon approached, the wind barely rippled the sail. Knowing he wouldn't be able to go any further, Tom steered to the starboard bank. After securing the bow to a small willow tree, he collected his belongings and set off along the bank to Denver. Going was easy, mostly level and well-trodden by boatmen and horses. Making good time, he arrived at the inn just before dark. A few river craft were tied up close by.

There was no wind now and dampness in the air was beginning to chill the early evening. A shroud of grey smoke slowly drifted horizontally over the buildings, making no effort to reach the steel grey sky after struggling to leave the inn's chimney. Two working horses stood patiently tethered to a fence. The thatch on the building had grown several generations of moss, making the inn look poorly maintained.

When Tom entered, he coughed. The air was blue, and the smell of smoke was intense, causing his eyes to smart. With a lack of draft, smoke drifted from the open fire where lumps of peat smouldered. Two old men sat by the hearth, trying in vain to warm themselves while a group of other men sat around the long table with tankards of ale. They turned to see who had entered.

Tom's "good evening" received no response and they returned to their conversations.

"Oh, you're back?" the landlady said with an edge of sarcasm.

Tom was taken aback and wanted to say, "No, it's a wooden replica of myself," but thought better of it, asking himself why landladies were all so rude in these times. "Yes, I'm afraid so. Do you have a room?"

"You must be joking. Some of these men have to share as it is. If you want to stay, it will have to be in the stables or the barn-like afore!"

Tom accepted. Two of the men at the table laughed, making him feel even less welcome.

"Stables are the best place for anyone on the king's business," someone said, deliberately loud enough for Tom to hear.

"Or the pig sty," someone else added. They laughed again.

Tom was surprised that he had been remembered. Although offended, he ignored the comments and ordered a tankard of ale which he took to the fireplace. As he stared at the smouldering peat, he wondered if it was safe to stay there without a skipper to keep an eye on things.

"Don't worry yourself about them at the table. Where is your master?" one of the old men asked.

"I was with a man named Hutch, but we stopped a few miles back and he went ashore. I waited a while but he didn't return, so I walked the last few miles."

The landlady overheard. "You want to watch out for that old bastard Hutch. He's a bloody rogue if ever I saw one, 'e still owes me for his last stay. Cleared off afore sparrows-fart, he did."

"Don't worry, Maud. We'll make sure he sees you right," one of the skippers called.

The old men looked at Tom. "So, you are the man who's running errands for King John, are you?"

"Not exactly, I'm a friend of his physician. I went to Ely to fetch medicine from the monks."

"That's what we 'eard. Not much goes unnoticed hereabouts, and news don't take long to get around.

Tom chuckled, thinking not much had changed over the years.

"Skipper Martin told us about you when he passed through yesterday. You're not from around here, are you?"

"No. Foreign parts."

"Trouble is, that king o'yours is bleeding us dry with his bloody taxes, so he's none too popular. Nor is anyone what's with him."

Maud busied herself lighting candles and oil lamps about the room.

"Not as bad as that old bastard Longchamp. A proper bully he was when it were tax collecting time. Have his men bash you about he would if you couldn't pay. Then steal a cow or a pig or two for their trouble," the other old man added.

They nodded to each other in agreement. At that moment Maud passed by.

"What's to eat today, Maud?"

"Pike and eel Pie. Old Will'm here caught a couple of big'uns, so he's on a few free ales just now. Says he'll try and get a duck or two on the morrow. That'll be a treat."

The old man raised his tankard in acknowledgement and smiled with pride, revealing a single yellowing tooth in the front of his bottom jaw.

Tom dragged a stool from the end of the table to sit with the old men. "My name is Thomas. Everyone calls me Tom."

The old men didn't offer their names but the one Maud had called William spoke: "So what'a you up to now, Thomas?"

"I'm on my way back to Bishop's Lynn."

"Your old king has gone from there now. You better go look for him afore he gets lost."

Both men laughed.

"You are probably right, but I have some other things to do there."

"So how you gonna get there?"

"Walk or get a lift on one of the boats, I suppose."

Before he could add anything more, William called across the room to the boatmen. "Man 'ere needs passage to Bishop's in the mornin'."

"What's it worth?"

Tom couldn't tell who had called out. "I'll pay for your bed and food here tonight."

"Buy me a tankard of ale and it's a deal!" A short skinny man with a grey beard rose from the table.

"Done!" Tom said, reaching to shake his hand.

"Me name's, Richard. Named after a proper king, I were."

"Hello, Richard, I'm Tom. I suppose you will be leaving at first light."

"No, not until the tide turns, unless there be a strong wind from the south to help fight the run of it."

Tom sat at the table to eat when his pike and eel pie arrived. He sensed these men had many questions, especially as he was in the service of the king, or so they believed. He explained that he was not as important or as close to the royal court as they might think, telling them he had never actually met King John. They seemed more accepting of him now. Diverting their conversation away from himself, he asked about their work and the new cathedral.

As Maud took his bowl away, Tom asked if she had an apple or any other fruit.

"No, that's it for today – unless you mean the fruit o' me loins, an my old man'd kill you if you try to get near 'em."

Everyone laughed aloud while Tom gave an embarrassed smile. It had been an eventful day and he was tired from the long walk. After a while, he excused himself for his bed. Picking up the blanket Maud had provided, he made his way to the stable.

"Being one of the king's men, I'd have thought you would give him a room, Maud," one man said.

"That's the very reason he's in the stable. Anyway, I'd have to turn one of you lot out." Then, with a big grin and raising her voice, she asked, "Is anyone 'ere volunteering to give up their nice warm bed for this 'ere king's gentleman?"

The men fell silent.

She walked away, pleased with herself.

When she had gone someone muttered, "She's in good form today, a bit sharp though."

Tom was not feeling well when he padded hay into a comfortable bed. Lying there for a while and gradually feeling more unwell, he knew he would soon vomit. Rushing, he barely made it past the stable door before his pike and eel pie splashed at his feet. Then, after taking a few deep breaths of the cold night air, he felt a little better. Shivering, he returned to his straw bed and the welcoming blanket. Sleep didn't come easy, but when he woke it was early morning. Before opening his eyes, and now feeling much better, he considered the contents of the pie.

Chapter 23

It was with a start that Tom discovered he was no longer in the stable at the Denver inn but back in his barn in 1924. His sense of urgency to reach Bishop's Lynn was still with him, and he swore his disappointment aloud. He had to return to the 1200s as soon as possible. But first, he would talk to Dora. Rising to his feet and steadying himself for a moment, he crossed the yard. The house didn't have its usual homely glow. All the curtains were closed and no smoke was coming from the chimney. He found the door locked, which was unusual; he couldn't remember the last time it had been. He lifted a flower pot by the door to find a key. The house was exactly as he had left it, except for two letters on the doormat. Obviously, Dora had not been there since he had left. He wondered who had locked the door. Locking doors and closing windows was never necessary before, and where was Dora?

Previously, he had assumed she had gone out for the evening, but now he was seriously worried. It was not like her to go off without leaving a note of some kind. But there was nothing, no clue to where she may have gone. Once again, Tom was faced with an agonising decision. Should he return to the children or raise the alarm that Dora was missing?

Knowing the children were safe in the convent, he decided to delay his return. First, he went to his mother's cottage hoping to find Dora. He knocked and entered in a single movement. Ma was bent over the stove stoking last night's ashes for hot embers to help start today's fire.

Without rising, she looked back to see who had entered. "Where a you bin? People a bin a-look'n all over for you, my lad? The police have even bin'ere with a lot of questions."

"Why? What's going on? And where is Dora?"

"You might well ask, young man! You mean you don't know?"

"Don't know what? Come on, Ma, where is she?"

"You better sit down then."

Tom didn't want to sit but knew his mother wouldn't say anything until he did. She continued poking the fire, placing newspaper and small pieces of kindling on the embers. When they flared, she put larger pieces of wood on top. Ma was quite aware that she was holding Tom in suspense. "When it gets going I'll put a bit a coal on." Only then did she take one of the kitchen chairs and sit across the table to face Tom.

Tom tapped his fingers on the table, "Come on Ma, where's Dora?"

"Well, to tell you the truth, they found her a-floatin face down in the river yesterday."

"What!" Wide-eyed, Tom leaned towards her.

"I know, I know. We are all shocked about it, a terrible business."

"Dear God, what happened?"

"We don't rightly know yet, not till the coroner has done his report…an the police want'a talk to you afore they say anything. So don't you go a-clearing off a'gin."

"No, Ma, but what do the police *think* happened?"

"We can't be too sure. They're not saying much just now, but they seem to think it's all a bit strange. They say there were no signs of a struggle on her, so thinking it might be suicide, but they can't find no note. They said there's always a note when it's suicide. Anyway, they wanna talk to you."

Tom was silent while he struggled to comprehend. Then quietly he said, "I suppose I'd better go and talk to them." He felt weak, his hands trembled and he was cold. His life was becoming more upsetting and stressful by the hour. Thinking, *It never used to be this complicated, not even during the war. What the hell happened to Dora? I hope the police can tell us. They'll want to question me and to know where I've been?* He didn't want to lie but hoped it would buy some time if he maintained his story about visiting his cousin in London.

"Has Dora gone, Ma? Is she's really dead? I can't believe it!" His tears welled and he knew he still loved her, even though their relationship had long since been strained. It dawned on him that he had all but lost his children, and now his wife was gone too. How was he going to tell Susie and Alfie their mother had died?

Ma made a pot of tea, then called up the narrow wooden stairs to tell Peter a mug was waiting for him too. "Oh, and Tom's 'ere," she added.

Two minutes later, the door creaked open when Peter entered.

Tom was pensive and sat in a fixed, unseeing stare at the hot coals beneath the kettle.

Peter greeted him quietly whilst seating himself at the table. "Hello. I suppose Ma has told you about Dora. I'm very sorry, mate."

"Hello, Pete. Thanks…yes, she has, but I don't know what to make of it."

"It's all very queer, a bloody mystery if you ask me. Poor Dora. Where have you been these last few days, Tom?"

Tom looked into his brother's eyes with a stare that said, *Don't ask. I can't tell you in front of Ma.*

Peter got the message, whilst Ma's curiosity got the better of her. "Yes, where have you been?"

Tom moved in his seat and looked away.

"Well come on then, where have you been? You should have been here, she persisted.

"Okay, okay, I'll tell you. But you have to swear that you won't utter a word to anyone. Not ever!"

"I can't see why not. It can't be that bad. Not after what's happened to your Dora.

Tom's frustration was beginning to show. "It's not *that bad*, Ma. It's not bad at all, it's deadly serious and unless you give me your solemn promise not to say a word to anyone, I won't tell you." He knew he would eventually regret speaking to his mother that way.

Ma rocked her head from side to side and pinched her lips, before struggling to say, "All right then, I won't say a word to anyone!"

"Good…and you have to mean it, Ma! Peter already knows and I'll tell you what I've told him, maybe perhaps a bit more."

"Knows what?"

"That I've found Alfie, Susie and the other missing children."

Staring at Tom, she placed her hand over her heart while her mouth rested half-open.

Tom explained about the container and the potion.

He said where he had put it, adding that the children must have found it. "Of course, I didn't know then what it would do. I sniffed it to see what it was, and in less than half a minute I fell unconscious. When I woke up, I had been transported to Bishop's Lynn, Kings Lynn to you, Ma, back in the time of King John, only a day or two before he lost his treasure in the Wash.

"You're mad, my boy, completely bonkers!"

"And that's why you can't tell anyone, Ma. If you do, I'll get locked up in the madhouse. The police'll believe I'm involved in the kids' disappearance and be all over me. Not only that, just imagine the uproar in the village. You tell one person, and within ten minutes the whole village'll know. Our lives won't be worth living!

"Anyway, after a day I found myself transported back here again. Can't you see, Ma? I had to go back again to find out if the kids were there. So I sniffed the stuff again and went back. Then, almost by accident, I found Alfie and Susie. Well, to be honest, they found me and took me to the other missing kids. Now I've got to find a way of getting them home again."

Ma stared at him in astonishment.

"Like I said, just imagine what would happen if the village people knew what I've told you. Then again, most people wouldn't believe it anyway. They'd think you were off your rocker too."

"I'm not surprised!" Ma smirked.

"You simply can't say a word because there might not be a way of getting the children back. The parents would be upset and get false hopes. Not to mention blaming me. The only good thing is that it would let Peter off the hook. I have to go again, and I need you to cover for me when questions are asked about where I am."

Ma scratched her head. "If this is true, and you have managed to come back, how come the children can't?"

"Because you only come back if you sniff the stuff. If you taste it like they did, you stay there."

Tom explained about Rauin, how he had lost the flask and what the monks had told him. He saw no point in mentioning his involvement with the Knights Templar or his journey to Ely.

"Now, about Dora. It looks like I have to stay here for a while, or the police'll get suspicious. Anyway, I want to see her and to be at the funeral. The police will ask where I've been, and I certainly can't tell them. So I need you to stick to the story about helping my cousin in London."

Peter interrupted, "You are right, the police will think you are off your rocker. But you don't seem as upset about Dora as I thought you would be."

"To be honest, I've got a lot on my mind. My head is spinning and things have not been good between us for a couple of years. We seem to have, sort of… drifted apart. Dora went cold towards me. There was no affection any more, and she was always grumpy. No doubt I'll have to go and identify her."

"No, you don't," Peter said. "You weren't here, so I did it."

"Thanks. It couldn't have been easy."

"Believe me, I have seen a lot worse. She looked peaceful, even younger, funny that."

Tom sighed. "I'll go to Ely this morning and present myself at the police station."

Ma sat heavily on a chair. "A fine business this is. I dunno what we're coming to. My son keeps disappearing, my daughter-in-law has drowned, and now I gotta lie to the police."

Sergeant Bowles was at the front desk. "Ah, Mr Harrison, we have wanted to talk to you for a couple of days. You'd better come through to the back office." His tone was officious and nothing in his voice implied sympathy over Dora's death.

Tom was uneasy as he followed Bowles past the front counter. The back office had a desk, three chairs, a filing cabinet, and was lit by the light from a high barred window. A single unlit light bulb hung from the ceiling.

Sitting opposite each other across the desk, Bowles shuffled papers in silence, eventually putting a blank sheet on top. He then produced a pencil, followed by a penknife from his pocket. He turned to face a waste bin and sharpened the pencil without speaking.

Tom wondered if this was a deliberate ploy to make him uneasy. If so, it was working, even though he had nothing to feel guilty about.

Bowles seemed to be enjoying the theatrics and eventually looked up. "So, Mr Harrison, what do you know about your wife's death?"

"Nothing. I was hoping you could tell me what happened."

"All in good time. Right now I want to know what *you* know about it."

"Like I said, nothing. I've been away and when I got back, my mother told me she had drowned."

"Quite so. Where were you at the time?"

"London."

"Doing what?"

"Helping my cousin."

"Doing what?"

"I was helping him with some personal matters."

"Can you prove it?"

"Look, Sergeant, what does it have to do with my wife's death? I told you I was not here at the time! Although I certainly wish I had been."

"Ah, but we only have your word for where you were!"

"If you don't believe me, why don't you ask my family?"

"I did." The sergeant looked down to make a note.

"Why don't you ask my mother or my brother, or anyone else in the village if I was seen there in the last couple of days?"

"As I said, sir, I already have, but I want to hear your side of the story and know where you were."

"There is no *story*, and I have told you where I was."

"What would you say if I told you the ticket clerk at the railway station has no recollection of ever selling you a ticket to London, or anywhere else for that matter?"

"Who said I went by train? Now look here, Sergeant, I have a right to know what happened to my wife!"

"As it happens, we received the Cambridge coroner's report just an hour ago and it poses just as many questions as answers. I can confirm that your wife drowned, but we don't yet know the circumstances. We can't be sure if she committed suicide, had an accident…or was helped, if you understand my meaning.

Tom was shocked at the mere thought Dora might have killed herself or been murdered. "What do you mean?"

"The report confirms that she drowned in the river she was found in. You see, we always send a sample of the water to see if it matches what's found in the lungs. There are no signs of a struggle on her body or any indication of how it might have happened. However, did you know she was approximately twelve weeks pregnant?"

Tom stared at Bowles, his shoulders dropped, he went pale and trembled as he stared down at the desk. Things were getting worse. He and Dora had not made love for well over a year.

"Judging from the look on your face, you had no idea. I'm surprised. Most wives can't wait to tell their husbands."

Tom couldn't stop himself. "Not if it's not his."

Bowles sat up sharply while Tom realised what he had just said.

"Do you know who the father is? I hope you can tell us. We had assumed it was you."

Tom was upset, angry, and confused. He wanted to cry, scream, walk up and down and punch something, anything would do. This was too much on top of her death. So many questions rushed through his head, none of which had answers, leaving him unable to think rationally.

"Well now, Mr Harrison, this adds even more intrigue to the case and maybe a motive for the drowning. Who knows, she might have committed suicide out of shame and embarrassment, or even the fear of facing you? On the other hand, you might have found out and done away with her yourself. Or her lover may have decided he didn't want any part of it and helped her on her way. There are lots of possibilities."

"You left out the possibility of it being an accident. But that wouldn't be exciting enough for you, would it?"

"Now then, sir, let's not adopt that attitude. Just remember that until this is resolved, you are considered a suspect in a very serious matter, possibly even murder."

You gotta be kidding me!"

"I'll have to contact the chief constable and get a

detective down here. In the meantime don't go dashing off to London. We'll need to talk to you again."

"Oh, I promise I'll not go to London. Not until we have got to the bottom of this. Can I go now?"

"Unless you can add something more at this stage, yes. If you are truly not the father, think of who it could be."

Going back to Ma's cottage Tom couldn't stop thinking about Sergeant Bowles' final words, his mind raced. Who did Dora know or have any close contact with? The boss, other workmen, anyone else who may have visited the farm? Dora had not been interested in love-making for a long time. Perhaps her affair had been going on for a while, which is why she had not been interested in him. It could have been anyone. It was a bloody well-kept secret, especially for this village. By the time he reached the cottage, he was bristling with questions.

Ma asked how it went.

"Interesting. Very bloody interesting!"

Ma immediately cut him short, "Don't talk to your mother like that."

Peter interrupted, "So tell us."

"They just got the coroner's report. They said there were no signs of a struggle, but that she was twelve weeks pregnant."

"She hid that well," Ma said with a twinge of sarcasm.

Tom continued, "Listen, embarrassing as it is, Dora and me have not had sex for more than a year! So who the bloody hell is the father?"

Ma blushed. "Oh dear me…and you know I don't like that sort of language in my house."

"Sorry, Ma, but imagine how I feel. Now the police

are thinking she might have committed suicide, or even been murdered, perhaps by me."

Ma went pale. Peter stared at Tom with his mouth open, then frowned saying, "Bugger!" Ma gave him a dirty look.

Tom was in a high state of mixed emotions. Dora had been unfaithful, and now she had died. He couldn't tell which hurt the most. He felt anger, sadness, betrayal, and outrage all at the same time while wondering who the father of her unborn child was. All this, whilst at the back of his mind was the promise he had made the children.

"What are you going to do?" Peter asked.

"Buggered if I know!"

"Tom!" Ma snapped.

"Are you aware of her seeing anyone else while I was away?"

"No. Anyway, it would have happened long before you started disappearing," Ma said. "As far as I know, the only people who go to the farm are your boss, some of the workmen, me, and our Peter, of course."

Tom paced the room. "In a village like this someone is bound to know something. When they find out she was pregnant, the place will be full of rumours and gossip. It'll be in all the newspapers too. You can see it, 'Dead Woman's Mystery Pregnancy' splashed across the front page! Not only that, I can't go back to the children any time soon or it will look as though I'm guilty of something. The police already want to talk to me again. They are even sending for a detective." He paused. "Has anyone made the funeral arrangements?"

Peter spoke quietly. "I talked to the undertaker and the vicar, so they know, but they can't do nothing until her body is released, and I don't suppose they'll do that for a day or two."

There was a knock at the door. Ma went to see who was there. Constable Cornwell was holding a brown paper bag.

"Can I come in, Mrs Harrison?"

Ma stepped back and beckoned him forwards.

"I'm pleased you are all here. I've got something to show you." He opened the bag and produced a muddied lady's shoe.

"Do any of you recognise this?"

Tom and Peter shook their heads.

Frowning, Ma sat down. "Yes, it's one of Dora's. Where did you find it?"

"I was looking along the river bank again, not far from where Mrs Harrison was found, and I came across it stuck deep in the mud at the water's edge. It looked as though someone had got stuck, lost their balance, and fallen into the river leaving their shoe behind. I didn't see any other footprints or find the other shoe."

"So do you think it was an accident?" Tom asked.

"I can't say, Sir. I'll have to give this to the sergeant. No doubt, he will want to come and see where I found it."

"But Dora knew these banks like the back of her hand. We used to play on them as kids. She wouldn't go near any of the muddy edges."

"I reckon it will be up to the sergeant to decide what happened, thank you. I'd better get this shoe back to Ely. Best you all wait here in case Sergeant Bowles wants to talk to you."

Later in the afternoon, Sergeant Bowles arrived with Constable Cornwell in tow. Ma's kitchen seemed small now. The officers declined the offer to sit. Bowles was clearly enjoying the moment as he raised his chest to speak. "Well now, it seems we are making some progress. As you know, the constable here has found where the unfortunate Mrs Harrison went into the river. Are you absolutely certain the shoe Constable Cornwell found belonged to Dora Harrison?"

"Yes, we already said it did." Ma was impatient.

"Then I must ask to see your shoes, gentlemen."

"What for?" Tom asked.

"To see if there are any traces of the same mud found on the shoe the constable recovered."

"You can't be serious! You've been reading too many detective novels. This is farming country. We all have the same mud on our shoes and boots at some time or other, even the kids do!"

"That'll do, Mr Harrison, just remember you are still a suspect."

Tom was silent as he reluctantly took his boots off.

Peter handed a boot over.

"And the other one, if you please, sir!" Bowles demanded.

Constable Cornwell interceded, "Er, excuse me, Sergeant. But if you remember the gentleman only has one leg."

"Do you want my leg as well?" Peter scoffed.

Bowles hesitated, flushed and cleared his throat. "Well then, this one will have to do."

Tom and Peter gave each other looks which said, *idiot*. They decided the sergeant didn't know what he was looking for, and it became obvious that Bowles had realised it too.

The boots were returned after a superficial inspection,

only done in an attempt to help Bowles save face and recover his failing credibility. "Well now, we can't be too careful, can we? We have to explore every avenue to get to the truth."

Tom didn't hesitate. "You really are hoping this will turn out to be something more than just an accident, aren't you, Sergeant? I suppose it would put a little excitement in your dull life, ey?"

Bowles ignored the comment and prepared to leave. "Thank you. Now don't any of you go running off until we get to the bottom of this, do you hear?"

Over the next two days, there was much coming and going by the police. Many people in the village had been questioned, but no significant information was forthcoming or evidence found. Apart from one farmworker who said he had seen Dora walking along the river bank on the day she went missing. However, as Dora's handbag and none of its contents had been found, "a robbery gone wrong" was quickly dismissed. It was concluded that the handbag was lost in the river and might simply wash up one day, if at all.

After the third day, Dora's body was released to the undertaker and her funeral was conducted by Vicar Parsons in the local church two days later. He spoke well of Dora but didn't mention how she had died, only to say her passing was unfortunate and untimely. The eulogy was read by her friend Anne Brown, as Tom, in his distress and distraction, didn't know what to say. Dora was buried in the village cemetery immediately afterwards. As was customary, almost everyone in the village attended.

Tom was upset, but it was at the graveside when he

began to feel the true depth of his loss and the finality of Dora's passing. When they left the cemetery, Tom again considered if he should try to discover who Dora had been seeing or return to the children. He thanked Anne, telling her she could help herself to any of Dora's clothes, or other ladies' items she might like. Anne felt awkward and declined.

After the burial, people were invited to the church hall for tea or sherry, and cakes to, as the vicar put it, "celebrate Dora's life."

Tom thought the expression inappropriate as Dora only had a few really happy adult years and was mostly under the dark cloud of depression. Villagers offered the Harrisons their condolences but asked few questions. Conversations were polite but stilted, self-conscious, and unnatural. Ma took the opportunity to chat with her older lady friends. Peter was uncomfortable and left early. Few people had spoken to him as suspicion still hung over his head regarding the children. Some were still convinced he knew more than he had revealed, and that he was involved in some way. Tom was equally uncomfortable, not quite knowing what to say to people. Albert, his boss, asked when he would be returning to work.

"I don't know, but I will get back as soon as I can."

"Look, Tom, I know it's not a good time to ask, but it would be helpful to know when. The field work is getting done, but it's putting more pressure on the others and I don't want to get behind."

"Look…I'll do my best to get back to work soon."

Albert hesitated a moment. "I know you must be upset at losing Dora, but do you know who the father is yet?"

"So you know about that, do you? I bet the whole bloody village does too! Why don't people mind their own business and just be sad at Dora's death rather than worry about scandal?"

"Sorry, Tom, I didn't mean to upset you. I was only asking. It's just that I thought you'd be onto it by now."

Tom glared at him. "It seems you are one of only a few people who ever went to the farm when I was not there!"

"Steady on, mate, you don't think…"

"Well, at this moment I don't know what to think about anyone!"

Tom was frustrated at not having the answer to Albert's question, and disgruntled because he didn't know how or where to start looking. It seemed he would have to wait for village gossip to come up with suggestions. Village speculation often contained an element of truth. As in most villages, rumours were never forgotten, and in the minds of some, they became fact, true or not.

Albert grunted and walked away. After an hour all the village folk had left the hall.

Ma and Tom returned to the cottage where Peter was waiting, clearly disturbed. "Tom, I got something to tell you. Can we all please sit down?"

"What's this about, Pete?" Tom looked into his brother's troubled eyes.

"Tom, I don't know what happened to Dora, but I do know who the father is."

"Who", Tom sharply asked.

There was a moment of hesitation.

"Me." Peter stared at the floor, unable to look Tom in the face.

Ma reached for Tom's arm to hold him back.

"What! You?" Tom shouted. "Christ! How long has this been going on?"

"Nothing has been *going on* as you put it. It only ever happened once. Afterwards, we were both ashamed. I still am, and very bloody sorry about it too. I went to the farm, as usual, to feed the chickens and do a couple of little jobs. Dora invited me in for a mug of tea. We got chatting. She were upset and tearful about Susie and Alfie, so I embraced her for a bit of comfort. It had been a long time since I'd felt a woman that close. She was warm and comfortable against me. I couldn't help getting aroused, and she must have noticed. Then one thing led to another. I think she felt something too, 'cos afterwards she said she hadn't made love for a long time, and it was nice. I was relieved 'cos I thought I had been clumsy. We vowed to never do it again and not tell anyone what we'd done."

Ma's face was ashen, and she couldn't speak.

"Shit, Peter, my own brother! My own bloody brother!"

Peter was in tears. "I know, I know. I'm sorry, Tom, so very, very sorry…and Dora was too. Not to mention embarrassed. We just got carried away in the heat of the moment."

"I should kick your arse to kingdom come, but it won't solve anything now, will it!"

"I'm sorry, Tom, really sorry."

Tom's breathing steadied. "I don't know what to think of you, Peter…my own brother! So far, there are only three people who know, and that's us here, so let's keep it that way, shall we!"

Ma was deeply shocked and didn't know what to say, so she did what she always does in a dilemma and put the kettle on.

Chapter 24

Influenced by Sergeant Bowles' suspicions, the chief constable sent a detective from Cambridge to conduct a more thorough investigation. He was never happy until a logical conclusion to any mystery had been reached.

The arrival of a detective in the village increased speculation and rumour to a point where some of the gossip became ridiculous. The detective listened to it all and decided there was little credibility or evidence in any of it, considering the tales to be no more than village gossip. Nor could he find anyone who openly disliked Dora or carried a grudge against her. She was simply accepted for who she was and for her place in the community.

After interviewing Tom, Peter, and old Mrs Harrison, he went with Constable Cornwell to where Dora's shoe had been found, hoping to interpret what was left of the marks in the mud. He concluded there was no real evidence, circumstantial or otherwise, to justify any consideration of a criminal case. To him, it looked as though Dora Harrison had simply lost her balance and fallen into the river.

Before returning to Cambridge he went to see Dora's doctor in Ely who said that as far as he knew Dora was physically healthy and that, due to patient confidentiality, he was limited in what he could divulge.

"Doctor, a woman is dead and I need to know more about her. How she died is known, but we don't know why, or if anyone else was involved. Did you know she was pregnant?"

"Yes, of course."

"Are there any medical circumstances which, in your opinion, would cause her untimely death?"

The doctor thought for a moment. "Given my records and having seen the coroner's report…medically speaking, no, but if I may generalise: sometimes people who are depressed have been known to do themselves harm."

"Was she depressed?"

"I believe so."

"Why?"

"I can't tell you, officer. However, it is a matter of public knowledge that her children went missing a while back and have never been found. Naturally, she would be distressed. Then, of course, most women of her age do not wish to have more children, so the thought of being pregnant again can be upsetting, even traumatic for some. I have known women to take drastic measures to abort a foetus."

"Apart from that, can you think of any other reason why she may have been stressed or depressed?"

"No. However, it does not mean there is no other reason."

"So in your opinion, you don't think she was capable of taking her own life?"

"I didn't say that. We are all 'capable', officer, under one circumstance or another. Now if you mean 'likely', in my opinion, I doubt it, but who knows. When she came to see me last it was for a voluntary check-up. She said she was not feeling herself. She told me she had fainted, suspecting pregnancy as the cause. Women often faint in early pregnancy, you understand. So I examined her and confirmed what I believe she already knew. We both knew fainting was not unusual, so I told her to sit, or better still, to lie down if she felt faint again or suddenly came over weak and light-headed. I advised that if it happens more than once or twice more, she should come back to see me, and I would prescribe tablets to fortify her blood. It sometimes helps."

The detective included his interview with the doctor in his report. In his summary, he stated that no suspicious evidence was found, but acknowledged the possibility of certain background circumstances surrounding her pregnancy which might cause speculation. At the same time, he emphasized that having met those close to Dora, and many of the village folk, in his professional opinion nothing untoward had taken place. The chief constable recommended the report and other relevant materials be lodged with a magistrate for a hearing and a subsequent decision on whether or not to take the matter further.

An inquest was to be held one month later at the Ely Magistrates Court. For Tom that month seemed to drag on forever. All he wanted was to get back to the children and had considered going to them and returning before the hearing. It tormented him, but he dismissed the idea believing that if he disappeared again at this time, it would encourage more speculation and questions from the police.

At the inquest, the police were represented by Sergeant

Bowles and Detective Constable Chase, who presented their findings and answered questions. Sergeant Bowles was keen to offer his opinion but was quickly silenced by the magistrate.

"We are here to reach a conclusion based on facts, Sergeant, not speculation or theories."

Bowles was embarrassed and thereafter answered questions directly and as concisely as possible. Detective Chase was clearly more experienced and remained factual. Dora's doctor was also called but was unable to offer any more detail than he had already told the police.

Tom answered questions from the magistrate and was relieved not to be asked where he had been at the time of Dora's death. He was only required to answer questions concerning Dora.

"Did you know she was pregnant?"

"No."

"It's unusual for a husband not to know if his wife is pregnant, Mr Harrison."

"She could be secretive sometimes. Dora would have told me when she was ready. I expect she wanted to be absolutely sure first."

"I'm not at liberty to say how it came about, Mr Harrison, but there is some speculation that you may not be the father. How do you respond to that?"

Tom was furious and taken by surprise. It was all so public. Someone had opened their mouth, but Ma and Peter had promised not to talk about it. Sergeant Bowles and the detective must have included it in their reports. Then he remembered that his boss had asked him and realised the whole village would know.

"I have heard the speculation, sir," he replied.

The magistrate hesitated as he turned the pages in

front of him. "But what do you make of it, Mr Harrison?"

"I'm confused and upset. I don't know what to think."

"All right, Mr Harrison, you may relax, we will not pressure you further on this delicate point. You are not on trial here, nor is your wife's conduct. What can you tell us about your wife's mental health and your relationship?"

"She has not been the same since our children disappeared. That's when she got depressed this time."

"This time, Mr Harrison?"

"Yes, she had previously lost a baby and was depressed for about a year."

"I hate to ask you, but do you feel she was capable of taking her own life?"

"Definitely not."

Much to his relief, Dora's pregnancy and the suggestion he might not be the father was not raised again. Peter and Ma sat uncomfortably through the entire proceedings but were not asked to give evidence. At midday the magistrate ordered a break of two hours, allowing him an opportunity to consider his opinion.

When the hearing reconvened there were more people in the courtroom than previously. Newspaper reporters from Ely, March, and Cambridge stood with pencil and pad in hand at the back of the room, all anxiously waiting to hear the result. Under normal circumstances, only the local newspaper would report the matter, but this was different. It was an event connected to the village of the missing children, and the mother of two of them.

After basic formalities, the room fell silent when the magistrate prepared to speak. Then, in a calm matter-of-fact manner, he announced his findings: "I have reviewed all the evidence provided before me from Mrs Harrison's doctor, the coroner, and the police. I have listened to the

323

evidence provided here today and conclude that Mrs Harrison's untimely death was indeed an unfortunate accident."

A murmur went through the court. It grew louder as people began to talk openly to each other, while reporters frantically scratched at their pads. A clerk called for silence and after a moment or two, the magistrate continued.

"I have considered all the evidence and reached my conclusion based on the following: I understand that it is a common event for women to faint at least once in the early part of their pregnancy. After extensive investigation, the police have found no evidence of foul play. Therefore, I must conclude that Mrs Harrison fainted while by the river, causing her to fall into the water, so leading to her untimely death. I declare this matter closed with a verdict of accidental death."

Chatter immediately broke out amongst the public while the reporters frantically continued their shorthand notes before dashing out. However, one approached Tom to ask about Dora's pregnancy. Tom ignored him. Ma dabbed the corner of her eye with one of her best embroidered handkerchiefs. Tom's shoulders slumped in relief, while Peter stared at the floor, relieved he had not been called to comment and that it was over.

The three hardly spoke on the bus back to the village, although Ma had muttered, "I'm glad it's finished with now." But she knew the relationship between her sons would never be the same again.

Tom's attention was now on the children and any possible way they could be brought back. There would certainly be no way in the twentieth century. He accepted that what had happened was an accident, a side effect and getting them back would be difficult, even impossible, just as he had been told. Yet he couldn't overcome the nagging question: If they could be sent back in time with a potion, then surely one could be found to bring them forwards again? He considered that if he went back for long enough, he might go to Denny Abbey and talk to the nuns himself. Or maybe get the nuns and monks to work together. Although that seemed unlikely as they only just managed to tolerate each other, even then it was with very little trust.

As the bus trundled on there was still no communication between them. Each deep in their own thoughts.

Peter was full of shame and regret, giving him grave concerns about his relationship with his brother, whom he had greatly admired and respected. Guilt reminded him that Tom had always trusted and loved him as his little brother. Like Ma, he knew things would never be the same again. Now their conversations were few and often abrupt, but he hoped it would change in time. He knew his mother was disgusted and disappointed with him, but she still treated him as a loved son.

Ma, with a mother's wisdom and intuition, knew he would be troubled by his conscience. Not something he needed while still adjusting to his disability and feelings of inadequacy.

At the back of Peter's mind was the irrepressible feeling of guilt. Firstly, for taking advantage of Dora when she was in a low state and needed a friend. Secondly, for betraying Tom and their family's trust. Most of all it was that if he had not got her pregnant, she wouldn't have fainted and fallen into the river. It was all his fault.

As his anxieties festered, he wanted to tell Tom and Ma how desperately sorry he was and ask for their understanding and forgiveness. However, his conscience teased him saying he didn't deserve it, and that it would change nothing. He wondered if he would ever find the right moment or the courage.

As the bus pulled into the village, Ma made no secret of her priority to put the kettle on. "I've been a-gaspin' for a cuppa this last hour or more. I expect you'd both like one too."

As usual, Peter sat in his father's old carver by the stove. Tom stood a moment before sitting at the table, while Ma opened the curtains to let more light in. The silence in the little kitchen was oppressive.

Peter decided to break the ice, knowing that if ever there was a time to say his piece, it was now. "Ma, Tom, please listen to me. I need to tell you how sorry I am for causing all this. I feel absolutely wretched. I can't think straight any more and…"

Tom cut him short. "I don't want to hear about it, Peter! Not now, not ever! What's done is done. There is nothing we can do about it and nothing more to say."

Peter felt worse, believing this may have been his only chance to explain his feelings.

"Let him speak, Tom," Ma begged.

"Hell, no! I don't want to hear his crap."

Ma bit her lip and stared angrily at him.

Peter was shocked at Tom's tone but not his rejection, which he understood. Believing it better not to pursue Tom, he said no more.

Ma continued to stare at Tom. Saying nothing, she allowed her eyes to speak for her in the hope that Tom would relent. But he stared back in defiance. Then, after a little reflection, he turned to Peter.

"The truth is that Dora and me have not had a

psychical relationship for a long time. But it don't mean I didn't care about her, or that I'm not upset she's dead. The thing that hurts most right now is that you betrayed me by having sex with my wife! Your own brother's bloody wife!"

Ma interrupted, "We'll 'ave no more of that swearing or dirty talk in my house if you please! Now let that be an end to it. We got more important things to worry about, like getting them children back."

Chapter 25

Sitting by his kitchen stove, Tom was pensive, knowing he had promised the children he would return and had not done so within a reasonable time. He was also worried, fearing there would be no way of getting them back. In his torment, he speculated on what seemed to be the most likely opportunities, but just as before, there was no acceptable answer. To him, the whole thing was like a bad dream - a nightmare - and it was his fault.

After a gentle tap on the door, Peter entered. Neither greeted the other. Peter broke the silence. "Can we talk, Tom?"

"What about?"

"Well, the things that have gone on in the last few weeks are doing my head in, and I need to try and explain it to you. There's a bit more to this than you know."

"What makes you think I'm interested?"

Peter ignored the remark and pulled a chair towards the stove to sit facing his brother. Tom saw the sorrow in his glazed eyes and relented.

"You do know that I don't want to talk about what happened between you and Dora, don't you?"

Peter waited a moment saying, "Yes, I know, and I can understand why, but there are a few things you don't know that you need to know."

"I suppose you'd better tell me then."

"What me and Dora did was wrong, very wrong. I know nothing'll change that, but there were other things. You see, she was already upset at Susie and Alfie's disappearance. She was terrified at what might have happened to them, tormented with anxiety because they had not been found and probably never would be. There was no closure for her. Then on top of that, she said you were cold towards her."

"Shit! That's how she was with me."

"I don't know, Tom. She thought you were having an affair with Rosie and felt she had been rejected for a younger, more attractive woman. So you see, it was easy, even natural for her to find a bit of comfort somewhere else. I also think that in the back of her mind she might have wanted to get back at you for betraying her with Rosie. Not that you did. But at least it would make her feel better."

"What happened to family respect, loyalty, and our marriage vows? What about you respecting your brother?"

"I don't know what I was thinking or if I was thinking at all. I guess I felt sorry for her and wanted to comfort her. Then one thing led to another. Like I said, it wasn't planned, and we were both embarrassed afterwards so vowed to never do it again, or tell a soul. To tell you the truth, we were ashamed of ourselves. I still am, and if she hadn't fallen pregnant nobody would have ever known, not even you. Now I feel responsible for her death. I feel so bloody wretched, Tom, I really do." Peter sniffed and rubbed the back of his hand under his nose.

Tom didn't say that he accepted Peter's apology but

his attitude to his brother began to soften. "Let's leave it there, shall we? I have other things to worry about right now, like finding a way to get those children back."

Peter slowly reached for Tom's arm. "What can I do to help?"

Tom moved his arm away. "You only know part of what has been going on, and there's nothing you can do."

"I don't suppose we'll ever know if I can help unless you tell me the rest. Anyway, two heads are better than one."

"If I tell you more, you'll have to keep your mouth shut like before. I need to know I can trust you, but after recent events, I'm not sure if I can."

Peter was unable to respond to Tom's remark and seconds passed as he gazed around the room, almost as though looking for somewhere to hide. "I can assure you my lips are sealed. I'll not say a word to anyone, not even Ma." Then swallowing the lump in his throat: "I want you to trust me again. Please, Tom, I need you to."

Tom stared into his brother's eyes. "I know you are going to find this hard to believe but I assure you it's all true."

"Try me," Peter begged.

Speaking slowly and carefully, Tom added details of events to what he had previously explained, telling about Rauin, the Knights Templar and their horses, King John, how the children had actually found him, the monks, the abbot, the nuns at Denny Abbey, and witnessing the building of Ely Cathedral. Then rubbing his chin he frowned. "So you see it's my carelessness that caused the kids to disappear."

"Well, dear brother, it seems we have both been blessed, or cursed, with a conscience and have our own crosses to bear."

The comment resonated with Tom, making him feel he had no right to judge his brother as neither of them was perfect. It now seemed wrong to be casting the first stone or to cast one at all.

"What you say is certainly hard, if not impossible to believe. Can you prove any of it?"

"Just look at all these notes I made along the way. They are all dated."

"I hear you, Tom, but you could have written them anywhere and at any time."

Tom rummaged in his pocket and produced a small leather pouch, closed at the top with a draw cord, and gave it to Peter.

"Do you remember when I said that Rauin gave me money for the trip to Ely? Take a look inside. Look at the coins and ask where else would I get them?"

Peter's eyes widened. "You wouldn't be having me on, would you?"

Tom exhaled heavily. "Do you think I would tell you and Ma I had found the children if I hadn't? It would be a sick joke, and I'm not that cruel."

"I know, Tom, but where is the flask now?"

"Here." Tom lifted his rucksack from the floor, removed the flask and handed it to Peter.

"Be careful with it. Don't take the lid off."

Peter thought a moment. "Okay, just 'suppose' I believe you."

Tom rolled his eyes.

Peter continued. "I think it would help to know what that stuff inside is, so how about we take it to one of the university laboratories in Cambridge? I hear St John's is up on that chemistry stuff."

"I suppose you are right. We have to start somewhere."

"Let's take the bus to Cambridge in the morning." Peter was now more motivated than he had been since returning from France.

Finding St John's College was easy. The grand entrance was impressive, looking more like an ornate medieval castle gate than a college entrance. They were stopped by a man dressed like an undertaker on his way to a funeral.

"Can I help you, gentlemen?"

Peter introduced themselves by their first names. "We would like to see the head of Chemistry please."

"Do you have an appointment?"

"Sorry, no."

"The professor is a very busy man and is unable to see anyone without an appointment."

"But we have come a long way and it's important," Peter persisted.

Tom looked away.

"We have an unidentified substance we found in a medieval cask and would like someone to identify it for us."

"Ah, then you should talk to Dr Roberts. He's your best man. If you would like to wait here, I'll see if he's available."

Returning minutes later, he directed them to a heavy wooden door some thirty yards away. As they approached, a tall thin, grey-haired man wearing a white coat was looking in their direction.

"I am Doctor Roberts. I believe you wish to see me?"

"Yes, sir."

Tom had not called anyone "sir" since his army days. However, given the doctor's posh accent and title, he thought it appropriate, especially as he wanted his help. They introduced themselves and explained why they were there, trying not to give too much detail.

"I work the land and I found this container which I think could be medieval. It's got a strange substance stuck at the bottom. We thought you might be able to tell us what it is and what it's made from.

"Ah, there's nothing like a good mystery. Come in, come in, gentlemen."

Roberts led them to a small laboratory. "This is my little hideaway where I play and get up to mischief. May I see the container?"

Tom took the flask from his rucksack and handed it to Roberts.

Taking it to a high work bench by a window, he perched himself on a tall stool and held the cask up to the light. "Mmm, a most interesting item, I must say. As an amateur historian, I find this sort of thing fascinating. It certainly looks very old. I've not seen one like it before, most unusual. Have you shown it to the museum?"

Before Tom could answer, the doctor had followed his instincts, removed the lid and sniffed the contents. Tom grabbed Peter's arm while staring at the doctor, who put the flask down before resting his elbows on the bench. Then after rubbing his temples and groaning, he disappeared.

Peter was wide-eyed in disbelief. "Shit, Tom! What the hell is going on? What's in that bloody thing? It's not possible!"

"I suppose you believe me now?" Tom said with satisfaction.

"Too bloody right I do. What'll we do?"

"Nothing, just get out of here."

"What about Doctor Roberts?"

"He'll be all right. He only took a small sniff so he might be back after a few hours, or maybe tomorrow. But he's in for a bit of a surprise. Come on, let's go."

Tom replaced the lid and put the flask back in his rucksack before they calmly walked out. Smiling, he thanked the man at the entrance as they left. They spoke in whispers on the bus back to Ely.

"Bugger me, Tom, I didn't know if I should believe you, but now I've seen it with my own eyes. I don't know what to think, I'm really worried."

"It's strange all right!"

"When they discover the doctor is not here, do you think they'll come looking for us? Remember we were the last people to see him."

"They might wonder who we are, but they don't know anything about us." Tom grinned. "I wonder if he'll tell people what happened to him, or where he's been when he returns. I'd guess not, or people would think he's lost his marbles!"

"But he completely disappeared!" Peter exclaimed.

"Precisely, he wasn't seen to leave with us, was he? And there's nobody to be found. I'm sure we're okay. They won't necessarily think there's any mischief involving us. They'll just think he's gone off somewhere, which of course he has," Tom said with a chuckle.

"What's so funny?"

"You have to have been there to know. He'll turn up in the early thirteenth century wearing his horn-rimmed glasses, his long white coat with his pencils in his top pocket, and with that posh accent of his, he'll stand out like the balls on a whippet. He won't know where he is, or if he's coming or going," Tom laughed aloud.

"But what's he gonna tell people when he comes back?"

"I don't think he'll say a single word. In his confusion, he'll probably think he had a dream when he finds himself back on his perch. Wouldn't you love to be a fly on the wall at that moment?"

Peter smiled and began to relax. "But we still don't know what that stuff is, do we?"

"No, damn it. To make matters worse we can't take it to anyone else and forewarn them or they will think we're mad. Imagine saying, 'Don't sniff it or you'll disappear.' They won't believe it and before you know it someone else will be shooting back in time."

"Is it dangerous back there?"

Peter listened wide-eyed in silence as Tom explained. They were almost back in Ely by the time he had finished describing Bishop's Lynn.

"One thing that impresses me is that they seem so unsophisticated in some ways, even primitive, but much more advanced in a lot of others. Just look at Ely Cathedral. We think it's huge and impressive, even beautiful. But just imagine that a thousand years ago someone sat down with a blank sheet of paper and designed it from scratch. He was a master architect and would put a lot of our blokes to shame. How many of our buildings are going to last a thousand years? They understood what we call structural engineering and all that technical stuff. Then they had to build it. You should have seen 'em, Peter. Hundreds of 'em, maybe a thousand or two, men, women, and children hauling, cutting, and shaping great lumps of stone and timber. All done by manpower and horses, they had no machines or heavy cranes. Their scaffolding was nothing more than rickety poles lashed together. Just look how high they went. The ladders looked none too safe either, but they did the job. Remember it stood on a hill in the middle of a great swamp. Bloody amazing if you ask me."

Chapter 26

As they cycled back to the village from Ely, Tom explained that he must go return the children very soon.

"Can I go with you?"

"Absolutely not…and don't ask again. I'd like to take them something. What do you think they'd like?"

"A few sticks of barley sugar and bars of chocolate would go down well."

"Yes, and if I take enough they can share them. I'll pop back into Ely in the morning. They'll have a better selection than the village shop. Not only that, old Mabel will think it strange if I go buying loads of children's goodies. She likes to know everything and will ask who they are for."

"You could take Susie and Alfie their favourite toys. I know Susie loved that old doll of hers. As for Alfie, he didn't have many toys, but he loved that catapult I made him."

"A good idea," Tom replied.

Nothing more was discussed until they reached Tythe Farm.

"Would you mind if I stayed here with you tonight?"

Tom raised his eyebrows. "Okay, but why?"

"Sentiment, I suppose. Things have been difficult this

past week or more. Maybe I'm being a bit melancholy. I just want to try and make things better. It helps to be closer to you."

"You can have Alfie's bed."

Peter explained to Ma that he was going to stay with Tom that night and finished by saying, "I love you, Ma."

She blushed. "What's come over you, young man? Get off with you before I box your ears."

Tom bought four bottles of brown ale from the pub to help the evening along. Their conversation was congenial, but it didn't flow easily. Both tried to avoid the subject of Dora and any connection with her that would dampen the atmosphere. Peter asked questions about the children, wanting to know how they were and how they were coping with the strict regimes of the convent.

Eventually, Tom looked at the clock. "Well, I'm off up the wooden hill. It's been a long day. See you in the morning, Peter."

"Okay, I'll just sit by the stove a while longer before I go up."

Tom rose before daylight intending to stoke the stove, empty the ashes, and make breakfast. As he lit and pumped the Tilly Lamp, he saw a folded sheet of writing paper on the table. Sitting, he opened it and read a letter from Peter.

My Dear Brother,

By the time you read this I will have died centuries ago, hopefully after a long life.

I'm going to taste the residue in the bottom of the flask so I won't return, and I'll take the flask with me. It could be useful in finding an antidote for the children. Please don't be upset or angry with me.

My life here seems worthless, and I'm forced to be reclusive to avoid the villagers' scorn. It's not always spoken, but I feel it and see it in their eyes. Some even turn their backs to me.

I have disgraced our family. I can't stop feeling guilty about betraying you and find it hard to deal with. I couldn't have wished for a better brother, so thank you for being there for me. You taught me almost everything I know, especially about horses, so I guess I will be able to find work back there. But this is not my main reason for going. It just makes my decision easier.

I love those children and they trust me. I want to take care of them, and I think they will be happier if someone they know, and like, is always with them. I'll give them the love and caring which I doubt they are getting now. At the same time, I'll do everything I can to find a way of getting them back to you. God willing, you will see them again, but of course, there are no promises, as you said, it might not be possible but you and Ma will always know someone is trying.

I don't want to smell the potion because I would be back and forth, and it wouldn't be fair to the children. Also, the potion might run out or be lost, and I don't want to risk them being left alone again, so I'll taste a good amount to keep me there. I'll be doing something worthwhile with my life without the stress and ridicule I have here. Please don't be upset with me. It's what I want. I feel I have a purpose in life now.

Please try and explain to Ma and give her my love.

Your loving brother, Peter.

Shocked, Tom didn't move from the table and with a huge sigh, he read the letter again. As it was all beginning to sink in he muttered, "Peter, you silly big-hearted sod! You'd better not be playing games!"

Tom grabbed his rucksack to find the flask was gone.

He swore aloud, wondering what he should do.

Almost immediately he jolted upright. "I wonder..."

Rising quickly he went to the children's bedroom where he was unable to find Susie's doll or Alfie's catapult.

"Peter, this is just like you!"

At that moment Tom felt a wave of compassion for his brother. Peter had sacrificed his life here for the sake of the children, in the certain knowledge that he would never see his family again, not to mention embarking on a strange life full of uncertainty.

He took a deep breath. "Okay, Peter, good luck, mate, I really admire you. God Bless you, little brother, I do love you." He was saddened that Peter would never hear those words.

Tom tried to explain to Ma as best he could but she didn't understand and kept asking, "So when's he coming home?"

Eventually, rather than tell her the whole truth and upset her more he said, "I don't know, Ma. Probably when he can get the children back, but it could take a while yet."

Ma shed a tear but asked nothing more. In that conversation, Tom began to recognise Ma's condition for the first time. He considered her age and now began to remember that in recent months she had often asked the same question twice or more times in the same conversation. He'd thought it was simply absent-mindedness, but he was now concerned it may be something more.

"Ma, I've been thinking. I have to go back to work and I don't have Dora now, so I need someone to look after me and things at the house."

He knew Ma would be thinking ahead of what was

being intimated. He was right. While straightening her back to sit upright, she tried not to smile too widely. Feeling needed and useful again took her mind off Peter. She would take pride in her new responsibilities.

"So why don't you move in with me, Ma? You know it won't be easy with all that cooking, keeping the place clean and tidy. I suppose it will be like old times. Do you think you are still up to it?"

"Huh, don't be so cheeky. I've still got a few good years left in me yet."

Three days later she moved into Tythe Farm. Now he could keep an eye on her and hopefully provide the support she would eventually need.

Ma was up first every morning. She had the stove hot and a mug of tea waiting on the table for Tom when he came down. By the evening she was tired and often fell asleep in a chair by the warmth of the stove. One morning, a few months later, Tom came down to the kitchen to find Ma still sleeping in the old wooden carver.

"Hello, Ma, you okay?"

She didn't reply. Tom gently shook her shoulder, "Are you alright, Ma?"

Her head slumped forwards, resting her chin on her breast.

Ma was buried in the village cemetery four days later.

Chapter 27

It was six months before Tom had settled into a routine of living alone. Sitting at the kitchen table with his notes, newspaper clippings, and school exercise books spread out before him, he wondering what he should do with them. Should he destroy them? Put them away for someone else to ponder over in the future? Or should he continue to compile them into the sequence of events? Since he didn't expect anyone to believe his story, he considered if the latter would even be worthwhile. Although he could provide an honest answer to where the village children had gone and how it had all happened. No, they would most likely believe he had fabricated the story from things that were already public knowledge. Some might even consider it in poor taste, causing the villagers to relive the tragedy of their losses.

Then to occupy himself as much as anything else, he organised and numbered them in order. By the time the papers, clippings, and notebooks were sequenced it was late, but the exercise had rekindled his enthusiasm to do something positive with them.

The tilly lamp spluttered and dimmed. "Needs more paraffin," he grumbled to the empty room. He was tired and wanted his bed. Most evenings were spent drafting and compiling information to link relevant facts where necessary. After many hours of diligent work, he was satisfied, but still not sure what to do with the pile of papers which had now grown.

He wanted people to know the truth but didn't want to get into arguments, be mocked or made to look a fool, and certainly not to be blamed for the children's disappearance or be interrogated by the police again. Even with these frustrations, he felt the truth should eventually be known. It was a few weeks later, while grooming a horse, when out of the blue a solution came to him. He would write a story, a book of fiction, a novel, and leave folks to interpret or believe as they saw fit. Using a pseudonym, the author would remain unknown. Perfect! He had to consider when and where the book should be published, but for now, he would begin the story.

Tom was no scholar. He knew what he wanted to say but fumbled with words and phraseology in his schoolboy English. After six months of evening dedication and much use of a dictionary, he finally had a completed manuscript. It took a further two months of reviewing and correcting before he was totally satisfied.

Thursday was market day in Ely, a day of great activity. He had previously enjoyed appraising the horses and cattle which stood patiently in their pens. In the past some farmers had asked his advice before bidding on a horse, which he had found flattering, so would willingly oblige. However, this Thursday would be different. With his manuscript in a bag, he entered the offices of Baxter and Baxter, Solicitors. There was only one Mr Baxter now as young Mr Baxter had been killed in the Great War. However, out of sentiment, the old man had not changed the firm's name. He had expected his son would join him and eventually take over the practice. Keeping the firm's name unchanged now kept his son close and symbolised the sentimental denial of his loss.

Tom detected the smell of musty rooms while being greeted by an austere middle-aged woman, who displayed a misplaced air of superiority. She looked Tom up and down with disdain, suggesting his appearance was not entirely appropriate for a visit to her employer.

"Can I help you, sir?"

"Yes, I'd like to see Mr Baxter, please."

"Do you have an appointment?" She looked over Tom's head knowing he didn't but wanted to make a point of it, and of the honour of seeing Mr Baxter, so enhancing her own perceived privileged status.

"No, do I need one?"

Still staring into space above Tom she said, "It is usual, sir, but I will see if Mr Baxter can spare a moment for you. Who shall I say is calling?

"My name is Thomas Harrison."

"Please take a seat, Mr Harrison," she said turning to leave.

With a smile, Tom remembered what the old man in the Denver inn had said: "I'd hate to wake up with her beside me every morning."

She soon returned. "Mr Baxter will see you in about five minutes." She walked away before Tom could respond, and then disappeared through a door next to Mr Baxter's office.

After ten minutes she reappeared. "Mr Baxter will see you now," she said with a tone of superiority as she opened his door.

Mr Baxter was an elderly man with thinning grey

hair who looked as though he should have retired years ago. His dark suit was a little grubby, and his manner suggested he was tired, yet trapped by the momentum of his portfolios.

"Take a seat, Mr Harrison. What can I do for you?"

"I'm not exactly sure, Mr Baxter. You see, I have written a story, and I want someone to store it safely before it's published. Can you do that for me?"

"Why do you not want it published right away?"

Tom adjusted his seating position. "Well, to be honest, although it's only a novel, it could cause upset for a lot of people just now, and unwelcome problems for me. Maybe at some time in the future it would be acceptable.

Baxter looked at Tom inquisitively over the small round spectacles that perched on the end of his nose.

"What is so upsetting about it?"

Tom hesitated. "Do you remember the village children who went missing, not long back?"

"Yes, of course."

"Well, it's about what happened to them." Then quickly but awkwardly added, "That is to say, what I *think* happened to them."

The old man rubbed his chin. "Mmm, I see what you mean. It could certainly be a little insensitive this soon after the event. When would you consider having it published?"

"Not for a long time."

"How long?"

"Ninety years."

Baxter pulled his head back and stared at Tom. "Mr Harrison, is it possible that you know rather more than the average person about the matter? Have you discovered something the police should know about? Is there anything in your manuscript that would lead them to finding those poor children? Or at least, to know what has happened to them?"

"No! Definitely not," Tom lied. "I should tell you that my own two children were the first to go missing. If I knew anything that would help the police, I would have told them long ago."

"Yes, I see, of course. But ninety years is a very long time, and I seriously doubt if anyone living today will still be here. In fact, I'd suggest none will be, including your good self."

Tom looked the old man in the eye. "Exactly."

"Well, Mr Harrison, we can certainly secure it for you for that length of time, but I hope it will be discovered in the timely manner you request. There will certainly be nobody here to remember it."

"I understand that, but when it's found I'd like it to be handed, unopened to a publisher."

"Do you have any other conditions?"

"Only one. If the children should return to the village sooner, I would like the book published straight away."

Tom thought it would clear Peter's name and might even make him a hero. At that moment he felt a sense of relief, for as far as he was concerned, apart from his conscience, the whole affair would then be over.

Baxter suggested that a letter of conditions should be attached to the bundle to ensure it would be properly dealt with when the time came. "Otherwise, who knows what might become of it."

The manuscript was placed in a buff folder and securely tied with red tape. Mr Baxter wrote a note which read: *'Not to be opened until January 2010 unless all five missing children are found before.'* He signed it, printed his name, added the date, and stamped it with his firm's name and address.

"I'll get Miss Church to seal the tape with wax after she has typed my letter with your instructions. She can then tuck it under the tape before archiving. May I suggest you leave information directing your descendants to the document, perhaps a note in your will would suffice? Do you have a will, Mr Harrison?"

"No," Tom said feeling that perhaps he should.

Baxter looked over his spectacles again. "Then I will be happy to draft one for you if you would care to give it some thought. In the meantime make an appointment with Miss Church on your way out. Is there anything else I can do for you, Mr Harrison?"

"No, that's it. Thank you, I'll make an appointment to come back when I know what I want to say in my will."

"Good, I'll not bill you for this consultation. We can deal with that after I have drafted your will."

Tom left the office and strolled to the cattle market. As he walked it came to him that he had no descendants to name in a will. He had no children, Ma was gone and it was highly unlikely that Peter, Susie, and Alfie would ever be seen again. He did not return to Baxter and Baxter Solicitors.

Six months after Tom's visit, old Mr Baxter sold his practice to a Cambridge firm wanting to open a satellite office in Ely. He retired immediately after the sale was concluded. In 2009 the former offices of Baxter and Baxter were to be demolished to make way for more modern, functional premises.

As the building was being cleared, Tom's manuscript was discovered in a small room where archived documents had been stored. Mr Baxter's letter, containing Tom's instructions, was examined and the transcript was eventually presented to a publisher under a signed agreement. Part of which said that should the manuscript be published half of any profits should go to Dr Barnardo's Children's Homes.

The publisher was enthralled with Tom's account and considered it a work of fiction based on real-life events, many of which could be verified in public records. The publisher expected that it would achieve good commercial success, especially in the Fen area of East Anglia. An author was commissioned to review and edit the work into a publishable format. Tom Harrison had called it "The Secret Book" but the publisher changed it to "Lost in Time."

Chapter 28

It was early morning when Peter Harrison woke in the stables at Bishop's Lynn. To his relief, he had arrived where he had hoped and the searing pain through his temples had gone, even though he was a little disorientated.

Rising from a bed of hay in the dim light, he looked around. It was quiet, only two horses were stabled. Clearly, the ostlers had not yet arrived. The main door creaked as he slowly pushed it open. He hesitated a few moments in trepidation of what he might find outside.

The track leading to the stables was deserted and the only signs of life at this early hour were a few smoking chimneys. Sniffing a deep breath of the chilled air, Peter steeled himself for what the day might bring. Cautiously, he made his way into the town.

He felt guilty at taking the pouch of silver coins Rauin had given Tom. Although he knew his brother would have offered them if he had approved of what he was doing. But Tom would not approve, so how could he tell him? He could have apologized in his letter, but with so much on his mind, he had missed the opportunity.

Within a few minutes, Peter had reached the market square where he recognized the octagonal shelter Tom had described. Nearby a few oxen and horse-drawn carts began to pass to and from the quays. He decided to wait for the town to wake before venturing further. Sitting in the shelter he remembered what he was told about the Knights Templar, pleased he wouldn't have to contend with them. He had arrived in Bishop's Lynn with no constructive plan, other than to see the children, do everything he could to care for them and try to send them home. How he and the children would survive day to day only now hit home.

The day was growing lighter from under a steel grey sky and activity in the square was increasing. Most people were not wealthy, most being poorly dressed. Realizing he would stand out in his twentieth-century clothes he was reluctant to approach anyone for directions. Then relaxing, he remembered what Tom had said about people thinking he had come from one of the foreign trading ships and hoped it would be the same for himself. He stood, arched his back, stretched and wandered the streets, eagerly taking in all that was unfamiliar.

On seeing a more respectably dressed person, he hesitantly approached. "Excuse me, sir. Could you please tell me where the convent is?"

The man hesitated as if deciding whether to answer or walk away. There was a period of silence whilst he looked Peter up and down, making him feel self-conscious.

"I'm sorry to bother you, sir, but I'm looking for the convent."

Clearly intrigued by Peter's appearance and speech, he pointed and said, "Follow this road and you will find it to your right side."

He turned and walked away before Peter could thank him. Now more apprehensive than before, he walked slowly along the cobbled street, wishing he had his big brother's worldly confidence. It didn't take long to reach the convent, although he didn't recognize it until two nuns carrying bags came through a heavy wooden door, followed by the sound of heavy bolts being secured behind them.

"Excuse me, ladies, is this the convent?"

Once again, he received strange looks.

"Yes. What is your business here?"

"I've come about the children in your care."

"You had best bang on the door and ask for Mother Superior."

Peter thanked them and did as he was directed. They scurried away chatting excitedly, then after a moment or two looked back at him. A panel behind the barred viewing hatch opened almost immediately.

"Yes?"

"I'd like to see Mother Superior, please."

"What is your business here, my good man?"

"I want to talk to her about some of the children you care for."

The hatch closed without further comment. He hoped the nun had gone to fetch Mother Superior rather than rejecting his request, leaving him vacantly standing there. After patiently waiting, the hatch opened again.

"Mother Superior wants to know your concern about the children."

Peter felt a twinge of frustration. "I am Mr Harrison. You have five children staying with you from a different… from deep in the Washes. Two of them are my nephews. They are a little different to other children. I need to talk to Mother Superior and see…"

The hatch banged closed.

Again he was obliged to wait for it to reopen.

"Mother Superior asks if you have come to take them away."

"In a manner of speaking, yes, but…"

The hatch banged shut again. Peter clenched his teeth. Eventually, he heard bolts being released, and when the door opened he was beckoned in.

"I am to take you to a room where Mother Superior will see you, sir."

"Thank you," Peter said with a sigh of relief.

After being invited to sit, and waiting several minutes, Mother Superior entered.

"You are not Mr Harrison! Who are you and what is it you want here?"

"Ah, you must have thought I was Thomas Harrison, my brother."

"Then pray what is your name and business here?"

Peter was feeling awkward and a little intimidated.

"I am Peter Harrison. I'm the younger brother of Thomas Harrison, who you met before. Tom is the father of two of the children, Alfie and Susie."

There was a moment of silence while she considered. "You dress in a similar fashion to Thomas Harrison, and you speak in the same manner. I can see similarities in your features, but can you prove your relationship?"

"No, I have nothing with me. Why don't you ask the children if they have an Uncle Peter and if there is anything unusual about him, especially his legs? Surely that would prove something?"

Standing, Mother Superior looked at him sternly. "Legs, is it! I'll be back."

It was a full five minutes before she returned.

"Well, Mr Harrison, the children rather excitedly

confirmed they do have an Uncle Peter. Although I understand you are not a true uncle to all of them. They said you have an artificial leg. Alfred wanted to know how I knew about you. I did not say."

"That's right, I am only a true uncle to Alfie and Susie, but the others call me uncle too."

Peter rolled up his trouser leg to reveal his pink prosthesis limb. Mother Superior looked on in amazement when he tapped it with his knuckles making a hollow sound.

"Well then, Mr Harrison it seems you are who you claim to be. You will excuse my caution as it is not unknown for children to be kidnapped for service on foreign ships or eventual slavery. I have to say that your brother was a great disappointment. He promised to return for the children but, as you must know, he never has. The children became distressed and difficult at times through their disappointment."

"Tom really wanted to come back, but his wife died causing a lot of problems, so I have come in his place."

"I am sorry to hear of his wife. What is it you now want with the children, Mr Harrison?"

"I'd like to care for them, but before I do anything, may I please see them."

"You shall. But please do not cause an upset. Wait while I fetch them?"

For Peter, the next few minutes were full of excited anticipation, yet tinged with reserve of how they would receive him.

Mother Superior had not told the children he was there in order to watch their reactions on seeing him. When the children entered, her remaining reservations disappeared.

Alfie and Susie immediately called, "Uncle Peter," and were the first to run to his open arms. Overjoyed, tears ran down Peter's cheeks while he found it difficult to speak. Almost immediately Polly, Mary, and Alan rushed to him, clambering for his embrace. When the first minutes of the emotional reunion had passed, Mother Superior told the children to sit, which they immediately did. From that small interaction, Peter could see that discipline was strict here.

"I'll leave you a while with the children, Mr Harrison."

Immediately after she had left, Susie and Alfie jumped up to stand close to their uncle. Sitting, he put his arms around them, pulling them to his sides. Susie buried her face in his neck, where he felt her tears run down to his collar. Again he found it difficult to speak.

It was several minutes before Alfie asked, "Why didn't Dad come back like he'd promised?"

"He desperately wanted to, Alfie," Peter spoke quietly, "he really did. But so much was happening at home that he wasn't able to come, but he was intending to keep his promise. He said he felt terrible at not coming after promising he would. Anyway, I came so that you'd know you've not been forgotten." Peter felt obligated to explain why Tom had not been able to return, but he would not do it now.

"Will you go away like Daddy?" Susie frowned.

"No, sweetheart, I'm staying right here with you, I promise."

Susie gave him another hug. Her soft, innocent touch to his cheek brought another surge of emotion. "Why didn't Daddy come back?"

Peter hesitated. "Oh, it's a long story. I'll tell you all about it another time."

"Will you take us home, Uncle Peter?" Polly asked.

"To be honest, I don't know if I can, but I'm going to do everything possible to."

There was a chorus of "Please, Uncle Peter, we want to go home."

"Peter looked at the floor, "I know you do, I know, I'll do my best, I promise. But it may take a while." Then, trying to lift the atmosphere, he smiled at them. "It's wonderful to see you all again. The best Christmas present I could ever have."

"Is it Christmastide - I mean Christmas?" Alfie asked.

"Not yet, but it will be soon." Peter now wished he had brought sweets and chocolate. "Why don't you tell me what you have been doing since you arrived here?"

Between them, the children described life in the convent, their chores, the nuns' treatment, and how strange they found the town.

Excitedly, Alan Fletcher added, "Do you know what, Uncle Peter? Nobody smokes here. We have not seen one person with a pipe or a cigarette. When I told the nuns about smoking, they laughed. "Why would anyone put leaves in their mouth and set fire to them?" they said to make fun of me.

Peter chuckled, but before he could comment Mother Superior returned.

"Come children, it's time for your Latin and scripture lessons. No doubt, you will see your uncle again before long."

Peter saw their disappointment. He nodded, winked to them and held out his arms to give them each a final hug. Susie clung on. "Go with Mother Superior, sweetheart, I'll see you later."

"Thank you, Mr Harrison, I shall return shortly."

Peter took the time to regain his composure.

"I must ask you, Mr Harrison, what are your intentions regarding the children?"

"Most importantly, I want to take care of them myself here in Bishop's Lynn, but I've only just arrived and not yet found work or a place to live."

"Do you not wish to return them to their homes?"

Peter had to think quickly and replied, "Yes, eventually. But we will stay here for a while. I need to find work and earn coin to take back. As you might know, our islands are very poor."

"Very well. Where will you sleep tonight? What work do you do?"

"I'll find an inn for a night or two. I have been caring for horses. Thomas taught me."

There was silence for almost a minute as she paced in thought. Peter watched, wondering what she would ask next.

"Are your intentions honourable, Mr Harrison? Do you sincerely intend to stay here a while and care for the children?"

Peter didn't hesitate and said, "Yes, absolutely."

"Then call here this evening. I may be able to assist you in your endeavours."

"Thank you. May I see the children then too?"

"Yes."

Peter thanked her and left to explore the streets. It didn't take long to find an inn with food and a bed for a few nights. Being a stranger here made him feel vulnerable and insecure. After eating, his explorations found him at the quays where he lingered a while, fascinated by the scene.

As he returned to the inn, his mind raced with

questions as realization hit home. What had he done? Is this my life now -where I'll stay until I die? Where will I live? What will I do for work? How will I look after the children? How will I get the kids back home? If I can send them, will I be able to go too?

Someone shouted at him. Startled, he was shaken from his thoughts and quickly jumped from the path of a cart hurrying into the quay. The jolt hurt his stub, making him limp. He stopped at the market square and sat in the shelter to wait for the pain to subside. People came and went. Some tried not to appear inquisitive but when he smiled at them, they quickly looked away. An old man approached and, without speaking, offered Peter a fish from his basket while holding out his hand for payment. A gentle shake of the head and a smile sent the old man shuffling away. Before long Peter left. Stopping at a blacksmith's shop, he watched as a horse was being shoed, thinking little had changed in seven hundred years.

"Do you shoe many horses?"

The man didn't look up, just answered, "Four or five a day."

"So you must know most of the owners?"

The blacksmith looked to see who the stranger was. "Not all of 'em, the wealthy ones send their grooms with their beasts. Not too happy with them wealthy folks, they want the job done immediately, but force me to wait long for payment."

"Do you know anyone who needs a groom?"

"None what I'd recommend." He watched with interest as the stranger left.

It was getting cold, so Peter decided to wait at the inn until evening. Checking his watch he saw it was past 6 o'clock, it had been dark for more than an hour. After eating a steaming bowl of broth with bread, he decided it was time to go to the convent.

The nun who peered through the inspection hatch recognized him, unbolted the door and beckoned him in.

"Welcome, Mr Harrison. Mother Superior is expecting you."

He thanked her and followed her to a reception room.

"Please sit. Mother Superior will be here in a moment."

She entered with a smile, helping Peter relax. "Well now, Mr Harrison, if we may confirm my understanding. Your intention is to establish yourself here in Bishop's Lynn with suitable employment and a home where you will care for the children. Is that correct?"

"Yes, it is."

"Good, then I may be able to assist you. Bishop Pandulph Masca has extensive stables and needs assistance. The man who previously managed them left with the Knights Templar some weeks back and left no word of his return. I have arranged for you to meet the bishop's secretary on the morrow at mid morn. His name is Gilbert Clarke, a scholarly man, who will probably decide on you quickly as his need is pressing. Of course, it will be up to you to convince him of your knowledge and skills. What do you say, Mr Harrison?"

"Wow, blimey! Thank you."

"Your speech is stranger than your brother's, Mr Harrison."

Peter grinned as he offered his thanks and appreciation.

She smiled back. "It will be good for the children to be with their own kind."

Peter asked if he could now see the children, and the next blissful hour was spent with them. After listening to their stories and desires, he again assured them that he would not desert them, repeating that he would do everything he could to get them home. By the time the children were ushered to their bedroom, they were happy and full of optimism.

This was the most relaxed Peter had been since arriving. He felt good and enjoyed a tankard of ale at the inn. His contented sleep came easy.

He woke early to the sound of horses' hooves and the clatter of carts on the cobbled street below his window. After eating a breakfast of salted pork, eggs, and bread, he asked the landlady for directions to the bishop's mansion.

"What do want there?"

Peter was surprised at her abrupt, almost rude manner, and taken off guard for the want of a cheeky answer, so told the truth, "I have an appointment."

"With the bishop?" she asked.

"If you don't know where it is just say and I'll ask someone else."

Disgruntled, she begrudgingly gave directions. "You'll know if he's there 'cos his flag'll be a-flyin' if he is."

Peter was becoming oriented to the town and easily found his way. He couldn't miss the impressive stone mansion with its high walled courtyard. As he approached the large doorway, a man stepped out and asked his business. On explaining that he had an appointment with Gilbert Clarke, he was shown into a small room off the entrance hall. He didn't know this was where Tom had almost met his end at the hands of the knights.

It was several minutes before a tall man dressed in

a dark flowing robe entered, introducing himself as Gilbert Clarke. Peter's interview was quick and informal. Clarke was only briefly interested in his knowledge of maintaining horses, much to Peter's relief. That he had previously worked with horses seemed enough.

Clarke took him through an archway leading to a large cobbled courtyard at the rear of the mansion. Further away to the left he was shown the stables. Opposite was a thatched cottage with an adjoining barn.

"There are four to sixteen beasts stabled here at any one time, depending on His Grace's movements and our number of guests. You are expected to attend to all animals equally. You have a staff of three: an ostler and two juveniles. The latter do much of the cleaning. You are required to see the courtyards are maintained daily, to order in hay and other feed as required, and see to the animal's ongoing health. Do you understand?"

"Yes. Do I understand that you are offering me the position?"

Clarke raised his eyebrows. "Do you not accept?"

"Yes, of course, thank you very much. It's just that you didn't actually…er, yes, I'm very pleased. Thank you."

"You may show your gratitude in your performance." He pointed to the cottage. "Over there is your accommodation where you will live and be available at all times. Is that clear?"

Peter's eyes sparkled with pleasure. He had landed in clover and couldn't believe his luck, never expecting to have accommodation provided with a position. "I have children" he said cautiously. "Are they allowed to stay here with me?"

"Naturally, it is usual. The previous occupant had his wife and children here also. If you have a woman, she may be required to assist in the main kitchen at feast times. It is incumbent on you to ensure your children's appropriate behaviour at all times and for them to stay out of the way. I must advise you that your entry and departure from the manor precinct will always be by the rear entrance. Do you understand?"

"Yes. Thank you."

"Now I must return to the house. Inspect your accommodation if you wish. You will start at first light on the morrow."

Without asking, Clarke had assumed that Peter could start the next morning. Then, with a sweeping flourish of his cloak, he turned and headed for the manor, leaving Peter to his own devices.

First, he explored the cottage. Although expecting little, he still found it basic: bare whitewashed walls, two small windows to the front, and the underside of the thatched roof formed a sloping ceiling. The largest room had a fireplace for warmth and cooking. On a bench to one side were two pots, a wooden bucket, a few plates, and utensils. There was a rustic-looking table and four chairs in the centre of the room. A door to one side led to a smaller room containing two single beds. This in turn led to a smaller room containing a single bed. Not quite what Peter had hoped for, but he was pleased to have somewhere to live. Wondering how he would manage with five children, he convinced himself he would find a way.

Next, he visited the stables where he found four horses, all in good condition. Their stalls were clean and stocked with feed. The empty stalls looked as though they had not been used for some days. Two teenage boys pushed past him with a wheelbarrow. Neither spoke.

"Excuse me, what are your names?"

"Who wants to know?"

Peter was surprised at being spoken to in such a way by someone so young and responded in a tone to establish his authority.

"I'm your new master. So, let's show a little respect, shall we?"

They looked down, quickly grabbed their hats from their heads. "Sorry, sir."

"That's better. Now, what are your names?"

They talked for almost a quarter of an hour. Peter had many questions and needed to know how things were done here. In conclusion, he said, "If you work well without me chasing you, we'll get along fine."

The boys nodded. "Yes sir. Thank you, sir."

He spent the afternoon cleaning the cottage with whatever he could find. Brought in firewood from a stack behind the barn and made kindling.

Returning to the convent that evening, he explained recent events to the children. He told them he would not be able to take them for a few days. As expected, they were disappointed and impatient but understood. He thanked Mother Superior for the introduction she had made, telling her that he had been offered and accepted the position, that he now had somewhere to live and make a home for the children.

"Unfortunately, the cottage is small and almost bare, so I have to find furniture and make it more homely for them. Would you please keep them here for a day or two longer?"

"Yes, of course, but only for a few days, you understand."

"Of course, thank you. I really do want to take care

of them myself, but they need beds, mattresses, and other things. I'll take them as soon as I can."

"We can give you sacks. Perhaps you could fill them with hay for mattresses? It is market day in the town, and at this time of the year there are always traders selling woollen blankets."

Peter thanked her and asked if he could see the children each day until he was ready to take them. She agreed.

He went back to the inn to eat but decided to spend the night in the cottage to save his coins. It was cold with dampness in the air, so he lit a fire. It didn't take long for his eyes to adjust to the dim flickering light that made mysterious moving patterns on the walls. He had no blanket, so dragged the single bed from the small room to near the fire. It was not as comfortable as his bed at the inn, but he slept well. It had been a fruitful, yet tiring day, and not without a little tension, but he was delighted at having achieved something positive.

It was dark when Peter awoke. He knew dawn would not be long in coming as the distant sound of a cockerel heralded its approach. Cold, he rekindled the fire and thought of what the day might bring. First, he would see what the boys and the groom were doing, then go to the market to buy food, blankets, and other items, such as he could afford. As the greyness of dawn appeared, he heard voices outside. On opening the door a middle-aged man and the two boys were waiting.

"Mornin' sir." the man said. "Me name's William. Most call me Bill. These here are Michael and Jeffery. Mick and Jeff, if you please. I hear you met 'em yesterday. Good lads, just as long as we keep an eye on 'em. Thought we should introduce ourselves, proper like.

What with you bein' new an all."

"Thank you, Bill. I appreciate that. It's nice to meet you."

The boys looked down and fidgeted with their caps in front of their stomachs. Bill looked Peter in the face.

"Can I show you around, sir?"

"Yes, that would be fine. Thank you."

Bill turned to the boys. "Don't stand there all day. Get started on mucking them stables out." Then looking back at Peter he said, "I keeps an eye on 'em, sir, t'make sure they do things proper. It never hurts to push 'em along now and ag'in."

The boys scurried away while Bill took Peter to the stables and to where the hay was stored. To the side of the stables was a well, the main source of water for the cottage and the stables. It looked quaint to Peter with its wooden winch and bucket. Bill explained that he and the boys know what to do most of the time but liked to be told what more was expected when the bishop was in residence or when they had visitors.

"He's not always here, spends a lot'a time in Norwich, you see. An 'we don't always get a lotta warning when he's a comin' back."

Having completed a tour of the yard and outbuildings, Peter invited Bill into the cottage where they sat at the table. Peter explained that he was new in Bishop's Lynn and needed to familiarize himself with the place. He didn't say where he had come from or how. Given Peter's speech and dress, Bill was clearly inquisitive but he didn't ask, confident that he would eventually be told. Bill had a pleasant, honest demeanour which encouraged friendship and trust, and Peter already found himself liking the man.

"I should tell you a little about the way I see things, Peter said. "First, you don't work *for* me. Nobody is any better than anyone else. We work together. We just have different jobs and responsibilities. But having said that, I have to take the responsibility for what goes on here, so I expect my instructions to be followed."

"Yes, sir, certainly. I got a wife and three children, so I needs this job. I worked at the quay for a while, and hated it. This 'ere job is a godsend with better pay and conditions. So I won't be a-lettin' you down.

"Good. Thank you, Bill. I'll be relying on you, especially in these first few days. Perhaps you could help me right now. As you can see, the cottage is rather bare and I need to get a few things."

Bill explained where to go and how much to pay for the things Peter needed. So, with Bill's help and generosity over the next few days, he was able to equip the cottage ready for the children.

Chapter 29

It was a few days before Christmas when the excited children moved in. Peter slept in the small room, Susie, Polly, and Mary in the back room and the boys in the main room. Their beds were brought in from the girls' room each evening. Although Alfie and Alan complained about the chore, they were happy to be in the warmest place.

Each of the girls was allocated daily tasks. Polly, being the oldest, would maintain the fire and anything to do with preparing food. Susie and Mary would keep the cottage clean and tidy, including bringing in water and wood. The boys were set to clearing a patch behind the cottage ready for planting spring vegetables. After a little thought, the boys were disconcerted at the notion of spring planting.

"Are we going to be here that long? We thought you were going to take us home, Uncle Peter?"

"I want to, but right now I don't know how to, or how long it will take. Anyway, it would be nice to have fresh vegetables if we are still here." He could see the boys were not entirely satisfied. "Tell you what! Why don't I tell you one of my stories before we go to bed this evening like I used to when we were by the river?"

There was a resounding, "Yes, please."

Their first evening meal together was satisfying. Bill's wife had sent a loaf of homemade bread and a pat of butter. Harold, the bishop's gardener, gave vegetables from the private garden, offered with a wink and instructions not to tell anyone. "We can't let them lit'luns go hungry, can we? That bishop's got lots more'an what he needs. Anyway, he's not here to see, is he?"

Later, sitting by the fire, Peter was satisfied. He had seen the children fed, they had enjoyed his story and were now sleeping peacefully. He reached for his bag to find the mysterious container that had brought him here, two of Tom's books on the care of horses, Susie's doll and Alfie's catapult. It was now his first opportunity to examine the container closely. He decided it didn't look exceptional, although its contents were another matter.

Christmas was only a few days away, so he wanted to do something special. Gifts for the children and Christmas dinner needed planning in secret if he was to make it a surprise. Presents for Alfie and Susie were easy. He would give them the catapult and doll, knowing they would be pleased. After some thought, he decided to make a bow and arrows for Alan and hand puppets for Mary and Polly. He would do it over the next few evenings after they had gone to bed.

The children were excited to hear that Christmas was so close and had fun decorating the cottage with holly, ivy, and a few pine cones they had managed to find. Peter was impressed and congratulated them on a job well done.

In the hours whilst sitting quietly by the river, he had often whittled away at pieces of wood and had become adept at carving with his shut-knife. So making two puppet heads didn't take long and cutting off part of his shirt sleeves to make gloves was easy. He tied the cloth to the wooden heads and made two small holes from which fingers could protrude. Alan's bow and arrow were made while the children were about their chores. All were then hidden under Peter's bed until the right moment came to surprise them.

Although he was pleased with being able to celebrate Christmas with gifts, when he looked at them he felt sad and a lump choked his throat. "Poor little devils," he muttered, "this is all they are getting for Christmas. Perhaps I could get them some warmer clothes to fight this bitter northerly."

The bishop was to spend Christmas in Norwich conducting services in the cathedral. His secretary went with him to manage his entourage, so the manor house was empty but for the cook, her maid, and a servant. No indication of when they would return was given, but Gilbert Clarke had paid everybody before they left. To Peter's delight, he had been given a small Christmas bonus on behalf of the bishop.

On Christmas Eve the cold north wind brought a flurry of snow with the threat of more to follow. That morning a matronly middle-aged woman wrapped in a heavy shawl had knocked on the cottage door.

"I'm Maggie. I cook for His Grace. It's time we met, not seen you around much, you must'a been busy, they say your name is Peter." All said in a single breath.

Peter confirmed his name with a smile. "I'm pleased to meet you, Maggie."

She took another breath. "Thought I had better tell you we got a bit of a tradition here come Christmastide. Everyone what works for the bishop gets dinner in the manor house on the day. So don't you go making no other plans. Them children a'yours get to come an'all." She gasped for breath before continuing, "It's good fun, but makes a lot'a work for me and the girl, especially when His Grace is here. Then we have to do it after his supper. He won't be coming in to say a prayer over us this year neither." She puffed and gasped as though she had been running.

"Would you like one of the older children to help you?" Peter offered.

"No. We can manage, we done it plenty'a times afore."

"What time shall we come?"

"Early evening. Come to the servants' quarters. We don't get to use the main dining hall."

With that, she turned and headed back to the house. Obviously, he and the children were expected to be there. "Well, that's Christmas dinner taken care of," he thought with pleasure.

As he had hoped, it snowed overnight, and a few inches lay across the yard and gardens when the day broke. The children would have a white Christmas. Anxious to go outside, they hurried their breakfast, but he held them back.

"It's Christmas day today, a time when we give presents." Peter had lost his faith during the war, so didn't mention the true meaning of Christmas or how the tradition of giving presents came about.

"Although I haven't been here long, I have managed a little present for each of you. Wait here whilst I get them." First, he brought the puppets for Mary and Polly. They immediately put a hand inside and waggled their fingers through the holes. With big smiles, they nodded the puppet heads to each other, making strange speaking sounds before falling into giggles. Next, he gave Alan his bow and arrows. Peter saw that Alfie and Susie were getting impatient and smiled as he playfully held them in suspense. "I think you will recognize these."

Alfie was thrilled with his catapult, pulling it back a few times to shoot imaginary rabbits.

Susie yelled, "It's Lilly! My Lilly! I had forgotten about Lilly! Thank you, Uncle Peter."

After a few moments, Susie looked up at him with sad eyes. "But Uncle Peter, we didn't get you anything."

Peter returned a warm smile. "Well, it's not too late. There is something I would like more than anything else…you could give one of your lovely big hugs and a big kiss on the cheek."

Later in the yard, they all helped make a snowman and had a snowball fight. Peter joined in and when he slipped and fell, they pelted him with snowballs. It was great fun and everyone laughed. Alan took delight in shooting their snowman with arrows. The girls called, telling him not to spoil it. After a while, their hands and feet were cold, so they went into the cottage to warm themselves by the fire. They complained of pain while their hands warmed. Peter told them not to worry, "It's called hot-aches. It'll go away as soon as your fingers are warm." He had forgotten what hot-aches were like, and it reminded him of his childhood.

In the afternoon a cord was strung across the room just above the girls' heads, and a blanket was draped across it. Mary and Polly were invited to stand behind it and give a Punch and Judy style puppet show. Everyone laughed at their funny voices and the silly things they said.

Still clutching Lilly, Susie scrambled onto Peter's lap. After a while, she kissed his cheek and sorrowfully whispered, "Uncle Peter, I still wish we had got you a proper present."

Peter felt her warm glow of love and affection. "Being here with you is the best present I could have wished for. So I am very happy, sweetheart."

She hugged his neck and blissfully snuggled into him. He thought she might be getting a little too big for this, but he liked it just the same.

Peter produced five small rounded pebbles and taught them to play five stones. After they had all tested their skill, a decision was made to have a competition to see who would be the five stones champion. Much cheering and laughter filled the little cottage as they played. After an hour, Alfie was congratulated on his new status and was allowed to keep the stones.

That evening they went to the gathering of the bishop's employees in the servant's hall. It was a jolly affair, and the children were able to meet Bill's children. Much to their delight, Alfie taught them to play five stones, and they all felt they had made new friends. The food was outstanding with roast pork and swan, with a range of mixed vegetables. Baked apples and fresh cream followed. With some discretion, the adults were permitted to taste a little of the bishop's wine. A prayer of thanks was said, making Peter feel awkward, while Maggie was repeatedly congratulated on her cooking. Although pleased, she blushed. "Oh, it's nothing really. I just did it for us instead of His Grace. Anyway, there's lots of stuff here what would go to waste if it wasn't eaten."

Peter suggested that Maggie and her "girl", as she called her, should sit and relax a while, noting that her girl was, in fact, a young woman. Then to Maggie's delight, he asked the children to wash the plates, pots and pans. In a quiet moment, Maggie suggested they finish the evening by singing Christmastide carols. It was late when they went to their beds, all feeling happy and fulfilled.

Mary said, "I think this is the best Christmas I have ever had."

Peter smiled with satisfaction, and his mind drifted. "I don't want them to spend another Christmas here, I must think about getting them home."

Chapter 30

The next day brought work as usual for Peter, Bill, and the lads. With only two horses in the stables, the work was finished well before noon. The stalls were clean, horses groomed, covered with blankets, given clean water and fresh hay and a pile of steaming horse dung lay in the snow nearby.

Peter smiled, "It's funny how you get used to that smell, Bill. It clears your nostrils and is never really offensive."

"It's all right until you step in it. It stinks a lot worse then."

Peter laughed. "I've never thought about it, but you are right. There's not a great deal to do with only two horses here."

"You wait till His Grace gets back. The stables will be nearly full, and when visitors come there'll be even more. There will be his coach to clean up too. We'll be busy from dawn to dusk. Best we make the most of it now while we can."

"Why don't you and the boys take the rest of the day off? I can keep an eye on things here."

The bishop returned in mid-January. Bill was right. There was a lot to do, and everyone was kept busy.

At the end of January, Gilbert Clarke announced that His Grace would make a pilgrimage to Rome in the spring, emphasizing that the coach, wagons, and horses must be in their very best condition for the journey. Everyone was pleased at the prospect of a more relaxing time that would follow. Especially knowing the bishop would be away for many months, or even a year. At the same time, they knew there would be much more to do before His Grace left. Peter decided that once the party had departed it would provide his best opportunity to go to Ely.

As spring approached, work on the bishop's coach and wagons intensified, most of which was done by Bill and Jeff. The health and fitness of the horses were attended to by Peter, while Mick cleaned and maintained the stables. As winter drew to a close, hay became scarce, but being for the bishop's stables sellers were obliged to part with it. There was an unspoken obligation to support the church, which often came with a twinge of resentment. Common people were expected to pay taxes and relinquish their animal feed without complaint. Peter empathized with their plight and hoped the spring grasses would soon appear in the paddocks.

They were given seven days' notice of the bishop's intended departure date, causing a great flurry of activity. Peter invited Bill to help make a list of things that still needed to be done. On seeing Peter's list, Bill's curiosity got the better of him and he asked where Peter was from. He was impressed that Peter could read and write, and was fascinated by the style of his writing. Although Bill was illiterate, he recognized the difference between what Peter was writing and what he had seen from the bishop and his secretary.

Maintaining his story, Peter explained that he was from an isolated island deep in the Washes where things were done differently. Although a little doubtful, Bill accepted the explanation.

As the week progressed, urgency and tensions grew in ensuring everything was perfect for the bishop's journey. On the day of departure, the staff respectfully lined up by the carriage to say farewell and wish the bishop a safe journey. This was one of only a handful of times when Peter saw the bishop. Maggie shed a tear for the man who had always treated them with respect and kindness, afraid for his safety on the long journey. Saying nothing, the bishop smiled with a gentle nod of acknowledgement before climbing into his carriage. They waited and watched as the small train departed. It was then that Peter first recognized the cook's "girl" as a pleasant-looking young woman of about his own age. When he smiled at her, she blushed and turned to see if Maggie had noticed, then looked down as she hurried back to the house. A welcome calm fell over the gathering as each returned to their duties. But Peter's mind was on Maggie's assistant.

It was not long before Peter found an excuse to visit the kitchen in the hope of seeing Maggie's girl. She was reserved and kept her back to Peter much of the time as she went about her chores. Although in a few fleeting glances, there seemed to be an attraction that her shyness denied. Peter found it a little frustrating, yet endearing. However, he took satisfaction from knowing he had been noticed. He wanted to ask her name but considered it too forward, especially in front of Maggie.

"Bring me that metal tray, Eva. Gentleman here wants me to make some sweet stuff how he told me, what he calls brittle toffee, for them children."

"Oh, Maggie, please call me Peter. I'd prefer that."

He was pleased to know the young woman's name and that she now knew his.

Maggie noticed him watching Eva. Her intuition brought a smile, and in her usual breathless rush, she said, "I got plenty'a sugar blocks…did you say you want me to put a few chopped nuts in there too? There's a bag or two in the bishop's pantry. He don't know what's in there, and if he did, he'll 'ave forgotten by the time he gets back."

"I'm sure the children would love to have nuts in it. Thank you".

"I'll do it how you told me but you'll have to wait for it to set proper. You'd better come back later."

Peter smiled, already knowing he would need to go back. Later, on his return, he found Maggie and Eva inquisitively inspecting the, almost transparent, brittle. He turned the shallow tray upside down and banging an edge on the table, the toffee dropped out in one piece. After breaking some off, he invited Maggie and Eva to try it. Their delight showed in their faces. Eva didn't appear so shy now and looked Pete, "Thank you, sir. It's very nice."

"I'd be pleased if you would call me Peter."

"My name is Eva.

"Thank you, Eva. I'll remember that."

They smiled at each other while Maggie grinned in amusement at their interaction. Peter thanked Maggie for making the toffee and put some aside for them before leaving with the children's special treat.

Over the next few weeks, Peter and Eva found themselves meeting "casually" while going about their work. Although Maggie could see there was nothing casual about it.

As spring neared, Peter thought more of going to Ely, so he asked Bill if he could manage for a few days without him.

"I managed well enough afore you come." Bill laughed saying, "Go and do your business with them monks and don't worry about what's happening here. We'll be fine."

Later that day Peter went to the quay to arrange a passage to Ely. Conveniently, he found one that would not leave until the day after tomorrow, giving him time to prepare and explain to the children why he was going.

By now Peter had formed a warm relationship with Eva and made a point of openly spending time with her. Knowing that he would miss her was a strange feeling, one he had not experienced before. He sensed that she felt the same, especially when she told him to be careful and asked him to return soon.

The next evening Eva presented him with a package. "Some food for your journey." Then, in a quick movement, she kissed his cheek and blushed. Susie, Polly, and Mary giggled.

The children were excited. Hoping he would be successful and come back soon. At three-thirty in the morning, he quietly left the cottage to catch the boat leaving on the flood tide. The journey was interesting but uneventful, apart from the overnight stop at the Denver inn.

He had not been there long before one of the old men sitting by the smouldering peat fire spoke.

"Not seen you here afore?"

"No, just passing through."

"Off to Ely, I suppose?"

"Yes, I have some business with the monks there."

The other man joined in. "You sounds like that other fella what were here a while back. Dressed a bit like you an'all. Said he were working for King John, or som'ut like that. He were off to Ely an'all."

"Ah, that would have been my brother, Tom."

"Come to think of it, he looked a bit like you, only pr'aps a bit older." The old men were content at having identified the stranger.

"You can't be working for King John, 'cos he's dead and gone. Thank the Lord. Mind you, we now got a nine-year-old. King Henry III, a big title for a little fella. Dunno what he's gonna do."

Peter smiled. "He'll probably do what he's told. I work for Bishop Eustace at his manor in Bishop's Lynn."

With their curiosity satisfied, the old men settled down to talk between themselves.

They had arrived in the early evening and although he'd done little during the day, Peter was tired after getting up so early and felt lucky to have a real bed for the night. The next morning brought another early start and later that day he was in Ely. No one took notice of him in the evening light as he made his way up the muddy tracks towards the hill top. Stopping occasionally, he was fascinated to see carts drawn by as many as eight oxen.

By the time he reached the top, the evening sun had gone, making it a priority for him to find an inn for the night. There was still a hive of activity in the failing light with craftsmen and builders still going about their work in earnest. Peter asked a coster, peddling leather aprons, where he might find a place to eat and sleep but received only a strange look accompanied by a grunt.

Assuming the man had not understood, Peter continued his exploration and soon discovered that although inns were plentiful in the town, they were full. It was dark, and an hour had passed before he found an alehouse on the southern outskirts of the town that would provide him with a bed.

On entering, he noticed a short, rotund man wearing a once-white apron and holding a very large jug, standing to one side to survey the scene, looking for guests needing more ale. Peter assumed this was the landlord.

"Good evening, landlord…."

"Not from round here, are you?" the landlord interrupted.

"Well, as it happens, I…" Peter checked himself with a simple, "No."

"Thought not. What can I do for you?"

"I'd like to stay here for the night if you have room, maybe for a few nights."

"It must be your lucky day, sir. I got one left. That'll be two silver pennies…in advance if you please. Can't have you foreigners running off at dawn without paying, can we? We got enough of that going on as it is."

"What about meals?"

"Pay when you eat, same for your ale. Take it or leave it!

Marian, that's me wife, will show you where to sleep."

After being paid, the landlord strutted off to fill a tankard for a customer who had waved his empty vessel. Moments later a short skinny woman entered carrying a tray of steaming bowls and a plate of bread. In a deep voice that didn't match her appearance, she called, "Two braised ducks, one eel pie!"

Three men each raised a hand from one of the small

tables. It was then that Peter noticed there were women there too, but after watching them flirt with customers, he realised why they were there. Sitting at the only vacant table, he waited for the skinny woman's approach.

"Yes?" Her aggressive tone deterred him from asking what she had. But he managed to say, "Duck, please."

She held her hand out for payment.

"And an ale."

"He gets the ale!" As she gestured towards the man in the dirty apron.

Minutes later she returned with a large bowl of what looked like vegetable soup with a quarter of a braised duck in it. Turning to the landlord, she called across the room. "Man here wants ale!" He raised his eyebrows, annoyed at the need to be called to provide service where he'd failed to notice.

Peter surveyed the scene as he ate, wondering about their unfriendly attitude. Maybe there are more than enough customers to keep them busy without the need to be polite to any of them. He was warm and fed, but tired. When the woman returned for his empty bowl, he asked if Marian would show him to his room.

"That's me!" she said as she pointed to a small door in the corner of the room. "Through that door, top of the stairs, second door on the left is yours. Take a candle off the shelf afore you go."

Peter rose slowly, adjusted his jacket, and made for the door. He had not previously realised there was an upper floor. On entering his room, he could see why. The roof space had been converted into a series of tiny rooms where he could only stand upright in the middle. A simple framed bed and a wooden stool occupied most of the floor space, leaving barely enough room to manoeuvre. There were no sheets, just a crude mattress and a woollen blanket. After removing his boots, jacket, and trousers he ducked beneath the sloping beams to lie on the not-so-comfortable, bed. With his hands behind his head, he stared at the underside of the roofing thatch and pondered how to go about things tomorrow. It was noisy. Voices from downstairs were as clear as if they were coming from outside his door. He was tired and hoped the racket would not last.

Breakfast was stodgy oats with goat's milk.

"Do you have any eggs?"

"They cost extra," Marian replied as she walked away with disinterest, suggesting she didn't want the bother of preparing them.

Longing for a mug of Ma's tea right now, he was shocked at the realisation that she would not be born for another seven hundred years, and he for a little longer. Such notions took some getting used. So for now he closing his eyes he shook his head to clear the befuddlement.

Chapter 31

Peter explored the town for a while, not sure of the difference between a bishop and an abbot. As he wandered, his thoughts were continually distracted by the sights and sounds of Ely. It was like nowhere he could ever have imagined. Still, with no idea who to ask for, he had no option other than to approach one of the monks he saw at the construction site.

Unsure how to pose his question without appearing ignorant, his question came out wrong. "Who is the boss of the monks?"

The shocked monk stepped back, taking a moment to look Peter up and down. "What is your business here? Who are you?"

"Sorry," Peter said awkwardly. "I didn't mean to be rude but I just need to talk to whoever is in charge at the monastery."

"The Abbot fulfils that role. But you are a stranger here, young man. What is your business with the Abbot?"

Peter wondered what business it was of the monk.

"I've got private things to discuss, which I'm sure the Abbot wouldn't want me to divulge."

The monk was indignant. "You speak strangely."

"Can you please tell me where I can find the Abbot?"

"In the abbey or at the monastery, of course."

"And where are they?" Peter stared at the man.

"Go to the south side of the construction and you will see the monastery."

"Thank you." Peter was satisfied with how he had managed the situation.

At the abbey door, Peter was greeted by a novice monk who, without speaking, studied his dress. Then, believing his manner might be offensive: "I'm sorry, sir…but you present yourself in an unusual way for these parts. One I have seen only once before. I did not mean to offend."

"No offence taken, I assure you. I would like to speak to the Abbot please."

"Certainly, sir. I will see if he is free. You dress and speak in the manner of another gentleman who was here last year. He also wished to speak with Abbot Blackthorne."

Peter smiled. "That must have been my brother, Thomas. I'm his younger brother, Peter."

"Yes, yes, that's it. Thomas, Thomas Harrison was his name. But I digress. Please wait here while I let the Abbot know you wish to see him."

It was only minutes before the door opened again. A middle-aged man, clothed in long black robes with a white rope tied about his waist, offered a smile.

"Peter Harrison, I believe?"

"Yes, sir - I mean, Abbot."

"If you are truly the brother of Thomas Harrison, you are most welcome."

"I am. Thank you." Peter shuffled nervously.

"Yes, I see the likeness. Come in, come in. We shall talk in private. I hope you are not going to hurry away as did your brother. I have many unanswered questions."

He followed the Abbot to his chamber. As they entered, Blackthorne turned to the young monk, instructing that they should not to be disturbed. There were three chairs, two in front of a large table covered in scrolls and other documents, a third, much larger chair, stood on the far side.

"Please be seated, Mr Harrison."

The Abbot sat on one of the smaller chairs and gestured his visitor to sit on the other. Peter was relieved and a little perplexed at the eagerness of his welcome. Clearly Tom must have made a good impression.

"Now, Mr Harrison. What brings you here?"

"Well, as you remember my brother…"

The Abbot's enthusiasm didn't allow Peter to finish. "Yes, I could hardly forget him. Your village children fell victim to an ageing potion concocted by one of our monks. Unfortunately, we were not able to assist him in his quest to reverse its effects. However, our discussions were most intriguing. I was reluctant to believe him until he produced evidence of his transportation to our time. I was finally convinced when certain of his prophesies, or historical facts as he called them, materialized. In particular, those of our previous king's demise and the loss of his wealth." He paused to regain a more serene composure. "Please tell me how you also come to be here."

"I arrived here the same way my brother did, as I'm sure you must know. Tom found himself here by accident and discovered our missing children. I came deliberately because of the children…and for other personal reasons." Before the Abbot could ask his other reasons, Peter quickly added, "One big difference is that he sniffed the potion and travelled back and forth a few times, that's how we knew what had happened to the children. But I tasted it, so I can't go back."

"Your brother was most anxious to find an antidote which would send your children to your own time, but as I said, it was not possible. I do hope you are not on the same quest."

"Well actually, I am. But I can wait and will pay for the research."

"I regret that payment will make no difference. May I ask why you tasted it knowing you may never go back to your own time?"

"Tom said it was impossible to find an antidote. So if that was true, then I wanted to stay here and look after the children."

"That is very noble of you, Mr Harrison, but how would you have financed the research? Although, as I said, payment will not aid your quest."

"I work for Bishop Eustace in Bishop's Lynn. He is a kind man and pays his staff well."

"I know Bishop Eustace and agree that he is most honourable and can be generous."

"Abbot Blackthorne, if your monks had been set the task of making a potion, such that when it was tasted or smelled, it would send that person back hundreds of years in time, would they know what to do? Or believe that it could be done?"

"Well, my immediate expectation is of their jest at it being ridiculously impossible."

Peter leaned forwards holding the Abbot in a stare. "But we know it's not impossible, because that is exactly what they did!"

The Abbot pulled his head back, knowing where his visitor's argument was leading.

"So why then, if your monks were clever enough to achieve what they once consider impossible, even if by accident…"

Blackthorne raised a hand to stop Peter from saying more. With his fingers spread wide and their tips pressed against each other in front of him, he stared at the ceiling for what seemed an eternity.

"You make a good point, Mr Harrison. After all, in the Christian church, we are familiar with miracles and know them to be possible. But for miracles, we would have no saints. Please allow me time to consider and talk with the monk in question. The poor fellow was incarcerated for some weeks after the unforeseen power of the original potion was revealed. He lived with visions of being burned at the stake after it was suggested he had delved in witchcraft." The abbot grinned.

"When will you see him?"

"On the morrow, after morning dedication. You are aware, Mr Harrison, that if your quest is to be fulfilled it could take a very long time, even years if it can be achieved at all."

Peter frowned. "Yes."

"Of course, it may also take a season or two to gather the appropriate ingredients as and when they may be required, many of which are cultivated at Denny Abbey. I'm afraid the abbess there is very protective of their produce and imposes heavy charges for the most rare and difficult to cultivate."

"Please don't be concerned about payment, I'll pay for them."

"Then leave it with me, Mr Harrison. You may return midday tomorrow. I regret that I am unable to offer you the same hospitality as I did your brother. We currently have many guests, a delegation no less, who require our hospitality and seek my attention. You were indeed lucky to arrive between debates while our scribes record events thus far."

The next day Peter waited for almost an hour in the Abbot's chamber before he blustered in.

"Ah, Mr Harrison. Please accept my apologies for keeping you, I can spare but a few moments. I have spoken with the monk in question and instructed him to investigate the possibility of your request. His name is Ambrose. You should address him as 'Reverend Sir' if you wish to be correct. He can be found in his cell at the rear of the abbey. I have committed you to visit him periodically to enquire of his progress, and to provide funds for any purchase he may be required to make. I might add that it may serve your purpose if a personal gift from you was occasionally forthcoming. Your visits will also serve to aid his continued focus on the matter. Please understand that progress, if there is to be any, will be slow, for his unusual knowledge of the Latin scriptures is often in demand, so will distract him."

"Thank you, Abbot, I'm very grateful. I'd like to meet, Mr. Ambrose, I mean the Reverend Sir right away, if I may."

"Of course. Naturally, you will wish an opportunity to negotiate your terms. I will have him brought here if you care to wait in the outer hall. Now if you will excuse me, I must respond to other duties."

Peter stood and thanked the abbot again for his time and assistance.

Chapter 32

After his mother's death, Tom had become reclusive. Not unsociable, but content to be alone with his innermost thoughts and memories. It was nine years since Ma had passed away and, although he didn't feel sorry for himself, he still felt the pain of losing his wife, mother, brother, and children. His feelings of guilt for contributing to Susie and Alfie's disappearance only added to his pain. Modernization on the farm and his reluctance to acknowledge it as progress did not help his demeanour. He struggled to admit that his beloved horses were becoming redundant, and believed this was why he had not been promoted to farm manager when the position had become vacant.

Early evenings were mostly spent grooming and talking to his two remaining mares, after which he'd find something to eat. Preparing simple meals had become monotonous as a result of his reluctance to cook. He relaxed by the stove, sitting in the old carver, listening to the wireless. He had nailed Dora's old clothes prop high on the back of the wooden toilet hut and run a wire from the kitchen to the top to make an aerial. Taking his time to read the newspapers on Sunday mornings had become a ritual, and when he folded the large pages back he'd still say, "Sorry, my duck, I'll be done in a minute." At other times he was frustrated with himself for feeling guilty at smoking more than one pipe in the kitchen, knowing that Dora wouldn't approve. Then he would chastise himself for being silly.

The last of the wheat harvest had been gathered and the haystacks were built, allowing Tom to finish early, and not at sunset, which was normal at harvest time. After returning his horses to their stables, he went to fetch them fresh hay from the big barn. As he approached he saw two people standing just inside, partly in shadow. Apart from himself and other workers, nobody from the village had been in there for years, and certainly not the local children. The villagers would have had it pulled down by now if they could.

As he moved towards the barn the two stepped into the light. Tom stopped in his tracks, shocked, not knowing what to say. In confusion, he tightly closed his eyes for a second and stared again.

The shorter of the two, a girl of about eleven or twelve, hesitated before stepping towards him, stopping at arm's length. She could see the confusion in his rapidly glazing eyes as realization sunk in. The boy, in his early teens, followed a pace behind her.

Tom's vision blurred.

"It's me, Daddy! It's me, your Susie."

She threw herself into his arms. Alfie, who was too emotional to speak, embraced them both as they all stood in tears. Tom felt his heart pound and knees weaken as they had never done before, not sure if his mind was playing tricks, and if this was truly real.

In a surreal flurry of emotion, they made their way to the house where it took a long time for them to regain their composure. Alfie and Susie struggled to comprehend that they had actually returned and had so much to tell. Tom was beside himself with joy and had a million questions, yet choked by emotion, not knowing where to begin, he stared hard at them to convince himself they were real.

It was Alfie who broke the silence.

"Nothing has changed here, Dad. Everything looks just as I remember it."

When Tom tried to speak, his throat knotted and he was only able to croak out a few unintelligible words.

"I was so little when we left that I only have vague memories of being here, but I certainly remember you, Daddy," Susie said.

They sat, arms reaching across the kitchen table with their hands linked tight. Tom clung to them as though he would never let them go again. Desperate to know what had been done to get them back, it was his first question.

"Uncle Peter got the monks to make another potion."

Alfie cut in, "It wasn't that simple, Susie. Uncle Peter went to Ely at least twice every year to see the monk who was trying to make a new potion. On his last visit, the monk finally told him it was impossible, that he was exhausted trying, and there were no more possibilities. Uncle Peter got upset, so the monk said that although he had not found a reversal potion, he had made one that might dilute the effect of the first one. That if it worked, it might cause us to revert to where we came from. The monk hadn't tested it, but Uncle Peter took it anyway… and as you see, it worked!"

Tom looked down and gently shook his head. "Peter," he muttered, "you little devil, you bloody did it! Bless your beautiful heart." He looked at the children. "What about the others? Are they coming too and what about Uncle Peter?"

Susie answered. "Uncle Peter was cautious about the stuff because we didn't know what else it might do, so it was decided that one of us would test it first. Alfie was the only one to volunteer, and I didn't want to be parted from him, so I insisted that we try it together. Uncle Peter wasn't happy about it but we managed to persuade him. We drank some of the stuff yesterday about this time, so I suppose it takes a day to work."

"What about the others?"

"It was agreed that if we disappeared, then they would take some at the same time the next day. So if we're lucky, they could be here about this time tomorrow."

Tom's heart pounded. "And is Uncle Peter coming too?"

Alfie's expression changed to a frown. "Uncle Peter decided not to come back. He met a really nice lady where we lived and married her. We'll tell you more about her later, but he is happy and has children of his own.

"How is Uncle Peter?"

As Alfie replied, Susie searched inside her shawl for a parchment. "He is all right. He's happy and has a job with the bishop in Bishop's Lynn. He loves Eva. That's his wife's name, and he adores his children. We'll miss them all."

Susie passed Tom a rolled-up parchment. "He wrote you and Grandma a letter."

"I'm very sorry, but I should tell you that your grandma passed away a few years ago. Did Uncle Peter tell you that your mum had died too?"

Susie looked at her hands. "Yes, he said she had

accidentally fallen into the river. He was very upset and didn't want to talk about it."

Tom understood but didn't explain; just read Peter's letter.

Dear Ma and Tom,

If you are reading this letter you will know that we eventually found a way to get the children home. They are all well, and I have done my best to care for them over the years. I have tried to improve their education in English, Arithmetic, and other general subjects. No doubt, you will be surprised to hear that they all know Latin, courtesy of the nuns.

I won't return with them as I have found happiness here, more than I could ever expect back in our village. I have married a wonderful lady named Eva, and we have two lovely children of our own named Thomas and Dora. (I can see you smiling). I'll leave it to Alfie and Susie to tell you about them. They could never come back with me to your time, and there is no way I would leave them as they are my life's love now. I hope you understand.

Your loving son and brother, Peter

Tom's eyes glazed again as he rolled the parchment. Susie squeezed his hand. On looking up, he sniffed, stood, and turned his back to face the stove saying, "I'd best put the kettle on."

Alfie smiled. "Uncle Peter always said tea was for all occasions."

The atmosphere soon returned to one of joy and excitement with much to discuss. It was not until the small hours of the morning that anyone mentioned being tired.

"Your room is just as you left it," Tom said with a grin.

He doubted that he would sleep tonight with so much adrenalin charging through his veins so sat in his old carver and recounted the day's events. Lighting his pipe was difficult due to the stubborn lump in his throat. He gently put the pipe down in awe of his good fortune, when a thought startled him. He stiffened and sat upright in the chair.

'What would he tell the villagers? What will they think? How could he tell Mr and Mrs Brown and Mr and Mrs Fletcher that their children may be coming back in a few hours? Should he tell them in advance? He speculated that if they simply turned up and went to their homes, the news would be around the village in minutes. The police would be asking millions of awkward questions and the answers would never be believed. Then there was the press. They would have a field day. No, there had to be an agreement on how to deal with this.

The next morning Tom was too emotional to eat, but it was with the greatest pleasure that he cooked two hearty breakfasts and watched with pride as Susie sat at the hearth with the toasting fork. The look of joy on his children's faces as they ate would stay with him forever. "I can't begin to tell you how wonderful it is to have you home again, but we have a bit of an issue. How shall we announce your return and the possibility of Polly, Mary and, Alan coming back?" Alfie and Susie didn't see a problem, so Tom explained.

After much discussion, it was decided that Tom would go to each of the parents and invite them to his house to discuss their children. It was Sunday, so he knew that if he went early they would be at home preparing for church. He was hesitant at making the initial approaches as the Harrison name was still considered with some disdain. Many believed they had been involved in some way. There was a connection with their big barn and Peter, especially as he had also disappeared leaving most to believe that he was guilty and had run away rather than be found out and face the consequences.

Nonetheless, on Tom's insistence that he had something of importance to discuss regarding their children, curiosity overcame their reluctance. It was agreed they would all meet at Tom's house at mid-day. His urgent request for them to tell no one only heightened their curiosity.

Chapter 33

Tom waited until everyone was present before explaining why they were there, which meant that Susie and Alfie would have to wait out of sight. By five past twelve, all the parents had arrived. It was crowded in the little kitchen, so they were invited into the "best room".

Brian Fletcher was the first to speak. "What's this all about Tom?"

"I really don't know where to start, so I'll come straight to the point." He took a breath in anticipation of the impact his words were about to have. "There is a very good chance your children will come back to the village later today."

There was stunned silence while they all stared at Tom, who waited for his words to sink in. "If they do come, we need to talk about how to handle things afterwards."

Mrs Fletcher and Mrs Brown, standing shoulder to shoulder, clasped each other's hands in shock, then stared wide-eyed at each other before fixing their stares back onto Tom.

Brian Fletcher was sceptical. "How do you know? I bloody well knew along you Harrisons' had something to do with them kids going missing! So how do you know?

Where are they now? You'd better not be pissing us about!"

Tom spoke quietly. "Relax, Brian, it's not what you think. The truth is I have known where they are for a while but none of you would have believed me in a million years if I'd told you. And if I had told the police they would have had me locked up in the loony bin, and they would still not have been able to get your children back."

"Why didn't you tell us anyway?"

"Look, as I said, it's difficult to know how to tell you even now but here goes…" Softly, Tom cleared his throat. "They were accidentally transported back to the early twelve hundreds, to the time of King John."

"Bullshit! You are out of your tree, Thomas Harrison!"

"You see, Brian, you don't believe me. Well, let me tell you that my Alfie and Susie came back yesterday, and your kids could come this evening!"

"So where are your kids now?"

"Wait here."

Tom left the room and called for Alfie and Susie to come down. When they walked in, still wearing medieval clothes, the women gasped, recognizing them inspite their added years. The men were sceptical at just seeing a boy and a girl strangely dressed. Mrs Fletcher and Mrs Brown's knuckles turned white as their grip on each other tightened. Brian Fletcher demanded to know what was going on.

"Shut up, Brian! Shut the hell up!" his wife demanded, full of tension, anticipation, and wanting to believe.

Tom turned to Alfie and Susie. "This is Polly's, Mary's, and Alan's mum and dad. Would you please tell them where you have been and how you got there?"

They all listened, dumbfounded as Alfie and Susie hesitantly told their story, afraid of being ridiculed.

Brian Fletcher attempted to interrupt several times with demanding questions but was told by Tom to wait until he had heard the whole story.

Alfie and Susie explained how they came to be transported, how their Uncle Peter had looked after them all, and how they had come back. The rest would be told in good time.

"As unbelievable as it sounds," Tom added, "it does explain why there has been no trace of them or any leads to discover what had happened."

Trembling, Mrs Brown believed their story, and remembering, suggested that it explained the medium's experience. "So where will they be when they come back?"

"Where they left from in the big barn, I expect," Tom speculated.

Still agitated, Brian Fletcher asked where the "stuff" that did this had come from and where Peter Harrison was now.

Tom explained that he had found a medieval container while ploughing. He looked away when he said he'd left it in the big barn where the children had found it. Before there could be any comment or question about his mistake, he continued, savouring the next moment.

"As for my brother, you can stop blaming him for having anything to do with their disappearance. He came back from the war in a bad way, both physically and mentally. He had a mountain to climb, needed affection, love, caring, and understanding. But all you did was to cause him more pain and suffering. The poor lad almost went out of his mind."

Tom felt his blood pressure rising, but he didn't care. He had stored his emotions for too long. He would say what had to be said. "I can tell you that he felt he had no future here and knew he was being blamed for the children's disappearance, that nobody would listen or try to understand. Why? Because you didn't want to! You had made up your minds and that was that. He loved and cared for *all* the children, and they adored him. So he tasted the potion himself, knowing that he may never come back again, not even if he wanted to. He went so he could look after *your* children and hopefully find a way to get them back to *you*. And that is exactly what he has done! My brother is a bloody hero, and I'm very proud of him! You should all be ashamed of yourselves!"

As Tom's words sunk in there was a lingering, embarrassed silence which dared to be broken by some brave soul. They simply looked down, afraid to catch Tom's steady, but glazed stare as he turned to each of them. He hoped he had shamed them while it took a few moments for him to calm himself. Then, in a more relaxed tone, he said, "Now look, God willing, there is every reason to suppose your children will come back this evening, so we have to come up with a plan to deal with it."

Brian Fletcher interjected, "We don't need no plan. Let's get them back home and tell the whole bloody world."

"That's just what we can't do. Can you imagine what the press would do with this story? They'd make us look like idiots and say we are all inbred, mad villagers. They would pester the life out of us forever and a day. Nobody will believe us. It'll be too outrageous for them. More importantly, the children will be pestered to death. They would never be left alone and probably wish they were back with my brother."

The room fell silent for a few seconds, followed by murmurs of agreement. Tom paused before adding, "And what about the police? How on earth would we explain it to them? Can you imagine trying to convince Sergeant Bowles! He would have us locked up in the madhouse, or have the children taken from us thinking we are all lunatics. My guess is that the police would think we had secretly imprisoned them all this time for some bizarre reason or other. They would be bound to think of something, and we'd all be in trouble. Who knows what they might come up with? No, we have to agree to keep all this quiet, as hard as it might be."

Brian Fletcher had calmed. "You are right, mate, but what about the other people in the village? They'll soon find out."

"I've given it some thought, and I think we have to keep the children out of sight for a little while. We'll tell the village folk in our own way and explain the seriousness of why it has to be kept secret. Some will believe the truth but most won't. Either way, they have to keep their big mouths shut."

Mrs Fletcher made an obvious observation: "I can't see everyone keeping it quiet for long. Someone is bound to talk."

Tom had a ready answer which hinged on hope and trust. He scanned the faces around the room while they stared expectantly back at him. He spoke cautiously in the knowledge that his reasoning carried great risk. "This is a very small village and, apart from the vicar, everyone was born and bred here, some families for generations. I know we are an odd lot at times, but now the chips are seriously down we need to be here for each other. If we explain properly and ask for their support, we might just get away with it. We might also tactfully suggest that if anyone does speak out, then others will have nothing more to do with them. They'll be made to feel like outcasts having betrayed the village, be ostracized and encouraged to leave.

"That's a bit harsh," someone suggested.

"Then ask yourself how much you value your children, their sanity and their future lives? Do you have a better idea? Perhaps you would like to move away and settle somewhere else."

No one answered, but their body language said they understood.

"Okay then. According to Alfie and Susie, if they do get back, we can expect them in the early evening. We can't let them go wandering off when they arrive, so I suggest we meet here again at about five-thirty. My Alfie and Susie will wait for them in the big barn and bring them to the house. Your kids know mine so will trust them.

Everyone agreed it was the best thing to do and left with many unanswered questions. The news was so unexpected and sudden that it created a confused numbness in a surreal situation. Even the village looked different as they returned to their homes. None could fully believe this was happening but hoped and prayed it was.

The parents arrived at Tythe Farm early. Few had little to say and all were unsure of what to expect, all nervously impatient, knowing they may have an agonizing wait.

Susie and Alfie went to the barn in hopeful anticipation. Once inside, Alfie's memories flooded back but Susie said she hardly remembered the barn. "Is this where it all started?"

Choked, Alfie looked away.

By seven-thirty, the parents were becoming restless. Tom tried to explain there was no control over when, or if, the children might arrive and asked for their understanding. In his heart, he prayed for the children to come. Trying to distract everyone, he offered tea, but it didn't work. As one of the ladies took over pouring, more fears flooded his mind. If the other children didn't come, there would be no way of keeping Alfie and Susie's return quiet. The parents would make sure of that. The police would be involved, the press wouldn't leave him alone, and his children would be mercilessly hounded. It could be him that was forced to leave the village. He looked at the ceiling and said a silent, pleading prayer, "*Dear God, please let them come. Please bring them back home for everyone's sake.*"

After another hour, frustrations were beginning to boil over, and more tea did nothing to quell the tension. Tom knew that Brian Fletcher would soon have something to say. It was only a matter of time.

"Look here, Tom, I hope you are not mucking us about? 'Cos if you are, you'll know about it! We've been here for ages, patiently waiting, saying little, and for what? Bugger all! It's not funny and bloody cruel too. Look at the state of my missus!"

Tom tried his best to explain again but to no avail.

"Let me go and have a word with Alfie and Susie to be doubly sure that I got the time right."

Tom returned minutes later. "Yes, the time is correct but please remember that it's only an approximation."

Several people began to speak at the same time, but

Brian Fletcher's voice dominated, "I dunno about the rest of you, but I'll give it to nine-thirty then I'm off home. Or maybe to the pub, I could do with a pint or two after this crap."

Sounds of agreement came from the gathering. Tom's knees weakened as the minutes passed in silence. He tried not to keep checking the time, but the constant ticking of the clock on the mantelpiece only aided his torment. Anger and disappointment crept into the room. Optimism and patience were gone, and the intense stares Tom received were painful with each pair of eyes asking if this was a cruel hoax. He searched helplessly for answers but was unable to explain.

At nine-thirty Mr Fletcher put his cap on. "Right, that's it, I'm off! Damn you, Tom Harrison!"

Everyone had something to say at the same time as hats and coats were donned. Tom's pupils narrowed along with his feelings of despair, frustration, and vulnerability.

Through the hubbub, he heard a familiar sound and raised a hand for silence. All eyes followed his to the door. The latch clinked again before the door slowly opened. Susie and Alfie entered without speaking. Behind them came Polly Brown, Mary and Alan Fletcher still wearing their short hooded capes. There was a deafening silence with nobody moving. The children's eyes focused on their parents, as did the parents' on their children. As recognition of their older children sank in, a scream from one of the ladies triggered a crescendo of uncontrollable joy which the small room could hardly contain.

Oblivious to the screams, tears, embraces, and the emotional sounds of rejoicing, Tom's shoulders dropped with relief as he slumped into his old carver. Leaning forwards, he placed his elbows on his knees and with his face in his hands, he sobbed with relief. Alfie and Susie moved to his side, each resting a comforting hand on his shoulders. It was finally over.

History and Geography

A scenic paradise, dense forests of oak and beech proudly stood unmolested. Sabre-toothed cat, hyena, woolly mammoth, wolf, elk, bison, and bear roamed freely in this world of plenty. Then came the ice, building up to a mile thick, creeping slowly southward over the land to devour this pristine habitat. Giant glaciers contoured and reshaped the land beneath their colossal weight.

Creatures were forced south as lush landscapes were crushed and compressed. The great forests were flattened, and for 120,000 years the temperature did not exceed freezing point. Then, just as this mighty force reached its peak, the Earth's axis changed, allowing the sun to warm the planet once more and so the ice began to recede. As it melted, sea levels rose by three hundred feet and when it was finished the landmasses of the planet were shaped quite differently.

By 12,000 BC, the melting had stopped, and the planet settled once more. In Britain much of the melted ice and spill from the North Sea had drained onto the flat, lowland areas of East Anglia to create vast wetlands covering more than three thousand square kilometres, some of which to the north, became tidal saltmarshes. The warming sun encouraged the regrowth of vegetation and the formation of a new and different habitat, allowing life to return to what had once seemed an inhospitable environment. But the giant trees did not return. The great swamps and waterways became the natural homes of fish, eels by the trillion, and wildfowl. Reeds grew tall and plentiful. Willow trees, brambles, and shrubs began to grow on the few shallow hills which had become Fenland islands.

Although a harsh damp environment, hardy people migrated to this seemingly inhospitable place. The Neolithic, Bronze and Iron Age, Roman, Saxon, and Medieval periods saw populations grow on the periphery of the Fens and on its islands. The Romans recognised the potential to reveal rich, peat-laden farmland if only the Fens could be drained. But their attempts failed.

In 1634, King Charles I approved the 4th Earl of Bedford to carry out works that would drain these huge marshes. His initial attempts were unsuccessful, so in 1650, the experienced Dutch engineer Cornelius Vermuyden was commissioned to undertake the task.

The people of the Fens were unhappy to see their livelihood of wildfowling, fishing for eels, reed cutting, weaving willow into baskets and traps all disappear. They clashed with the workmen and their masters while trying to preserve these wetlands. Their fighting was so fierce they became known as Fen Tigers. These people were hunters and gatherers and the Fens economy depended on the currency of eels, reed for thatch, and willow-woven goods.

A group of shallow hills towards the south became known as the Isles of Eels. Hence, the name Ely came naturally for the capital of this Fenland region.

Land shrinkage occurred as a result of removing the

water. This continues today and is measured in tens of feet from the days of the earliest records. As the land shrank, artefacts and objects from the distant past have neared the surface to eventually reveal themselves at the turn of a sod. Even remains of the great forests of giant trees, now called Bog Oaks, feel the sun again. Other strange, unidentified, mysterious objects from medieval times now see daylight for the first time in many centuries. Who knows what secrets they hold, or stories they could tell? Yet the mystery of why King John's treasure has not revealed itself as other items have, remains.

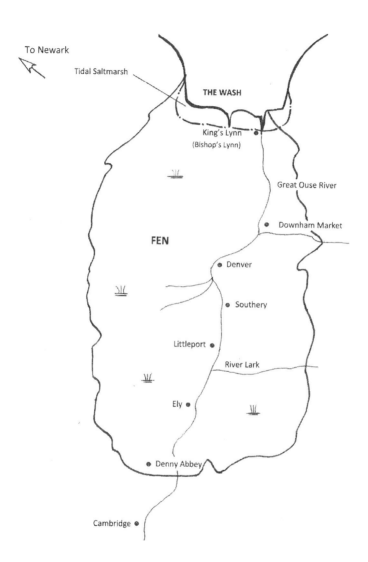

To Newark

Tidal Saltmarsh

THE WASH

King's Lynn
(Bishop's Lynn)

Great Ouse River

Downham Market

FEN

Denver

Southery

Littleport

River Lark

Ely

Denny Abbey

Cambridge

407

Printed in Great Britain
by Amazon